GRIMOIRES AND GUNSMOKE

THE OHIO INCIDENT

BY
S. DUDLEY

Grimoires and Gunsmoke
The Ohio Incident

ISBN (print): 979-8-88993-049-5
ISBN (e-book): 979-8-88993-048-8
Library of Congress Control Number (print): 2025934311
Edited by S. Adusumilli

Published 2025 by MoonQuill
Arlington, VA
www.moonquill.com

Table of Contents

THE OHIO INCIDENT

Chapter 1

A lord dined alone in an opulent yet empty banquet hall. Methodically, he cut each bite of food before slowly bringing it to his long, feathered, dragon-like snout. His brilliant white feathers shimmered with each bit of succulent meat. The feast table was laden with a broad selection of dishes, but the lord gravitated toward his comfort food, plucking morsels only from the platter of seared, still-bleeding meats.

To the casual observer, it was merely another grand feast for another person of importance. But to a solitary human servant with a keen eye, it was anything but ordinary.

The servant woman instinctively adjusted the sleeves of her uniform. She brushed her hand over her splendid platinum-blonde hair, tied neatly into a bun, ensuring her appearance was immaculate for the lord's gaze. Clasping her pale hands behind her back, she pursed her lips as she sensed the tension brewing in the room. This imposing dragon-like humanoid, adorned with opalescent feathers that shaded from white to gold, seemed stressed out of his mind as he poked at his food, lost in thought.

The servant gathered her courage and shifted. "Y-Your Grace, Varian?" she said hesitantly. "Is there an issue with the meal? Would you prefer I have it remade?"

Her voice pierced the dragnoid's stupor. His gaze shifted from the window, through which the sprawling city beneath his gargantuan castle could be seen and focused on the servant. "Ah... I appreciate the thought, Luva," Varian began, absently smoothing out a ruffled feather. "But no, the meal is exquisite, as always. It's just these earthly pleasures. They seem to have faded in their allure."

Luva felt a surge of anxiety. Emotions coursed through her at the remark, and her eyes began to swim. Was the food that bad? Was he displeased with her service? Luva's mind raced with doubts.

As a newcomer in the halls of the main castle, she was acutely aware of her insignificance. Here she was, standing in the presence of Emperor Lord Varian of the Seraphic Empire, a being whose decisions shaped the destiny of millions. She felt like an ant in his presence and feared that any slight could lead to her swift dismissal—or worse. Yet, instead of the scathing rebuke she expected, her lord offered her a magnanimous look and lifted his hand, gesturing for her to speak her mind.

"Go on, ask your question," he encouraged, his face neutral. Varian knew from experience that mimicking a human or an elf's smile would inspire panic rather than confidence. His rows of razor-sharp teeth and long maw made it seem more like he was trying to devour rather than comfort her.

"Y-Your Grace," she began softly, choosing her words with care, "p-perhaps... Perhaps it's my ineptitude diminishing your appetite?"

The lord chuckled lightly at that, the sound deep and resonant, echoing through the grand hall. "No, no, no!" he replied immediately, dispelling her misconception with a wave. "There's nothing wrong with what you're doing. It's just... the burden of responsibility is getting to me."

A blank look clouded Luva's face as she blinked in surprise. "Oh!" she said, bowing her head deeply. "I apologize, Your Grace! I didn't mean to presume."

Varian waved her off again. "There's no need to kowtow, Luva," he said with a gentle exhale, amused. The tips of his incisors showed despite his neutral expression. "You're doing wonderfully. I'm just stressed from overseeing such a vast empire. Some of the burdens I bear and expectations I have to meet are too profound for any mere mortal."

Luva cautiously met Varian's gaze. Behind the lord, an enormous gilt painting of his celestial parents loomed, their watchful eyes framing him. His sire, the dragon who carved the Seraphic Empire from the ruins of a decades-long civil war, was the embodiment of authority and imperial majesty. His dame, the Elven Mother, the Ethereal Goddess of Magic, also loomed larger than life, dwarfing their flesh-and-blood son.

Luva was struck by his resemblance to his father, though he was humanoid rather than full dragonkin. She could feel the immense pressure he faced living up to such an extraordinary lineage. His parents were beings of myth—creatures that humans and even elves whispered about in awe and fear. Carrying the blood of a goddess and the oldest celestial dragons meant expectations were not just high— they were practically impossible. Every decision and action would be scrutinized not just by his subjects or court but by the history and legacy of his ancestors.

"To be born of both sky and earth, divine and draconic, is both a blessing and a bane," Varian groaned as he brought another piece of meat to his mouth.

Luva froze, feeling like he had plucked her thoughts from her head and answered them. "Your Grace, might there be any way I can lighten your load?" she finally managed to squeak, gathering the courage to speak.

Varian paused for a moment, his gaze resting on Luva with a mix of appreciation and resignation. "You are very kind and dutiful, Luva.

But no," he said, his voice carrying the weight of centuries. He stood, his towering form casting a long shadow in the flickering light of the banquet hall. He slid his chair in with a quiet scrap against the stone floor and added, "I think I'm done for now."

Luva watched the lord walk toward his chambers. Something tugged at her, a desire to alleviate his burden. "Is there nothing I can do to help?" she called out, a hint of desperation in her voice.

Varian stopped just in front of her, turning to regard her for a moment. The look of concern was etched deeply on her face, and he couldn't help but feel satisfied with her devotion. "Well, if you really want to help," he began, looking her up and down.

The servant's face reddened slightly under his scrutinizing gaze, but she stood firm, determined to offer whatever assistance she could.

"I may ask you to stop by my chamber to help me... de-stress," he finally said, his voice low and earnest.

A mix of emotions coursed through Luva as her eyes widened at his request—surprise, uncertainty, but above all, a steadfast resolve to serve. She knew that helping a lord might extend beyond the typical duties of a servant. It could mean lending an ear to his troubles, offering words of comfort, or providing other forms of relief. However, she had never imagined a dragonkin would show interest in anyone other than his own kind.

"Of course, Your Grace. I will be there," she replied almost immediately, lowering her head in deference.

Varian nodded, approval gleaming in his eyes. "Very good," he responded in his deep, resonant voice. "I expect you within the hour."

As he turned to leave, the dragonkin's tongue flicked out, running across his maw in hunger, while Luva bowed once more.

When the emperor made his way to his regal chambers, Luva's heart pounded with fear and excitement. Never in her wildest dreams had she imagined something like this would be possible. As the grand doors to his chambers closed behind him with a quiet but definitive thud, she was left alone in the vast, echoing hall.

Once within the confines of his private sanctuary, Varian moved toward the massive window overlooking the bustling castle grounds below. From this height, the people of his empire looked like mere ants as they went about their duties.

Duties which *he* dictated.

Something about that thought made the emperor's heart flutter with excitement. Ordering a mere mortal to carry out any command—mundane or complex—was a power Varian could turn into reality with a single thought. Whether it was making the most powerful lords bend their knees, compelling a soldier to take their own life for his amusement, leading entire legions to war, or...

Having a being of another species spread their legs.

Within the borders of the great Seraphic Empire, his will was unchallenged, his authority absolute. The law of the land was a fabric woven from his desires and expectations. People worked, celebrated, and lived at the whim of his silent commands. But as Varian's gaze drifted to the massive statue erected in honor of his mother and father, a sense of dread replaced his anticipation. The ever-present reminder of the weight placed on his shoulders by these two divinities gnawed at him.

His dragon-like maw remained motionless, but his jaw tightened, and his feathers rippled before smoothing flat again. Varian knew he had not yet earned the honor of standing among the divines, but he fervently promised himself that would be remedied soon. His gaze left the window and fell sourly on the ornate hourglass in the corner of the chamber. Golden grains of sand dribbled through the tapered glass, accumulating in a massive pile below.

Time. There was not much left. He bitterly reflected that time was an ever-grinding constant that brought everyone to their knees, whether beggars or kings. Even *he* couldn't escape it without help. But soon, his time of greatness would come to pass.

Lost in circling thoughts, he waited until, at last, the chamber's fireplace roared to life, flames ferociously spewing from its mouth and illuminating the room with dancing shadows.

"Ah, Alastor," Varian's sonorous voice broke the room's stillness as he turned back to the window, pointedly ignoring the spectacle of flames. "How wonderful it is that the Herald of the Hells graces my sanctuary once more," he said without even turning around. "You devils certainly know how to make an entrance."

Clad in refined attire a century out of date, a human with sharp, chiseled features walked from the flames and performed an elegant bow to the emperor's indifferent shoulder. "When a being of such unparalleled splendor calls, even the infernal depths stand to attention," he declared, his tone dripping with honey.

Palpable tension filled the air. This encounter was another move in their long-running game as they navigated their layers of veiled, intertwined agendas.

With a deliberate flourish, fiery sparks shot out from Alastor's hand, and an ornate scroll slowly materialized. The ancient yet crisp parchment was sealed with an emblem that combined Varian's quetzal rampant and Alastor's personal seal, his silhouette in profile executed in crimson and gold. As it unfurled, the words etched upon it seemed to move and shift, encrypted against the casual glance. The scroll delineated their grand deal: an agreement to facilitate Varian's ascension beyond the pedestrian boundaries of mortality so he could stand alongside the pantheon of gods. Varian, already a demigod but still hungry to prove himself against the immortal legacy of his parents, sought the final pieces of power to solidify his divine stature.

"I have fulfilled my part," Alastor said, voice dripping with dark amusement. "Now, I ask you to fulfill yours." Sparks crackled from the devil's mouth, and an intense blaze filled his eyes.

"It is my understanding you have The Banished One in your possession. Give her to me," Alastor demanded as he stood staring at Varian's back.

Varian slowly turned to face Alastor, his eyes radiant with the new power flooding him as their deal neared consummation. His gaze fell on the scroll in the devil's hand. The infernal document wasn't merely parchment; it was alive—a breathing testament to the promises and debts woven between the two formidable beings.

As Alastor emphasized his demand, the scroll reacted in kind. From its ancient surface, blazing letters rose, hovering midair, forming a mesmerizing holographic tableau that portrayed their binding agreement in the infernal script.

"I am well aware of our arrangement, Alastor," Varian replied, his voice smooth yet authoritative. Every syllable he uttered caused the letters on the scroll to dance as if responding to their master's voice. "And you will have her in due time... But tell me, why do you desire her so fervently? Surely, you could wait another week or two."

Alastor's demeanor shifted slightly, betraying a hint of impatience and outrage. The room grew hotter as his voice dropped to a venomous whisper. "Every moment she remains out of my grasp, the chains that the infernal realm has on your soul pull tighter. Time, Varian, is a luxury you cannot afford." The devil squeezed his fist tighter to emphasize his point, and the letters spelling out the contract burned brighter, casting the entire chamber in a pulsing cherry glow.

Varian tore his gaze from the scroll and directed his full attention to Alastor, attempting to discern the devil's intent beyond this immediate gambit. The dragonkin smirked as he finally spoke, revealing a row of needle-tipped teeth. "I have yet to break our agreement, Alastor," he replied, eyes glinting with a mix of amusement and defiance. "I may have ascended beyond mere mortality, but I have not forgotten our pact—nor do I take lightly the tether you hold over my soul."

The light in the room shifted uneasily; the furnishings appeared to quake and jump, a trick of the wildly flickering fire glow. The effect intensified as flames licked around Alastor, and his long, barbed tail materialized, belying his human mask. For the first time since entering the opulent chamber, Alastor's poise slipped. A trace of uncertainty flitted across his chiseled face, fleeting as a windblown ember. "Then tell me, Varian, why this delay?" Alastor's voice was eerily earnest, lacking the bombastic honey he'd opened the conversation with. "What do you hope to achieve by withholding her from me?"

Varian's smirk grew wider, his majestic presence radiating confidence. "Did you truly believe my ambitions were limited to becoming a demigod?" He gestured broadly with both arms, and the feathered crest on the back of his head echoed the regal gesture, golden plumes rising and spreading to catch the firelight. "While our agreement holds weight, I have been thorough in my reading. There is no time limit on when I have to deliver The Banished One, and her powers have a purpose far beyond what the mortals understand."

Alastor's eyes narrowed as the fire defining the contract collapsed back into an ordinary paper scroll. His pretty face tightened in a scowl, his human mask slipping further. The devil's tail twitched irritably, and the air in the chamber grew thick with heat and the sulfurous reek of the abyss. "I do not know what you are planning, Varian, but you tread on dangerous ground," Alastor growled, his expression dark against the perfectly sculpted features. "The powers you speak of are unpredictable. Chaotic." He showed his teeth, his words clipped and emphatic. "Beyond your comprehension."

The feathered emperor drew himself up, sensing how close he was to winning this round. His eyes sparkled with anticipation and excitement, the ravenous hunger of his ambition driving him recklessly. "Risk is the price of ambition, Alastor. Did you think I would be satisfied with half measures?" Varian leaned forward, his voice iced with resolve. "My scholars have felt it—a pulse, a whisper from the beyond. The Unclaimed. They believe we can create a bridge to this uncharted realm, teeming with untapped souls."

"Madness!" Alastor roared. His elegant mask ripped away entirely as he contorted into his dark, true form. Obsidian skin stretched over tight muscle, punctuated with jagged bone spires up his spine. He unfurled expansive, leathery wings and beat the air in frustrated rage. His face retained its angular perfection, but grotesque horns crowned his head, and his eyes burned incandescent. "You gamble with the very fabric of existence, Varian! Meddling with such realities risks not just your empire or this world but the balance of all realms!"

Varian let out a condescending chuckle, pleased that he'd provoked the devil into losing control. He flicked his hand, and the contract obeyed, levitating between them, no longer in Alastor's grip. Glowing ethereal letters pulsed vividly, highlighting the clauses that bound them both. "Ah, Alastor, your memory seems a tad rusty. Might I remind you of this little stipulation?" He gestured toward a line on the contract that shimmered brighter than the rest. "As long as this contract stands, no harm shall befall me by the hands or will of the Hells."

Drawing himself up to his full height, Varian's feather-crested mane fluffed with newfound arrogance. "Your dire warnings and threats fall on deaf ears, *Devil*. I will pursue the path to true godhood, and no demon, celestial, or whatever else comes crawling out will stand in my way." Dismissing Alastor's misgivings with a wave, he added, "If you are concerned about our agreement, I suggest you assist me in ensuring its success rather than mewling about prophetic magics."

With a calculated glint, Varian turned and gestured towards the giant, ornate hourglass at the corner of the chamber. The golden sands within were on the verge of running out, the final grains ticking down to the imminent opening of the rift.

"See there, Alastor? Time is almost upon us," he mused, beaming with pride as the pieces came together. "My plan is already in motion. Beyond those borders," he continued, pointing to the vast map spread out on a table behind him, "lands are teeming with resources and glory that await my legions. Unclaimed souls are looking for a new god. A new world, ripe for the empire." The dragonkin's voice dropped to a whisper as his taloned hand slid across the map and settled on the wild lands.

Varian's fingers traced the borders of his sprawling empire and lingered over certain marked regions, indicative of his contingency plans. "Here," he began, pointing to fortified castles and fortresses marked in gold, "my loyal vassals, ever ready to defend our honor and legacy." He then moved his hand over a wild, untamed area of the map. "And these wild lands... Unpredictable, yes, but they serve as a buffer. If the worst comes to pass, they will be the first to face the wrath, the first line of defense—or, if need be, the first sacrifice."

Alastor's mind raced, thoughts swirling in a storm of dread and frustration, paralyzed by the terms of the contract to stop the disaster in motion before him. Into the morbid silence that hung between them, his internal musings thundered unfiltered. "It's a tragic paradox of mortal kind: Deny them their freedom, and they label you a despot. Grant them autonomy, and they become the oppressors they once condemned." Though bound by the ironclad clauses of their contract, the devil's demeanor shifted again from suppressed rage to earnest desperation. "Varian," he implored, his fiery gaze searching the emperor's eyes. "Do not let pride and ambition blind you to the cataclysms that may unfold. Can't you see? Even as a spawn of the hells, I warn you that your quest for power could unleash chaos on a scale you can't even fathom!"

The devil's voice dropped to a haunting whisper that echoed off the walls, his tone chilled as he reexperienced memories of past tragedies. "Were you not taught of the events that led to The Banished One's imprisonment in the first place?! There were cataclysms, Varian—shattered, gods fallen! Countless souls lost to oblivion, never to be claimed again!"

Drawing closer, Alastor's infernal aura pulsated, his form shifting between his elegant mask and monstrous nature, reflecting the conflict within. "Beyond whatever rift you create," he continued, his eyes darkening, "lies not just untapped potential but abominations unknown even to us—terrors that would make The Banished One seem like a mere petulant child. Do not let your avarice drive us all to ruin. Even we devils do not wish to rule over rubble and wastelands!"

A flicker of doubt crossed Varian's eyes but vanished almost as quickly as it came. He defiantly met Alastor's gaze.

Would he heed the devil's warning, or would his ambition overpower reason?

Varian cast a dismissive glance at the empty hourglass, his voice dripping with disdain. "Do you truly believe your fanciful tales of horror will deter me, Alastor? My empire is vast, and my legions are unmatched. We are more than equipped to conquer whatever 'abominations' lie beyond the rift."

Alastor snarled, his infernal form trembling as a strange blend of anger and dread coursed through him. "Your arrogance blinds you to the peril you beckon!"

But Varian's face remained a mask of unwavering resolve. "Your words are nothing more than the desperate cries of a fool who fears change. My ascent is inevitable, Devil." He turned back toward the hourglass, smiling as the last grains of sand slipped to the bottom.

At that precise moment, Alastor felt the boundaries of the mortal realm ripple and distort. Like a stone cast into still water, a pulse of energy spread outward, tearing apart the very fabric of time and space.

"What have you done?" the devil whispered, his blazing gaze fixed on the now-glowing hourglass.

Unbeknownst to Varian, the rift he had recklessly opened extended far beyond his comprehension. The shockwave reverberated, breaching dimensions and tearing a gateway into another realm.

In Cambridge, Ohio, the early evening sky darkened briefly before brightening again as though a partial eclipse had momentarily dimmed the setting sun.

* * *

As the evening sky filled with radiant blue light, ringed with sunset gold clouds, Bix, a scruffy, balding man with pale skin characteristic of his Appalachian roots, drew a long, exaggerated snort before expelling a plug of spit onto the tall, waving grass.

"C'mon, Bix... We just need a small dab of ice, a'ight?" a painfully bony and long-haired man said as he stepped forward a bit. "I knows yous got a little, so—"

"I don't give two shits what any y'all peckerwoods need," Bix snarled at the cluster of twitching, equally scruffy people standing outside his property line. "I done told you, we ain't. Done. Cookin'! Now git before I put some buck in ya!"

Bix pumped his shotgun, the intimidating sound echoing through the silence. He then pointed the weapon towards the group, making his threat all the more real. A yelp of fear broke from the crowd of people as they scurried away, knowing full well Bix wasn't bluffing.

Another glob of mucus hit the dirt as Bix slung the shotgun over his shoulder and turned toward the dilapidated structure he called home, grumbling to himself, "Goddamn junkies... Can't even wait a day to get they fix."

Bix glanced at the rundown, one-story shack that had long lost its battle with time and weather. The whitewash had faded to gray streaks, the paint chipping and peeling, exposing the word-out wooden skeleton beneath.

"I ain't got no patience to deal with this shit," Bix muttered, yanking on the front door, which groaned under its weight.

Once inside, the interior was obsessively tidy compared to the house's derelict exterior. The floor and walls were lined with plastic sheets, neatly duct-taped at the corners. The air was pungent with the smell of chemicals—a stench that burned the nostrils and stung eyes.

At the center of it all, standing amidst an assortment of makeshift chemistry equipment, was Beau, Bix's younger brother. He was dressed in a hazmat suit, its bright yellow standing out against the shack's worn gray interior. His eyes, hidden behind the protective goggles, focused on a boiling flask before him.

"Gettin' close, Beau?" Bix asked, shutting the door behind him.

"Goddamn crackheads are already outside beggin' for—" Bix was cut off by a large concussive force that rattled everything in the house.

Beau was quick to react, grabbing the glass beakers and flasks to keep them steady. "What in the name of the lord was that?!" he shouted, his voice muffled by the gas mask as he turned to Bix.

"It's the Fourth, Beau." Bix shrugged. "You know how folks be 'round these parts, probably just some idjit," he finished nonchalantly, his gaze falling back on the desperate figures loitering at the boundary of their property. "Anyway, how much longer ya got on the cookin'?"

"Another couple of hours, at least," Beau replied, still holding onto the flasks. His eyes darted anxiously between them, making sure nothing was damaged. "The yield won't be any good if I rush it, Bix."

Bix groaned in frustration, his gaze flicking back to the rickety screen door. He was about to dismiss his brother's worries and go back to keeping watch when another explosion—closer and brighter this time—shook the ground beneath their feet.

The beakers and flasks rattled even more violently. Still, luckily, Beau was quick enough to grab the most volatile one before it crashed to the floor. Glass and lab equipment scattered all over the floor as Beau turned to his shotgun-wielding brother, fury in his eyes.

"Bix! You best go out there and tell them goddamn peckerwoods to stop. They owe us fuckin' money, or you better kill 'em!" Beau shouted, his voice muffled by the gas mask and the reverberating rumbles that seemed to shake their entire world.

Bix rolled his eyes and gave a disgruntled sigh. "Always the money with you, ain't it, Beau?" He slung his shotgun over his shoulder and headed for the screen door. "A'ight, a'ight. I'll go shoot some dipshits," Bix grumbled as he shouldered open the door. About to step off the porch, he froze in confusion. The land on the horizon looked... disjointed and warped. Where the familiar Appalachian hills and forests had been, there was now a vast, flat expanse of strange vegetation unlike anything he'd ever seen. He blinked and rubbed his eyes, wondering if he'd inhaled some spilled product.

The landscape wasn't the only thing that was off. A group of people—strangers—stood just outside his property line. They were gesturing wildly and yelling in a language Bix couldn't understand. They looked as confused as he felt.

"What in the hell?" he mumbled under his breath, taking a moment to reassess the situation. He missed his step off the porch and stumbled into the tall grass. His first thought was these were junkies, and he was definitely high from a chemical leak. Shaking his head, Bix shouted at the strangers, "Hey! You! What the hell y'all just do?" He raised his shotgun and aimed it at them.

The strangers turned towards him, equally puzzled. They muttered amongst themselves in their strange language before one of them—a tall, thin man, oddly clad in full metal armor—stepped forward.

He began speaking, but the words were foreign, nothing like the Appalachian drawl Bix was used to. Bix squinted, annoyed by his lack of understanding, but then noticed the speaker's pointed ears and the folk around him. "I don't know what the hell you're saying, but y'all cosplayin' fucks owe us some goddamn money for whatever the hell y'all just did! Ya understand?!" Bix demanded, but all he got were more confused looks.

The armored figure exchanged a few heated words with his companions before drawing a sword. Another one started swinging his hands in the air, and suddenly, small balls of ice and fire appeared at their fingertips. The sight was utterly captivating, but Bix had no idea what he was seeing. He stood rooted in place, eyes wide in disbelief.

"Aw, hell no. I must be high as a kite," Bix muttered, pointing his shotgun at the armored fellow with ice forming on his fingertips and pulling the trigger.

A deafening crack rang out, and one of the armored figures fell. The rest immediately sprang into action. The nearest stranger dragged their fallen comrade away as others formed a defensive line. In unison, their arms rose like a shield wall and conjured a brilliant, nearly impenetrable barrier.

Behind this shield, the fire-casting man didn't hesitate. His hand motions quickened, his chanting much harsher, as the fireball in their hand grew brighter and more prominent.

Meanwhile, Beau stormed out of the house, ripping off his respirator. "Goddammit, Bix! Why'd ya kill someone here?! Now we gotta—What the?" Beau froze, staring at the bizarre scene before him. "Bix, what the hell is that?"

"I dunno, Beau, I thought I was high, but it looks like the cosplayers are—" Bix was cut off by the fire-caster launching the fireball directly at them. Instantly, their world was engulfed in searing heat and blinding light. The last thing they saw was their shanty house being consumed by the massive fireball.

The crackling flames and screams faded, replaced by the steady hum of an aircraft engine.

"A la verga... What the hell are we getting ourselves into?" Corporal Luis Santiago, a Puerto Rican with a tanned complexion, muttered as he saw his M2A4 Bradley Infantry Fighting Vehicle chained to the cargo plane's floor.

Chapter 2

After Corporal Santiago's little outburst, no one in his platoon could come up with a reasonable answer. They all had the same question as they sat there staring at their machines of war: rows of M2A4 Bradley Infantry vehicles locked, loaded, and ready for a combat drop.

"I mean, let's face it—it's aliens," said Santiago, the driver of one of the vehicles, as he turned his head to his Sergeant First Class. "We're definitely being invaded by aliens."

Santiago's vehicle commander, Sergeant First Class Erik Hofmann, let out a deep sigh, his pale face reddening with irritation. Even though his corporal made some good points, not even their commanding officers knew what the hell was going on. The only thing anyone knew for certain was that there were attacks on the mainland, and they all needed to pile into C-17 Globemasters with enough ammunition to level a city.

"Shut the fuck up, Santiago," Hofmann retorted, leaning back against the wall of the cargo plane.

"C'mon, LT, get my back here," Santiago replied, undeterred, gesturing to the three Bradley IFVs. "Nobody just pops out of nowhere unless it's aliens!" he yelled down the line at the lieutenant, who looked more exasperated than anything else.

Lieutenant Jayden DuPont, already bumping his head against the wall in an effort to suppress his agitation with Santiago's rambling about aliens, finally straightened up and looked at his corporal. His dark skin contrasted with the plane's dim, metallic surroundings. As the aircraft hit a patch of turbulence, the deafening clang of chains echoed through the cargo bay, and everyone paused until they could hear again.

"We don't know that, Santiago," DuPoint replied in a monotone voice once the noise had returned to its usual deafening roar. "Now, do what Hofmann told you to do and shut the fuck up."

"I'm just sayin', sir." Santiago shrugged, leaning back in his own seat. "They just popped out in the middle of nowhere and started blasting, you know?" His voice trailed off as he raised his hands like his favorite History Channel "expert."

"Maybe it's those little green pendejos. Or the tall gray—"

"Santiago, if you don't shut the fuck up, I'm gonna throw you out of the back of this goddamn plane," growled Sergeant Daniel Kim, the Bradley's Korean American gunner. "Do yourself a favor and stop while you're ahead."

The corporal put his hands up in surrender after receiving Kim's glare. "Alright, alright, I get it," Santiago said as he reclined in his seat, crossing his arms over his chest. A few of the forty men on board muffled their laughter, but a harsh look from Kim quickly silenced it.

The cargo bay soon fell into silence, crammed only with the sounds of the droning hum of the turbofan engines and the occasional creak of the three nearly thirty-ton war machines. Santiago's gaze drifted back to his Bradley, his face growing serious for a moment. His eyes traced the vehicle's features, noting the two live missiles stowed on the side of the turret. He couldn't help but wonder what exactly they were heading into. They were an armored unit, not an airborne one, so a combat drop wasn't exactly standard procedure, at least not one that they were trained to do. And yet, here they were.

"He has a point, though. What if it's actually—" Private First Class Lukas Kowalski broke the silence but was immediately cut off.

Lieutenant DuPont didn't even bother looking at the man when he barked, "Shut up, Kowalski," eliciting laughter throughout the cabins once again.

Kowalski sank further into his seat, deciding it was better to keep his thoughts to himself for now. "Roger that, sir," he responded, adjusting the rifle slung across his chest. His fingers grazed the cold metal of the firearm, tracing its edges as a strange comfort amid the uncertainty that hung in the air.

Hofmann ignored the tense but still somewhat jovial atmosphere. His gaze drifted down the line, taking in the rest of the platoon. As the gears in his head turned, Santiago's words lingered in his mind. As far as Hofmann was concerned, there wasn't a single country on the planet with the technology to materialize an invasion force in the middle of a landlocked country.

Were they moving to put down an uprising?

That didn't seem right. Any uprising would have been plastered all over social media or the news long before things escalated. Plus, handing it would be the National Guard's responsibility, not a heavily armored unit flying out of Texas.

Seeing that they were part of the latest iteration of the heavily armored "penetration" division concept that the brass had slapped together, Hofmann surmised that this was probably some kind of test. The 1st Cavalry Division had been redesigned to be the Army's spearhead in any major conflict. Hofmann's division was composed of advanced and heavily armored vehicles and specialized infantry units with the explicit goal of breaching enemy lines and continuing the assault.

The platoon sergeant gently bumped his head against the plane's hull and closed his eyes, hoping to take a quick catnap. There was no point in overthinking the situation. They'd soon find out whether the Chinese had figured out how to materialize out of thin air or if Santiago was right and it was aliens, after all.

But Hoffman's rest was short-lived. The sharp crackle of the plane's intercom pierced the quiet.

"Brace for approach. We're going into a tactical landing pattern, and we're coming in hot," the pilot's voice echoed through the cargo hold.

Tactical landing.

They were going into a hot zone and going in fast.

DuPont's gaze never wavered from Hofmann, even as the initial surprise gave way to a grim understanding. Everyone snapped into work mode. "You heard the man!" Dupont shouted aggressively and called out to the rest of his soldiers, his voice cutting through the rising tension with calm, steady assurance.

"Secure your shit and strap in tight! This will be a rough descent," he ordered, tightening his own harness. "We're going in hot, so be ready to move and get the vehicles decoupled as soon as we touch down!"

"Takashi, Cooper, Diego, Thornfield!" DuPont continued, his piercing gaze sweeping each NCO in turn. His voice cut through the noise of the humming engines and was a blade of authority in the chaos. "Help Hofmann decouple his Bradley. We need him out of the way as soon as the bird touches down! Understood?" DuPont grabbed his rifle, racked the charging handle, and chambered a round.

The soldiers snapped to attention, their bodies taut with the adrenaline of the impending drop. "Roger that, sir!" came the unanimous response, each man springing into action.

Staff Sergeant Takashi, a quiet Japanese American, pointed to a few of his men and started issuing orders to prepare their own Bradleys for decoupling when they landed. Diego, Thornfield, and Cooper followed suit, assigning squads to their respective vehicles.

The roar of the engines and the whistling wind outside made it hard for the soldiers to hear one another as the aircraft descended rapidly. It felt as if their stomachs were left hanging thousands of feet above them, a sensation only worsened by the anticipation of the unknown.

"The fuck is going on, sir?" Santiago asked again, his voice barely audible over the noise. His knuckles were white from gripping the straps of his harness, his eyes wide as he looked to his lieutenant for answers. But DuPont, strapped into his seat, gave nothing away. His gaze was fixed on the slowly approaching ground below them, a hardened expression on his face. He'd been in this kind of situation before, and he knew better than to make promises or assumptions.

"I don't know, Santiago," DuPont admitted, gazing at the worried corporal. "But I'm sure we'll find out soon enough. Now get your fuckin' helmet on."

The rapid descent continued, the lights of the land below growing closer and more defined. No one said another word as they all realized they weren't landing on an actual airstrip but a small strip of grass used as a makeshift runway.

The usually talkative Santiago swallowed hard and simply nodded, his fingers fumbling to strap his helmet on. The unit's lighthearted banter had given way to a somber tension. Each man was lost in his thoughts as the landscape below approached with alarming speed.

As the soldiers held their breaths, the aircraft shuddered and jolted. The undercarriage screamed in protest as it made contact with the uneven ground. The pilot, however, skillfully decelerated, and the transport bounced and shook as it barreled down the grassy field. Once the plane had ground to a halt, officers barked orders, and the soldiers unbuckled themselves, springing into action. They had half of the bindings securing their vehicles undone before the cargo bay doors even touched the ground. The doors banged open, revealing a starlit night punctuated by intense gunfire and explosions echoing in the distance.

The sudden sounds of conflict outside caught everyone off guard, momentarily freezing them in their tracks. The soldiers' heartbeats echoed in their ears, drowning out the distant sound of gunfire. The booming echo of an explosion somewhere off in the distance jolted them back into motion.

"Move! Move! Move!" Lieutenant DuPont yelled, reigniting the sense of urgency among his men. "Get this shit off the plane! Section Two still has to land!"

Remembering that the rest of their company was still in the air, the soldiers swiftly got back to work. The rumble of heavy diesel engines filled the air as the first metal beasts roared to life while a new wave of soldiers flooded in to assist in decoupling the vehicles. With the first Bradley free of its chains, the massive vehicle thundered down the ramp, churning up dust and grass in its wake.

The second Bradley followed as Lieutenant DuPont walked down the ramp, shaking hands with one of the men directing the vehicles. "1st Lieutenant DuPont," he said as he introduced himself, sizing up his counterpart. He took in the CCT patch on the other officer's chest, indicating him as part of the Air Force's elite Combat Controllers.

"Technical Sergeant Anthony Pena," the airman replied, returning DuPont's firm handshake. "I'm sure you want to know what the fuck is going on, but you're better off seeing it for yourself." The CCT started walking, motioning for the lieutenant to walk with him, then pointed south. DuPont turned, narrowing his eyes at the mention of fighting. His mind whirled with questions, but he maintained his composure, focusing on what the CCT was saying. "We've got everything from Special Forces and Rangers to the National Guard fighting along the 77 on both sides of the road, trying to reach Cambridge."

"Wait, wait, wait. What?" DuPont pressed his fingers against his eyebrows before glancing back at the cargo plane taxiing to take off. "The 77? As in Interstate 77? Sergeant Pena, what the fuck is happening?"

"I'd like an answer to that too, Lieutenant," Pena replied grimly. "Something is attacking us." The CCT shook his head in disbelief. "We've got these... things. Creatures. They're not from around here, that's for sure. They hit us hard and fast, taking the town and killing civilians. The Rangers were the first to respond, and now we're all here, trying to hold them back."

Dupont noticed Pena's voice had an edge to it, a certain tension that went beyond the normal stresses of combat. His eyes were steely, his jaw set. "And before you ask, no one has the faintest clue. One minute, everything's normal. The next... well, you'll see." Pena turned toward the cargo plane as it was starting to take off. "If it doesn't look like it belongs on this planet, shoot it. If it doesn't look right, shoot it. If it doesn't have an IR strobe, shoot it." His attention shifted to the next cargo plane lining up for landing. He raised his hand to his radio to communicate with the incoming cargo plane, tacitly dismissing the lieutenant.

DuPont stood there for a moment in complete and utter shock as he let the information sink in. "Jesus... Santiago was right." He turned around and jogged to the lead Bradley, his mind racing with thoughts of preparation and action.

"Fuck, Santiago was right!" DuPont shouted as he climbed up the IFV's ramp, joining the rest of his squad.

Sitting in the vehicle's command chair, Hofman snapped his head around. "What?!" Hofmann's face contorted in disbelief. "Santiago was *what?!*"

DuPont let out a series of frustrated grunts as he struggled to fit into the only available seat. "The goddamn corporal was right. We're being fucking attacked by aliens!" he replied hurriedly, shoving a soldier's M240 machine gun out of his way to make room for himself. "We've got unidentified hostile... somethings out there!"

The Bradley's ramps finally started to lift, sealing the occupants inside the dimly lit interior. The dull roar of the engine filled the silence left by DuPont's revelation. The usual banter, the jokes, and the sounds of soldiers preparing for a mission all felt muted. The gravity of the situation hit like a mortar, leaving the men dazed.

Did humanity even stand a chance against a space-faring enemy attack? Everyone in the unit had grown up playing video games or watching media about alien invasions, and their imaginations ran wild with what-if scenarios. The very idea that an extraterrestrial race had the capability to cross the vast expanse of the cosmos, reach Earth, and launch an assault was terrifying. Their technology, strategies, and physiology could be beyond anything they could comprehend.

Santiago's voice broke through the oppressive silence. "I always imagined it'd be like Mass Effect, you know? Cool weapons, shiny ships, maybe even a few good-guy aliens on our side or something." He tried to laugh, but the sound quickly died, and silence reclaimed the Bradley once again as it rolled towards the road, grinding the grass beneath it to mud.

DuPont completely ignored the comment and focused on accessing his end-user device, a phone mounted to his chest. The man did his best to access the tactical map and other intel available via the digital interface. The device provided real-time updates from the higher command and fellow units, but everything coming through now was disorganized. DuPont concluded that everything was a cluster fuck.

"Goddamn it..." the lieutenant muttered as they finally reached the road. He tried to figure out who to talk to amidst the random bursts of chatter in his ear. Distressed voices cried for help, sharp commands rang out, and desperate attempts to rally scattered troops added to the mess. The cacophony made it nearly impossible to discern if there was any kind of cohesive command. It felt like they had just been dropped into a free-for-all.

Hofmann opened his mouth, ready to chime in on Santiago's joke, but something surreal flashed across his commander's screen before he could speak. Just two hundred meters away, several soldiers with infrared strobes on their heads sprinted out of the treeline, making a mad dash to the other side. At first, Hofmann thought they were trying to break contact to get to the other side, but he soon realized they were running away from something.

"Gunner!" Hofmann yelled desperately as an enormous armored beast, rivaling the Bradley in size, burst through the forest edge and onto the asphalt.

The damned thing had an eerie resemblance to a wingless, bipedal dragon whose massive claws scraped and sparked against the road's surface. It skidded out on the asphalt like a dog on polished wood. The sight was ridiculous and awe-inspiring, like something you'd see from a fantasy story. Its muscular body was covered in dark scales that seemed to reflect and absorb the ambient light, casting eerie shadows around it. Powerful, clawed limbs dug into the road as it righted itself, revealing rows of sharp, gleaming teeth in a maw that seemed to stretch endlessly. Its fiery orange eyes scanned the area hungrily.

With a predatory speed that defied its size, the creature surged forward again, giving chase to the fleeing soldiers. The beast's raw power was terrifying; each bound it took covered an alarming distance.

"Tracking!" the gunner, Sergeant Kim, yelled in response, quickly getting a bead on the creature.

The Bradley's 25mm Bushmaster chain gun roared into action as Kim unleashed a rapid barrage of high explosive rounds. Each round struck true, causing the creature to falter momentarily with every small explosion against its thick scales. But, the monster's resilience was astounding; while a few hits caused visible wounds in the softer and fleshier areas, the barrage was far from enough to bring the creature to a halt.

The beast, now enraged, turned its gaze toward the Bradley, its eyes glinting with malevolent intelligence. Muscles rippled beneath its armored hide as it repositioned itself, sizing up the armored vehicle as its new primary threat. It let out a deafening roar that echoed across the battlefield, sending an involuntary chill down the spines of every soldier within the vicinity. The sheer power and volume of the roar caused the Bradley's hull to vibrate.

"Armor piercing! Fucking use AP!" Hofmann shouted as he saw the thing sprint toward them with mind-boggling speed.

Sergeant Kim reacted instantly, switching ammunition. "Loading AP!" he called back, his voice desperate. Just as a mechanical clunk signified the switch in the chamber, the sergeant held down on the trigger once more, and the Bradley's chain gun released another furious volley. Each shot struck with a more noticeable effect than before; the rounds found their mark, digging into the creature's thick hide. A series of high-pitched metallic pings could be heard as the AP rounds made contact, some ricocheting off but several penetrating deep into the monster's tough exterior. Dark, viscous fluid, reminiscent of blood but with an odd luminescent quality, spewed from the beast, painting the asphalt as it crashed to the ground, slamming into the IFV before sending it skidding back.

The force of the impact knocked several of the crew off their seats, and the Bradley screeched to a halt several feet away. Hofmann was momentarily dazed, his vision blurred, and his ears rang from the brutal collision.

"Out! Out, now! Everyone dismount!" DuPont yelled, his voice sharp and urgent. He grabbed the lever to lower the Bradley's ramp and pushed it with all his might. With a mechanical hiss, the ramp slowly descended, revealing the hazy atmosphere outside.

The soldiers scrambled out of the cramped vehicle, some on their feet, others rolling to the ground. Even as the infantry tried their best to shake off the dizziness from the impact, the sound of the 25mm Bushmaster cannon continued to roar, engaging other targets down the road. By this time, the second and third Bradley in their little convoy had come to a halt, forming a makeshift defensive line along the main road. A cacophony of fire erupted from each vehicle as soldiers poured out of their respective vehicles and sprinted toward the treeline to escape the open ground. The world around them had descended into a blur of pure chaos.

Chapter 3

Lieutenant DuPont was among the first of his platoon to reach the tree line, with the rest of his men close behind. As he darted past the first tree, he collided with something solid yet slightly squishy, sending him tumbling to the ground.

Recoiling, the lieutenant looked up to see what he had hit and found himself facing a small humanoid creature, barely as tall as his chest. Its large yellow eyes blinked in surprise, and a long reptilian snout, somewhat akin to a dinosaur, jutted out, with a row of small, pointed teeth visible even when its mouth was closed. Its sleek, lithe body shimmered with a deep blue hue where the light struck, entirely covered in black, protective scales. Thin, frail-looking limbs ended in clawed hands and feet, giving it an appearance both delicate and deadly.

DuPont and the creature locked eyes briefly, neither registering the other's existence, until one of the lieutenant's men screamed in panic, "Contact! Contact!" Almost immediately, the forest erupted in a cacophony of gunfire, bullets whizzing by, tearing into trees, underbrush, and the creatures that suddenly surrounded them.

In a fraction of a second, DuPont shoved his weapon into the small creature's face and pulled the trigger. A bang echoed amidst the chaos, and the creature's head snapped back before it went limp.

"Check your fire! Check your fucking fire, goddamn it!" Lieutenant DuPont barked, trying to regain some kind of control of his squad as he pushed the lifeless creature off him and scrambled to his feet, his heart racing. He briefly glanced at the fallen creature, eyes widening in disbelief. But as he surveyed the chaos around him, the feeling only intensified. His squad was battling identical monstrous reptiles, desperately trying to keep them at bay.

The situation improved only when the rest of his platoon entered the forest, laying waste to the creatures with a coordinated onslaught of gunfire. Whatever small monsters weren't cut down fled into the dense underbrush, disappearing into the shadows of the trees.

DuPont did his best to take stock of the situation, peering down at his chest-mounted phone. The tactical battle map, which was supposed to track friendly units and mark enemy positions, was completely useless. From the look of things, they were in a full-blown clusterfuck, with friend and foe mixed in disarray. And it didn't help that the relentless sound of gunfire and explosions echoed from all directions, leaving them disoriented and directionless.

"W-What do we do now, sir?" Staff Sergeant Takashi asked, stepping over the bleeding humanoid reptile on the ground. His eyes were wide with confusion and fear as he looked at his platoon leader for guidance.

The lieutenant bit back a sardonic chuckle as he wiped the reptilian blood from his face. Glancing at his men and back at Takashi, a single thought echoed in his mind: *That's a good fucking question.*

More deafening thumps echoed through the forest as the Bradley IFVs fired again, sending a volley of shells toward enemy concentrations and larger monsters. DuPont popped his head out of the tree line, watching as the rounds shattered smaller reptiles and more humanoid figures.

"Takashi, take your squad and cross to the other side of the road!"

DuPont barked orders as he darted back into the cover of the trees. "Don't let our Bradleys get flanked!"

Staff Sergeant Takashi nodded and sprang into action, pressing down on his push-to-talk button. "2-3 on me!" he yelled as he and a large swath of men darted out of the tree line.

DuPont turned to Staff Sergeant Cooper and issued another set of orders. "Cooper, take this flank. I'm taking 2-1 to provide close-in security for the Bradleys. Make sure none of these squirmy fucks flank us. Copy?"

Cooper gave a sharp nod. "Roger, sir. 2-2." He immediately went to work. "2-2, you heard him! Get your asses moving and fan out!" he shouted, waving his hand for the men to disperse.

As DuPont's orders were carried out, Cooper rallied his squad and sprinted toward the IFVs. Amid the storm of gunfire and explosions, DuPont experienced a strange moment of stillness. He shook his head, trying to clear the fog of uncertainty. The unfamiliar terrain, the bizarre creatures, and the blurring line between friend and foe. None of them had trained for anything like this, but then again, the military was notorious for putting its men into situations they hadn't trained for.

They just had to roll with it and make it up as they went.

"Gunner, Traverse right twenty degrees! 150 meters, enemy in the open!" Hofmann shouted as a large group of humanoid reptiles emerged from the forest. "Light 'em up!"

A metallic thunk resounded as Sergeant Kim switched the ammo from armored piercing to high explosive rounds and adjusted the turret accordingly. "On the way!" he shouted back, pressing the trigger. The vehicle rocked as the 25mm cannon fired.

With the platoon's fourth Bradley catching up, the vehicles unleashed a barrage of firepower, their shells screaming through the air before tearing through the invaders. The resulting carnage made the surviving reptilian creatures panic, scattering them in every direction.

As the strange monsters lay dead or dying, Hofmann kept a vigilant watch on the thermal readings on his command screen, searching for any lingering threat. The only signatures that dominated the display were vivid bursts of distant explosions and a vast expanse of fire consuming the landscape. Towering columns of smoke rose, casting haunting silhouettes against the backdrop of the continental United States, causing Hofmann's stomach to drop.

But the sergeant first class didn't have time to dwell on the grim scene. There was still work to be done and aliens to kill. The immediate threat might have been neutralized, but the radio chatter indicated that this battle was far from over.

"Wrecker 1, this is Bravo 2 Actual, interrogative!" DuPont's voice crackled over the radio, gunfire audible in the background. "Is your Bradley still operational?"

"Roger that, Lieutenant," Hofmann responded crisply. "She's a bit dented, but she's still roaring."

"Good to hear, Wrecker 1," DuPont's voice came back, a hint of relief audible even through the static. "Alright, I've got a hold of something resembling command. I need you and your boys to push forward slowly. They're a bit further up ahead—cut off and surrounded.

Hofmann tightened his grip on his commander's hand station as he scanned the surrounding area. "Copy, Bravo 2 Actual. Any intel on what we're walking into?"

"Negative, Wrecker 1," DuPont shot back. "The only thing I know is that everything's fucked and there's shit everywhere. Now, start moving. Out."

With that, the squad radio went silent, replaced by the chaotic noise of the battlefield.

Exhaling deeply, Hofmann did his best to clear his head and steel his nerves. "Alright, you heard the man," he began, addressing his crew inside before pressing the push-to-talk for the other Bradleys under his command. "This is Wrecker 1 to all vehicles. We're going to start pushing forward—slow and steady. Stay alert, maintain a line, and don't crunch any of our boys. They're using us as cover."

The driver, Corporal Santiago, sighed as he adjusted himself in the forward compartment. "We're all going to fuckin' die."

"More like you're going to fucking die, Santiago." Sergeant Kim chimed in, a smirk evident in his voice. "Your dumb ass jinxed it, so you're the one that's going to pay." He continued teasing as the Bradley lurched forward, its engine growling and tracks churning the dirt beneath.

"Hey, fuck you, pendejo," Santiago shot back, steering to avoid the strange but dead, tank-sized dragon in the middle of the road.

The other Bradleys in formation followed suit, maintaining a spaced but uniform metal wall as they advanced up the road. Each turret was pointed differently, ensuring 360-degree security in the uncertain landscape.

As the soldiers trailed behind them, the platoon slowly crept forward. Once they passed the bend, a scene of destruction awaited. The air was thick with smoke, and the scent of molten metal and burnt flesh was almost overpowering. The once-busy interstate, typically filled with commuters and families, was now an apocalyptic wasteland. Bodies belonging to both humans and these strange aliens were strewn across the roadway in a macabre, chaotic jumble. Cars and armored vehicles of all types had their metal frames twisted and contorted from the intense heat and explosive force.

"Fuck," Kim cursed, using the gunner's sight to take in the full scene. "What the hell is even happening?"

"First contact," Santiago replied grimly. "And it didn't go well."

The platoon maneuvered past the charred remnants of a Bradley, its front appearing as though it had been subjected to an intense, searing heat that caused it to melt and cave inwards abruptly.

Popping open the commander's hatch, Hofmann pulled himself out to get a closer look at the destroyed vehicle and furrowed his brow. "Goddamn," he muttered as he watched a few soldiers from his platoon peer inside the back.

However, the men immediately recoiled away from the wreck, shaking their heads in disgust as if they had just seen something absolutely horrific. "Yep, no one survived that shit," one of the men said, stepping over a still-red-hot glob of molten metal.

Hofmann drew a deep breath against the acrid smell of burnt metal and rubber, scowled, and retreated back into the confines of his vehicle. The man shook his head, trying to dislodge the visceral images from his mind's eye. "Keep your eyes open and TOWs ready. I don't want what happened to them to happen to us," he commanded, his voice carrying an uncharacteristic tremor.

A series of affirmations from each of his subordinate Bradleys resounded over the radio as they slowly maneuvered through the still-burning hellscape. Even though the sounds of battle still raged in every direction, the men of Bravo Company, 2nd Platoon, advanced toward the heart of the conflict, where it was the most intense.

Peering around at the destruction, the lieutenant couldn't help but wonder where their air support was. The fact that they weren't all already dead meant the invaders hadn't gained air superiority. By all accounts, the United States Air Force should have thrown everything they had—including the kitchen sink—at these creatures. Yet, the vast majority of distant booms didn't quite add up. This wasn't the sound of artillery, and DuPont saw no obvious signs of bombardment.

Something was different.

That's when it clicked. The source of the cacophony wasn't just from the ground. Instinctively, DuPont looked up, and what he saw left him utterly speechless.

The sky, usually a haven for human airpower, was now its own battlefield. An array of dragon-like creatures, some as large as the vehicles he commanded, others dwarfing even the largest planes he'd ever seen, clashed and dove among the clouds. Fiery breath met icy blasts in mid-air, resulting in explosions that made the ground battles look like minor skirmishes. What caught him completely off guard were the projectiles—missiles from unseen SAM sites and fighter jets—zigzagging between these creatures, trying to find a mark and keep their distance.

DuPont had been unfair. The Air Force was indeed in play, and they were struggling just as much as he was. At that moment, a giant explosion lit up the night sky as one jet strayed too close to a dragon and paid dearly for it.

"Those damned things are intercepting our missiles by... breathing fucking flames?" DuPont said, dumbfounded. The rest of his squad gave him odd looks before they, too, turned their vision skyward, their expressions shifting from initial disbelief to mounting horror.

The chaos unfolding overhead was as mesmerizing as it was terrifying. Sleek, state-of-the-art jets, designed with the latest stealth and maneuverability features, were struggling against these flying behemoths. A massive volley of missiles was launched simultaneously, only for most to be met with searing flames or chilling blasts of ice.

Despite their mythical reputation, the dragons had an uncanny knack for intercepting advanced human weaponry.

Only a handful of missiles managed to breach the dragons' aerial defenses, and their impact varied *greatly*. While the colossal creatures remained unscathed, their smaller counterparts weren't as fortunate. The mid-sized dragons were momentarily stunned, briefly plummeting before regaining their composure and flight. In contrast, the smaller, car-sized dragons were affected, erupting in a gruesome spectacle that showered the sky with debris and gore.

Lieutenant DuPont had seen a lot of shit during his time in the army, both as an enlisted man and an officer, but never had he seen anything like this. These dragons, once confined to fairy tales and epic poems, now dominated the airspace with unparalleled agility and ferocity. It was a scene stranger than a fantasy novel, yet its grim reality was inescapable.

"What was the saying?" DuPont muttered, shaking his head as he marched onward. "The only difference between fiction and reality is that fiction has to make sense?" He motioned to his men to keep moving and to catch up with the Bradleys.

"Hurry up. We can gawk when we're dead," the lieutenant barked, determined to stay focused on the mission. After all, they were still in the midst of a battle, and the enemy on the ground hadn't paused just because the skies had become a new kind of battlefield.

One of DuPont's men, Private Schwarez, always quick with a retort, replied, "Sir, I'm pretty sure we're not gonna see shit when we're dead." He secured his helmet tighter as he jogged to close the gap between him and the Bradleys.

"Shut the fuck up, Schwarez," the lieutenant responded in a monotonous tone, shaking his head.

As the unit pressed forward, they reached a bend where the

sounds of battle became more intense. The immediate staccato of gunfire replaced the distant roar of dragons and the scream of jets, shouts, and the ominous thuds of explosions.

Rounding the bend, the soldiers froze, their training and instincts momentarily overridden by sheer astonishment. Less than fifty meters ahead, a massive, wingless, dragon-like creature—unlike any they had seen thus far—towered over the tree line, glaring angrily at the forest. Standing on four powerful legs covered in gleaming obsidian scales, its large, horned head rocked back as its mouth began to glow as if it were trying to swallow molten metal.

Suddenly, three explosions rocked the beast, causing it to stumble back. It accidentally spewed molten slag onto the friendly forces below—small reptile-like creatures and larger humanoids of varying shapes and sizes. Screams of agony echoed as they were scorched by the very creature they had been supporting.

Rockets and machine gun fire hissed out from the shadows, striking both the larger beast and any armored humanoid creatures still standing. The iconic chops of M2 Browning .50 caliber machine guns added to the battlefield's thunderous chorus, their bullets tearing through the invaders as they struggled to recover from the bout of friendly fire.

"TOW! All units, TOW it! TOW it, now!" Hofmann shouted into the intercom, his eyes locked onto the massive creature wreaking havoc. "Gunner!"

Sergeant Kim responded immediately. The whirring of the Bradley's TOW Anti-Tank Guided Missile system came to life as its launcher popped out of its housing. "Tracking!" he shouted, the sophisticated optics lining up the enormous creature in its crosshairs. "On the way!"

Several deafening hisses resounded as each Bradley launched its TOW missiles in rapid succession. Trails of smoke and fire crisscrossed the battlefield, homing in on the towering beast.

Four deafening explosions echoed as the gargantuan beast screamed in agony, thrashing wildly in its torment. Its massive, clawed limbs crushed everything in its path, inadvertently squashing scores of its own allies beneath its bulk. The smaller reptilian creatures scurried in panic, only to be caught under the colossal foot of the beast or flung away by its violent tail swipes. The larger humanoid allies, attempting to assist the wounded beast, became collateral casualties as they were either trampled or smashed by its uncontrollable movements.

Then came the second volley from the tree line. The explosions were smaller in comparison, reminiscent of shoulder-fired weapons, but their precision was uncanny. Each missile struck the beast's softer underbelly, causing it to howl in even greater pain.

And then came another volley of missiles from the Bradleys, their warheads leaving trails of white smoke against the darkening sky. Four more devastating explosions rippled through the air, some striking the creature directly in the head, causing it to go limp and collapse with a ground-shaking thud. Dust and debris flew up, creating a smokescreen that momentarily obscured the aftermath.

"Light 'em the fuck up!" DuPont's voice boomed over the radio as a hurricane of gunfire erupted from the Bradleys, joined by the rapid chatter of machine guns and rifles from the infantrymen. The smaller creatures and humanoid allies, which had previously swarmed to support the massive creature, were now exposed and subjected to a well-coordinated hailstorm of lead.

In desperation, the car-sized monsters the platoon had faced earlier tried to close the distance, but each step was met with ruthless firepower. Though some shells from the Bradleys' main cannons bounced off their armor, most of the armor-piercing rounds tore into the beasts, spraying the asphalt with their blood.

The battle-scarred terrain transformed into a grim mosaic of fallen beings as the remnants of the once-fearsome creatures attempted a frantic retreat. However, fate was a cruel mistress. Their avenues of escape were swiftly cut off by the unyielding hail of gunfire from the tree line, tearing into those who dared to flee, leaving none standing.

Innumerable streaks of burning red tracers barked out of the tree line, ripping through the creatures and causing them to collapse. Clearly, this particular spot had been prepared well in advance for such an onslaught, and these monsters were caught in a classic L-shaped ambush.

"Cease fire!" DuPont shouted, waving his hand as he walked among his troops. "Cease fire! Save your ammo!"

As the gunfire began to peter out, an eerie post-battle silence descended. Only the distant screams of the wounded creatures and the crackles of distant battles filled the air. Emerging from the tree line was a mass of figures clad in the very same camouflaged uniforms as DuPont's men. The soldiers lowered their weapons but remained alert as they slowly advanced toward the carnage, finishing off any creature still showing signs of life.

"Must be the National Guard," one of DuPont's men remarked, eyeing the sorry state of their gear.

"Yeah, probably," another responded, glancing at the mismatched equipment and faded uniforms the new group of soldiers wore. "But they held their own, I'll give 'em that. Come on, let's meet the Nasty Girls." DuPont motioned for his men to approach the battered defenders.

DuPont made it a point to keep a couple of Bradleys behind in a supporting position as they moved toward the National Guard soldiers. His tactical instincts never took a backseat, even in moments like this. It was always best to leave a supporting element in place in case of a counterattack.

"Man, we owe you one," one of the defenders chuckled, walking towards the lieutenant, his face smudged with soot and grime. "Didn't think we'd see the cavalry coming our way. Captain Duggen." The man extended a dirty, gloved hand toward DuPont.

With a nod, DuPont returned the handshake with a firm grip. "Lieutenant DuPont. And trust me, it wasn't a one-way street. You guys gave us the window we needed."

"We didn't do shit. They did," the captain said, pointing toward the tree line.

Following Captain Duggen's gesture, DuPont's gaze landed on a group of extremely well-equipped figures. Two held Carl Gustafs, shoulder-launched weapons designed for armored targets. Their advanced helmets, fitted with night vision, tactical lights, and state-of-the-art comms, gave them an ethereal quality. Their modular vests, meticulously organized with specialized electronics and ornate knives, complemented the customized guns in their hands, each equipped with high-end optics.

But what stood out the most were the beards many of them wore.

"Hey, Eli!" an operator said, nudging another. "Go see what the dude wants. He's pointing at us."

CHAPTER 4

Beyond the violent and chaotic battle on the other side of the rift, a magnificent and enormous sovereign—a type of celestial dragon—unfolded its golden, feathered wings, casting an intimidating shadow over the luxurious enclave it had claimed as its resting ground.

The empire's expeditionary forces had spared no expense or effort in constructing its vast sanctuary, which stood in stark contrast to its utilitarian tents. The massive pillows being rested upon were embroidered with the finest threads the mortal realms could offer, and they lay atop expansive, padded ground mattresses requisitioned from the army. With this particular patch of the military encampment transformed, the sovereign was as satisfied as a being of its stature could be with its new haven.

At least it was until some petulant mortal disturbed its slumber.

Before the creature of legend knelt, a dragonborn general, his form covered in a cascade of dark, iridescent feathers. He bowed in fervent reverence, his proud frame dwarfed by the celestial dragon's grand form.

The general immediately lowered his head to the ground as the hateful eyes of the ancient creature flared at him, furious at how such a lowly being could fathom interrupting its leisure.

"Korthax," the dragon's earth-shaking voice echoed like a symphony of thunderous clouds and flowing rivers. I assume you come with words of victory and conquest?" the sovereign asked, narrowing its radiant eyes.

But the atmosphere grew heavy instead of the expected answer as silence reigned. Korthax, a warrior of unparalleled might and a heralded strategist among his peers, found himself kneeling and trembling like a leaf beneath the sovereign's increasingly hostile gaze.

"No, my Sovereign..." Korthax finally managed to utter, his once-confident and commanding voice reduced to a mewl. His eyes swirled with conflicted emotions—shame for his failure, humiliation for misjudging the threat, and unmitigated fear as he met those burning golden eyes that seemed ready to disintegrate him. "The dwellers of this realm... have a resilience we did not anticipate."

The colossal being let out an irritated huff, leaning forward to create a majestic, menacing canopy over Korthax. "Speak, you unsightly cur! And let not your words falter, for your failure on the battlefield is mirrored tenfold in your cowardice now!" The Sovereign's booming voice echoed throughout the enclave, causing the ground to shake as its eyes bore into Korthax.

The fiery orbs seemed to pierce into the very core of Korthax's being, seeking to ignite a flame where now only smoldering ashes of doubt remained. He could feel every vertebra in his spine crystallizing with an ancient, primal dread born from legends of yore.

"Their constructs," Korthax blurted hastily, his voice fluctuating between desperation and awe, "might make the green-flamed furnaces of the mountain-born dwarves flicker with envy! M-Metal beasts at their command, crawling through their lands, exhaling fire and devastation with unyielding precision and—"

"Inane ramblings and craven justifications!" the sovereign snarled, its voice like a thousand storms, cutting Korthax off as he quaked in fear where he knelt.

The vast wings of the sovereign unfurled menacingly, a living tapestry of golden hues engulfing the twilight, replacing its gentle warmth with darkness that echoed his fury. "You kneel before me, spewing these infantile fairy tales, Korthax!" Flames shot from the celestial dragon's nostrils as it bared its teeth. "You dare speak of mechanical beasts roaming the lands when you command legions of my scaled kin who control the skies!" The Sovereign sneered.

Korthax trembled like a fragile leaf before a hurricane, his gaze fixed on the ground in deference. Yet, within him, a fragment of the courage he once held remained as he opened his mouth to speak the truth. "M-My Sovereign, it is with a heavy heart that I admit... that we have not taken control of the skies," he confessed, his voice barely more than a whisper.

He inhaled deeply, gathering the remnants of his shattered resolve before continuing. "There is an omnipresent force, a pervasive gaze that finds all wherever they soar. It's as if..." Korthax paused as he heavily gulped, aware that his very life hung on the whims of the ancient, whimsical entity before him. "It's as if there's an all-seeing eye watching everyone and everything."

"Our dragons, our wyrms, and even the wyverns feel a prickling, unsettling itch that claws at their skin and senses," the general elaborated, his face incredulous as he spoke, unable to fully believe his words.

The dragon's immense nostrils flared again, shooting flames as high as the ceiling as it listened to Korthax's faltering words. An unbearable heat radiated from the sovereign's mouth as it moved its head closer, its maw opening slightly, promising a terrifying inferno.

"An all-seeing eye?" An amalgamation of simmering and cracking plasma bubbled within the dragon's mouth as it spoke. "Do you take me for a fool? Do you expect me to swallow tales spun from your maddened mind, Korthax? You come here filled with stories of ghosts haunting the sky, believing I would heed such childish ravings?"

After a few moments of silence, the sovereign raised its massive arm, unfurled a single taloned finger, and deliberately pointed directly at Korthax. "Hear me well, Korthax," the dragon's eyes burned like portals to the infernal realm as they regarded the small, prostrated dragonkin.

"I, the Grand Relor, Sovereign of the Empire, Servant of Emperor Varian, shall grant you the benefit of the doubt." He reared his head back, looking down at Korthax with disgust. "You shall receive a sliver of my trust, a fragment of belief in your frantic utterances. I will seek out these phantoms you speak of myself and witness your ineptitude with my own eyes."

Relor's face drew closer until Korthax could feel the searing heat of the dragon's breath, a furnace threatening to consume him in its fiery depths. "But know this, you pitiful shard of a once-great lineage. If I find a trace of deception in your words, a hint of delusion or incompetence..." The dragon's voice dropped to a growl, reverberating through Korthax's bones.

"I shall extend your life and set ablaze the very flesh clinging to your pitiful frame. I will render your skin a canvas of agony and ruin, and you shall serve as a living testament to the price of falsehood and cowardice—a beacon of suffering for all to witness." The sovereign's voice was cataclysmic, more of a promise than a threat.

A moment passed between them as Korthax absorbed the sovereign's words. The sense of impending doom wasn't the right combination of words to describe how the general felt. If he were honest with himself, he doubted any language could express the feeling of eternal torment looming over him, especially knowing Relor could deliver just that.

"May the gods and the emperor have mercy upon your soul, Korthax, for I shall grant you none if your words prove empty," the dragon decreed as its giant wings began to unfurl, expanding like the heavens themselves, stretching to the very edges of the enclave.

Relor launched skyward with one ferocious downbeat, sending a vortex through the haven, turning it into a whirlwind of chaos. The roof of the enclave shattered immediately under the sheer force of the sovereign's ascent.

Caught in the gust, Korthax tumbled, tossed like a leaf in a storm, before careening through the large, ornate doors. His form finally came to a halt just outside the celestial dragon's sanctuary and into the camp proper.

After regaining his bearings, the general stood, dusted himself off, and looked skyward, trying to shake off the dizziness. His eyes didn't take long to refocus on the sovereign's silhouette, glowing radiantly from the reflected sunlight as it shot toward the ominous rift on the horizon. The behemoth surged forward with a speed that defied its size, each powerful beat of its wings propelling it faster, leaving a trail of scorching gold in its wake.

The tear in the fabric of reality was even more majestic, playing tricks on one's eye. At a glance, the two realms appeared as if a tailor had seamlessly stitched them together. From one angle, the world presented its regular, sunlit panorama, the familiar canvas of mountains and sky that Korthax had always known. Yet, barely a breath away, the other side of the rift was shrouded in night, dotted with alien constellations that gleamed with an uncanny luminescence.

As Relor surged into that alien world, the ancient celestial dragon felt a pulse reverberate through the fabric of his being. It was a sensation unlike any he had ever felt, as though an infinite number of tiny pricks and prods stabbed at the sinews of his anatomy.

Relor's nerves twitched with acute awareness, his consciousness attuned to the fact that the sky was no longer a sanctuary of open space and freedom. Each beat of his majestic wings stirred unseen forces that followed him everywhere. He could feel the whispers of this "all-seeing eye" brushing against its feathers—an insidious caress seeking to invade every inch of his being.

A fearful cry suddenly pierced the air. "My Sovereign!"

Caught by surprise, Relor turned to see one of the scaled dragon thralls marked by subjugation and service. Though a minor entity compared to the gargantuan Relor, the thrall was still formidable, capable of laying waste to armies or cities.

The scaled dragon spiraled upwards, its scales reflecting an array of twilight hues as it approached Relor with a frantic urgency. "You mustn't venture closer, mighty one! The mortals of the realm grow stronger the further you move from the rift! They see everything, feel everything!" Its voice cracked with panic.

Stopping mid-flight, Relor locked his formidable gaze on the scaled thrall, incredulous that a mere servant would address him so flippantly. Glaring harshly at the offender, Relor decided to punish this one later for its insolence. For now, they were on a battlefield.

"Why should the dragons fear the mortals?" Relor's voice thundered, disbelief and curiosity intertwining. "Since the dawn of time, we have soared the skies unchallenged. What strength do those beyond the rift possess?"

"They have woven a net across the sky, a net of metal and fire! I-It can see us, track us, hunt us," the smaller dragon stammered, but its voice gained strength as it continued. "Their metal beasts roar with a fury that rivals the greatest storms, spitting deadly darts that pierce the scales and flesh of even the wyrms!"

Relor's eyes blazed with stubborn fire as they flicked across the battlespace with intense curiosity. The enormous feathered dragon opened its mouth to reply but was abruptly interrupted as he felt a new and much more uncomfortable sensation.

Caught off guard, Relor shifted in discomfort as dozens of significantly more focused "eyes" seemed to bore into his very soul. An electric crackle tinged the air, and the atmosphere thickened with an unknown, alarming pulsation. Every dragon that littered the sky snapped their heads in different directions, their keen senses zeroing in on multiple sources of this concentrated intrusion.

Their eyes widened, and their pupils dilated as the flight-or-fight instinct took hold. Clearly, this strange sensation was only the prelude to the rumored lethal darts the metal beasts had released.

Another, even smaller dragon's voice roared, urging Relor into action. "My liege, we cannot remain here! Their aim is true, and their numbers are many!"

The skies erupted into chaos as dragons, wyrms, and wyverns veered in every direction. It was a mesmerizing yet heart-wrenching sight as majestic beasts, once masters of land, sea, and air, twisted desperately to evade whatever was hurtling toward them.

An echo of understanding flashed through Relor's ancient eyes as they narrowed, focusing on the distant horizon. The air was alive with the burning streaks of darts moving at impossible speeds for any mortal realm.

As the first darts neared the dragons, Relor unleashed a power only a few had ever seen and survived to tell the tale. His mouth glowed like molten metal, radiating a primordial heat of creation and destruction. With a guttural roar, he expelled a plume of flame—no ordinary fire, but plasma. The incandescent brilliance arced around him, stretching hundreds of meters and consuming the darts in its path.

But even Relor's might could not shield everyone. The horde of wyverns, already at a disadvantage by their diminutive stature and lack of robust defenses, were hit the hardest. Many perished instantly; their bodies vaporized in blinding flashes of light. The studier wyrms, though wounded, survived—scales splitting, wings tearing, but still able to fight.

The shockwaves had thrown the dragons off course. Disoriented, some flinched, but they remained capable of flight and battle.

Relor, too, was not exempt from the onslaught. Several of the darts managed to pierce his defenses, exploding against his thick feathers and causing him to growl in pain. Yet the mighty dragon pressed on, undeterred. His body surged forward with an acceleration only dragons possessed.

"Quickly! Close the distance!" the sovereign roared as he sped ahead, his wings creating a gust like a thunderclap. The other dragons followed suit, their bodies streaking through the sky at impossible speeds. As they accelerated, the sky transformed into a sea of monsters, harnessing their innate power to reach a velocity that usually seemed unattainable.

With their eyes ablaze with fiery determination, they bore down upon the source of their torment. Just ahead, Relor finally spotted them: hordes of metal beasts with wings of steel and hearts of fire, spitting death with unerring precision.

But the dragons' charge had not gone unnoticed. As they closed the gap, another volley of missiles erupted from the flying machines, each targeting the soaring beasts with calculated efficiency. The sky became a storm of fire and metal, each side unleashing its fury in a desperate battle for dominance.

Realizing the raw power bearing on them, the metal beasts tried to break contact. Their engines roared to life, jets of flame propelling them as they climbed steeply or banked sharply, trying to widen the distance. But they had underestimated the primal might and agility that fueled the dragons.

Relor led the charge with a fierce cry, his mouth glowing like a forge. A torrent of molten fire erupted from his jaws, engulfing the closest metal monsters in seconds, melting their steel exteriors.

To his side, another dragon used its raw physical strength, stretching its limbs to seize a fleeing machine. With a fierce swipe, its diamond-hard claws sheared through metal, ripping off a wing and sending the craft spiraling to the ground in flames. The machine became a tumbling mass of fire and debris, a testament to the dragon's unforgiving strength.

The sky was a canvas of chaos—roars, alien weaponry buzzing, fire and lightning swirling, and explosions lighting up the night as the two groups merged. For every dragon that fell, a metal beast ended in a symphony of destruction. It was a battle that defied reality, where ancient might clash with modern steel, threatening to tear the very heavens.

Amidst the destruction, a glimmer of unity emerged. Relor's commanding presence surged through every dragon, binding them as one. Together, they became a unit, a formidable force that wielded elemental breath and scales flying with synchronized mastery.

The smaller dragon, who had spoken earlier, found its voice again, shouting instructions and encouraging its comrades with newfound courage. The dragons began to utilize tactics they had never needed before, working together to outmaneuver and overwhelm their metal adversaries with superior speed and coordination.

Relor could feel a unified pulse of intent and will flow between him and the flight of dragons. Together, they formed a single force entity, a tapestry of flames and scales bound by a shared goal to preserve their lineage and reclaim the skies.

Yet, the metallic intruders also exhibited an eerie semblance of unity. Even as the dragons reduced their bodies to molten wrecks, the horde of machines maintained their relentless assault, their maneuvers precise and calculated.

From the dragons' perspective, the flying beasts appeared devoid of life but bore a sinister intelligence. They capitalized on their distance, striking from afar before the dragons could reach them.

Everything above the clouds was locked in a dance of death. In the pulsating heart of the battle, Relor and his brethren fought with a fury that echoed the ancient conflicts of their ancestors. Their cries filled the sky, a symphony of raw power reverberating across the heavens. Despite the ferocious onslaught, the dragons moved gracefully, a ballet of fire and wind defying the metallic monsters that sought to claim their domain.

Memories of battles from long ago flooded Relor's mind—when kin clashed against kin, feathers against scales, in a whirlwind of fire and fury. Those battles had been personal, a tumultuous struggle for power and dominion. But this this was different. The metallic adversaries bore no emotion, no sentiment, no regret. They were instruments of destruction, each move calculated, each strike executed with admirable and terrifying precision.

Relor roared, fury rising at the sight of soulless, mortal-made machines striking down his majestic kind as if they were mere prey. A blistering anger surged within him, an inferno threatening to consume his very being. Yet within that rage lay a well of ancient determination, a force capable of carving valleys and sundering mountains.

Dragons and their kin were the rightful rulers and caretakers of all the realms. They were the guardians of ancient lore and the protectors of mortals—creatures who graced the dreams and stories of the very beings that arrogantly sought to deny them.

And as the metallic demons advanced, converging from the darkening horizon, ancient, untamed energy surged within Relor, rising like an unstoppable tide.

With his massive wings outstretched, Relor lifted his head toward the heavens. From the depths of his soul, a roar resounded, echoing with magic that pulsed through time and space. It was a cry infused with the wisdom of the ancients, a harmonious blend of power and grace that sang the song of creation and echoed the heartbeat of the universe itself.

The dragons around him felt it—a resonance that struck deep, fusing with their very essence. It awakened a latent force within them, a wellspring of power that strengthened their bodies and ignited a flame in their hearts that even death could not extinguish.

A golden aura radiated from the gargantuan, feathered dragon, emitting a tangible energy that spread outward in undulating waves, wrapping each of his kin in a warm embrace of light and might. Every dragon, every wyrm, and even every wyvern became a beacon, a luminous entity that mirrored the golden fire burning within Relor. With the sovereign at the head of the pack, they advanced toward the metal monsters, breathing fire upon the numerous deadly darts hurtling toward them.

Chapter 5

Within the bustling confines of the makeshift command post, a rhythmic symphony of artillery fire and frantic crew movements provided a grim backdrop as Brigadier General Lawrence Hargrove wrestled the landline from its cradle. His face, lined with the stress of leadership amid the chaos, grew taut as steel cables when he spoke.

"Sir, I'm doing everything possible to contain the situation," Hargrove said while his aids engaged in their own frantic conversations with field commanders. "But I've got no lines. I've got everything from the rangers to the local police mixed with the enemy out there." He paused for a moment before bringing a hand to his face. "I don't know how long we can hold out, but it won't be long. I need those reinforcements, and I needed them yesterday."

On the other end of the line, General Vincent Turner's voice echoed with the weight of the nation's highest military echelons. The shouting in the background hinted at the magnitude of nationwide mobilization.

"I hear you, Lawrence." Turner's voice was like ground steel, unwavering amid the pandemonium. "We've got a total recall from Poland to Japan beelining it to Ohio, but they need time, time we desperately need you to buy."

Hargrove's jaw clenched, a muscle twitching in his cheek as he surveyed the hectic room. Reports of units being overrun streamed in while his aids scrambled to regain control of the situation. "Time isn't a luxury we can afford, Vincent. The Air Force is keeping the... the dragons at bay, but they're taking heavy losses. And if those beasts come down in full force, we don't stand a chance. We're holding on by a thread here."

A long silence followed, filled only by the distant thrum of artillery and the frantic activity within the command center. The maps spread on the table seemed to pulse with a life of their own, bearing witness to a clash of worlds that was as brutal as it was unimaginable.

Vincent's voice crackled back, carrying a somber weight that mirrored the dire circumstances. "I understand, Lawrence, and I want you to know we're moving heaven and earth to back you up, but..." The Chairman of the Joint Chiefs of Staff sighed deeply. "If these things break through and reach any of the major population centers, the President has authorized a nuclear strike."

The words hung heavy between them. General Hargrove sat down, placing a hand on his head. "God, Vincent," he muttered in horror. "I never thought I'd live to see the day when that would be an option on our own soil." His voice nearly cracked as his mind raced to find any other way to prevent such a cataclysm.

He could almost picture Vincent on the other end, in the well-lit rooms of the Pentagon, surrounded by the nation's brilliant military minds, all grappling with the unimaginable. Yet, here it was, unfolding in real-time.

"We'll hold, sir," the brigadier general declared, cradling his head. "We'll hold, or we'll die."

After a moment, Vincent's voice came through, frayed but steady. "Elements of the 1st Cavalry Division and the 82nd Airborne are already in theater, but their full strength won't be there another 24 hours." His words hit Hargrove like a gut punch. The seconds stretched painfully as the weight of leadership pressed down on him. "ISR reports the enemy's main body is pushing north. My recommendation is to start pulling back. Godspeed, Lawrence."

After the line fell silent, Hargrove slammed his field phone down and immediately stormed over to the sprawled map on the table. He meticulously examined the crucial locations between their current HQ and Cleveland. "We need to implement a 'defense-in-depth' approach," he directed, his voice firm. "Draw them close, extend their lines, and bleed them relentlessly at every juncture."

The officers in the tent rushed over as the general highlighted Zanesville, Wheeling, Marietta, and New Philadelphia. "Pull our boys back to these positions. These towns will act as our secondary line of defense and buy us some breathing room."

Hargrove continued, sketching defensive points with swift, precise movements. "We'll stagger our defenses, using the natural terrain and any urban environments to our advantage."

"We can use the highways as choke points," Colonel Reynalds, his executive officer, suggested. "Fortify the overpasses and intersections. They'll become kill zones for artillery and close air support."

"I don't know about that, sir," Major Lee, the operations officer chimed in. "The big lizards may be preoccupied, but there's still plenty of those small bastards flying about. They've already proven they can pick apart our rotary aircraft."

Hargrove shot a firm glance at Lee. "Listen, gentlemen," he began, his voice gravelly and commanding with a gravitas that drew immediate attention. "We aren't in a position to worry about the attrition rate of our aircraft. I want everything in the air—we can't afford to hold back."

"We need as much of our forces *intact* when we reach New Philadelphia." The general slammed his finger down on Akron, just below Cleveland. "Because that's where we're making our last stand. We hold there, or we die there."

Silence settled heavily upon the room, the gravity of Hargrove's words sinking into every officer present. They exchanged stoic glances even though a storm raged within each of them. With a silent nod, the HQ staff dispersed to get to work, leaving Hargrove standing alone, leaning heavily over the map.

* * *

BRRRRRRRRRRRRRRRRRRRT!

A thunderous roar resounded overhead as an A-10 Warthog cut through the smoke-filled sky, executing a devastating strafing run. Its 30mm Gatling gun unleashed hellfire upon the fantastical horde in the open field, mowing down waves of monstrous creatures and armored beings. The sheer force of its firepower carved a clear path in the battlefield, granting DuPont and his men a brief reprieve from the relentless onslaught.

But as quickly as the Warthog had entered the fray, it began to climb and bank sharply, its engines howling in response to evade the new threat. Two massive, winged monsters erupted from the dense tree line, their wingbeats creating gusts that knocked over smaller creatures below. With a horrendous snarl, the beasts fixed their predatory gaze on the retreating aircraft, their leathery wings slicing through the air with alarming speed for their size.

Instant recognition flashed across Lieutenant DuPont's face as he saw the Warthog's merciless gun *devastate* the enemy force's right flank. "Reset left!" he bellowed to his men, pointing toward the exposed vulnerability in the enemy lines.

"Reset left!" his men echoed as they quickly repositioned. In their rush to reinforce their decimated flank, the enemy had left a glaring gap in their formation. Their magical barriers flickered inconsistently and then failed completely as a torrent of machine gun and rifle fire ripped into them.

Suddenly, a titanic figure surged from the chaotic depths of the enemy lines. This humanoid behemoth towered nearly fifteen feet tall, its large, portly abdomen in stark contrast to the masterfully crafted armor it wore. Wielding a colossal metal shield in one hand and a menacing metal club in the other, the brute charged furiously across the open field toward the tree line.

Friend and foe alike shifted their attention to the armored monster. In response, a relentless hail of gunfire turned toward the giant, but the massive shield deflected every round with ease. Even the normally devastating .50 cal rounds effortlessly bounced off as the ground shook with each of the creature's thunderous steps.

"Back blast! Back blast!" one of the Special Forces operators DuPont had met just an hour prior shouted as he aimed his Carl Gustaf at a monstrous figure.

A deafening blast rang out with a squeeze of the trigger as the anti-tank warhead streaked through the air, finding its mark. The giant barely had time to react before a searing white-hot jet of molten copper pierced the massive shield, carving through the creature's flesh.

But the giant wasn't the only casualty. The explosion tore violently through its body and ejected out whatever bone fragments and shards of metal into all the beings behind it; small lizards and armored figures were showered with the deadly debris.

Seizing the opportunity, DuPont bolted from behind the fallen tree he had been using for cover and dashed to the nearest machine gunner. Tapping the side of his helmet he pointed to the group of exposed magic users and shouted, "Light them the fuck up!"

Without even skipping a beat, the machine gunner shifted his fire left, spraying a group of robed individuals who were hastily erecting a new line of magical defenses. The machine gun chattered incessantly, and each bullet that slammed into the glowing barrier sent out ripples of distortion—until a few rounds punched through.

The robed figures, a mix of individuals with varying degrees of skill, lost their coordination under the relentless hail of gunfire. The entire left flank's barrier crumbled, and in its absence, death followed. DuPont's platoon and the National Guard seized the moment, unleashing everything they had on the exposed horde.

No mercy was given as the enemy's morale broke and their formations collapsed. The shimmering blue barrier fell completely, leaving the enemy defenseless as they fled toward the opposing tree line. Exposed and vulnerable, they were torn apart by DuPont's platoon and remnants of the entrenched National Guard.

The chatter of machine guns and the blasts of shoulder-launched munitions scythed through the horde, leaving nothing but devastation in their wake. Soldiers, who moments earlier had clung desperately to their lines, now avenged their fallen brothers by mercilessly cutting down the invaders.

"Cease fire!" Captain Duggen's voice suddenly rang out as he ran up and down the line. "I said cease fire!"

With reluctant obedience, the symphony of violence and destruction dwindled to a grim silence, punctuated only by the moans of the wounded and the crackling of burning debris. Soldiers hesitated, fingers hovering near their triggers as they surveyed the shattered remnants of the horde, wary of a potential counterattack.

Taking position beside DuPont, Captain Duggen swiftly brought up his end-user device and glanced down at the dynamic tactical battle map displayed on its screen. "Command's ordering a retreat," he stated tersely, his eyes darting between the device and the aftermath of the battle. "We need to use this lull to get the fuck out of here, and I need you and your Bradleys to hold the rear."

The thumps of the Bradleys' main guns echoed in the distance, engaging whatever was on the main road. "I've got too many wounded and too many civilians to move fast, and you're the best equipped to shield us as we fall back," Duggen continued, his brows furrowed.

"Roger that, Captain," DuPont replied, glancing down at his own end-user device.

He hadn't noticed it, but his platoon was several kilometers away from the main body of their battalion. Zooming out on his tactical map, he nearly gasped at the sight: a sea of red blinking icons indicated heavy enemy positions and lines of contact, yet their immediate vicinity was relatively clear. Somehow, they had ended up in a pocket of minimal resistance while the bulk of the enemy forces concentrated around Cambridge High School just a mile or two away from the main road.

Shaking his head, the lieutenant turned back to Captain Duggen. "It looks pretty clear from here to the marked staging area," DuPont said, snapping his device shut against his chest and looking around at his men. "We won't have much time, but we can load the wounded in the Bradleys and make our way back to the rear."

DuPont's gaze then shifted to the main road, where he saw massive muzzle flashes from one of his Bradleys between the gaps of thick brush. "Plus, those things have been firing non-stop. They should be pretty low on ammo by now."

The captain nodded gravely, realizing their window of opportunity was far too narrow for comfort. "Fires and air support are sparse, too. They're concentrated in other areas—it was already a miracle that one of the special forces guys got a fast mover to even respond." He sighed, bringing a hand to his head. "We need to move now before it's too late."

With a decisive nod, DuPont picked up the radio and began issuing concise commands, setting the withdrawal into motion. The captain mimicked the action, ordering his men to start corralling the civilians and prepare the wounded.

The encampment erupted into a flurry of action as soldiers worked tirelessly, moving equipment while preparing the wounded and civilians for evacuation. The air was thick with urgency, the harsh undertones of barked orders and the mechanical roar of vehicles coming to life forming a tense atmosphere that permeated the entrenched position.

A little farther from the buzz of activity, the group of special forces soldiers kept their eyes trained on the areas where the invaders had retreated, waiting patiently for anyone foolish enough to stick their head out.

SNAP!

The muffled yet still loud report of a suppressed rifle pierced the morning air. Behind the trigger was Richard Schwarz, the team's resident sniper. A towering and pale figure with a wild, untamed beard reminiscent of a Viking, he was a living testament to the strength and perseverance of the Jäger of old.

"Dipshit," the operator sneered as a figure with what looked like rabbit ears clutched their chest and retreated back into the foliage. "Hey, Cole, I dunno if my rifle is penetrating these guys. I didn't exactly bring anything other than 7.62," he said, turning his head to Major Patrick Coleman, leader of the Special Forces Operational Detachment-Alpha (ODA) team.

Coleman bore the kind of features that could easily blend into any crowd yet held an innate quality that demanded respect. His platinum blonde hair was neat and closely cropped, the picture-perfect definition of a leader of elite soldiers. His short beard, more a golden stubble really, was meticulously maintained, adding a rugged charm to his otherwise unassuming visage.

Looking over to his right with his crystal blue eyes, Cole acknowledged Schwarz' concern with an annoyed grunt. "Maybe we are, maybe we aren't," he said, shifting his position slightly, keeping a keen eye on the ever-moving boundaries of the forest. The underlying tension seemed to have multiplied, becoming almost palpable.

"But it seems to be doing something since they're dipping their heads back in after we hit 'em." the major continued, stretching his neck to the side. "Just keep popping them. It's not like we can do anything about it right now."

Schwarz shook his head in disbelief. "I mean, I'm still in fucking awe," he said, shifting the rifle in a more comfortable position. "When they first threw us out here, I expected aliens, not... Lord of the Rings bullshit."

As the strained sounds of suppressed laughter rose, Bennett Moran, the ODA team's engineer, couldn't hold back any longer. Tall and lanky, he was a sharp contrast to the muscular builds of some of his team members. "Yeah, maybe we can ask one of the dragons if Sauron's behind this," he quipped with a mischievous smirk.

"I mean, I wouldn't count anything out," Elijah Drake, the team's medic, chimed in, rubbing his thick, scraggly beard. He rolled up his sleeves to cool down on the hot summer night, his earthy brown skin glistening in the heat. "I did blast a fatty cosplaying as a Balrog with a Gustaf," he added, smirking at Coleman..

Coleman simply shook his head in derision. "Fucking nerds," he muttered before refocusing on the tree line.

"You're just jealous we have hobbies outside the Army," Elijah retorted, the grin evident in his voice even as he kept his eyes peeled on their surroundings.

Bennett chimed in, "Yeah, Tolkien is a masterpiece. Besides, it'll go a long way to get familiar with our new friends here, since we're effectively being invaded by Narnia."

"No, no. Cole's definitely right," Schwarz interjected as he squeezed the trigger, dropping another scout too foolish not to keep their head down. "You're both nerds."

"Fucking nerds, to be exact," Coleman corrected.

A silence fell, punctuated only by the sounds of distant gunfire and explosions. Occasionally, a stray artillery round or streak of magical energy whizzed overhead, a surreal reminder of the blend of technology and mysticism that defined this conflict. The team hunkered down, the forest offering them a semblance of protection and camouflage against the chaos of the outside world.

"Do you think they have elves?" Elijah suddenly spoke up. "I'd do an elf."

Before anyone could respond, Bennett gave the medic a side-eye. "You'd do anything, degenerate."

Coleman placed a hand on his head, trying to subdue a growing headache. "Oh, for fuck's sake." He sighed, knowing another round of their incessant bickering was about to start. And like clockwork, Elijah turned his head and narrowed his eyes at the engineer.

But Major Coleman interrupted before the medic could speak. "Alright, shut the fuck up now, please," he begged more than commanded, rubbing his temples in evident frustration.

Amused snorts from unseen members of the ODA team echoed further down the line. Another bout of silence reigned as they waited for their conventional counterparts to finish their preparations.

However, Elijah couldn't help himself. "Fuck you," he muttered.

"No, fuck *you*," Bennett immediately shot back, knowing the insult was coming.

Coleman's growl of annoyance was drowned out by the crackle of their radios coming to life. "Baron, this is Viking. Be advised that a large mass of enemy forces is starting to converge on your location. We're going to saturate the area with artillery, ETA 20 minutes. How copy?"

After glaring at the two idiots, Coleman grabbed his push-to-talk and responded, "Roger that, Viking. Baron copies all. Baron out." He turned to Elijah, jerking his head toward the makeshift encampment. "Alright, let's do this shit."

Without needing further prompting, Elijah stood up and followed Coleman to help speed things along.

As the two navigated through the dense brush, Coleman looked up and frowned. He couldn't quite process the sight of the enormous, building-sized dragons chasing after fighter aircrafts that were trying desperately to keep their distance. It felt like a fever dream, especially when his eyes fell upon the absolutely gargantuan golden dragon spitting fire like a fire hose, twisting and turning as if physics were merely a suggestion.

"Maybe we are being invaded by Narnia," he muttered, picking up the pace.

CHAPTER 6

A melancholic chill filled the air as DuPont and his platoon sat atop the Bradleys, traveling north.

However, he and his platoon weren't alone. Everywhere DuPont looked, soldiers and guardsmen clung to their vehicles, gripping their gear and weapons. Each vehicle, from Humvees to larger transport trucks, was packed to capacity with wounded soldiers and civilians. Many were in visible distress, their faces pallid with shock and fatigue. Children clung to their parents, trying to comprehend the chaos around them. Medics worked tirelessly, tending to the wounded even as they moved, stabilizing injuries, and offering what little comfort they could.

The freeway was a sea of military and civilian vehicles. As far as the eye could see, the lanes were congested with a seemingly endless convoy, all heading in the same direction. Pickup trucks, SUVs, and even the occasional school bus—repurposed to ferry evacuees—rode alongside tanks and artillery units. Every so often, helicopters pierced the skyline, blades thundering as they provided aerial support and surveyed the ground below.

As they fled, DuPont turned his gaze south toward the dark horizon lit by the fires of the town they'd been tasked with defending. Some would call the retreat organized, but he figured it only seemed that way because everyone was running in the same direction.

Cambridge was lost the moment that rift opened, and those monsters poured out. No matter how he or anyone else deluded themselves, DuPont realized there was never any real chance of holding that town. But he couldn't stop thinking about all the people they'd had to leave behind.

Captain Duggen had managed to keep some semblance of order, but DuPont couldn't tell whether they were obeying his command or just doing what seemed best. They followed the freeway to the next town, the horde close on their heels.

Not too long ago, DuPont learned that those monsters had their own version of artillery, and some of it had already landed in the area. He looked around and saw a small country home that was similar to his granny's house just outside of Atlanta. A cute, dainty home now turned into blackened slag with its garden and white picket fence still intact.

That was when it truly hit him. They had been invaded.

The scream of low-flying aircraft unleashing missiles before steeply climbing back into the sky knocked DuPont out of his reverie. The missiles arced up, illuminating the horizon with blinding flashes as they struck unseen targets.

Cries of fear rippled throughout the convoy as civilians huddled closer together, trying to shield themselves and their loved ones from the impending danger. Children buried their faces into their parents' chests, their tiny bodies trembling with terror.

"I've never thought I'd see the day where we're the ones retreating while the Air Force charges headlong into the fray," Hofmann's gruff voice came over the commotion, a mix of awe and disbelief evident in his tone.

Thankful for the distraction, DuPont turned his gaze toward Hofmann, who was perched in the commander's cupola of the Bradley, his eyes fixed on the distant aerial ballet of fighter jets darting through the sky. "They're the tip of the spear right now," DuPont said with genuine admiration. "The Air Force and the Air National Guard have been throwing themselves at those things just to keep the bigger ones off our ass."

Hofmann frowned, adjusting his helmet slightly. "The bigger ones? How much bigger are we talking?" He leaned back, glancing up at the sky as another set of fighters fired more missiles. "Those fuckers in the forest were as big as F-16s."

DuPont grimaced, his blue eyes reflecting the weight of the intel he'd heard. "Big enough to take out an Abrams. Heard it over the net that Delta was screaming about how some big piece of shit slagged an entire tank platoon with a single breath."

A deep sigh escaped Hofmann as he closed his eyes and hung his head momentarily, absorbing DuPont's words. "Fuck me. Slagged? As in melted?"

The lieutenant nodded slowly, the soldiers around him shifting nervously. "Melted, vaporized—whatever you want to call it. The tank armor didn't stand a chance. Reports suggest that the metal just liquified."

"But that's not even the worst of it." DuPont glanced south, where faint plumes of smoke marked their previous encounters. "Reports are coming in that they're getting smarter, adjusting their tactics. With every move we make, they respond faster and adapt. Their ground forces? They're no longer standing out in the open like they're reenacting some ancient battlefield. They're using cover, flanking, and coordinating."

Hofmann's brows furrowed in frustration. "You're saying they're learning from us?"

DuPont shook his head. "I'd say it's more like they're starting to pay attention to what works and what doesn't." He sighed, adjusting his rifle. "Command thinks they underestimated us and waltz in here thinking they could just burn a few towns, awe us with their size and might, and then watch us kneel. They probably expected a swift and relatively bloodless victory on their part."

"And now they've realized we're dangerous after we bloodied their nose," Hofmann mused, gazing at the horizon.

A silence ensued, broken only by the distant roar of jet engines. Suddenly, Hofmann squinted at the sky, noticing a formation of lower-flying fighters launching missiles toward the horizon. "By the way, why are they flying so low?" Hofmann questioned, pointing upward.

DuPont followed Hofmann's gaze, recognizing the pattern. "Those fuckers are hiding in the trees," he explained with a grimace on his face. "They're blasting any of those smaller dragons whenever they pop out of the forest."

Hofmann's eyes widened in realization. "Great, so you're telling me these dragons are VTOLs, hiding in the goddamn trees and ambushing us whenever they feel like it?"

"Yep." DuPont nodded grimly. "It's harder for the flyboys to detect them when they're so low and nestled in the foliage. Even our recon drones have been having a hell of a time spotting them until they're practically airborne and right on top of our units."

DuPont leaned back, feeling the vibrations from the Bradley beneath him. "And that's not the only problem. Once they take off, they're nimble, fast as fuck, and can change direction in a heartbeat." A few of his men on the Bradley laughed at the absurdity. "And they can *feel* fucking radar, apparently. Our SAMs have an okay hit rate, but not enough that makes anyone feel comfortable."

After that piece of news, no one felt like asking more questions. A depressing silence swept across the convoy, broken only by the droning rumble of tracks and the deafening hiss of missiles fired from jets overhead. Soldiers exchanged worried glances, gripped their weapons tighter, and hunkered down, each lost in their thoughts.

For once, they were going into battle without overmatch capabilities, a situation the U.S. military hadn't faced in quite a long time.

As the convoy continued its steady advance, the battered defenders finally drove into New Philadelphia. Signs of a somewhat organized military presence were palpable here. Still, it was a hodgepodge of rapidly deployed units and chaotic reorganization, all working toward the same goal of survival.

The streets were lined with military and civilian vehicles, and schools and municipal buildings had been hastily converted into field hospitals and command centers. Everywhere DuPont looked, he could see service members from the Army, Air Force, Marines, and strangely enough, even the Navy were working alongside local law enforcement and first responders. The usual distinctions between units had vanished, replaced by a singular objective: defense.

Tanks and armored vehicles were positioned at key intersections, vigilantly watching the distant tree lines and skies. Nearby, a group of Seabees worked to construct barricades, turning the once-peaceful town into a veritable fortress.

Despite preparations for the impending battle, another operation was also in full swing. Emergency services were in a frantic race to evacuate the remaining civilians from the potential war zone. Buses, vans, and even regular sedans were being readied to ferry families, the elderly, and anyone not directly involved in the defense efforts out of harm's way.

DuPont's attention was drawn to a familiar group as the Bradley maneuvered through the town's main thoroughfare. In a cleared-out parking lot stood the special forces team he had spotted earlier, rapidly refitting and re-arming from crates of weapons and supplies offloaded by an endless stream of helicopters.

Adjacent to the team, a few Blackhawk helicopters and V-22 Ospreys sat with blades still spinning, engines emanating a low growl, indicative of their recent return from some mission. Ground crew darted around the choppers, refueling and performing quick checks to ensure they'd be ready for the next sortie.

DuPont narrowed his eyes as he watched the team's efficiency. They didn't waste any time as they shoved grenades in their pockets, magazines in their pouches, and water in their packs. Within seconds, the elite soldiers departed toward an Osprey full of fresh Marines, its rotors churning up dust from the asphalt.

Hofmann leaned closer to DuPont, shouting over the cacophony of helicopters and armored vehicles, "Damn, they're not wasting any time!"

DuPont nodded, his eyes fixed on the rapidly departing rotary aircraft. "Yeah, they've come to fuck!" the lieutenant shouted back.

Before they could continue discussing the special forces team, the ground vibrated as a procession of M1A2 Abrams tanks roared into view. These mechanical beasts moved in perfect synchrony, their powerful engines whining in unison and their heavy treads churning the battered streets as they sped toward the front line.

Hofmann felt a rush of pride as the behemoths rolled by. "Looks like we've come to fuck too," he muttered with a half-smile.

"Let's not keep them waiting, then!" DuPont, catching the sentiment, nodded in agreement. "C'mon, let's drop off the wounded and get resupplied. We've got lizards to kill!"

The Bradleys roared to life once more, storming toward the aid station and assembly area. It wouldn't be long before the platoon joined the heavy machines, all converging to a pre-designated staging area. Soldiers checked their gear, commanders reviewed the battle plans, and everyone prepared for the coming offensive.

* * *

"Mages and healers to the front!" bellowed Rhyzukar, a service-bound dragonkin commander.

The commanding voice echoed across the expansive plain, filled with Drakoni legions and the empire's vassal forces. Marks of servitude adorned his scaled form. Silver shackles covered in ethereal flames were tattooed around his muscular forelimbs, a spectral symbol of the ancient oath binding him and his kin to the empire's service.

"Make haste, lest the enemy's winged monstrosities and iron chariots overrun our brothers!" Rhyzukar's fiery eyes darted about, surveying the mayhem below as his forces faced the might of magicks they could hardly fathom.

Yzael, standing below the elevated commander, looked up, her face contorted with concern and disbelief. Her striking platinum hair cascaded in elegant waves, a striking contrast to her ethereal, nearly translucent skin. Her elongated ears, characteristic of the high elves, stretched out nearly as long as a forearm. They had a slight, elegant droop to them due to their weight, making her appearance even more unique and striking. The gentle curve of those ears gave her an appearance of regal grace, but at this moment, they quivered with anxiety.

Yzael turned to her direct superior, Lord Jrazem, who had trained, studied, and mediated with the Seraph Empire on behalf of the vassal states for months leading up to the invasion. All intelligence had pointed to an easy conquest, a realm devoid of any potent magic that could challenge the might of the empire and its tributaries. But after what she had seen earlier, her confidence in victory was shaken.

The celestial seraphic dragon, one of the empire's sovereigns, had soared through the sky and into the rift. Initially, Yzael thought it was an eccentric inspection of their immediate victory, but their anticipated triumphant return never came. Instead, urgent cries and desperate calls to strengthen the barrier protecting the small foothold they established on the other were all they heard.

"I thought this was supposed to be easy," said a voice behind Yzael.

The high elf turned around and saw one of the largest humans she had ever known, a towering and brawny figure named Gideon. A warrior from her side of the rift, he was one of the many unaffiliated freelancers contracted by the independent principalities, city-states, and small kingdoms to assist in the invasion.

Clad in heavy iron armor that had seen better days, the plating was scuffed and marred from countless battles, adding a layer of history to the already fearsome appearance. Despite its worn state, Gideon stood firm and unyielding, his massive axe resting on his shoulder.

Stretching his rough, scarred face into a smile, Gideon shifted his scrutinizing gaze toward the rift in the distance. "They said it'd be like hunting fawn in an open field, right?" he teased, slapping Yzael's shoulder with a heavy gauntlet, causing her to stagger slightly. "I guess it serves 'em right in bein' so damned arrogant."

The sheer force of Gideon's jovial pat sent a shudder through Yzael's delicate frame. She cast him a sharp glance, her eyes like amethysts glinting under the uncertain light filtering from the chaotic sky. "This is no jesting matter, Gideon," she hissed, her voice laced with apprehension. She smoothed her opalescent robes, the fabric shimmering with ethereal lights as she righted herself. "The empire had a veritable horde of dragons, let alone wyrms or wyverns, and now they're trying to scrape together every mage they can!"

"By the hells, they've even sent their sovereign in, which was *hours* ago!" Yzael snarled, gripping her grimoire tightly.

Gideon's laugh echoed loudly across the field, clanging metal and desperate commands providing a chaotic symphony in the background. His laughter, devoid of mirth, bore the bitterness of a warrior who had seen the folly of many campaigns.

But the mirthful demeanor soon dwindled, his face hardening by the unspoken worries mirrored in Yzael's wide eyes. He watched the desperate scramble further ahead, the once-mighty legions in disarray, dragons and their kin limping back into the encampment with wounds that seemed impossible to inflict.

"Aye," he grumbled, his gaze hardening as he took in the chaotic panorama unfolding. "They thought to tame another world, bind it in chains, but look now. They're caught in their own snare."

His attention shifted back to Yzael, his face devoid of emotion. "They were fools to think they could just march into another realm and claim it as their own. Fools to underestimate the power that dwells in unknown worlds."

Yzael's eyes were shadowed with foreboding as she stared at the confusion and turmoil unraveling amongst their ranks. "But we are bound in this folly now, Gideon. Our fate is intertwined with theirs—" Her words were soon cut short by innumerable flashes of light in the direction of the rift.

Then came the sound of deafening explosions as the barrier protecting the growing outpost on the other side of the rift glowed a bright blue. Yzael felt it; the barrier screamed in agony as it absorbed the concussive forces, its ethereal membrane shimmering in and out of existence as it struggled against the overwhelming onslaught.

A torrent of hushed whispers rippled through the mass of mages as Yzael's eyes widened, fixated on the mesmerizing, terrifying display.

Her heart thundered in her chest, the cacophony of explosion magic assaulting her senses. "By the ancients," she whispered in horror.

That was not the familiar, heated embrace of fire magic. The violent concussions and blinding light bore the hallmarks of the ancient and forbidden art of explosion magic, a power so uncontrollable and deadly that only archwizards or dragons dared wield it.

Yet here it was, unleashed with precision by a realm that was supposed to harbor no magical essence.

Though unversed in the intricate lores of magic, Gideon sensed the extraordinary nature of the assault. The blows that reverberated through the earth spoke of immense, fearsome power. "What in the realms is happening, Yzael?" he inquired, his voice tinged with the unfamiliar sting of dread. Once staunch and unyielding, his steel armor now felt like a fragile shell in the face of this boundless onslaught.

The high elf's visage, painted in hues of despair and awe, met Gideon's questioning gaze. "Explosion magic." Yzael gasped, her voice almost lost amidst the cacophony around her. "How do they command such power?"

"Well." Gideon hefted his axe into his hands. "Suppose we're 'bout to find out, ain't we?"

With trepidation, the armies of the vassal states marched forward, the draconic and seraphic commanders leading their units as the vanguard. The elite legions moved with unwavering discipline, starkly contrasting their disorderly vassals.

And so, the armies crossed the threshold, their forms bathed in the astral luminescence of the barrier's embrace. They emerged into the unknown, the realm beyond whispering a cold and deadly welcome.

Chapter 7

Looking up at the alien night sky, Yzael and Gideon watched as the formidable forms of dragon flights, fresh from their realm, soared overhead. The two felt a distinct unease seeing such power concentrated in one place. Even just one of these creatures could bring a city to its knees, and here they saw a veritable horde flying over these foreign lands...

And they were trouble.

"I bet ya an entire gold we won't live to see the morrow," Gideon said with a derisive laugh, his gruff voice cutting through the silence. He might have continued his pessimistic musing, but Yzael's sharp reprimand interrupted him.

"Be silent, brute!" she barked, her eyes focusing on the sky.

While most of the flights headed further into the heavens to reinforce their brethren, Yzael noticed several dragons lingering near the barrier and the outpost under construction. The majestic beasts were fixated on the horizon, their eyes shimmering with a spectral glow. The sight filled the troops below with a cold, unsettling sense of expectation.

"What are they waiting for?" Gideon muttered, disregarding Yzael's earlier admonition. He squinted towards the distance, trying to discern what had captivated the dragons' attention.

"Hush!" Yzael hissed, clutching her grimoire tightly to her chest as she too strained to pierce the distant haze. The smoke from the still-burning town filled the night sky, leaving much to be desired.

As they watched silently, a deafening roar erupted from one of the dragons, which hurled itself toward the horizon with frightening speed. With one powerful beat of its wings, it disappeared like a comet. Others quickly followed suit, their forms shrinking into the distant gloom, leaving only the echo of their wings in the air.

The troops watched the breathtaking scene unfold as each dragon unleashed its unique might upon an unseen adversary. Through the murky air, a spectacular array of colors blossomed. Fiery plumes of red and orange mingled with vibrant torrents of icy blue and white while bolts of lightning interlaced them, stitching the sky with threads of electric gold.

Yzael's eyes widened at the mesmerizing spectacle, displaying a dance of beauty and destruction. "By the ancients," she whispered in awe. Despite the gravity of the situation, the sight held an elegance, a testament to the dragons' diverse elemental fury.

But soon, the mesmerizing lights faded, replaced by the low roar of something... alien.

Suddenly, Yzael and the others spotted them. Uncountable numbers of metallic creatures, their bodies narrow and arrow-like with stubby wings, silhouetted against the otherworldly moon as they sped across the night sky. Yzael's heart pounded as the world around her seemingly drowned in the ominous roar of these impossibly fast, alien entities.

They darted through the air with an unnatural, mechanical precision, moving in unison like a school of fish. Half as long as a wyvern, the entities emitted no aura of life, and their cold, metallic bodies seemed to drain the very warmth from the air as they passed.

As the swift metallic creatures reached the barrier, the ethereal shimmer of the magical wall halted their advance. Upon contact, enormous explosions blossomed against the barrier, each detonation casting violent ripples of blue energy across its surface.

The luminescent shield absorbed most of the impacts, its hue flickering erratically with each successive strike. However, these explosions' sheer magnitude and frequency began to take their toll. Fissures of raw magical energy started to form, spider-webbing across the barrier's surface. Soldiers, mages, and all onlookers watched in horror as the protective wall briefly flickered out.

With a sound akin to a shattering crystal, a section of the barrier faltered and collapsed, and a new wave of metallic entities broke through, with dragons in hot pursuit. The advancing legions watched in horror as explosions tore through the staging area just in front of the rift.

Yzael nearly fell to her knees at the sight of the destruction. She couldn't imagine the number of mages lost, let alone the casualties. The barrier should have been near impenetrable with the amount of magic the sorcerers and wizards forced into it.

Gideon was the first to react, his voice booming above the maelstrom as he tried to restore order. "Rally! Form ranks, we need to end whatever is spitting such hatred!" he ordered amidst the cacophony of explosions and the incessant shrieks of the alien projectiles still streaming in, with dragons desperately chasing them.

The commanders of the retinue echoed the command, their voices amplified by magic and vibrating with urgency.

"Keep moving! We aren't the targets!" their commander, Lysandra, clad in her magical armor, called out. "But be prepared to erect a barrier on my command!"

The legions, shaking with fear and anticipation, gathered their wits at their commanders' orders. Gideon and Lysandra's indomitable will shone like a beacon through the chaos as they approached the town.

Heaving a deep breath, Yzael stepped forward and began chanting. Strange energy gathered at her fingertips as they moved deftly through the air, weaving intricate patterns. A faint whistling grew louder until the smoke started to shift.

What started as a gentle breeze swiftly transformed into gusts, pushing back the smoky tendrils that had sought to obscure their path, revealing a scene of carnage. The acrid scent of burnt wood and liquified metal filled everyone's nostrils.

"What do ya think this was?" Gideon asked, moving to stand beside Yzael, his heavy boots crunching over someone's charred remains.

Yzael's equally curious eyes fell on a burned-out, misshapen metal hulk. "I even cannot fathom," she said somberly. The outline was odd, alien to their realm, and marked by strange symbols scorched and barely visible on the malformed metal. "This thing appears to have wheels, so a vehicle or carriage of some sort?"

Gideon's eyes followed her gaze to the shrunken and molten blobs that had once appeared to be wheels. "Where would one latch the beasts to pull it?" he mused aloud. "Seems awfully inefficient for a carriage."

Yzael furrowed her brow, scanning the area for their commander. Her eyes finally landed on Lysandra and her magical armor. The domineering woman was deeply engrossed in a conversation with a draconic commander, whose towering form loomed over her. The dragonborn, clad in dark, earthy scales, spoke in urgent, resonant tones.

Lysandra's face was drawn with worry as she listened to the dragonborn speak frantically. Yzael had never seen a being of their species look so panicked before in her life, and the sight added to her growing anxiety. She and Gideon finally approached them cautiously, their steps hesitant as they got closer to the duo.

"If you hear the whistling of the wind, you must take shelter!" the draconic commander said, his voice sharp and urgent. "If you're out in the open, seek any cover possible, be it a ditch or depression in the land! Spread out your ranks! Bunching together will lead to catastrophe!" The draconic commander's voice spoke with urgency, a sharp contrast to his usually calm and composed demeanor. His vibrant, golden eyes flicked from face to face, ensuring his words sank deep into the hearts of the two commanders in front of him.

"If there is no shelter or cover, dig holes as fast as you can and stay low. Do not linger out in the open. Above all, keep communication as quiet as possible! Those *things* lurk in the shadows. They can see in the dark as if it were day!"

Lysandra clenched her hands tightly, absorbing every word with a difficult look on her face. Had anyone else spoken about these warnings, she might have marked them as the ravings of a madman. But the warnings from dragons were deeply unsettling. They are creatures known for their unyielding bravery and stoic demeanor. Their servitude branding only made their advice much more credible.

"Thank you for the warning, my liege," Lysandra said, her voice full of skepticism yet layered with deep respect. "We will take your advice to heart. Our people and our realm are unfamiliar with these adversaries and their methods of warfare. We must rely on each other's strengths and knowledge if we are to protect our lands."

The draconic commander nodded, seemingly expecting her skepticism. "You do not believe me. I, too, was in disbelief when I first faced these creatures, but I've witnessed the devastation they bring firsthand. Trust in the experiences of those who have faced them. They are unlike any foe our world has ever seen."

With a hard expression, Gideon asked, "What are these *things* you speak of? Are they the reason behind the mangled remnants we found earlier?"

"Gideon, know your place!" Lysandra snapped as she clutched her sword tightly, giving the giant a stern look.

The draconic commander intervened, sensing the mounting tension. "No, it is quite alright. I take no offense." His eyes remained locked on Gideon as he took a few steps closer.

A maddened look crept into the dragonborn's eyes. "They take the shape of humans, like yourself," he said darkly, maintaining eye contact with Gideon.

A deep silence enshrouded the group, and everyone felt as if they had just been slapped in the face. The flickering light of the burning town cast long, eerie shadows around them, and the draconic commander's words hung in the air.

"Now, if you'll excuse me," the commander mumbled, limping past them. "I must see to the wounded." Despite his injury, his massive frame moved with surprising grace, his scaled tail leaving a shallow trail in the dusty earth.

An uncomfortable pause followed his departure. The group's silence was amplified by the distant cries and whimpers of the wounded and the constant thunderous booms in the distance. The imposing presence of the draconic commander had been a temporary barrier to those outside noises; now, they seeped back into their awareness.

Lysandra's gaze followed the commander as he limped away, the sturdy thud of his footfalls in sync with the heartbeats echoing in her ears. The smell of charred wood and pungent blood permeated the air, a grim reminder of their situation. The destroyed village, now a shadow of its former self, seemed to weep silently under the bright moonlight, its agony merging with the desolate landscape around it.

Gideon broke the silence, his voice strained but steady. "What do ya think?" he asked, anxiously rubbing the leather strap of his axe. "Do any of you think the lizard is talkin' crazy-like?"

No one said anything about Gideon's insubordination, and his words hung in the air while the legion of freelancers and volunteers shifted nervously in the background.

Deep in thought, Yzael sighed heavily. "Whether a flight of madness or an unsettling truth, there's a resonance in his words that we cannot simply ignore," she said grimly, turning towards the rift. "We all saw those projectiles, or whatever they were, slam into the barrier."

She gestured toward the dim, shimmering rift hanging in the air, the barrier holding back unknown darkness and despair. The ethereal glow cast eerie shadows, creating gaunt silhouettes upon the broken earth, their forms a spectral dance of despair. "There is a power here beyond our understanding, a malevolence that even sends the dragons into a panic." Her voice trembled, but she continued. "The commander speaks of iron beasts and fearsome foes disguised as men, and I, for one, believe him."

A murmur of agreement rippled through the gathered warriors, and unease spread like a current through the crowd. The air hummed with tension, punctuated by the distant bombardment, painting the sky orange with each explosion.

Lysandra's mind was in turmoil as she grappled with the weight of leadership. A scowl crossed her face as she gripped the pommel of her blade. The commander faced an impossible decision. Every fiber of her being urged her to turn back before it was too late, but she was bound by contract and oath to march on and subjugate whatever lay on the other side.

Her contract, however, never mentioned metallic horrors or magic powerful enough to challenge a sovereign. She sighed, glancing up at the night sky. The majestic golden dragon twisted and turned in the air, battling a swarm of almost imperceptible enemies compared to its size.

Explosions lit up its brilliant feathers. The dragon roared, a sound that vibrated through the bones of every being within miles, a haunting echo of fury. Amidst the dazzling dance, some of the sovereign's glimmering feathers fell like molten gold, scorching the land as the beast struggled to protect its horde from the relentless assault.

Gideon's hand rested on her shoulder, a solid, warm presence in the cold, chaotic night. "We never signed up for this, Captain," he murmured, his voice a low rumble that mirrored the distant, ominous booms.

"No, we did not," she whispered back, her gaze still fixed on the aerial tragedy. "But here we are, bound by words inked on parchment and coin."

Lysandra could feel the eyes of her men and women on her, their uncertainty and fear mirroring her own. The weight of their need for direction pressed heavily on her already burdened shoulders.

She turned from the celestial carnage, her gaze sweeping over the anxious faces of the freelancers. "We will make contact," she declared, her voice unwavering, her stance unyielding. "Be they monsters of iron or flesh."

Spinning hot on her heels, she marched toward the other legions, her cape billowing behind her as she moved with purposeful strides.

The rhythmic tramp of her company's boots followed, heading toward the horizon, aglow with explosions.

Yzael reached into her pocket, pulled out a single gold coin, an entire month's pay, and placed it into Gideon's hand. "I haven't agreed to your little wager, but it seems you've won."

* * *

Sitting in the cockpit of an F-16C, Captain Kai "Skunk" Wu tapped his fingers impatiently on the side of the cockpit while his plane idled on the highway of a makeshift runway. "C'mon, C'mon, hurry the fuck up!" Captain Wu growled, watching the ground crew scramble to rearm and refuel his plane.

He observed as his wingmen taxied down the improvised tarmac—an orchestra of men and machines under still-burning flares acting as runway lights. His eyes darted to his right, where a small makeshift control tower had been hastily set up, and combat controllers worked frantically to manage the chaotic ballet of landing and launching aircraft.

Headsets clamped to their ears, their voices never wavered as they directed pilots, coordinating the organized chaos with a calm precision that belied the dire circumstances. "Skunk 2, you're clear for takeoff on Runway One. Skunk 4, taxi to holding area. Skunk 3, prepare for immediate launch after Skunk 2." Captain Wu's headset blared to life.

Despite the chaos, there was a semblance of order. The roar of jet engines drowned out every other sound. Bright orange flames jutted from the F-16 as it lurched forward, causing the highway beneath the aircraft to become a blur of gray and white.

Wu glanced restlessly at the ground crew still working to mount missiles onto his fighter as the rest of his team took off one by one. The air vibrated with the hum of machinery and the crackle of communication devices. Despite his impatience, Wu couldn't help but feel a surge of admiration for the ground crew and combat controllers. They worked like a well-oiled machine, each moving with purpose amidst the orchestration of warfare.

His attention snapped back as he felt the final click of his armaments being secured. The crew chief signaled their completion with a thumbs up, followed quickly by a salute. The captain returned the gesture as his canopy closed and his gloved hand gripped the throttle.

Noticing the last plane of the flight was ready to go, Control radioed in. "Skunk 1, Runway 2 cleared for unrestricted takeoff. Happy hunting, dragon slayers."

CHAPTER 8

As Captain Wu pulled his aircraft alongside the rest of his flight, his radio crackled back to life as the Airborne Early Warning and Control transmitted orders to his headset. "All Skunk elements, ascend to angels 25, vector 2-2-0, maintain formation. Vul time, Vul time."

Wu felt his heartbeat echo in his ears as he gripped his flight stick tighter. Vul time—vulnerability Time—was such an oddly poetic term for such a lethal context. Essentially, it referred to the period when one's forces were most exposed to adversary action, the window where risk was at its peak.

Even after just taking off, they were already in range to engage these dragons, or whatever the hell they were, with long-range missiles. The F-16's advanced radar systems and other sensors worked synchronously, offering a high-resolution view of the airspace ahead. A swirl of colorful indicators and graphics painted his multifunctional displays, each symbol representing a different aircraft or projectile—friend or foe.

The AWACS continued to relay vital information, and their overarching view of the battle space was invaluable in these trying moments. "Skunk 1, Darkstar, group bearing 2-2-0, 30, 28,000, hot hostile." The AWACS code-named Darkstar relayed the bearing, range, altitude, and aspect of the enemy in the sky. "All players, weapons free."

Wu's eyes snapped to the radar screen as his hand instinctively moved to the weapon control system. He scanned the screen, identifying the group the AWACS referred to. He visualized the skies from the coordinates relayed, knowing the AWACS marked and verified the hostile targets in real time.

"Copy that Darkstar. Vector 2-2-0, 28,000, 30, hot hostile." Wu's voice was firm over the radio. His F-16 banked sharply, aligning its path with the specified vector. The other members of Skunk Flight followed suit, their jet trails painting intricate patterns in the sky.

"Puke 1, north group, 32,000, 36,000, hot hostile." The radio crackled to life again as the AWACS instructed other unseen flights.

Captain Wu and his flight were now fully meshed within the battle's intricate network. The communications channel became a flurry of directives, confirmations, and updates, each piloting a node within this complex web of airborne warfare.

From the sound of things, it was a complete free-for-all from 10,000 to 40,000 feet, with every wing on the East Coast joining the fray. The multitude of AWACS aircraft were trying to maintain control of the situation, but it was more akin to trying to control kites in a storm.

The alien entities defied traditional combat strategies with their agile and unpredictable movements, leaving even the most seasoned pilots baffled. The best solution was to keep their distance and snipe the little shits from the skies, but they had to close in for the merge to keep those bastards off the ground forces.

Captain Wu's eyes darted between the radar screen and the integrated battle network. Everyone was either here or already on their way. The F-35s, embedded in their various roles, were exploiting their advanced sensor suites to act as command and control, providing targeting solutions for everyone while sniping away at these things themselves.

Soon, his own aircraft was provided targeting solutions, and they were all focused on the giant golden fucker twirling in the sky.

"Skunk 1, Fox 3."

"Skunk 2, Fox 3."

"Skunk 3, Fox 3."

"Skunk 4, Fox 3."

As the callsigns echoed in his ears, Captain Wu felt the familiar jolt of his F-16 releasing its payload. The advanced AIM-120 AMRAAMs, a quartet of radar-guided death, hurtled into the skies, homing in on the golden beast.

The flights watched as the missiles disappeared into the distance, only for the gargantuan golden monster to snap his head and liquefy the damn things with its molten breath. This was not unexpected, but it was still frustrating. They had repeated the same song and dance for hours now, and it seemed that every one of these damned things had built-in Radar Warning Receivers.

Captain Wu and his flight were forced to switch targets as they flew closer to the fray. "Skunk 1 north group, maneuver," he instructed his flight as he banked right toward a cluster of smaller dragons attempting to break through the main formation, desperate to provide support for their struggling ground forces.

But the flight of F-16s wasn't going to allow any of them to do as they pleased. They sped through the turbulent skies, their radar systems locked onto the smaller, serpentine entities below. Captain Wu's eyes were glued to his heads-up display, watching as the targeting reticles aligned with the swiftly moving opponents. The HUD displayed range, speed, and estimated impact time, constantly adjusting with each minuscule movement of the dragons.

"Skunk 1 Fox 3, northern, north group, 22,000," Captain Wu intoned calmly into his headset, feeling the shudder as another

AMRAAM disengaged from the aircraft's underbelly, hurtling towards its target. The rest of his flight followed suit, their own missiles screaming through the atmosphere, leaving behind trails of white smoke as they rushed toward their targets at slightly different altitudes.

Time seemed to stand still as the missiles streaked through the sky toward the massive monsters, twisting and turning in an attempt to avoid the oncoming destruction. The pilots watched as the missiles struck true, each target jerking and screeching with pain. One of the dragons went limp and fell from the sky as the others snapped their attention to the oncoming F-16s.

In the cramped cockpit of her F-16, Skunk 2, also known as Lieutenant Kara "Pampers" Bell, watched her radar screen as the dragons turned to meet the assault.

As the dragons pivoted to face the jets, their heat signatures bloomed on her infrared detection system, their immense bodies throwing off heat like volcanic eruptions. They closed in fast—too fast for comfort, and Bell's hand moved with practiced ease as she prepared to engage. The screen split, one side showing the thermal signatures, the other a more conventional radar view. She noticed the creatures moving in formations that seemed almost strategic, almost military.

"Fox 3, Fox 3, northbound, north group, 24,000!" the woman called out as she fired another AMRAAM. "Heads up, north group, turning hot!"

"Skunk 1, tally, two dragons, left eleven high!" Wu's voice crackled over the comms as he alerted his wingman to the incoming threat dropping down from the left. "Skunk 2 anchor, bullseye 2-7-0, 2 miles, 24,000!"

Captain Wu barked through the radio, his eyes darting between his HUD and battle management system. "Skunk 1, *merge*, hostile dragon!"

The call to "merge" signaled that they were in the thick of it now—a phase where radar screens turned into a kaleidoscope of swirling icons, a whirl of friends and foes spinning in a chaotic aerial ballet. The skies were alive with the roars of jet engines, the snarl of dragons, and the staccato blasts of cannon fire.

"Skunk 2 break left, flare! Skunk 2, your 6 o'clock, low, 1 mile, bandits on you! Skunk 3, press!" Captain Wu struggled to continue to issue commands as his aircraft banked sharply, trying to keep visual on Bell as she dumped flares, hoping to distract the beast.

"Skunk 3 is engaged!" Skunk 3 replied as their F-16 afterburners lit up the night sky. The jet turned sharply, trying to get a lock on one of the dragons chasing Bell while their wingman slotted in behind the other. "Skunk 3, Fox 2!"

However, noticing it was being targeted, the trailing beast used its incredible agility and acceleration to dodge, sending the missile sailing off into the void. The dragon then shifted its course with an otherworldly speed, doubling back to charge straight at Skunk 4 as they lined up a missile.

"Skunk 4, break! Break right, break right, now!" Lieutenant Bell's urgent shout pierced the radio, a desperate bid to alert the vulnerable pilot.

But it was a fraction of a second too late. Skunk 4's F-16 banked hard to the right, engines screaming as the plane tried to escape the incoming wrath. The dragon, a maelstrom of scales and wings, belched a torrent of plasma-like fire. The ethereal blue flame surged through the night air, a streak of deadly brilliance homing in on the scrambling jet.

Skunk 4's aircraft was engulfed. The plasma fire enveloped the plane, the heat instantly slagging the cockpit. The once sleek and angular jet transformed into a molten wreck in milliseconds. The canopy bubbled and warped, sealing the pilot inside a cauldron of molten metal.

There was no time to mourn the abrupt loss; one errant move could seal the fate of any pilot. However, the dragon that had incinerated Skunk 4 swooped low, savoring its deadly victory and twisting to douse the burning F-16 with another breath.

And that proved to be a fatal mistake.

Captain Wu was already turning his plane to engage the beast. He lifted his head to put the dragon in the holographic head-up display in his helmet. Utilizing the labored, sharp breaths of the Anti-G straining maneuver, he locked onto the damned monster's massive thermal signature.

He would see to it that the dragon's little celebration would be short-lived. "Skunk 1, Fox 2!"

The missile left the rail with a violent hiss, its motor igniting a split-second later and propelling it toward the serpent-like behemoth. The advanced infrared seeker of the AIM-9x Sidewinder sailed almost a mile, homing in on the dragon's intense heat signature as it twisted and spiraled in a desperate attempt to evade.

The monster howled in pain as the warhead detonated, scoring a lucky hit on its wing. The explosion tore through the sinew and scale with a violent eruption of flame and shrapnel, leaving the beast flailing in the air, marred by the smoking, tattered remnants of its once majestic wing. It tumbled through the sky, screeching in agony, struggling to regain control. It eventually evened out and glided away, but it was clearly crippled.

"Skunk 1, Splash 1, left-hand turn!" Wu shouted, braking hard left, trying to avoid collisions with his wingmen as they twisted and turned in the battle space.

But the skies were far from clear. The cacophony of battle was overwhelming, with aircraft and dragons mingled together as far as the eye could see. Captain Wu's Sidewinder had hit its mark. Still, no one had the time or the opportunity to capitalize on the injured beast as even larger dragons surged from the clouds, threatening to overrun their formation.

Before they could be flanked, Captain Wu noticed the dragons suddenly taking erratic evasive maneuvers. Streaks of white smoke blues blurred overhead as missiles sailed past the dragons, but a few found their mark, causing the beast to howl in pain and anger.

Several flights of Navy F/A-18E Super Hornets mirrored the tactics he used in his flight. Two of them flew a few hundred meters overhead, hauling ass to get the dragons to chase them while their wingmen sniped the monsters out of the sky.

No matter where he looked, Wu saw the same scene playing out. The sky was an absolute clusterfuck of jets and dragons chasing each other. Missiles darted around, fire, ice, and lightning crackled, while claws and teeth ripped through the air, swiping at jets.

If not for the intense G-forces forcing the blood from his head as he maneuvered his F-16, Captain Wu would have considered this a fever dream. The world had turned on its head, and the impossible was now a daily reality. Dragons, creatures of legend and mythology, were not only real but were fucking engaging them in aerial combat.

Snapping his flight stick to the left, Wu banked hard. His head tracked Skunk 2, who was acting as the low man, baiting out beasts with a tempting target by firing a missile or two and then breaking off. The fight drew them deeper into the brawl. Wu then spotted an F-22 with almost its entire tail liquified by what looked like acid.

He watched as the deadliest aircraft in the world corkscrewed and flipped wildly, dipping under the brawl before a bright burst of light illuminated the cockpit. The canopy explosively jettisoned, spinning off into the darkness. A heartbeat later, a figure was catapulted outwards as the pilot ejected.

"Wow, that was actually pretty fuckin' smart," Captain Wu muttered to himself, his voice carrying a mix of amazement and respect as his F-16 banked to avoid an F-15 that was in the middle of his own evasive maneuvers.

In this chaotic mess, pilots needed to stay a step ahead when the sky was full of teeth eager for a mid-air snack.

Turning his attention back to his Skunk 2, Wu found a pair of much smaller but brutal creatures on his six. Their wings were bat-like and sinuous, more agile than the larger dragons, with streamlined bodies that darted through the air. Their scales, while sturdy, lacked the dense resilience of their larger counterparts, making them *much* more vulnerable.

"Guns, guns, guns!" Captain Wu shouted over the net as he lined his jet up with the two and squeezed the trigger.

The M61 Vulcan cannon attached to Captain Wu's fighter roared to life, sending a stream of hot 20mm armor-piercing incendiary rounds tearing through the creatures' hides. Blood sprayed into the sky as their bodies jerked under the onslaught. The first beast's wings were shredded, and its body was riddled with bullet holes, causing it to plummet to the earth below, while the other was cleanly cleaved in half.

Wu didn't have time to celebrate the two rapid kills. The skies were still swarming with threats, and he had to maintain his edge if he wanted to survive.

It was going to be a *long* night.

* * *

Waiting patiently deep within a grove, Coleman and his ODA watched as a strange, lumbering creature clumsily traipsed into the forest clearing. Its bulk was immense, like a dump truck, and it moved on six thick, stubby, spider-like legs.

Despite the fur that covered its body, an unsettling exoskeleton formed a segmented armor over it, gleaming with an alien sheen. Elements of molten plasma or lava roiled beneath its chitinous plates, casting an eerie glow that painted the trees in sinister shades of crimson.

Coleman couldn't tell whether the damn thing was a crustacean or an arachnid. Its large, flat head was reminiscent of both, bearing heavy, frowning mandibles that clicked rhythmically. Multiple eyes glinted with that same otherworldly molten light. The creature seemed out of place in the cool, verdant forest—more like something carved from the heart of a volcano or nestled in a harsh desert.

"What the fuck am I looking at?" Schwarz whispered, his troubled eyes narrowing in disbelief as he peered through the foliage.

"A nightmare," Coleman replied impassively.

Though his expression didn't show it, Coleman shared Schwarz's sentiment as his eyes remained glued to the odd spectacle unfolding in the clearing, especially when the creature's tail lifted towards the sky. Its massive body was nestled into the dirt.

"Jesus fucking Christ," Elijah muttered, his face twisted in disgust and hatred. "Kill it all with atomic hellfire."

As the ODA continued observing, the activity in the clearing intensified. Rabbit-eared beings formed into ranks, seemingly preparing for some kind of assault. They moved with a strange synchronicity, as if controlled by a single mind, their motions fluid and precise. Smaller creatures scurried between the ranks of the rabbit-eared infantry, adding another layer of confusion to the bizarre scene.

Elijah couldn't help but let out a small chuckle at the absurdity. "Nah, bro, this is some Final Fantasy shit," he whispered with a shake of his head, his voice a mix of disbelief and amusement. Settling his rifle on a fallen log, he peered through the scope, trying to make out more details of the alien beings.

Coleman crouched nearby and kept his focus on the scene. "Fantasy or not, we should probably take that thing out before we figure out what it does." He turned to one of the marines who had just settled in beside them. "Can we get an ordinance on it? Tell fires it's a priority target."

The marine frowned and replied, "I don't think so, sir. Everyone's got a priority target." He grabbed his push-to-talk radio. "I'll try, but last I heard, artillery has been firing nonstop. They've practically melted their barrels, but I'll give it a shot."

"Worst they can do is tell us to fuck off." Coleman nodded, appreciating the marine's efforts despite the low odds. "And if so, we'll hit 'em ourselves."

While the forward observer worked on getting fire support, Coleman turned to Gunnery Sergeant Riley, the Marine NCO embedded with them. "They're probably gonna tell us to eat shit, so we'll have to do this the hard way." Coleman's voice was firm as he looked over at the monster, which was starting to burrow itself into the ground, shoveling dirt violently as it dug in.

The Staff Sergeant silently motioned for his marines to gather around as he assessed their options. His eyes were trained on the gigantic creature in the clearing, its unsettling movements creating an aura of anticipation and anxiety among the men.

With the marines gathered in the thicket, Major Coleman smirked as he scanned their faces. If they were going to pull this off, he needed the most rabid and unhinged group of degenerates he could get his hands on. Luckily, the Marine Corps was the only animal he needed.

"Alright, this is what we're gonna do."

CHAPTER 9

With precision, Coleman and his team glided through the thick underbrush, the shadows of the trees offering concealment as they approached the clearing from the flank. A squad of fifteen marines, weapons held low and eyes sharp, shadowed the Special Forces ODA, moving silently and swiftly. They were ghostlike figures, invisible under the protective cloak of night, guided by the white phosphorescent glow of their night observation devices.

The beast nestled in the clearing—a fiery scorpion-like creature—cast an eerie, magma-like light across the open ground, illuminating everyone and everything around it. Realizing that night vision was unnecessary, Coleman flipped his night observation device up, letting the natural, albeit bizarre, light from the creature illuminate the scene. His eyes peered through his weapon's optic as he focused on the handlers around the creature.

He noticed something peculiar about them. They stood around the monstrosity as though it were a piece of equipment, gesturing and engaging in a hushed, urgent discussion. These beings had rabbit-like ears atop their heads, twitching as they conversed.

Coleman narrowed his eyes, studying his enemy. For warriors, they were rather slim and petite beneath their armor, and there seemed to be a subtle hint of feminine curves. However, their faces and forms were obscured enough to make it difficult to discern what they were.

Suddenly, one with an air of authority and a large bird-like creature perched on their arm bellowed something toward their comrades and gestured towards the surrounding treeline. With hasty, odd salutes and gestures, the beings grabbed their spears and began spreading in every direction.

Realizing they were likely setting up a security screen, Coleman pressed down on his push-to-talk. "Status on our fire support?"

A brief, tense pause followed before a voice, edged with frustration, replied, "Just checked with HQ. No-go on artillery, sir. They're swamped. Every asset's engaged elsewhere."

A slew of curses left Coleman's mouth as he quietly turned to the others. "Yep, they told us to eat shit," he whispered, motioning to the marines to take up positions along the treeline. "We're doing this the old-fashioned way."

Clutching his push-to-talk again, Coleman began issuing instructions for their plan B: assaulting the damned thing themselves.

"Looks like we're assaulting the damn thing," he said, his voice steady and authoritative, a stark contrast to the irritation he felt inside. "We're gonna hit it hard, and we're gonna hit it fast. Go on my mark."

Affirmations crackled through his headset as Coleman returned his focus to the optic, homing in on the bird.

Something about it seemed important. Its eyes reflected an intelligent, almost otherworldly light. It was an avian, yet not quite. The creature resembled a hawk or an eagle but possessed an ethereal, almost spectral quality that set it apart from any Earthly bird.

Suddenly, a terse conversation broke out among the handlers, and with a fluid motion, the one with the bird lofted it into the night sky. The creature soared upwards with incredible speed and precision. The scorpion-like creature's tail twitched in response, quivering in anticipation.

As if reacting to a command, the tail shot upwards in the direction the bird had flown. Every muscle, every mechanical joint of the beast seemed in tune with the avian's movements. Meanwhile, the handler chanted a few words, their hands twisting and gesturing gracefully. As the chant grew louder, the eye sockets of their helmet began to glow a milky white.

"Call me crazy, but what if that person is somehow controlling or seeing through the eyes of that bird thing?" Elijah whispered, focusing his own optic on the handler's glowing eyes. "And what if this thing is their indirect fire?"

Coleman opened his mouth to say that was utterly insane but then immediately closed it. As crazy as it sounded, that conclusion fits perfectly with the weird fantasy bullshit they'd been dealing with—from flying dragons and land beasts to feminine-looking, rabbit-eared people controlling a fucking lava scorpion. Why wouldn't magical bird spotters and living artillery be a part of the package?

"Yeah, it's a stretch," Coleman admitted, scanning the clearing with renewed urgency. "But it's starting to make a lot of sense. That bird gives them the eyes in the sky, and this creature provides the firepower. We're dealing with their version of a Joint Terminal Attack Controller with airborne reconnaissance."

"That's one hell of a combo," Bennett remarked, sounding almost admiring.

"Yeahhh," Coleman muttered as he reached for his radio. "All the more reason to take them out as soon as possible."

The enemy security screen was meandering closer to their position when suddenly, the supposed spotter raised their head. Their eerie, glowing eyes fixated on something in the distance. With a jarring scream, they yelled in a strange language before swiping their arms down in a chopping motion.

Suddenly, the monstrous scorpion-like creature's tail began to quiver, the segments undulating in an unsettling fashion. Its once-hard carapace seemed to balloon outwards, glowing with an internal, fiery light that intensified. Then, with an ear-splitting pop, a massive, searing glob of plasma rocketed into the night sky, tracing a blazing path as it ascended.

Coleman's gaze followed the plasma's trajectory as it soared into the abyss above. He and his team were witnessing a mesmerizing and horrifying feat.

"Fuck me, you were right," Schwarz whispered under his breath.

"Everyone turn on your EUD and start recording this shit!" Coleman barked in hush tones as he grabbed his End-User Device and prepared the 8k camera functionality. Schwarz, Bennett, and the rest of the team quickly activated their devices, ensuring they documented every intricate detail of the bizarre spectacle unfolding before them.

At that moment, the spotter provided another series of instructions that echoed across the clearing. The spotter's tone was intense, hands weaving a sequence of animated gestures, conveying urgency to the monstrous scorpion creature. The alien beast, in turn, adjusted its tail and aimed at a slightly different angle.

"They're adjusting fire," Bennett murmured, narrowing his eyes.

The ground began to tremble faintly, resonating with the creature's energy buildup. Once again, that same ominous glow emanated from the creature, spreading like a heat mirage as the air around it shimmered. Once cold and dark, the night was warm and bathed in fiery light before another glob of plasma shot toward the sky.

Having captured the event, Coleman swallowed hard and pressed down on his push-to-talk. "Next time that thing balloons up, hit 'em."

"Roger that, waiting for your mark," the platoon of marines on the other side of the treeline responded.

Huddled amidst the brush and the looming shadows of the forest, Coleman's team watched an enemy patrol wander closer and closer to their position. They were slightly distracted as what they assumed was their leader bellowed out another series of orders, causing the massive scorpion to rumble and adjust its tail. Another surge of heat started to build within the creature as its tail began to balloon once more.

"Get ready. Shit is gonna get messy," Coleman said to his team before pressing down on his radio. *"Execute."*

Two massive blasts erupted from the treeline facing the scorpion as anti-tank warheads slammed into the massive scorpion's face, causing it to chitter and twist in pain.

Almost immediately after the first round found its mark, the platoon of marines engaged the enemy with overwhelming firepower and precision. The night was punctuated by the rapid chatter of machine gun fire and the sharp crackling of rifles. Tracers zipped through the darkness, cutting luminous paths toward the security screen and the mass of infantry around the creature.

Meanwhile, Coleman's ODA and his squad of marines waited.

Their ambush point had been meticulously chosen, a perfect spot toward which the enemy's wandering patrol had been aimlessly moving earlier. Now, with the security detail charging towards the larger fray, the coast was clear for Coleman's team to make their move.

Two operatives further down the line, each armed with MAAWS, swiftly moved into position, taking aim directly at the creature's vulnerable tail.

The impact was instantaneous—a deafening explosion as the energy within the tail was violently released. Liquid fire sprayed outward, cascading over everything and everyone nearby. The handlers snapped out of their arcane rituals, turned towards the fighting, and prepared another set of spells aimed directly at the offensive treeline. But it was far too late. Once the second set of warheads hit, their chants turned to shrill screams of agony as they were engulfed in the searing molten discharge.

Coleman took a quick, decisive look at the battlefield. The enemy was off balance, their ranks in disarray, but they were quickly starting to organize and began erecting strange magical barriers.

Now was the time to strike.

"Light 'em up!" Coleman yelled, signaling his team. The other side of the treeline burst with life as machine guns ripped through the flank of the reeling, otherworldly invaders.

Tube-launched grenades fired into the mass of combatants huddled together for protection. Their detonations spread chaos and disarray, opening gaps for the flanking marines to exploit.

Suddenly, the scorpion chittered and screeched in pain and distress as more warheads detonated against its exoskeleton. Turning away from the battlefield, it began a frenzied attempt to escape. Its massive legs pounded the ground, crushing unfortunate soldiers underfoot, adding even more chaos among its own ranks.

With the rout of their artillery piece, a domino effect followed, as formations crumbled and discipline was abandoned.

"Keep the pressure on, move!" Staff Sergeant Riley yelled, urging his marines forward. Seeing their enemy in disarray and seizing the momentum, the marines became a force of nature. They moved through the treeline, keeping in lockstep with the routing enemy, only stopping to pick off those who tried to rally and put up a resistance.

Squad leaders communicated among themselves, identifying points of contention and guiding their fireteams forward to ensure the enemy had no avenue of escape or regrouping. From the main line, the platoon of marines, led by Lieutenant Mitchell, bounded forward in a well-coordinated maneuver, ensuring the invaders were within deadly range and their barriers were constantly being peppered by machine-gun fire.

The once-confident otherworldly force was now trapped; if they turned to run, their only means of protection would flicker out and be subsequently mowed down. If they stayed where they were, their barriers would eventually buckle under the sustained gunfire, exposing them.

It seemed the decision would be made for them as a marine took aim with his M3E1 MAAWS and pulled the trigger.

The fin-stabilized projectile cut through the air in a gentle arc, heading straight for the dense cluster of enemy combatants. Upon impact, a deafening explosion resonated across the battlefield, sending a shockwave that shattered the invaders' magical barriers like glass under a sledgehammer.

Coleman and his ODA winced as the mass of soldiers dropped like flies under the relentless barrage of machine-gun fire. However, the sight didn't stop Coleman for long. "Move, move!" he yelled to his team, pressing forward, quickly getting on top of the enemy and ending anyone who still moved.

The ever-so-aggressive marines had the same idea and quickly pressed forward, their shouts mixing with the sporadic bursts of their weapons. Once upon the enemy, a new, eerie quiet swept across the clearing, save for the still-burning hisses of those drenched in plasma, the distant explosions in the background, and the dying moans of the defeated.

Marines and the ODA members regrouped and scanned the area for any remnant as the smell of burnt flesh, molten metal, and expended gunpowder hung heavy in the air.

"Clear!" the marines shouted one by one as everyone assumed a more relaxed but still ready posture.

Coleman took a moment to survey the battlefield. Dozens of bodies of the strange beings were scattered everywhere, along with their equally strange equipment.

"These are women," Elijah's voice suddenly cut through the quiet as he stared down at one of the beings, its helmet in his hand.

The Marines and the rest of the team turned to him with puzzled expressions. One of the marines crouched next to a body and pulled off its helmet. "Well, I'll be damned. He's right," the man muttered with furrowed brows.

Staff Sergeant Riley pulled the helmet off another fallen alien and stared down at the face. The being had a strikingly human visage, but what set them apart were the long, semi-droopy rabbit ears that sat atop their heads. They were covered in soft, velvety fur that matched their hair color.

"My God," whispered Riley, his rough fingers gently touching one of the ears. "They look so much like us."

A murmur spread through the troops as more rabbit-eared humanoids were revealed and more helmets were pulled off. Even the special forces soldiers found themselves taken aback by the uncanny similarity.

Kneeling by a still-coughing rabbit woman, a dark-skinned man carrying an M240 spoke up. "I thought dragons and lizard people were invading us." Master Sergeant Bernie Lister, the ODA's weapons sergeant, turned to the rest of his team. "I mean, that's what we've been mostly fighting so far. The hell with this shit?"

Elijah crouched down beside Bernie and pulled off his med pack. "Should I treat her?" he asked, looking at Coleman.

Coleman went silent as he looked around. "Uhhh. I, uhh, I

honestly don't know," he responded, scratching his beard in confusion. "How would we know whatever you do to her won't just outright kill her?"

"Does that even matter?" Elijah lifted an eyebrow, unzipping his med pack. "I mean, she's either going to bleed out or have a severe allergic reaction to whatever I give her."

Coleman's gaze sharpened. "You mean to experiment on her?"

"No? What the fuck?" Elijah looked up at his team leader in both outrage and confusion. "I mean to save her, man. Jesus, look!" Elijah pointed to the hyperventilating rabbit woman as she stared at the men. "She's scared, in pain, and dying. I can either treat her, and hopefully she lives, or just let her bleed all over the place."

"I just don't want to deal with any Hague bullshit, Eli," Coleman replied, pinching the bridge of his nose.

Another hush descended upon the clearing as Elijah's brow knitted and his eyes turned side to side in contemplation. "Are aliens even covered in the Geneva Convention?"

Master Sergeant Bernie chuckled under his breath, breaking the tension. "Now there's a question I never thought I'd ever fucking hear. International law and Amazonian space rabbits." His laugh grew louder as his hand hit his face. "What kind of fucked-up fever dream is this?"

The marine who had revealed the humanoid's ears piped in, "I think the convention covers 'persons,' doesn't it? Now, whether the international community would recognize them as such is another debate entirely."

"You can't fuck it, Jackson. You'll get space aids," another marine joked, drawing chuckles from the rest of their platoon.

Jackson, however, took it in stride. "Hey, look, I ain't said I would, but—" He made the famous hand gesture from one of the hosts of

Ancient Aliens on the History Channel. But, aliens." This gesture led to an uproar of laughter, easing the tension in the clearing.

"Whatever, man. Patch her up, I guess," Coleman finally relented, shaking his head at the absurdity of their situation before turning to Staff Sergeant Riley. "And make sure none of them fuck it, please."

Staff Sergeant Riley's expression shifted from amusement to the stern demeanor for which he was known. His eyes honed in on Jackson. "Jackson!" He barked, pointing directly at him using the classic Marine Corps "knife hand" gesture. "You're pissing off the Snake Eaters! Don't diddle the fuckin' space rabbit, or you'll be licking shit off all the latrines!"

Jackson's grin faltered a bit under the Staff Sergeant's fierce glare. "Aye, aye, Sarge," he replied, trying to keep his composure.

The sergeant continued, his gaze sweeping over the gathered men. "And that goes for all of you. You're all makin' us look bad, so stop being fuck-ups for once in your goddamn lives!" The intensity of his tone made his marines flinch.

Elijah immediately got to work on the rabbit woman's injuries. She seemed to be conscious but in obvious distress. The alien's ears twitched erratically, and her large, glossy eyes stared at him with fear and pain. After stripping her armor, his hands steadily moved as he assessed her injuries and started treating her.

A piercing scream echoed throughout the hall as the medic shoved his fingers into a still-bleeding gunshot wound. Coiling his medical dressing, Elijah pushed it firmly inside to stanch the bleeding. The rabbit woman's legs thrashed, another cry escaping her lips.

"Quit your yappin'. If you're screamin', you ain't dyin'," the medic said, causing everyone around him to cringe. A few of the marines turned away, their faces pale, clearly unaccustomed to such up-close trauma work.

"Goddamn," muttered Coleman, turning towards Staff Sergeant Riley. "Have your boys and your corpsman sweep the area for more wounded," he suggested, turning to the rest of the Marines. "If there are more like her, we should find them and radio for evac."

A nod came from Sergeant Riley. "Roger that. We could use as much intel as we can get." Spinning around, Riley looked at the rest of his Marines. "All right, you useless fucks! You heard the man. Go look for any survivors and make sure Baptiste doesn't get shanked!"

The men sprang into action while Coleman shook his head and looked down at his still-recording End-User Device. Bringing his hand to his radio, he switched channels to talk to HQ.

"Warmonger, this is Baron. Be advised that we have POWs and critical intel. Requesting immediate evac, over."

CHAPTER 10

The forces entrenched around New Philadelphia braced themselves against the veritable horde on their doorstep. But as the saying goes, when it rains, it pours.

"Gunner! Sabot, walker! 11 o'clock!" bellowed Staff Sergeant Jones, commander of the M1A2 Abrams tank named "Aggravated Assault." The turret swiveled as the gunner, Sergeant Alphonso Hendricks, got the mind-boggling quadruped land dragon into his sights.

The beast sprinted across the battlefield with frightening speed, closing the gap on an M2A4 Bradley and ripping the turret off after slagging another Abrams with its plasma-like breath. "Identified!" Hendricks yelled, his hands gripping his controls tightly.

"Fire!" Jones commanded as the beast snapped its head toward them

"On the way!" Hendricks responded, squeezing the trigger.

The tank roared, sending a fin-stabilized depleted uranium dart hurtling toward the creature. The round struck the dragon square in the chest, a burst of sparks and dark red blood showering in the air as it staggered back. However, the creature wasn't down for the count and let out a roar of agony and fury that echoed across the battlefield as it tried to regain its composure.

"Sabot up!" Private Derrick Miller, the loader, called, signaling another round was ready.

"Re-engage!" the commander yelled.

The Abrams turret realigned on the wounded creature, now bearing a gaping wound in its chest. The beast, dubbed a walker, managed to lock eyes with them. With another snarl, the creature moved to charge at the offender, but first, it had to close the massive gap between it and the Abrams.

"On the way!" Hendricks shouted, firing another round as the tank shuddered with recoil.

The projectile hit its mark, tearing into the beast's front limb. The walker howled in pain and collapsed, leaving a blood trail in its wake.

"Up!" Miller announced, loading another round 40-pound projectile as swiftly as the first.

Despite its grievous injuries, the walker was not about to back down. With its remaining strength, it bellowed and lunged toward the tank, covering the distance with surprising speed for its injuries.

"It's still fuckin' alive! Re-engage!" Jones's voice boomed through their headsets, the tension palpable.

"On the way!" Hendricks responded, firing once more.

This shot finally did the trick. The projectile struck with a violent burst of sparks, sending the massive creature crashing to the ground, tumbling head over tail just a hundred meters away.

Before anyone had a chance to celebrate the takedown, Jones's voice cut through their fleeting relief. "Right, right, right! Gunner, look right!" Jones yelled as he spotted a mass of people in his commander's sight. "Infantry out in the open, AMP!"

"AMP up!" Miller announced as he swiftly loaded the Advanced Multi-Purpose shell into the firing chamber.

The tank's turret swiveled, and the targeting reticle hovered over a decent group pushing forward with a shimmering blue shield just in front of them. The strange barrier was lit up like a firecracker as tracer fire from almost every direction slammed into it and other similar shields protecting different units of the alien forces. The barrage, while intense, seemed to only minimally affect the enemy's advance.

Beyond the initial infantry wave, more of those daunting walkers prowled the battlefield, flanked by a new type of strange creature. These quadrupeds bore a peculiar resemblance to a hybrid of hyenas and rhinos, yet they were much larger and sported a metallic sheen on their fur. But what was most frightening was they had their own distinctive shield that glowed with a reddish tint. These creatures led the charge, creating a path for the following infantry.

However, they had to take care of the infantry that managed to get within spitting distance first. These magic users were equally as dangerous and needed to be dealt with.

"Identified!" Hendricks replied, spotting one of the shimmering barriers, which seemed to be powered by several of these mages standing in formation and channeling their energies into the protective field. "On the way!"

The tank shuddered as it fired, the deafening blast lighting up the night as the fin-stabilized round hurtled toward its target.

* * *

Holding on for dear life, Yzael poured everything she had into keeping her shield up as the world around her dissolved into chaos and noise. Drenched in sweat, her outstretched hands moved intricately, fingers weaving through the energies around her. The chants she murmured, blending with those of other mages, barely held back the deadly streaks of magic that hammered against their fragile protection.

Behind the barrier, Lysandra barked orders, rallying the small band of freelancers to regroup. The battlefield was alive, with incessant chatter of death streaking through the air. Every time someone strayed too far from their designated mage, they were torn apart by infernal magic that spat fire and metal.

"Stay with your mages!" Lysandra shouted, her voice carrying over the clamor. "Healers! Use this opening to get the wounded back to safety!"

Yzael, her face strained with concentration and fatigue, grunted as a nearby explosion violently rocked her shield. The force of the impact nearly knocked her off her feet, her eyes widening in alarm. Sparks and embers flickered along the perimeter of the barrier as it wavered momentarily.

"C-Commander! They're not letting up," Yzael gasped, her voice thick with strain. "I—I don't know how much longer I can keep this up."

Ever the pillar of strength, Lysandra cast a concerned glance at the young mage before spinning around. "Elara! Rhonan! To Yzael's side! Form a bulwark!" she ordered, gesturing to two nearby mages deep in their defensive spells, defending smaller pockets of their comrades.

The two mages nodded, straining to move their barriers closer to Yzael's. As their shields merged, the energy intensified, forming a brighter, stronger barrier that pulsed and expanded to cover more ground.

Lysandra quickly moved to Yzael's side, placing a steadying hand on her shoulder. "Stay with us, Yzael. You're doing great. Our shield will be stronger with the three of you working together."

Yzael, however, cast a worried glance toward Gideon. "By combining our barriers, we're making ourselves a tempting target," she warned.

The hulking man beside her frowned and eyed the dug-in mechanical beasts looming in the distance, their cannons belching fire before quickly retreating. "It's the very definition of putting all our eggs in one basket," he said grimly.

Lysandra bit her lip, her gaze shifting to a nearby structure. Just beyond their position, the edge of a town appeared, the promise of shelter and defensive structures tantalizingly close.

If only they could just hold out a little longer.

"We have no choice! If Yzael exhausts herself, we're all dead!" Lysandra shot back, her voice tinged with urgency. "We have to make it to that town. It's our best chance, especially when there is something that can slay the empire's drake!" She gestured towards the massive land drake skidding across the ground after being hit by God knows what.

Doubt flickered in some eyes, but they also realized they had no other options. The relentless assault from this world's brutal warfare was just too overwhelming.

"Hurry! Push!" Lysandra bellowed, pointing toward a building up ahead. "We're almost there—"

Her command was abruptly cut short by a world-shattering explosion that upturned the very earth.

Yzael couldn't quite see, but she could feel herself flipping through the air like a ragdoll, each second seeming to stretch into eternity. The protective barrier they had maintained had shattered like glass, and when she hit the ground with a sickening thud, all the air was forced from her lungs.

As the mage tried to catch her breath, the taste of blood and dust filled her mouth. The weight of the realization crashed upon her: her shield had failed, and they were now vulnerable to the onslaught of this alien world.

In her mind, she screamed at herself to get up and use what little power she had left, but her body refused to listen. The chilling tendrils of shock and fatigue threatened to drag her into darkness, but Yzael clung to what remained of her consciousness and forced her eyes open.

Carnage surrounded her.

The once-organized ranks of her comrades were now a bloody mess of armor, flesh, and charred ground. Broken bodies, some recognizable, some not, lay interspersed with the twisted remnants of their equipment. The land was scarred with craters, and smoky tendrils rose from smoldering fires that consumed anything they touched.

Sounds became muted as if she were underwater. Yzael expected the cries of pain and clashing of weapons, but she could only hear silence and the incessant chattering of this realm's weapons.

Nearby, a soldier desperately tried to stem the bleeding from a wound on his comrade, using a piece of cloth to press against the open gash. He whispered words of comfort, his eyes darting around nervously, aware of the ever-present danger. Gideon managed to tie a makeshift tourniquet just as a burst of streaking lights cut through the air and peppered the man. The soldier gave a choked gasp, his body jerking with the force of the impact before collapsing heavily next to his already injured comrade, lifeless eyes staring into the sky.

"Why?" Yzael whispered as a lump formed in her throat. She was a freelancer, prepared for death ever since taking up this profession, but the cold, mechanical cruelty of this new world's warfare was something she had never imagined.

It was so impersonal.

Suddenly, strong arms wrapped around Yzael's waist, lifting her off the ground. The world blurred as she was swiftly carried toward the building they'd desperately been trying to reach. The sensation was familiar—too familiar. She felt like she could close her eyes and let the chaos of the day wash away, but she resisted, forcing herself to stay alert.

She knew that powerful grip—it could only be Gideon, that loveable brute. Relief surged through her as she took in his battle-worn face. Their bond, forged in countless monster hunts and bounty jobs, gave her a fleeting sense of momentary peace.

Once inside the building, Gideon gently set her down against a crumbling wall, slumping beside her with a groan of pain.

"G-Gideon!" Yzael moaned weakly, reaching out. "You're hurt!"

The large warrior gave her a weary smile in return. "Yep. So are you, lass."

Her eyes darted to her side, where she felt a damp warmth—blood was seeping through her robes. She had been so focused on her magic in the heat of the battle and hadn't even noticed the injury, but now the pain was catching up to her.

"W-Where's Lysandra?" Yzael asked, her voice thick with worry as she tried to push herself up.

"Honestly?" Gideon murmured, gently pressing her back down. He tore a strip of cloth from his own attire and folded it, pressing it against her wound. "I ain't got the faintest clue. Soon as I came to, I grabbed you and made a break for it."

Yzael winced and let out a painful moan as his hands applied pressure, sending sharp jolts of pain through her body. She gritted her teeth, trying to focus. "We really messed up, didn't we?"

Gideon glanced through the hole in the wall at the devastation that used to be their comrades. The man fell silent as he felt Yzael's hand grip his own.

"Gideon," the mage choked out. "Are we going to die?"

For a moment, only the distant roar of otherworldly weapons and thunderous explosions filled the void as the weight of the question hung in the air.

Yzael's eyes, clouded with pain and fear, sought solace in his. "G-Gideon. I don't want to die," she whispered, her voice trembling.

The large man followed her gaze to the shattered bodies strewn just outside. Her eyes fixated on Elara, one of their fellow mages whose body was blown in half and lifeless.

Shifting to block the view, Gideon pulled Yzael into a tight embrace, shielding her as best he could from the horrors. "I won't let anything happen to you," he vowed, his voice thick with emotion.

Turning toward a shattered window, Gideon saw that the empire had finally released the yoxen reserve. With their metallic fur and powerful frames, these fearsome beasts were already being pulled back. Their retreat was orderly, but the sounds of their handler's shouts mixed with the growls caused the last glint of hope in Gideon's eyes to fade.

A part of him wanted to succumb to his own despair, but the weight of Yzael in his arms anchored him. Her shallow and quick breaths reminded him that they were still alive, still fighting, and as long as they had breath in their lungs, they had a chance to survive.

"Gideon, it's quiet," Yzael said, peering around his massive form. "D-Did we manage to push up?"

Gideon wrapped his arm around Yzael's waist and lifted her to her feet, doing his best to ignore her cries of pain. Looking over his shoulder through the hole in the wall and the broken square windows, he saw that the battlefield had come to a momentary standstill. Smoke and dust danced in the night, painting a grim picture of the devastation they had just survived.

"No," Gideon murmured, surveying the wreckage. "I think they're regrouping. Or maybe they broke through on another front."

Leaning against him for support, Yzael followed his gaze. "Where are the others?" she whispered, hoping for some sign of allies amidst the smoke and ruins.

"We gotta go." Gideon's tone held an urgency that snapped her attention back to him. Even in the dim light, she could see the lines of worry etched deeply into his face. "These demons will soon be upon us. We can't stay here."

Yzael swallowed hard, nodding in agreement. The pain in her abdomen throbbed constantly, but all she could do was endure it for now. "O-Okay," she stammered with a shaky voice.

With a grunt of exertion from his own wounds, Gideon wrapped his arm around Yzael and helped her to the other side of the building, hoping to find a safe exit. They stumbled through a corridor, guided only by the meager moonlight filtering through broken windows. But the light from the broken glass, coupled with her concussion, seemed to play tricks on Yzael's vision. Shadows seemed to leap out at her, and she flinched each time they rounded a corner.

The living room was barely intact. Its walls were poked with tiny holes, and furniture was scattered in disarray, overturned and charred. As they moved forward, the muted sounds of warfare outside became slightly clearer. Drawn to the window instinctively, Gideon cautiously peered through the tattered curtains.

That's when he saw the massive iron behemoths the draconic commander warned them about.

Their heads swiveled as if scanning the horizon for more moving targets. The monsters moved steadily through the shattered streets, accompanied by groups of soldiers in strange, foliage-colored clothes. Their weapons were unlike any Gideon had encountered before.

One of the soldiers shifted, giving them a glimpse of a long, slender object made of dark, gleaming metal in his hand. The design was foreign and intimidating, with no blades or arrows in sight. Instead, it had a cylindrical front and a curious protruding stock that the soldier nestled into his shoulder.

"Those things must be enchanted," Yzael whispered, her voice laced with awe and terror. "They release their fury without incantation and no visible spellwork. It's like they've captured raw power in that slender metal staff."

Gideon scowled as they moved past the window toward what looked like a door. "As fascinating as it is, I ain't fixin' to stay and find out how it works," he mumbled, pulling Yzael along.

The woman groaned in pain, clenching her teeth as they hurried through the house, but she mustered enough strength to keep up with Gideon's brisk pace. Every step sent jolts of pain through her body, reminding her of her injuries.

Gideon grabbed the handle when they reached the door, but it wouldn't budge. He cursed under his breath, staring at the unfamiliar mechanism. Unlike the doors of their world, which either had simple latches or intricate magical locks, this one had a small metal slit and an oddly shaped rotating knob.

"Am I really going to be bested by a damned door?" Gideon grumbled, his fingers fumbling with the foreign device.

But before he could continue, Yzael urgently shook his arm, her face drained of color. "Gideon!" she hissed, pointing to the window. "They're coming this way!"

Without another thought, Gideon grabbed Yzael's sword from its scabbard, the blade gleaming with a deadly promise. Set in his stance, every muscle in Gideon's body tensed as he prepared for what he believed would be their final stand. Yzael, even with her injuries, gripped her dagger and summoned the last of her energy for the fight, tears rolling down her face.

Just as the first soldier stepped into the threshold, a resonant hum of magic pulsed from the opposite direction. Bright, radiant light burst forth, momentarily turning night into day. The soldiers, caught off-guard, immediately turned their attention to this new threat, opening fire with their metallic staves, causing the all-too-familiar snaps of death.

With the soldiers distracted, Gideon saw his chance. Without hesitation, he pulled back his leg and slammed his boot into the door. The strange wood weakened from the day's conflicts gave way under his force, and the door swung open violently.

With Yzael's sword in one hand, he scooped up the injured mage with the other, literally carrying her like a sack of potatoes as the hulking man darted to the other building. With the soldier's attention preoccupied with an obstinate stronghold, Gideon and Yzael slipped deeper into the town, covered by the shouting of commands and coordinated assault.

Then, just as the two reached the adjacent building, a roaring sound that seemed to shake the very earth caused them to stumble. The colossal iron beast released a devastating blast, blowing apart a massive section of the targeted building's wall and sending chunks of debris hurtling through the air.

Yzael screamed in pain, clutching her wound as they crashed through the front door. "I—I think I'm losing too much blood!"

Pulling Yzael into a more sheltered corner, away from the shattered windows, Gideon carefully brushed her blood-soaked hands aside to assess the wound. The sight was grim but not as dire as he had feared. Though the small projectiles had pierced straight through her torso, the bleeding wasn't as profuse as he'd expected.

It wasn't life-threatening—at least, not yet.

However, the shock and pain had driven Yzael's mind race to the worst-case scenario. "Gideon! There's... There's so much blood!" Yzael's voice quivered, her usually vibrant eyes clouded with fear. "It hurts so much. I can't—I can't die here!"

Gideon held her face in his hands, forcing her to meet his gaze. "Listen to me," he said firmly. "You are not going to die. This wound is bad, but it's not fatal."

"You're stronger than this, Yzael," Gideon murmured, tenderly stroking her hair, stained with the grime of their fight. "I've seen you face wyverns and chimeras, so I know you will prevail, just as you have before."

Yzael's breathing hitched, and her pale face was streaked with dirt and sweat. The mention of their previous encounters—those moments of life or death they had danced with countless times before—brought back memories of triumphant victories and narrow escapes.

A shaky laugh escaped her lips. "Wyverns and chimeras. Seems almost quaint now, doesn't it?" she replied, attempting a weak smile.

Gideon chuckled softly in response before returning to the battle behind them, which suddenly went quiet. "Come, we need to keep going."

Another moan of pain left Yzael's mouth as they stepped back into the chaos outside, leaving behind the semblance of safety they had found. With the flicker of hope of reaching their allies, they trudged forward through the war-torn streets of this damned city while the whistles of death resounded overhead, only to detonate in the distance from where they had come.

CHAPTER 11

A complicated mix of emotions surged through Lysandra as she stared up at the night sky.

If forced to name a specific feeling, it would most likely have been despair—or perhaps regret. Guilt was another strong contender in the whirlwind tearing through her. Each memory, every decision, weighed heavily on her chest, pressing her deeper into the cold ground beneath her.

The stars twinkled with indifferent beauty, their light seemingly mocking her fragile existence. They appeared blurrier than they ought to have been. Somewhere in the back of her mind, Lysandra registered the irregularity of their shimmering, the usual clarity smeared into near obscurity by her struggling vision.

Yet she remained trapped within the depths of her own torment. The warped stars above were nothing more than a fleeting distraction against the relentless tide of haunting faces. Echoes of her soldiers' laughter, the firm pats on her back, the unwavering trust in their eyes—all of it obliterated instantly by one disastrous decision and a searing flash of light.

Those eyes, once so full of life and excitement of a new campaign, now stared at her, hollow and lifeless. Lysandra hadn't noticed that she had turned her head toward the vacant gaze of one of the mages she had called to help with the barrier—or at least what remained of her.

"Elara," Lysandra croaked, reaching out to the barely recognizable body mangled by the explosion.

She had invited this doom upon them all. It was the only memory she could recall, and every moment of it was agonizingly clear. They were so close to a shelter, the seductive lure of safety just within reach, and her hasty decision to group them into a tight formation had sentenced them to a grisly demise.

"We're almost there. We just need to hold on a little longer," Lysandra had told them, her voice filled with false confidence. *"Once inside, we can fortify our defenses and tend to our wounded."*

But they never made it.

"A fool," she whispered weakly to no one in particular. A fool who had gleefully handed their enemies an opportunity they couldn't resist, turning hope into tragedy.

Lysandra wanted to cry, but her body wouldn't respond. Every fiber of her being screamed that she should be in excruciating pain, yet all she felt was numbness—that she almost mistook it for oblivion.

But something was off.

Her vision was strangely occluded. A patchy, nebulous fog clouded half of her sight, while the other was a blurred smear of light against the dark void. Confusion began to seep into her semi-conscious mind as she gathered what little willpower she had left, lifting a hand toward her left eye.

It felt like an eternity. Lysandra's right hand crawled, inch by inch, up her battered, blood-stained armor. The weight of her limb was nearly unbearable, but she pressed on, driven by sheer force of will.

Her fingertips brushed against her face, the sensation distant and muted, like a dream within a dream. But her breath caught in her throat when her fingers met a wet, sticky warmth—blood—and a lot of it.

The cold wind whispered secrets to her as she probed further, her hand stopping when it encountered a jagged gash across her brow and cheek, ending just above her unresponsive left eye.

A soft chuckle forced its way up her throat, though even that simple action seemed insurmountable in her weakened state. The once-renowned Thorned Rose, the cruel beauty of Aldenshore, had been reduced to this. The thought would have been laughable if it weren't so heart-wrenchingly tragic. Her fame and reputation, built over countless battles and bounties, were undone by a foolish gamble. She, who had always prided herself on always being one step ahead, was now literally half-blind.

The dampened sound of shuffling feet and barks of orders interrupted her thoughts. They sounded faint and distant, but Lysandra knew they were alarmingly close. Her heart rate quickened, and she started hyperventilating as the blurred outline of someone appeared before her.

She was trapped in her own body.

"Hey, we got a live one!" a voice called out in a language Lysandra couldn't make heads or tails of.

A pair of boots stopped in front of her, and Lysandra lifted her head with great effort, squinting to focus on the figure above her. Her vision, albeit compromised, allowed her to see something entirely baffling.

The man wasn't armored in the familiar steel and leather of the knights or warriors she had encountered in her time. Instead, he wore what looked like a strange woven fabric patterned in irregular earthy hues. His torso was adorned with a dense vest, clearly protective in nature but unlike any armor she had ever seen. Patches of strange symbols and designs were sewn onto it, and his helmet was made of some alien material, neither metal nor leather, with a transparent visor over his eyes. Gadgets and tools hung from his vest, none of which she recognized.

But then there was his weapon. The man pointed the strange, elongated device down at her, the gesture bone-chillingly casual and nonchalant. Though Lysandra couldn't comprehend most of it, the man's hand hovered near something resembling a trigger.

"Should I waste her?" the soldier yelled, glancing over his shoulder.

Lysandra realized the object in the man's hand was something akin to a crossbow, and she was about to die. The realization created a lump in her throat, and though she couldn't comprehend his words, their meaning was clear.

A single glistening tear rolled down her cheek, creating a stark contrast against the grime and blood that marred her face. It was a silent testament and plea for mercy, relief, and anything but this.

"No, you fucking idiot!" another voice barked, distinct from the young soldier's, carrying authority and deep exasperation.

A new figure stepped into view from the corner of her vision, brusquely shoveling the soldier aside. He raised his hand and delivered sharp, chopping gestures to his subordinates' faces—a disciplinary motion that struck Lysandra as strange and unfamiliar. His hand, flat and firm, thrust forward in a sharp, controlled motion as if to emphasize his authority.

"Just cause they're fuckin' aliens don't mean we get a free pass to fuckin' execute motherfuckers, Walker!" the newcomer, presumably his superior, snarled. "What the fuck is wrong with you?!"

With his weapon pointed away, Walker stammered, "R-Roger that, Sarn't. Sorry, Sarn't," the young soldier replied submissively, his face reddening from the reprimand.

"Last thing I need is to get the Lieutenant or, god forbid, the fuckin' CO on my ass because you dumbfucks want to commit war crimes!" The sergeant spun around, pointing at everyone in the vicinity, before turning back to his subordinate. "Is that what you want, Walker? A fuckin' court-martial?! A trip to the fuckin' Hague?!"

Walker stood at attention, his back ramrod straight. "No, Sarn't."

"That's what I fuckin' thought. Now get this elf a goddamn medic before I NJP your ass!" The sergeant barked. Walker, visibly shaken, scurried off, his boots pounding the uneven ground. "Jesus fuckin' Christ."

The sergeant exhaled heavily, attempting to stifle his frustration and regain composure. His eyes shifted back to Lysandra, lying battered on the ground. Her breathing labored, and her gaze dull with sorrow and fear.

He rubbed his temple as if warding off an oncoming headache, his eyes scanning the scene. He noticed the glint of the battered woman's pointed ears and the intricate craftsmanship of her armor despite its damaged state. Her glimmering cuirass, now discolored, was peppered with deep dents from the fragments of a recent explosion. Some shrapnel had torn through the armor below her chest line, leaving evident bloodstains that contrasted with the once-gleaming metal.

"What a mess," he muttered, turning to see a medic jogging toward him.

Before Lysandra could comprehend what was happening, another individual hovered over her, carefully stripping away her clothes and armor. A soldier meticulously cataloged each piece, ensuring nothing was misplaced.

In her weakened state, fear clouded Lysandra's judgment. The removal of her armor felt like the ultimate insult, a sign of impending doom. Although meant to be compassionate and helpful, the medic's actions took on a sinister light in her mind. She believed they were removing her belongings as a precursor to her execution, ensuring nothing of value would be wasted after her death.

But worse than the perceived indignity was the overwhelming weight of guilt and regret. Lysandra had committed the worst sin a commander could ever make. She hadn't just gotten herself killed—she had led her loyal comrades straight to their deaths. Perhaps the indignities were deserved.

Lysandra stared at the alien night sky as her body jerked around from the forcible disrobing. It would have been the ultimate insult to the woman if she could feel anything beyond the profound numbness that gripped her soul. Every touch, every tug of the fabric against her skin, failed to elicit a reaction. Her mind had constructed a barrier against the emotions threatening to break through.

Despite everything, she couldn't help but notice the stars. Even in this nightmare, they shimmered with an otherworldly beauty. The constellations were unfamiliar but still wondrous.

As she closed her remaining eye, Lysandra wondered if this was the part where they'd violate her. The thought made her smirk slightly. *"Even without an eye, I must still hold some beauty,"* she mused. *"At least there's that."*

With that thought, the former commander believed it was the last thing she would ever think or feel.

However, to her disappointment, Lysandra opened her eyes again. A deafening whine and strange ethereal whirls filled the air. Her arm was a maze of tubes and odd-looking gadgets.

She tried to move, but her body was restrained tightly against a cold metal floor. Slowly, she turned to the right, noticing another figure, one that was distinctly different from the soldiers from before.

His gear was different, though he bore the same earthy hues as his comrades. He sat casually, legs dangling over the side.

Lysandra's blurry vision remained locked on the man's back, the wind tousling his long, dark hair. Every detail, from the worn patches on his armor to the deliberate way he adjusted the unfamiliar weapon resting across his lap, radiated experience and precision. Even the faint tension in his shoulders carried a silent warning: to test or underestimate him was to invite death.

As her vision cleared, she took in the scene around her. Confusion clouded Lysandra's face as she realized she was surrounded by a small ragtag group of wounded daesyls—contracted servants of the empire. A slight tinge of sympathy coursed through Lysandra when she saw their already long, droopy rabbit-like ears fall even further in dejection.

Craning her head with great difficulty, Lysandra saw they weren't in a room but aboard an enormous airborne contraption. The vessel's edges were open, allowing the crisp air to flow in. Below, the world was a blur of green and darkness as treetops rushed by at astonishing speed.

A dizzying realization washed over Lysandra. They were airborne, at a height that would be deadly to fall from. The sheer speed and occasional jolt made her stomach churn, and the cacophony started to overwhelm her senses.

She tried to muster the strength to shout and demand answers but realized she didn't even have the energy to keep her sole eye open any longer. Every ounce of her being seemed to be pulled into a heavy, relentless fatigue that couldn't be shaken.

Soon enough, the darkness took Lysandra once more.

* * *

DuPont let out a deep sigh as he stared at the wreck of one of his platoon's Bradley's. Its glacis had a gaping fist-sized hole, indicative of a direct hit from a high-velocity projectile.

However, he knew the said projectile wasn't exactly a "material" to begin with. He'd seen the Bradley making the fatal mistake of using the same firing position too many times. Amid the battle, it employed the hit-and-run tactics synonymous with armored warfare, darting out from behind cover to unleash hell and brimstone before immediately wheeling out of sight. It was a tactic meant to keep the enemy off-balance.

At first, it worked well, as the armor engaged mixed targets of infantry and what appeared to be giant, magically imbued horned hyenas. But the monster's sheer size and ferocity drew the attention away from the enemy infantry, who closed the gap unnoticed.

Compounding the issue, the Bradley made the fatal mistake of repeatedly popping out of the same location. That predictability became its downfall. While most of the platoon focused on the hulking monsters, a robed figure began channeling energy. The air around the figure crackled, and with a swift motion, the magic user unleashed a torrent of violet energy.

DuPont watched as the concentrated bolt of energy struck the Bradley dead-on. Sparks from the impact flew everywhere as if a goddamn sabot hit the damned thing.

"Fuck," DuPont groaned, watching as his men pulled Corporal Evans, the driver, from the wreckage.

In the aftermath of the battle, the air was thick with the acrid smell of smoke, gunpowder, and burnt metal. The distant cries of the wounded, the occasional shout of a medic, or the barks of orders from NCOs filled the void.

Just a day ago, they were all back in Fort Cavazos, Texas, trying to fill their time vacuuming rocks, doing PT, and sometimes going on the occasional live-fire exercise. But now they were graced with the presence of warlocks, dragons, and other monsters.

Sergeant First Class Hofmann hopped out of his Bradley and walked over. "We got four KIA and six wounded," he reported, pulling off his helmet and sitting next to DuPont.

Neither said a word as they stared at the mass of humanoid and monstrous bodies that littered the field. The muted moans and cries of the wounded punctuated the eerie calm left by the retreating enemy.

"Who would've believed any of this shit, sir?" Hofmann questioned, taking a deep breath and exhaling slowly. "I mean, I've read about wizards and knights in books, seen them in movies, or fought them in games. But this? I feel like this is some kind of psychotic hallucination."

DuPont didn't answer at first, still staring at the field. "What the fuck do we even do with them?" he suddenly asked, looking over at the sergeant, gesturing towards the carnage. "Do we give them medical attention? Do we go and finish them off? They just fuckin' left them there."

Hofmann's gaze tracked alongside DuPont's, settling on a small armored figure with dark, reptilian scales and a snout-like face. Its labored breathing punctuated the hush that had fallen over the battlefield. "Never thought I'd find myself having to consider the Geneva Convention for whatever these things are," Hofmann said, disbelief evident in his tone.

The lieutenant let out a derisive chuckle, shaking his head. The absurdity of their situation was hard to grasp. It truly boggled one's mind.

Suddenly, the roar of an engine disrupted their contemplation. Captain Ward emerged from the haze of dust and smoke, driving up in a battered Abrams. As the lumbering vehicle came to a halt, the captain jumped out of his commander's cupola with a face lined with stress and irritation.

"DuPont, get your shit in order and start salvaging whatever you can find. We're pulling back to the secondary defense line," Captain Ward barked, standing atop his tank.

DuPont hesitated, casting a glance toward the wounded invaders. "Sir, what about them?" he asked, nodding towards the injured beings strewn across the battlefield.

Ward followed DuPont's gaze, his expression unreadable for a moment. Then, with a glance at his wristwatch, he responded, "Leave 'em. We ain't got the time or the means."

Hofmann and his platoon leader watched their commanding officer hop back into his tank and drive off, its turbine engine whining in the distance. And as the dust from the retreating tank settled, DuPont and Hofmann exchanged glances before giving each other a simple shrug.

"Well, fuck 'em, I guess," DuPont mumbled with a hint of resignation. "You heard the captain. Let's get this show on the road."

CHAPTER 12

Gideon grunted through the pain and supported Yzael across the street as hell broke out around them.

Already trapped behind enemy lines, Gideon and Yzael were driven deeper into the town by the retreating Indigenous forces and their metal beasts.

The air was filled with the noise of strange weaponry echoing from every corner, accompanied by terse and harsh commands from nearby soldiers. Buildings burned, explosions shook the ground, and screams rang out as fang and claw met flesh whenever those horrid Yoxen or formidable Weremen drew too close.

Ducking into another building, Gideon and Yzael tried to catch their breath but were met with a scene of sheer carnage. A lone fur-covered humanoid in the shape of a wolf stood huffing and puffing, glowing red eyes fixed on them as it loomed over the bodies of its kin and several soldiers from this realm. A low growl rumbled behind them, followed by feverish chants from the enslaved weremen as its massive claws extended.

"T-Those accursed beasts brought their shamans!" Yzael yelped in fear as the monster hunched over, positioning itself to leap.

The hair on Gideon's neck stood up as he clutched the sword tightly. He had hoped to cross the lines back into friendly territory, but with the blood-crazed were men under the influence of profane magic, it seemed there were no friendly lines anywhere.

Before either could react, the wolf-like creature lunged, its monstrous maw agape and claws aimed to strike. Suddenly, deafening noises rang out, causing the beast to stumble and crash into the wall, clutching its chest.

After turning toward the offenders and their infernal devices, the creature hurled itself at them instead, only to be mowed under a hail of gunfire. The beast writhed as the deafening chatter of strange weapons echoed through the halls of the dilapidated building. Once the wereman ceased moving, soldiers stormed inside, putting more rounds into its head to ensure it was down for good.

Gideon threw Yzael into the other room and dove in after her as the soldiers snapped their weapons toward them. Hisses and snaps from projectiles slammed into the walls as the two hugged the floor, praying the barrage would cease.

Gideon glanced upward and saw one of the soldiers emerging from the hole in the wall, aiming the weapon at them. Time seemed to slow as Gideon met the soldier's cold gaze, knowing their lives were seconds from ending.

But before the soldier could pull the trigger, the wall behind him roared to life—splintering wood and brick flying in every direction. A massive, horned wereman, wielding a colossal mace dripping with blood, burst through the structure, roaring in fury.

"Run!" Gideon screamed, grabbing Yzael's arm and pulling her away from the scrappy battle.

Snaps and hisses echoed around them as they sprinted through the smoke and dust, desperately trying to evade the enemy soldiers and the supposedly friendly Weremen.

As they ran through the smoke, they found themselves face-to-face with a monstrous metal behemoth blocking their path. Its massive form loomed crookedly, its long snout extending down the street.

Yzael's eyes widened in horror. "By the heavens," she whispered, her voice tinged with wonder and fear.

Before Gideon could voice his own concern, the long snout of the metal creature erupted into an enormous fireball that consumed everything in its vicinity. The shockwave from the explosion threw the two off their feet, sending their world spinning.

The ringing in their ears was intense. Both Yzael and Gideon screamed at each other as they scrambled to their feet, instinctively moving away from the source of the explosion, but neither could hear the other's voice. Their words were lost amidst the intense buzzing in their ears, which pulsated painfully.

Stumbling into a nearby structure, they slid across its unnaturally smooth floor, shards of broken glass slicing into their hands and legs. The thick smoke inside made them cough and wheeze as they struggled to regain their bearings.

Gideon, still gripping Yzael, checked her abdomen, gently pulling back the fabric of her clothes to examine the makeshift bandage he'd applied earlier. The cloth was soaked with fresh blood, but the bleeding wasn't as severe as before.

Yzael winced in pain as Gideon inspected the wound. "It still hurts," she croaked weakly, clutching his hand with trembling fingers.

Neither could hear a word, but Gideon scowled at the sight of her injury. It wasn't bad, but if left untreated, it would be. They were stuck in this hellscape with no resources and even fewer allies. Both sides wanted them dead. Gideon's heart raced from the adrenaline and the creeping dread that Yzael might not survive. Each passing moment felt eternal, the knowledge that a makeshift bandage was their only medical option weighing heavily on him.

Taking a shaky breath, Gideon tried to calm himself. Panic wouldn't help either of them. He held Yzael's face gently, forcing her to look at him. "Ya gotta stay with me," he implored, eyes shining with unshed tears. "Please."

Despite the pain and inability to hear, Yzael understood each word and nodded weakly. She was just a shadow of her once snippy, feisty self. Horror and fatigue glazed her eyes, but even in her dire state, her spirit wasn't entirely snuffed out. "O-Okay," Yzael squeaked just as another concussive blast shook the building's foundation.

The distant hum in their ears started to fade, replaced by the sharp noise of rapid detonations. The floor vibrated with each explosion, and dust drifted from the ceiling. As their hearing gradually returned, it became clear that the battle was far from over. The chorus of unfamiliar weapons and the clattering of armored clinks grew louder.

Peeking out of the broken building, Gideon watched more iron beasts with smaller snouts speed in, firing rhythmic bursts at targets further down the street. The fiery eruptions came at an alarming rate, like someone pounding war drums—except these drums shot through every fiber of one's being. And if that wasn't enough, the rear of the metal monstrosities opened to unleash soldiers dressed in irregular patterns to flood out into the streets and fire their strange weapons at faraway targets.

But what really terrified Gideon was the sight of a group of nine soldiers sprinting directly toward him.

Yelping in horror, Gideon quickly ducked back inside and slammed the door shut. He sprinted back to Yzael, panic in his eyes. "They're coming! We need to move. Now!" he shouted, frantically scanning for any possible exit.

However, the walls seemed to close in, offering no immediate escape as the sounds of boots and commanding shouts grew louder. The rhythmic pounding of their machines echoed through the hallways.

Yzael's eyes widened in alarm, sensing the urgency of the situation. "Where? Where can we go?" she rasped.

Seeing no good options, Gideon dragged her deeper into the building, navigating the maze of rooms. Yzael did her best to kick against the ground, propelling them forward, but every jolt sent a searing pain through her side, and she couldn't stifle the occasional howl of agony.

The cacophony behind them grew louder as the soldiers' weapons reverberated off every surface, their shouts echoing in a language neither Gideon nor Yzael recognized.

Rounding a corner, Gideon spotted a narrow set of stairs leading downward. Without hesitation, he steered Yzael toward them, praying they would lead to some sort of escape. The stairs descended into a dim, damp basement. The air was thick with the scent of mold, but it offered them a temporary refuge from the fighting above.

The howls of weremen and the sick yodeling laughter of the yoxen spread throughout the area. Amidst the cacophony, the town's once peaceful nights filled with chirping crickets were now distant memories. The gunfire, Yoxen's laughter, and wereman's roars melded into a haunting lullaby of war.

Yet, in a lavish tent surrounded by golden banners, a world away from this chaos emanated a different kind of laughter. Korthax, the supreme commander of the subjugation force, sat on his luxurious cushion, cackling. The general's feather-covered fingers, adorned with gold rings, tapped rhythmically against the side of his snout, the glint of precious gems catching the soft light of the candles illuminating the tent.

His laughter wasn't one of joy but rather a melancholic acknowledgment of the irony. Here he was, overseeing what was turning out to be the worst disaster in the empire's history. The ill-fated invasion was such a catastrophic blunder that it overshadowed previous military embarrassments, including the heavy losses during the border war with the Necropolis and the woeful attempt to subjugate the forest of those accursed druids.

"Ahhh," he sighed, his laughter subsiding as he poured himself a goblet of deep blue liquor, letting the aroma waft to his nostrils. "Who would have thought that even a sovereign would be brought to the brink of failure?" he mused aloud, staring into the liquid's depths as if seeking answers.

Korthax leaned back, taking a moment to reflect upon the reports spread out before him. Arcane maps depicted the strategic layout of the currently occupied land—this unknown territory proving far more formidable than he had ever even fathomed. The land was dotted with large structures and complex transportation networks that, while unfamiliar to him, exuded a sense of advanced civilization.

Picking the stacks of reports, the supreme commander singled out one detailing an encounter with machines that moved on their own, launching projectiles capable of decimating even the most hardened draconics. There were mentions of flying machines, too—ones that weren't wyverns, wyrms, or dragons but made of metal and emitting a thunderous noise. These humans seemed to harness an energy source alien to him, and this power was giving them an edge.

He needed to act fast.

One option was to dig in, fortify their positions, and hope for reinforcements. But given this civilization's unexpected might and resistance, he wasn't sure if it would turn the tide. Their unknown technology power had proven formidable. Reports mentioned metal beasts on wheels that spewed fire, high-reaching buildings impervious to damage, and a myriad of other weapons and devices that confounded and decimated his troops.

This option wouldn't just deal a severe blow to the empire's reputation—it could also embolden this new civilization to escalate its aggression. Their strange and formidable airpower was already chipping away at his forces along the contested lines, posing a growing threat.

However, the most pragmatic choice seemed to be the most heartless and politically painful.

A strategic retreat.

They would have to pull back vital assets like the sovereign, the enslaved dragons, and the primary draconic forces. Unfortunately, this would mean sacrificing the empire's tributaries, vassals, and mercenaries. With one last hurrah and the feigned notion of creating a breakthrough, he would pull back the empire's core contingent and leave everyone else to the mercy of the otherworlders.

Their loss would buy the main forces time to retreat and reconsolidate on the other side of the rift from whence they came. But such a decision, while tactical, bore the burden of significant political complications. There were allegiances, treaties, and promises. Sacrificing the vassals and tributaries wasn't just a military decision—it was a statement that the empire's word could be forsaken when faced with unprecedented adversity.

The ramifications were far-reaching. The tributaries and vassals had joined the invasion with the promise of shared spoils and the empire's protection. Leaving them behind would be seen as the ultimate betrayal and could sow the seeds of dissent among the empire's allies and subjects. It could unravel centuries of work to absorb these states peacefully. This strategic move could erode the very foundations of the empire's political landscape.

Trust, once broken, would be hard to mend.

But what choice did he have? Losing border territories paled compared to losing hordes of dragons, let alone a Sovereign like the one fighting in the skies of that forsaken world. If word spread that the mightiest of their kind—a celestial dragon—fell in battle against these otherworlders, sheer panic and chaos would ensue throughout the empire.

"Damn it all!" Korthax bellowed, sending his hand through the thick hardwood table, splitting it in half.

Servants and guards jumped at the sudden outburst, exchanging fearful glances. The once tranquil war chamber was now filled with tension. His advisors, well accustomed to Korthax's fiery temperament, took a deep breath to steady themselves.

"Forgive me," Korthax growled, reigning in his anger and pulling his hand from the wreckage of the table. Blood trickled from a few minor cuts, but they healed almost instantly, a testament to his celestial prowess. "The gravity of our situation is pressing, and my patience is wearing thin."

None blamed him, not even the advisors and dragonkin commanders gathered around the table. The burden of leadership weighed heavily on Korthax's broad shoulders, but they understood the stakes: the lives lost and the potential repercussions of this ill-fated invasion. Even the lowborn servants knew from seeing the unending stream of wounded flooding back through the rift.

Commander Lira, a red-feathered seraph with scars marring her once flawless features, stepped forward, her voice steady despite the dire circumstances. "Your lordship, I understand your plight. However, time is running thin." She glanced momentarily at the scaled dragonkin to her left. "We need to recalibrate our strategy. The vassals and tributaries expect a plan, and morale is crumbling."

Narix, the dragonkin to whom Lira had cast a glance, nodded in agreement, his scales glistening in the dim light. "She speaks the truth.

The forces are restless, and tales of the otherworlders might have ignited fear among those in the encampment, especially after the devastating strike on the rift's staging ground."

Korthax remained silent, tapping his snout to control himself as he stared at the destroyed table. Outbursts like this were rare for him. Known for his measured, even kind, demeanor in the face of dire situations, Korthax did not expect such an unprecedented scenario. He had led countless battles and intricate strategies against formidable foes, always emerging victorious. But facing an enemy with unknown capabilities and tactics from another realm had shaken even the most hardened.

"I have my own opinion, but what is the worst-case scenario if we cannot close the rift and these things choose to pursue?" Korthax finally asked, his deep voice echoing through the tent.

"I believe," Lira spoke first, her eyes narrowing as she pondered the potential outcomes. "If the rift remains open and the otherworlders flood in, our allies and vassal states would significantly slow them down if we shape the narrative in our favor," she replied carefully, glancing around the table. "We shouldn't be above the clever use of propaganda."

Narix added, "I'm inclined to agree, though I find it distasteful." His claws tapped the table. "Fear can go a long way, especially since these otherworlders' intentions are a mystery to us. We've witnessed their destructive power, so we know the threat they pose is real. Harnessing that fear may be our best chance."

A deep snarl left Korthax, his clawed hand stabbed down into the broken table, sending the splinters flying.

His eyes locked onto Lira's, then Narix's. His voice was firm and cold. "In light of our current predicament, desperate times call for desperate measures." He paused, the weight of his decision evident in the room's tense atmosphere. "I want the auxiliaries to break through the frontline immediately. The main body of our forces will fall back."

Narix's eyes widened in confusion. "But, General, our vassals would never stand for it if they find out they're to—"

"Die in our stead?" Korthax interrupted, his tone frigid. "I am well aware. But what do you think would happen if our dragons fell, or even a damned sovereign?"

From his seat, Korthax stood up with his feathers spread out, making him seem even more regal. "Even though we've yet to commit our sephanic forces, the cataclysm that would follow would be far worse than losing a collection of barbarian city-states and kingdoms on the border."

Silence reigned as they watched the supreme commander mull over his next words. The dim light cast long shadows over Korthax's stern face, deepening the creases of age and the scars from countless battles.

"Our dragons are not just symbols of power," Korthax continued, "they are the lifeline of our realms, the protectors of our cities, and the hope of our people. Even the loss of a single flight would demoralize our entire civilization and break the spirits of those we lead," he spat out, glaring at Lira and Narix. "And even the emperor would feel its repercussions if we lose a sovereign."

With her plumage ruffled, Lira stepped closer, her voice gentle but firm. "Your will shall be done."

Narix hesitated momentarily, his scales shimmering in the dim light, then finally bowed deeply. "Your will shall be done."

The general looked at them both before turning sharply and marching to his quarters. "Tell the auxiliaries and mercenaries they'll be reinforced the moment they make their push," Korthax ordered without looking back. "Promise them gold, lands, whatever it takes.

They need to believe that they are not being abandoned."

The tent flap fell shut behind him, leaving Lira and Narix with the weight of the task ahead.

Chapter 13

Every passing second was a nightmare that not even the most depraved hag could conjure. The basement was damp, the steady drip of water forming a maddening rhythm against the cacophony of destruction outside. Dust and debris fell with each explosion, the old walls groaning in protest, threatening to collapse.

Yzael's breaths came ragged and labored, her face a ghostly pale in the dim, flickering light. The pool of blood beneath her seemed to grow steadily with each passing minute, a stark contrast to the gray floor. Gideon's hands were stained red, pressing down on Yzael's wound, trying to stem the flow. His eyes, always so fierce and unyielding, were now filled with raw anguish as panic started to creep into his face.

"Gideon," she whispered weakly, aware that her end was slowly drawing closer. "I'm scared."

Gideon's heart felt like a solid piece of lead sinking into the deep abyss. Swallowing hard, the large, solidly built man forced back the tears that threatened to spill from his eyes. "I know," he whispered back, offering a comforting touch to her shoulder amid the terror surrounding them. "But I need you to hold on for a little longer. I'll keep ya alive, I promise."

Sensing he was about to leave, Yzael reached out and grasped his hand, her fingers weakly curling around his. "No! No, please don't go!" she pleaded as the world shook around them. "I don't..." Yzael's voice broke as she continued, "I don't want to die alone."

The blasts became more violent, causing the overhead beams to creak ominously. Bits of concrete began to fall, dust filling the air. Gideon shielded Yzael with his body, hoping to protect her from further harm.

Every tremor was like a ticking clock, and each second felt like a lifetime as Yzael's condition weighed heavily on Gideon's mind. He couldn't stay here, couldn't just watch her fade away. He needed to act.

Through the gaps in the basement ceiling, he could hear the roars of the weremen and the deafening artillery blasts. Their only hope lay outside, but that world was filled with chaos and uncertainty.

Summoning every ounce of courage, Gideon stood up, ripping himself out of Yzael's grip. "I-I need you to stay strong, Yzael," he said with a voice thick with emotion. "I-I can't let you die like this. I have to find help, even if it's the last thing I do."

"No!" Yzael yelled, trying to push herself up. However, the high elf was too weak and toppled over in pain. Smacking against the concrete floor, Yzael felt her vision blur as darkness threatened to overtake her, but she fought it off, reaching out to the closing door and squeaking her last plea, "Please! Please don't leave me alone!"

The door slammed shut, leaving Yzael in the ever-consuming darkness of the basement. The silence that enveloped her was punctuated only by the muffled sounds of the battle above and her labored breathing. The world seemed distant, surreal. Every nerve in her body screamed in pain, but a different kind of pain tightened around her heart—the agony of abandonment.

Gideon stepped out into the hellscape above through gritted teeth and grabbed Yzael's sword tight. Bodies of weremen and strange soldiers were scattered everywhere, and the once-solid building they had sought shelter in had been completely decimated. Half of the structure had crumbled into rubble, ash and smoke billowing from its core, while the remaining half stood precariously with fire licking its remaining walls.

As the large man turned his gaze outside, he was met with an apocalyptic scene. The streets were filled with debris, smoldering fires, and bodies. The ground was scarred from the force of spells, strange otherworldly weapons, and the tread of those metal beasts.

As his thoughts turned to that monstrosity, his gaze fell upon the massive remains of one slumped in the corner of the street, its large turret pointing toward the heavens in a silent, accusing manner. Atop its cold iron surface lay the corpse of an enormous yoxen, its thick hide ripped open, its deep red blood pouring over the construct, staining it with an eerie sheen.

Despite the horrid sight, Gideon knew he couldn't afford to be paralyzed by the chaos as the bark of otherworldly weapons resounded, accompanied by the roars of weremen. Every second counted with Yzael's life hanging in the balance, and there was no telling how much longer the basement would hold—or how long she could hang on. The very thought pushed Gideon forward, keeping his head low, Yzael's sword reflecting the orange and red glow of the surrounding fires.

Suddenly, to his left, a war cry rang out as a group of weremen burst from an adjacent building, making a desperate bid to run down the street. But before they could make it far, the ground shook again as deafening blasts, which seemed to be summoned from the skies, erupted around them. The earth trembled with each terrifying explosion, creating craters and sending clouds of dust and debris into the air.

Gideon ducked behind the partially destroyed wall he had been hiding behind and shielded himself as the chatter of the otherworlders' weapons accompanied the rain of death. He had seen

Yzael wield all kinds of powerful spells, but in all his time as a freelancer, he had never encountered such ferocity in battle.

Weremen, under the effects of their horrid shaman's bloodlust, were known to be near unstoppable. They were relentless, throwing themselves at formations and cutting them apart without fear for their lives. And here they were, systematically torn apart from a distance by unseen hands, by a power that neither magic nor brute strength seemed to match.

Turning around and pressing himself closer to the wall, Gideon surveyed the room and caught sight of several lifeless forms sprawled across the floor. The structure, though battered from the battle outside, was filled with fallen weremen, with the shredded bodies of otherworldly soldiers lying amongst them.

He knew that while weremen were brutal and vicious, their shamans often brewed potent potions and concoctions that aided them in battle. Some were known to cure ailments or even mend wounds, while others imbued the drinker with strength. If he could find just one of these vials, it could be the difference between life and death for Yzael.

Even a strength potion could potentially give her what she needed to survive long enough to get to healers.

Gideon began his frantic search, weaving through the piles of rubble and bodies. He held onto the faintest hope of finding something useful as he overturned each Beastman corpse. But as he checked one body after another, all he found were either empty or shattered vials, their precious contents wasted amid the chaos.

Even after going over each body three times, he realized that nothing was useful.

Fissures formed on the floor as Gideon's hand slammed into it. The warrior's breath became ragged, and his vision blurred from the frustration and desperation. The weight of the situation pressed down as he turned over another body and resumed his frantic search.

He felt defeated, exhausted, and on the brink of despair. How could he face Yzael, who was on the verge of death, with the news that he couldn't find anything to help?

Tears finally streamed down his face as he broke down, collapsing to his knees. The usually resilient warrior, who had faced countless perils and emerged victorious, now found himself shattered in the face of possible loss. The ground beneath him felt cold and unyielding, matching the frosty grip of hopelessness that threatened to choke him.

"I'm sorry," he croaked, slamming his hand against the ground as the sounds of battle continued to echo around him. "Yzael, I'm so sorry. I don't know what to do!"

Each sob that wracked his body carried the weight of every promise, every vow, every moment he had shared with Yzael. Memories of their contracts together, from battling monsters in the wilds to clicking mugs together in seedy taverns, flooded his mind. The juxtaposition of those cherished memories against the current reality felt like a blade twisting in his heart.

But as Gideon's sorrow filled the battered room, a blast wave from a nearby explosion jolted him back to the present. Dust and debris filled his surroundings, and the room trembled under the force, reminding him where he was.

Gideon sucked in a few deep breaths and recollected himself. His gaze turned toward the realm's soldiers, clad in their strange irregular uniforms and strange weapons scattered around. He felt a pang of irony in seeking aid from the very enemies he'd been fighting against, but desperation knew no bounds.

In the background, the barks and roars of the weremen were

silenced by the rapid chatter of the otherworlders' weapons. As much as these foul beasts pushed the defenders back, the otherworlders were slowly and steadily retaking ground. Gideon had to move quickly.

Pushing over one of the fallen soldiers, Gideon's hands swiftly rifled through the body's pockets and pouches, searching for anything resembling potions, elixirs, or any form of aid that could help pull Yzael away from the brink of death.

In his hurried search, Gideon's fingers slid across unusual items that felt alien and familiar. There were tight rolls of white fabric with sticky ends, which he assumed were some sort of bandages, along with small, sealed packets that, when torn open, revealed wet, oddly scented cloths. While everything was foreign, Gideon could clearly understand they were used as potential life-saving tools.

"A-Ahh, fuck it! I'll take them all!" Gideon shouted, shoving as much as he could into his pouches before jumping to the following body.

This one was slumped against a ruined wall, a large chunk of its neck torn away. Beside the corpse lay a large bag adorned with a strange red cross symbol. Gideon knelt and tried to open the bag without hesitation, but his fingers fumbled over the curious metal tracks that sealed it shut. Impatient and anxious, he took his dagger and deftly sliced the bag open.

"Blessed be the ancients! A healer's bag!" he cried out in relief, barely able to contain his joy. Clear, flexible bags filled with liquid and attached tubes were packed alongside the same strange medical implements he'd seen on the other bodies.

Before he could reach Yzael, the distinct sound of the otherworlders' language rang out. Within moments, the staccato of their weapons echoed loudly, drowning out Gideon's yelp as he instinctively threw himself to the ground, pressing as close to the floor as possible. The unnatural projectiles pierced the walls just inches above him, slicing through the wall like paper.

Suddenly, two massive weremen burst through the wall, one riddled with holes from the outside assault, flailing as it collapsed onto the healer's bag, crushing it under its weight.

Having already rolled out of the way, Gideon watched in horror as the contents splattered and crushed, rendering the once invaluable supplies useless.

"No!" the warrior screamed, snatching at the crushed bag in desperation.

The second wereman, though injured, wasn't crippled. Its frenzied gaze locked onto Gideon for a moment before it scrambled deeper into the building, bullets slamming into the wall behind it. It only took a few seconds for Gideon to snap to attention, realizing the creature was heading straight for the door behind which his critically injured partner lay.

Fueled by adrenaline, Gideon sprinted after the wereman, gripping Yzael's weapon tightly. Turning the corner, he watched as the beast grabbed the basement door handle and yanked it off its hinges. Gideon lunged just in the nick of time, catching it completely off guard and sinking the blade deeply into the creature's shoulder before tackling it over a countertop.

The force of the impact shattered the glass and sent various items flying in every direction as the two rolled and thrashed, knocking over tables and chairs in the confined space. The beast roared in pain and anger, trying to dislodge the warrior clinging to it, stabbing him repeatedly in the side with its claws.

Gideon let out a guttural scream of agony as he yanked out the sword and plunged it into the monster's chest. The blade sank deep, eliciting another bloodcurdling roar as the wereman writhed beneath him. But with a sudden surge of monstrous strength, the beast clasped Gideon's arm and, with a powerful yank, flung the man off like a ragdoll into a large shelf.

Despite the sword still embedded in its chest, the wereman scrambled to its feet to escape. But before it could move, the rapid chatter of otherworldly weapons echoed. Multiple projectiles slammed into the wereman's back, causing it to jerk and stumble forward with every impact. The monster let out a pained roar as it crashed face-first into a nearby wall, bits of plaster and brick scattering.

Within moments, the room filled with otherworldly soldiers, their weapons trained on the now-motionless wereman sprawled on the floor, riddled with bullets. Their relief was short-lived, however, as they turned their attention to Gideon. With their weapons trained on him, the soldiers closed in, shouting commands in a language he couldn't understand. Weakened and bleeding profusely from his wounds, Gideon struggled to stand.

It was difficult for Gideon to process everything around him. The pain, which should have been sharp, was replaced by a numbness spreading through his body, replacing the earlier adrenaline. Everything felt surreal, as if he were stuck in a waking nightmare.

Dragging himself up to his knees, Gideon shifted his gaze so his eyes met the soldiers'. Their gazes were hardened and unyielding but not entirely devoid of compassion. He could barely speak; every word felt like it was being torn from his throat. His breaths were ragged and shallow, but he needed them to understand.

"Yzael," he choked out, coughing up blood. With all his strength, he began crawling toward the basement, pointing desperately to the ruined door. "Please. Please... please help her..."

There was a brief pause before the soldiers' leader, a dark-skinned man, cautiously approached, his weapon still trained on Gideon. The soldier's gaze flicked to the wereman with a sword still lodged in its chest before quickly snapping back to the armored figure crawling on the ground, his movements labored and weak.

Seeing Gideon's critical state, the soldier's grip on his weapon loosened slightly. He glanced at his squadmates for a brief moment, exchanging silent signals. Two of them took a defensive stance, ensuring the perimeter, while another cautiously approached the basement door.

"S-She needs..." Gideon tried to get out another plea, but his body gave out, and with one last moan, he collapsed. Even in death, his arm remained stretched, pointing toward the stairs.

"Cooper, Murphy, Rodriguez! On me! We're gonna take this basement!" DuPont yelled, stepping over the body of that strange medieval-esque warrior, his boots crunching on shattered glass.

His soldier quickly formed behind him while the other held security as the squad descended into the basement. The dim light from the room above faintly illuminated the staircase, casting eerie shadows on the wooden steps.

They moved confidently but cautiously, making sure every inch of their descent was covered and cleared for threats. Each soldier was on high alert, attuned to every creak of the steps, every drip of water from the moist walls, and the faint echoes of their movements.

The basement air was thick with humidity and carried a metallic scent. The soft glow from a single bulb hanging from the room revealed a figure lying in a pool of blood.

DuPont furrowed his brows as he crept closer. The figure was an ethereal woman with sharp, elven features. Long silver hair spread around her, merging with the blood that had flowed from her wounds. She lay on her side, her deep violet eyes staring unfocused at a pile of boxes, seemingly completely out of it.

The rest of the squad swiftly spread out, checking each corner of the basement and ensuring they were not about to deal with any unsavory surprises. Once the area was secured, Murphy cautiously approached the injured woman, still keeping his weapon ready.

"Clear!" Rodriguez called after tossing aside a few boxes and stabbing another with the tip of his rifle.

With gentle hands, Murphy turned the woman onto her back. The pool of blood had soaked through her ornate clothing, and her breathing was raspy and shallow. As she was flipped, her eyes met Murphy's momentarily, a flicker of recognition—or perhaps a last plea—shining within them.

"Heavens... protect," she murmured, her voice barely audible, before her eyelids fluttered and she slipped into unconsciousness. "Gideon."

A deep silence settled over the entire basement as the soldiers exchanged uneasy glances. DuPont's voice echoed as he turned toward the stairs. "Medic! Garza, get your ass down here, now!"

Chapter 14

Yzael had always been an outlier among her high elven peers in her homeland. Her sense of adventure and disdain for her people's stifling traditions had led her to leave behind a boring life of study, seeking purpose and meaning among freelancers and taskers. But now, amidst the cacophony of the tavern, she felt that familiar sting of alienation.

The Gryphon's Tavern was notorious in the city of Aldenshore for its rowdy and sometimes dangerous clientele of freelancers. Fights were as common as ordering a pint of ale or a fresh slab of meat. The air was thick with the scent of sweat, booze, and the occasional whiff of a spell gone wrong. Rowdy laughter, drunken ballads, and boisterous tales of exploits filled the space, making Yzael's ears throb.

Sitting alone at a corner table, Yzael tried to appear nonchalant with her ale, but her sharp, elven eyes surveyed the room with disdain and curiosity. Warriors clad in cloth and iron clinked glasses together, regaling their tablemates with stories of close calls and glorious victories. Mages huddled in dim corners, their faces illuminated by the soft glow of their grimoires, discussing arcane theories and debating the best spells for specific scenarios.

Lost in thought, Yzael didn't notice a female figure with knife-like ears—characteristic of sun elves—plopped in front of her. "All by yourself?" the stranger asked, tapping the table.

The voice, soft yet commanding, pulled Yzael from her thoughts. The sun elf woman had a fair complexion that shimmered subtly under the dim tavern light. Her white hair, pure as freshly fallen snow, was neatly tied in a long braid that cascaded over one shoulder, adorned with intricate beads and feathers.

But what caught Yzael's attention the most was the woman's attire. She wore a thick, fur-lined tunic embroidered with intricate patterns of wolves and ravens, cinched at the waist by a leather belt with ornate metalwork. Her boots, made of weathered hide, were laced up tightly and reached her mid-calf, providing warmth and protection against the harsh northern terrains.

Yzael's eyes narrowed slightly, and she tried to place where she had seen such attire before. It was distinctively northern, reminiscent of the lands far beyond the snowy peaks and frozen fjords.

Noticing Yzael's scrutiny, the sun elf extended a delicate hand adorned with a silver ring that sparkled like morning light. "Ulina," she introduced herself with a smile, "I'm the tavern mistress here. Couldn't help but notice you've been sitting here alone for quite a while. And with a grimoire, no less. Are you perhaps waiting for your partners?"

Hesitation from her bruised ego caused Yzael to look off to the side, cheeks flushing. After a deep breath, the mage finally swallowed her pride, her fingers tightly gripping the edge of her grimoire, "I, um, I'm not waiting for anyone," Yzael admitted, her voice quieter than she liked. "I thought perhaps I might test the waters here."

Ulina's expression softened, her eyes showing a glint of understanding. "Ah, are you a solo freelancer, then?" she asked with genuine interest. "Or just looking for a group to join?"

It took her a moment, but after a few sips of ale, Yzael finally gathered her thoughts. "Well, I've always been more of a loner," she confessed. "But I'm not opposed to the idea of working in a team."

"Hmmm," Ulina hummed, closing her eyes and resting her head

on her hand. "Going at it alone has its merits," she continued after a brief moment of contemplation, "but it's a treacherous world out on the periphery. Even the most skilled can benefit from having allies."

With a sudden motion, Ulina knocked on the hard wooden table, startling Yzael in her seat. "Ah! I've got it!" the tavern mistress exclaimed as a thought struck her.

She scanned the bustling tavern, her gaze settling on a lone human seated in the farthest corner. The man was engaged in a heated debate with his mug of ale, gesturing as he argued with a dwarf about "superior brewing methods." He wore a scarred iron cuirass over a tattered gambeson. His scraggly dark brown hair was matted and unkempt, and a perpetual scowl seemed to be etched on his face.

"I'm telling you, you half-pint piss monger, this southern brew is way more refined than your gods-awful mountain swills!" the man exclaimed, sloshing his ale for emphasis.

The stout dwarf with a fiery beard that matched his temper slammed his fist on the table. "You wouldn't know a good brew if it hit you square in the face, you long-legged-lard bastard!"

"Gideon!" Ulina yelled as she squeezed through the crowd and made her way over. The woman's jovial voice seemed to pierce through the heated atmosphere like a beacon, drawing nearby patrons' attention. "What have I told you about picking fights over drinks, especially with Thrain? It's ale, for heaven's sake!"

Gideon glanced up at Ulina, a wry grin playing on his lips. "Ah, Ulina. Just providing some entertainment for your customers," he replied, gesturing dramatically to the surrounding audience.

Thrain huffed, adjusting his extraordinarily long, thick beard. "He started it," he grumbled, pointing an accusing thumb at Gideon.

"Piss monger," Gideon muttered just loud enough for those nearby to hear as he turned to Ulina.

"Lard-fucker." Thrain immediately shot back, turning to his drink.

Ulina, already feeling exasperated, placed a hand on her forehead and rolled her eyes. "By the gods, you two are like children! Every week, it's something new."

Before Gideon could retort, Ulina grabbed his arm and, with surprising strength, yanked him off his chair. Gideon stumbled but quickly regained his footing.

"Hey! What in the infinite hells?!" he protested, trying to free himself from her iron grip.

"Quiet, you!" Ulina scolded, her voice filled with authority, silencing even the noisiest patrons. "Or I'll make you settle your tab all at once."

The threat made Gideon's face pale. Everyone in the tavern knew of Gideon's infamous tab, an ever-growing list of drinks and meals Ulina had mercifully allowed to accumulate. The thought of paying it off all at once was more than enough to make even the most hardened freelancer cringe.

With the large man finally subdued, Ulina marched him across the dining area, weaving through the tables until they reached Yzael's corner. She shoved the man into the seat opposite the mage, who had been observing the entire scene wide-eyed.

"Why in the world are you so strong?" Gideon complained, rubbing his arm as he settled into the new seat.

Ignoring the comment, Ulina put on her best sale smile and turned to the frazzled mage, "I hope you weren't too attached to that quiet evening of yours!" the tavern mistress said with a wink, gesturing towards the still disgruntled Gideon. "Because I believe I've found the solution to your partnership problem!"

Yzael raised an eyebrow, glancing between Ulina and Gideon, trepidation on her face. "This is the solution?"

Gideon opened his mouth to protest, but a loud smack from Ulina silenced him.

"One more word out of you, and I'll double your tab," Ulina threatened.

Gideon muttered something under his breath and shrank into his chair.

Ulina took a deep breath, her expression softening as she addressed Yzael. "All right, hear me out. You came here tonight looking for a partner and potentially a few starter jobs to get your foot in the door, correct?"

Yzael nodded, "Ah. Y-Yes, and preferably someone experienced. But, with all due respect, him?" She glanced warily at Gideon, who seemed to want absolutely nothing to do with this.

Ulina smirked, "I know, I know. Gideon may not be the friendliest face around, but beneath that rough exterior is a man who's completed more jobs successfully than most in this tavern. He's reliable, skilled, and knows the ropes better than anyone."

"You're going to need someone like him," she continued, "especially as a mage just starting to cut their teeth. He knows the ins and outs of freelancing and can guide you through the potential pitfalls of dealing with taskers. And we need living, experienced freelancers—not dead ones!"

A half-smirk played across Gideon's face as he scoffed, "Well, isn't that the nicest thing you've ever said about me, Ulina? I'm touched."

"Shut up, brute," Ulina snapped and rolled her eyes, eliciting a giggle from Yzael. "No one's talking to you! I'm merely stating facts to help our mage friend make an informed decision here."

Yzael, still amused, pondered for a moment, brushing a strand of hair behind her ear. "I appreciate your concern, Ulina. It's just partnering with someone, which is a significant decision."

Ulina's eyes gleamed with intrigue. "Well, now might just be the perfect time to get to know each other," she said, leaning in. "I've got a job that needs doing, and the client is offering five silver coins."

Gideon, distracted despite his initial bravado, tried to focus on the conversation, but his gaze occasionally wandered to Ulina's exposed cleavage. The allure of the exposed skin caused his gaze to keep flickering back and forth, making him barely acknowledge the amount.

"Five s-silver, eh?" he stammered, trying to keep his voice steady but failing given the distraction.

Ulina grinned mischievously, catching on to his flustered state. "Indeed. Now, here's my proposal. I'll split it evenly between the two of you, which means two silver coins each and one silver as a finder's fee for the tavern," she explained, watching their reactions.

Yzael nodded, pondering the split. "That sounds reasonable."

Gideon was about to voice his agreement when Ulina interrupted with a playful smirk. "Though for you, Gideon, considering you got a free show," she teased, delicately placing a hand over the top's opening, "I think one silver will suffice."

The man in question flushed a deep shade of red as he snapped his head toward the woman. "Now, wait just a minute!" he nearly shouted. "That ain't fair, Ulina! That ain't right!" Gideon desperately tried to find words to defend himself but found it challenging amidst the chuckles and giggles from the surrounding tables.

"Oh, lighten up, Gideon!" Ulina laughed, slapping his back. "Can't you take a joke? I'm not actually going to shortchange you over some tits!"

The tavern erupted in laughter, and even a group of burly warriors at the next table joined in the fun. "You always fall for that shit, Gideon!" This was followed by a burst of laughter from the group.

Gideon could only slump in his seat, realizing there was no salvaging his dignity at this point. He muttered something under his breath, earning another round of laughter from the crowd.

Trying to keep a straight face, Yzael turned to Gideon with a playful glint in her eyes. "Though I must say, Gideon, you aren't going to leer at me too, are you?" she teased, placing a hand on her own modest chest. "I wouldn't want to have to brand you as a lecherous beast."

"W-What?! No!" Gideon replied, his head snapping between Yzael, Ulina, and the warriors. "Gods damn it!" He slapped his hands over his face in an exaggerated facepalm. "Why does everything always turn into a spectacle with you, Ulina?"

Looking around, Ulina saw that the entire tavern was now a mix of boisterous laughter, playful jabs, and even some patrons toasting and buying a round of drinks to celebrate Gideon's "lecherous" behavior. Even some of the more stoic regulars were trying hard to suppress their smiles.

She stretched her arms out with a flourish, gesturing toward the mage and the warrior. "See? You two are getting along already!" Ulina declared, laughing heartily. "Now, are you going to accept the job or not?"

Gideon groaned, rubbing the bridge of his nose as if trying to massage away the headache that was starting to form. "All right, all right! Fine!" he conceded, resting his elbow on the table. "Just give us the details before you go off and pull another one of your stunts!"

Yzael, still suppressing her giggles, looked between the two of them. "Well, with such a warm welcome, how could I refuse?" she said, sipping her ale.

Ulina beamed, her energy infectious. She grabbed a few items off another table and arranged them in the rough shape of the city and its surroundings. "The job's simple, at least in theory," she began, tracing a finger along a winding path on the map. "There's been a series of disturbances along the northeast route, just outside of town. Locals say it's haunted, cursed, or whatever, but my client believes that scroungers are actually to blame and that they've set up a nest somewhere along the road. They're causing trouble for merchants and travelers. My client wants someone to investigate and, if it is a nest, to clear it out."

She paused, letting the information sink in. Then, she used a wooden fork to mark a spot on the makeshift map not far from the town. "Here," she said while pointing to a spot. "This is where the majority of the disturbances have been reported." Ulina continued, looking at the two freelancers. "People attacked or went missing in the night—you know the deal."

Gideon leaned in, inspecting the marked area. "That's the old Dalrymple Trail, isn't it? Used to be a popular route for merchants until the landslides a few years back. Makes sense scroungers would make their nest there; it provides ample cover, and any commonfolk passing by are easy prey."

Yzael hummed in thought, her fingers tracing an arcane pattern on the surface of her grimoire. "Scroungers, you say?" Her eyes narrowed slightly, a flicker of recognition in her gaze. "I came across a few of those filthy things on my way here, on the northwestern road. Nasty little creatures with more claws than sense." Yzael wrinkled her nose as she remembered the scent of their burning flesh when she disposed of them.

Ulina leaned forward, her interest piqued. "Northwestern road?" She hummed and tapped her foot, seemingly connecting the dots in her head. "That all but confirms it, then! There's a scrounger infestation near the town, and you two"—she pointed at the pair with both hands—"are to get rid of it!"

"Right now?" Gideon asked with a hint of hesitation in his voice. "I was hoping for another ale and maybe some breakfast first."

A chuckle escaped Ulina's lips as she hung her head in mock exasperation, allowing the man another glimpse of her cleavage. Gideon's gaze lingered just a moment before he quickly caught himself, the memory of their earlier exchange fresh in his mind. He forcefully turned his gaze to the worn wooden table, feeling a hint of heat rise to his cheeks. It was clear he didn't want to revisit the teasing from earlier.

"Fine, fine," Ulina relented, righting herself and brushing her braid behind her. "I'll have some breakfast and an ale sent to your table on the house." She gave a knowing look and a wink. "Consider it a gesture of goodwill since I'm pairing you up with a newbie. But get her kitted out first." Ulina finished, tilting her head towards the door before spinning around and heading to the kitchen.

"Staring again, Gideon?" Yzael teased, a mischievous smile plastered across her face, having caught his brief moment of weakness.

Gideon grumbled, trying to deflect her teasing. "I don't know what you're talking about," he said as he quickly shimmied out of his seat.

"Oh, please. Your face was as red as a ripe tomato," Yzael chuckled, clearly enjoying the banter. "But don't worry, your secret's safe with me, seeing we're now partners."

"There's no secret to keep," Gideon responded quickly, a bead of sweat dripping down his neck. He tried to regain some semblance of dignity, adjusting his gambeson and focusing on the door ahead. Yzael got up after him, her giggles still lingering in the air, and followed close behind.

As they approached the door, Yzael's laughter faded into a more contemplative expression. "Is she always like that?" she asked, nodding toward the kitchen where Ulina had disappeared.

Gideon heaved a sigh. "Yes. Yes, she is. Every single time." He shook his head. "Her shieldmaiden friend, Azeline, is better at pushing buttons, to be honest."

Yzael chuckled, offering a sympathetic nod. "Well, I commend you for your patience then."

They neared the door, and Gideon paused before opening it, turning to Yzael. "Are you sure you want me as your partner?" he asked, his tone serious. "I'm not exactly the easiest person to get along with."

Meeting his gaze, Yzael tilted her head in wonder before offering a sweet smile. "You've been decent to me so far." She paused, her eyes reflecting sincerity. "Besides, everyone has their edges."

An awkward silence ensued as Gideon blinked in surprise, absorbing her words. The noise from the tavern seemed to fade into the background, and for a moment, all that existed was the space between them.

Rubbing the bridge of his nose in embarrassment, Gideon cleared his throat. "Well, little lady, don't worry, I'll keep ya alive." He pushed open the door, allowing the blinding sunlight to flood in. "You'll need some proper gear if we're headed out beyond the city. Armor, weapons, and provisions."

But as he continued, his words seemed to grow distant, like an echo fading into the vastness of an empty hall. Gideon's voice grew fainter, muddled, and indistinct. As he reached out to push the door open, a blinding light suddenly flooded in, momentarily overwhelming Yzael's senses.

The comforting, familiar environment of the tavern faded away, replaced by the stark and sterile whiteness of a place she couldn't recognize. The tavern ceiling's rough, rustic wooden beams gave way to a pristine, flat expanse overhead. The soft and ambient glow of lanterns was replaced by the harsh, clinical strips of light embedded into the ceiling.

"G-Gid…" Yzael managed to croak, her voice barely audible with the foreign tube in her throat. "Gideon?"

Chapter 15

Relor's immense form overshadowed the land beneath as he surged through the rift. The sheer magnitude of the majestic sovereign stirred the air, causing trees to sway and the grass to dance in his wake. His once resplendent golden feathers, gleaming with near-luminescent brilliance, were now sullied with ash, soot, and drenched in his own radiant blood.

He was among the last dragons to journey through the rift, joining those who had already passed, each bearing the wounds and weariness of a battle that had raged for over a day. Several of his kin lay sprawled on the ground, their once-mighty forms now heaving with the effort of each labored breath, completely drained from the exhausting ordeal.

Finding an expanse large enough for his gargantuan size, Relor began his descent. It was far from the regal display befitting a creature of his grandeur. The sheer force of his landing shook the earth, and as he tried to stabilize his massive frame, a sharp, agonizing pain shot through him, causing him to stagger dangerously.

A deep, guttural roar erupted from his throat, a testament to the severity of his injuries. His massive legs, which had always held him aloft, were now the source of anguish, prompting a string of ancient curses from his maw. His once-pristine form was a patchwork of gashes, bruises, and broken feathers, all inflicted by the arrival of those infernal mortals' newest weapons.

In the beginning, the "darts" they shot at him and his kin were painful but manageable. The things would simply burst upon contact, bombarding them with burning heat and rattling shock waves. Most dragons could continue fighting even after being struck multiple times. But as the conflict wore on, the damnable mortals adapted, switching to more potent and effective iterations of their weapons.

Unlike their explosive predecessors, these newer "darts" the otherworlders employed slammed into their targets with unmatched speed. By the time one realized their hellish "eye" was looking at you, it was too late—a solid bolt of vengeful fury, seemingly unleashed by the gods themselves, was going to strike. And even if you saw them coming, those damned things were far too fast to dodge reliably, especially in the midst of a battle with their metal locusts.

"You humiliate me with this retreat, Korthax!" Relor bellowed with uncontrolled rage as he limped towards the camp, a group of humanoids emerging from it.

Korthax, a white-feathered dragonkin and the supreme commander of the invasion forces was already making his way toward the Sovereign with his head bowed low. "I apologize, my Sovereign," the general said, his voice steady as he knelt in subservience. "But this decision was not made lightly. If the flights fell—or heaven forbid, you fell—whole swathes of the empire could be put at risk. I could not, would not, let that happen."

Relor's fiery eyes glared down at Korthax, his body trembling from his injuries and the fury and frustration boiling within. "Fight another day?" he spat, his voice dripping with disdain. "We're the mightiest of beings in all of existence, Korthax! Masters of the heavens! Rightful keeper of all realms! And now, we flee like prey from these mortals?!"

Korthax remained silent, kowtowed before the massive entity. The sovereign knew full well that Korthax's warnings about the overwhelming force beyond the rift had proved painfully accurate. He also knew the call to retreat was sound and the only logical course of action. Yet it infuriated Relor to his core.

His once-indomitable pride had been shattered, and the shame of this failed conquest seeped into his very essence. The air grew tense, electrified by Relor's raw anger. Suddenly, with an explosive hiss, Relor lunged forward, jaws agape, his sharp teeth mere feet from Korthax's face. Despite his initial shock, Korthax did not waver or show fear. He kept his head low, fully aware of the wrath he had invoked but standing resolute in the face of possible death.

The majestic being's blazing eyes bored into Korthax, searching, probing for any hint of deceit or weakness. Yet all he found was unwavering loyalty and grim determination.

With a guttural growl, Relor snapped his jaws shut, inches from Korthax's head, causing the general to flinch ever so slightly, though he held his ground. The sovereign straightened up, towering over Korthax, his breathing heavy and labored from his injuries and his barely contained rage.

"You dare to counsel me on matters of war, Korthax?!" Relor's voice was a dangerous whisper, filled with barely restrained anger. "You, who have led us into a failed campaign! You who have failed to gauge the enemy's true strength! And you presume to know what is best?!"

Korthax remained silent, fully aware that any misplaced phrase could seal his fate. He maintained his stance of submission, eyes lowered, yet his voice was steady and resolute when he spoke. "I bear the burden of our defeat, my Sovereign. The miscalculations were mine, and I do not shy away from the consequences of my actions."

Relor's fiery gaze bore into Korthax, the seething rage within him like a hellish inferno. Every muscle, every sinew of the sovereign's magnificent form, was coiled in tension, poised on the knife's edge between mercy and wrath. His wingtips quivered with barely contained energy, and his tail lashed out, displacing the air and creating minor whirlwinds.

In the end, the massive divine creature reared back and looked down at the prostrated general with disgust. "You should thank the emperor and the gods for mercy, Korthax," Relor growled, the heat from his breath making the air waver. "For if I were any less forgiving, I'd see to it that you and your entire lineage would be turned to ash."

If he was capable of sweating, Korthax would have felt torrents of it pouring down the back of his neck. These weren't threats from dragons as ancient and mighty as the one before him.

They were promises.

"You honor me with another chance, Your Greatness," Korthax responded, his voice unwavering. "I understand the depth of my errors and the weight of your expectations. I shall work tirelessly to ensure that my actions henceforth reflect my unwavering loyalty and dedication to the emperor and his empire."

The fury in the sovereign's eyes gave way to a calculating look. "Your words mean little now, Korthax, but I shall allow you to prove your worth." Relor's voice carried a tone of stern finality. "You have one chance and one alone. Fail, and there will be no mercy. No reprieve."

Korthax lowered himself further, pressing his forehead to the cold ground beneath him, signifying his utmost submission and respect. "Your Grace, I will go before the emperor and the council and admit my grievous errors. I shall spare no detail, holding nothing back, and will accept any punishment or duty they see fit to bestow upon me."

Raising his head just slightly, enough to lock eyes on Relor's majestic form, Korthax continued, "But, Your Grandeur, I must share a dire concern. I have felt the enemy's fury, their tenacity."

The general paused, carefully considering his next words. "I—I believe they will not rest on their laurels and will choose to be more problematic in the future."

"You talk in riddles! Speak plainly, wretch!" Relor boomed, his voice echoing across the vast landscape, causing the ground beneath them to tremble.

The general swallowed hard, his claws digging into the earth. "I fear they will not be sated with merely chasing us away. They may choose to pursue us, my Sovereign. Any civilization that powerful will not tolerate any kind of attack without retaliation."

Relor's pupils narrowed, reflecting a mixture of irritation and contemplation. The mere thought that their adversaries might dare tread upon their sacred lands was unsettling. "You imply that our strategic withdrawal could lead them straight to our empire's doorstep?"

Korthax pressed his head to the floor once more. "Yes, my Sovereign."

The silence that followed was palpable. The wind howled around, ruffling the dragon's massive wings and tousling Korthax's mane. The potential threat weighed heavily on Relor as he realized it was a very real possibility.

After what seemed like an eternity, the gargantuan dragon finally broke the silence. "Then we must be swift and decisive. Return to the capital and inform the war council. We cannot be caught off guard."

Korthax pressed his head even deeper into the ground, if it were all possible. "At once, my Sovereign. Your will shall be done."

With a pained groan, Relor painstakingly lifted his colossal body from the ground. The vast sky was soon filled with a mesmerizing tapestry of dragons, their scales reflecting the sun's rays in myriad dazzling colors. But not all dragons were capable of taking flight. Some, their bodies battered and wings torn from the earlier confrontations, could only muster enough strength to lift a few feet off the ground before collapsing back to the earth with a heart-wrenching thud.

Korthax looked up, following the path of Relor and the mass of dragons disappearing into the horizon, their forms becoming distant silhouettes against the setting sun. "I live. What a delightful surprise," the general murmured to himself, relief evident in his voice.

Lira, who had been standing a good distance away just in case, finally made her way to his side. "Congratulations on your survival, General," she said, her voice holding a hint of amusement as her iridescent feathers shimmered in the sunlight.

"Thank you, Lira. It seems fate has other plans for me," Korthax replied as he stood and dusted himself off.

His trusted adjutant nodded gracefully before darting toward the dragons still sprawled out on the ground. Her voice softened. "And what of them? Those who could not join the sovereign?"

Korthax's gaze followed hers as he saw the wounded and exhausted dragons, still struggling to muster the strength to rise. Firm and resolute, he replied, "Leave them. They will rest and, in time, find their own way."

Lira's gaze lingered on the injured dragons for a moment before she shrugged slightly and turned back to her charge. "Very well," she said before changing focus. "Now, onto the matters of our withdrawal. Do you want to pull back to the secondary line or—"

"I mean to pull out of the region completely," Korthax replied, cutting her off. "After reviewing the details of the enemy's capabilities, I've concluded that we are ill-equipped to face them in our current state."

He motioned for Lira to follow him as they walked towards the encampment, which was buzzing with activity. "I've read accounts of bandit-like raids that decimated the Daesyl's Emberthrower units," Korthax said, sighing. "They appeared out of the wooded areas like ghosts, launching lightning attacks with impunity."

Lira's eyebrows knitted with concern. "Emberthrowers? Are those enormous six-legged creatures that spit fire over the horizon? Don't they usually sit far behind the front lines?"

Korthax nodded gravely. "Yes, and those *bandits*, I assume, are likely highly trained units that move swiftly and stealthily. They attack during the darkest hours and see better than our own night-seeing creatures."

"Furthermore, those monsters can strike us with explosive magic seemingly from nowhere," the general added, putting his hands to his eyes to massage the forming headache. "They can hit critical units or our supply routes with more of those damned darts."

Lira grimaced, clearly disturbed by the implication. The general continued, "Their explosive magic is unlike anything we've encountered. Our barriers and protective enchantments don't seem to deter them. And these darts? They come from such distances and speeds, so we don't even get a warning."

Korthax gazed at the horizon, his expression exhausted. "But what truly baffles me is their omniscience. It's as if they have the eyes of a soulhawk perpetually hovering above us, watching our every move." He glanced at Lira, searching for any sign of recognition. "You remember the legends, don't you? The soulhawk—an all-seeing entity, invisible and omnipresent. I can't shake the feeling that they have something akin to it."

Shaking her head, Lira looked at Korthax as if he were crazy. "So not only can they strike from unseen distances, they launch raids with beings that can see in the night as if it were day, and they seem to know where all our units are and their every move. But how?"

Korthax stopped and stared at her for a long moment before shrugging and continuing his trek. "Hells if I know," he said with a laugh of disbelief, indicating he didn't believe his words. "But evidence suggests everything in that report is true."

Lira fell into step beside him. Her usual confident stride was now more measured and pensive. The encampment around them came alive as the sun dipped below the horizon, casting a golden hue across tents and dragons alike. Sparks from fire pits spiraled upwards, and the occasional roar of a restless dragon punctuated the distant murmurs of conversations.

"So we fall back to the empire, use the tributaries, vassals, and everything in between as a buffer?" she began, realizing what Korthax's plan truly was.

The general nodded and entered the command tent. "That's correct. And the barbarian territories also border the Necropolis and the forest of those damned druids." He sighed deeply, poring over the vast map across the tent's central table. "They're known for their unpredictability and hatred of intruders. If the enemy pushes through the rift into the buffer states, they'll most likely be drawn into conflicts on multiple fronts."

Lira's eyes widened with realization. "You're thinking of using the volatile nature of those in the area to our advantage. Keep these demons busy and embroiled in skirmishes while the empire formulates a proper response."

Korthax smirked, the corner of his mouth turning up slightly. "Exactly. Those areas are volatile, dangerous, and filled with the untamed. If those otherworlders believe we are the only threat, they'll charge right in, drawing the attention of the liches of the Necropolis or those damned druids in that damned forest."

"Hm," Lira hummed as she paced the tent. "Turning our less-than-friendly neighbors and the very nature of the lands against them, let them temper our enemies."

"And when they've exhausted themselves, we'll swoop in and kill three or four birds with one stone," Korthax declared, slamming his hands on the table. "We bide our time while they fight each other and then take everything for ourselves. Every power, every faction, every stray creature they encounter will bend the knee to the empire—or be eradicated."

Still deep in thought, Lira finally spoke, her voice tinged with worry. "Your plan is cunning, Korthax, but it also feels like we're walking on a blade's edge. If we miscalculate even once—if they're stronger than we anticipate—the losses could be unimaginable. We'd be gambling not just with our troops but with whole swaths of the empire as collateral."

She took a deep breath, the worst-case scenario running through her mind. "And let's not forget, our retreat won't go unnoticed. Other powerful kingdoms and empires have always had their eyes on our lands and resources. If we're routed again, they might be emboldened to strike."

Looking up, Korthaz met Lira's gaze with an intensity that seemed to pierce right through her. He leaned in. "I'm well aware, Lira. But this is not a hasty decision; it's a calculated risk. By letting the savage states act as buffers, they'll inadvertently shield us. While the otherworlders are busy trying to navigate hostile kingdoms and tribes, we'll be on our territory, watching and waiting. And while they're embroiled in their battles, our spies will gather all the intelligence we need."

"We'll even pay lip service to those vultures looking to grab land," Korthax continued. "We'll feed the Holy Dominion and those filthy beastkin selective information about these otherworlders. We can indirectly guide their actions—maybe even pit them against our new foes." He waved his hand dismissively. "It'll be especially easy with the plethora of equipment we've captured."

Korthax excitedly drummed the table as his brain kept churning. "And some kingdoms, as opportunistic as they are, would rather face a known empire than some otherworldly force. We can foster unofficial relationships with those who'd prefer to see these new aggressors put in check."

Lira remained unsure. She sensed layers of complexity they couldn't fully grasp, especially given the unpredictable outcome of this plan. "It's a sound strategy, Korthax, but we're venturing into uncharted territory. We know nothing of the politics or motivations of these otherworlders. There are too many 'what ifs' here."

Korthax sighed, hanging his head. "I understand your concerns, Lira. But we must also remember the damage these demons have already inflicted. They've easily slain full-fledged dragons and even managed to wound a gods-damned celestial. Their strength is not to be underestimated. Either way, there are vast risks."

Reflecting on the general's words, Lira paused, furrowing her brow. The deaths of adult and even elder dragons were already a significant blow. Crippling an eon-old celestial dragon-like their sovereigns was even more significant. The mere thought of a force capable of such feats sent chills down her spine.

She swallowed hard. "I can't believe they have the power to do that. What chance do our mortal soldiers have if they can harm celestials?"

Korthax nodded gravely. "Exactly. Our hand is being forced, and perhaps this gamble, with all its intricacies and unknowns, might be our best shot. We need to buy time, gather intelligence, and rely on the unpredictable nature of the savage lands to slow them down."

The adjutant general looked down at the map before them, tracing the territories with her fingers, feeling the weight of countless lives in her hands. The delicate balance of power, the unknowns, and the potential consequences was as intoxicating as it was overwhelming.

Finally, she looked up, her eyes filled with resolve. "All right, Korthax. I hate to admit it, but your plan may be our best shot. Let's draft a proposal for the emperor."

"Come, we'll hammer out more details as we go," Korthax said, gesturing towards their magic-imbued scrolls and ink.

CHAPTER 16

The first rays of the sun broke over the eastern horizon, painting the Ohio landscape with hues of orange and gold. Yet, in contrast to this serene setting, the AH-64E Apache helicopters of the 3rd Platoon, Bravo Squadron, surged forward, their rotors cutting through the morning air. Flying low and fast, they utilized the early morning light to their advantage, the sun at their backs casting long shadows ahead and masking their approach on the horde heading towards New Philadelphia.

"Warmonger, Rebound 1, heading 2-7-0," Chief Warrant Officer 4 Jessica "Rebound" Moore's voice echoed through the battle network. "Moving to engage the main body of the horde."

"Hold one, Rebound," came the stern reply from HQ, a hint of urgency in the voice. "Rebound, we need you to divert immediately to heading 2-9-0. The troops downtown are being overrun. They need air support ASAP."

Jessica's gunner, Warrant Officer Michael "Kanga" Rew, responded with a hint of skepticism, "Wait, what? What about the skimmers? Wouldn't we be sitting ducks further away from our formation?" he asked over the local net.

A brief moment of static ensued while Jessica mulled over the new instructions. The skimmers were fast, and there was something to be said about protection in numbers—especially with the Marines' AH-1Z Vipers flying around with sidewinder missiles.

"Warmonger, say again? Confirm you want us to break off?" Jessica inquired, concern thick in her voice. "We'd be extremely vulnerable on our own out there."

Another pause put everyone on edge before a reply crackled through the radio with the background noise of the operations center filtering in. "Intel reports that the skimmers, along with the main body of dragons, are being pulled back. Airspace over New Philadelphia is clear. But our boys on the ground don't have the luxury of waiting. They're in a tight spot. They need you there, now."

Michael threw his head over his shoulder, exchanging glances with his pilot in command before the woman returned to comms. "Understood, Warmonger. Breaking right, heading 2-9-0."

Switching to her platoon comms, Jessica started issuing instructions, splitting the platoon into flights of two. "Listen up, we're going to split into flights to ensure we aren't putting all our eggs in one basket in case the intel is off. Boomer, you're gonna pair up with Agony. Costco, you're with me. We're hitting them from the east. Boomer, you and Agony are gonna divert to come at them from the north, over the town."

A series of affirmatives came over the radio, each pilot acknowledging their new orders as the Apaches shifted seamlessly into their new formations. Jessica watched as two helicopters broke off, flying north to fulfill their latest orders. Still, her attention quickly shifted back to her path and the silhouette of Costco's Apache beside hers.

"We're totally going to die," Warrant Officer 2 Giovanni "Costco" Fontana, always one to joke when things seemed bleak, spoke up with a chuckle.

Jessica grinned, shaking her head at his familiar bravado. "Shut up, Gio."

As they steadily made their way to the town, the morning sun cast the shadows of both aircrafts over the small road below. The serene beauty almost tricked Jessica into thinking this was another training mission to get some extra stick time, but reality quickly set in as she spotted plumes of heavy smoke billowing over the horizon from the burning town.

Giovanni's playful demeanor shifted as he tightened his grip on the Apache's controls. "You seeing that?"

"Yeah," Jessica replied, narrowing her eyes at the distant dark clouds. "Looks like they couldn't hold them at the outskirts."

Their path had been strategic, keeping them low and close to the winding roads, which offered the protective cloak of the trees and terrain. But the urgency dictated a change in strategy. The spiraling plumes of smoke intensified as they drew closer, signaling that the town was bearing the brunt of the onslaught.

"Rebound, this is Costco. We should move faster. Drone feed shows things looking bad," Giovanni said, his tone grave as he immediately transitioned to their call signs.

Clenching her teeth, Jessica wrestled with the decision: keep things slow and maintain caution or go for a direct approach and pull up. The threat of skimmers still loomed like a shadow. If ISR was incorrect, they'd be on top of them like flies on shit. "Damn it! All right. Break the tree line. We're punching straight through and hoping that HQ hasn't fucked us over."

"Copy that, Rebound." The second Apache confirmed as both pulled up on their flight controls, sending the helicopters soaring upwards.

The duo elevated sharply, slicing through the morning mist that clung to the treetops. The sudden exposure brought heightened vulnerability, and the pilots braced for the worst. But as the horizon opened before them, the feared giant lizards were nowhere to be seen.

The expected threat didn't materialize.

"Horizon's clear, climb!" Jessica ordered, nudging her aircraft higher to find a better vantage point. Giovanni's Apache followed suit, their rotors humming in harmony as they ascended.

From their new altitude, the grim tapestry of the battle unfurled below. The once-tranquil town of New Philadelphia had become a maelstrom. Flames and explosions of varying sizes, some dwarfing the buildings themselves, completely consumed the town. However, what struck Jessica most was the bizarre interplay of colors within the chaos: unnatural greens, purples, and violets hinted at the otherworldly powers shimmering in the air. At the same time, hexagonal blue shields deflected or detonated ordnance prematurely.

"I've never seen anything like this," Giovanni murmured, a mix of awe and horror in his voice.

As they neared the town, the ground combat below resembled a blend of modern warfare and scenes from a fantasy film. Soldiers fired conventional weapons while mages, distinguished by the colors of their spells, hurled the elemental forces in every direction. The landscape was a patchwork of clashes: soldiers battling strange creatures, tanks confronting gigantic hyena-like monsters, and Bradleys trying to bring down the large marching blue shield.

"Rebound 1 and 2 checking in. Flight of two Apaches holding east five miles. Ordnance to follow," Jessica called in, informing ground forces that they were in position and ready to provide close air support.

A near-unintelligible voice crackled back on the radio through the intense background gunfire. "Roger! Be advised. We're—" The voice suddenly cut off as more intense gunfire drowned it out. "We're north of the river and west of the burning office building!"

Jessica and Giovanni flew closer, their gunners working sensors to identify the landmarks. Thermal imaging and laser rangefinders helped pinpoint the exact locations amidst the chaos.

"Got 'em," Michael called out, using the high-resolution sensor suite to zoom in on the soldiers' fighting positions.

And what he saw was an absolute cluster fuck. Burning and molten military vehicles dotted the entire town as friendly, and enemy lines mixed a chaotic melee. Explosives and elemental power tore apart paved roads, and intersections had become whirlwinds of combat, with soldiers overrun by otherworldly creatures.

The defenders barely held on by a thread, their lines crumbling under the flood of enemies.

"Be advised, you've got a whole bunch coming up from the south," Michael's voice crackled over the radio as he monitored the situation. "They're maneuvering on your position through the alleyways."

"Roger, you're cleared hot on any moving targets south and east!" the voice responded, the raging battle nearly drowning out his voice. "Be advised, we have friendlies to the north and the west! Commanders initial: Papa, Mike! Engage! Engage!"

Jessica tightened her grip on the flight controls, the weight of the situation pressing on her. Her aircraft maneuvered closer and hovered in place, providing Michael with a steady platform to choose his targets.

"Rebound 1 copies all. We will be engaging." Michael used his sensors to track dozens upon dozens of what looked like werewolves and one of those massive hyena-like creatures flooding the road toward friendly positions.

He painted the hyena with his rangefinder and laser before calling in. "We got a whole bunch of guys maneuvering. We're engaging," the gunner said as a hellfire missile slid off the rack with a deadly hiss, arcing toward the sky.

Michael could see the heatwave from the missile's rocket plume, and just a few moments later, a massive explosion encompassed the hyena, causing it to crumple and skid along the asphalt. Wasting no time, the gunner switched to his 30mm chain gun and went cyclic on the beasts sprinting up the road.

The helicopter shuddered with each shot as 30mm rounds were expelled at an astonishing rate. Each round created plumes of death as they hit the ground, showering everything in their vicinity. Beings that caught direct hits were blown apart, while others tumbled in disarray, clutching their bodies. Those that survived the initial onslaught scrambled for cover, disoriented.

With each turn of the head, the gunner reaped death using his Target Acquisition Sight, which was attached to his helmet. This allowed him to control the chain gun mounted beneath the fuselage with lethal precision simply by turning his head. His Forward Look Infrared system painted the world in black and white, illuminating heat signatures so no one could hide from his sight.

Giovanni mirrored the action as his own Apache loosed a hellfire missile at another large creature, this one resembling a towering ogre with a massive pot belly and thick, armored skin. The missile found its mark, igniting a ball of fire and leaving only a charred, smoldering carcass in its wake.

"Be advised, you still have a massive force converging on your position from south to north," Jessica warned through the radio, her eyes darting between the gun cam feed and their surroundings. There was still a high probability of being intercepted by a skimmer, and she needed to keep her head on a swivel.

Breathless, the soldier on the other end responded, "Roger, we're moving! We're moving west. Continue to engage!"

Jessica glanced at the navigation screen to get a bead on the soldier's new position. "Copy, covering your movement to the west," she replied as the aircraft shuddered from another long volley of 30mm rounds.

Michael was relentless. He continued focusing his fire, raining death on the largest clusters of enemies foolish enough to clump together. But then, something on his FLIR system caught his attention—a cluster of humanoid figures, each of varying sizes, was slowly progressing further down the road. They were grouped tightly around another humanoid figure distinct from the rest. Unlike the others, this figure emitted an unusual energy that barely registered on Michael's FLIR, revealing itself as a series of interconnected hexagons that formed a semicircle around the group.

Intrigued, Michael zoomed in for a closer look. The shield seemed to focus primarily on the direction of the ongoing conflict, protecting the figures behind it from harm. The energy source was complex, unlike anything he'd seen in the field before. It was clear that this shield was why this particular group was untouched by the ongoing firefight.

Hypothesizing that the figure at its center would be key to dismantling this defensive mechanism, Michael quickly switched to his hellfires. The gunner painted the target with his laser and loosed a missile.

The missile arced upwards, distorting the air in its wake before descending rapidly toward its target.

"Goddamn!" Jessica shouted in surprise as she saw the missile impact from her own feed.

The dull blue barrier flickered out immediately, accompanied by bodies and body parts flying in every direction. Meanwhile, Michael chose to show no mercy for the stunned survivors and switched back to his 30mm, raining down a deadly hail of high-explosive rounds.

Tiny explosions peppered the soldiers in formations, trailing behind where the barrier once stood. The two pilots watched from their aerial vantage point as the mass of alien soldiers panicked. The once-cohesive unit scattered, each fighter scrambling for cover and attempting to regroup.

"Rebound 2, this is Rebound 1. Eyes on a large enemy formation just north of the river, south of the intersection by the burning office building. Coordinating fire. Over." Michael's voice was calm and measured over the radio as he adjusted the Apache's fire toward the fleeing invaders.

"Copy, Rebound 1. Tally on your target. Engaging with Hellfires, over." The voice of Rebound 2's gunner crackled back.

Jessica banked the Apache slightly, giving Michael a better firing angle. "You're a fucking demon, Mike," she chuckled, watching the enemy troops scramble back toward their comrades as their escape avenue erupted into shards of death.

"Fuck 'em," Michael replied, maintaining the pressure on the retreating forces.

A sudden, intense flare of light broke the night as Rebound 2's hellfire missile streaked toward the ground. Just seconds before the missile made contact, Michael could feel the raw energy in the air. Indistinguishable. The ground trembled, even from their altitude. The missile detonated in the heart of the alien formation, consuming scores of the tightly clustered enemies in a catastrophic explosion.

Michael launched his own Hellfire and watched the concussive force of the explosion expand outward, turning every being within its radius into mere indistinguishable fragments.

From the northeast, the unmistakable roar of rotors heralded the arrival of reinforcements as two more Apache attack helicopters from their platoon emerged over the horizon, their silhouettes menacing against the burning town below.

"Rebound 1, this is Rebound 3. Looks like you've been having a party without us," joked the lead pilot of the reinforcing choppers. "Be advised, two more Apaches on station, ordnance to follow," he announced to the beleaguered ground forces.

Jessica grinned, adjusting her flight pattern. "Glad you could join us. We've been thinning the herd, but there's plenty left for everyone."

The morning grew even brighter as the newly arrived Apaches unleashed their own versions of hell onto the invaders. Alien ogres and the hulking, nimble hyenas were systematically wiped out by the air-to-ground missiles, leaving the poor infantry to face tank and machine gun fire with no support.

"Rebound 1, tallying your previous targets. We're taking the east side. Light up anything that moves," Rebound 4's gunner reported as their Apache banked smoothly to position for optimal fire.

"Copy that, Rebound 4. Watch out for the structures on the east side; we've had priority squirters holding up in there," Jessica advised, peering at the horizon once more. She tilted the Apache to provide Michael with the best firing angles possible.

As Michael continued dispatching his deadly rounds, Jessica's attention remained southward, always alert for any sign of the aerial skimmers they were so accustomed to encountering. It seemed odd, but the agile skimmers were usually their most prominent aerial threat. They were fast, nimble, and notoriously hard to shake off once they had you in their sights.

The realization dawned on her slowly—a mix of surprise and disbelief. Did they pull back? Were they too low on the enemy's priority list, or was something else at play? She glanced over the HUD, then down to the burning town and back up to the empty skies. "Maybe they've actually left," she murmured, more to herself than to Michael.

"What?" Michael asked, momentarily looking away from the targeting system.

"They've pulled back. The skimmers and the air support, they're gone. They've left their ground forces to fend for themselves," Jessica cringed as she watched another detonation in the street that sent people flying.

Michael refocused on his feed and let loose another round of 30mm, scattering the enemy's ground troops and causing them to retreat. "Good, fuck 'em."

Jessica could do nothing but let out another chuckle, making another pass over blunted enemy assault. Watching the desperate alien soldiers below, clearly overwhelmed and outmatched without the support they likely relied on, she almost felt a strange twinge of pity. But it was only an "almost." They had chosen to come here, after all.

"Poor fucking infantry, indeed," she laughed as the chain gun fired one more time, causing the Apache to shudder.

CHAPTER 17

If there was a word to describe how 1st Lieutenant DuPont felt at that moment, it was complete and utter exhaustion.

With the afternoon sun oppressively beating down on him, DuPont sat lazily atop a destroyed National Guard Humvee, his combat boots dangling over the side. The Humvee's desert tan paint was scorched and riddled with massive holes, a grim testament to the fierce recent battle.

Looking down at his combat fatigues, DuPont noticed they were smeared with dirt, sweat, and maybe even a bit of blood. He couldn't tell if it was his or someone else's. All he knew was that he was simply too tired to give any kind of shit at the moment. Instead, he briefly wondered if all of this had been some terrible fever dream or if someone had spiked his canteen with an extreme dose of acid.

DuPont drummed his fingers against the metal as his weary eyes took in another of his Bradleys, its front end and turret eaten away by what looked like an acid-like liquid. The vibrant emerald corrosion clashed with the harsh reality of the situation—another piece of heavy equipment lost, though thankfully, not the crew. After prolonged combat with various creatures, his men knew better than to stick around and see what happened after being sprayed by something.

DuPont felt a deep sense of loss and bewilderment as he scanned the once-quiet Appalachian town. What had likely been a lively, peaceful place filled with laughter was now in ruins after the sheer brutality inflicted on it. Buildings that once stood proud were now piles of rubble, collapsed under the combination of massive magical creatures and modern ordnance.

Fires raged uncontrollably, consuming what little remained of the town. The acrid smoke stung his eyes, and the heat was oppressive, even from a distance. DuPont could see cars and military equipment frozen in place in the middle of the road, their forms twisted and contorted in ways that defied logic. He couldn't even begin to comprehend the forces at play that could cause such destruction.

Turning his head, DuPont shifted his gaze to the street below, where carnage lay spread out before him—a scene straight out of a twisted fairy tale. An enormous ogre-like creature lay on its back with a gaping wound in its grotesque belly, surrounded by enough blood to fill up a public pool. Behind it, corpses of other beings were strewn in chaotic disarray.

A good chunk of them were humans or elves equipped with gear reminiscent of a fantasy game. Scattered around, DuPont noticed yellowish-skinned creatures that he could only describe as goblins among their ranks, along with those lizard-like kobolds and more of those suicidal werewolves.

Suddenly, a sharp hissing noise above interrupted his musings. Glancing up, he watched an FGM-148 Javelin missile suddenly drop a foot or two before its rocket engine ignited, sending it arcing into the distance from a nearby building. The once deafening sounds of warfare had largely dissipated into an eerie post-battle calm, but occasional skirmishes broke the silence—gunfire or the muffled thud of an armored vehicle's main gun echoing through the ruined town.

"Any idea why they just left their own to die?" Hofmann, DuPont's platoon sergeant, asked as he wandered next to him, equally worn out and disheveled. Hofmann hadn't even bothered to remove his tanker helmet. Leaning against the Humvee, he fished out a pack of cigarettes.

DuPont didn't respond immediately, too lost in his own thoughts and the sights before him. After a moment, he finally managed a tired shrug, his voice heavy with fatigue. "Who the fuck knows?" He glanced toward the horizon, where he'd expected to see skies filled with the chaotic dance of dragons and jets. But now, they were empty, eerily quiet.

The contrast between the expected chaos of war and the present calm was stark. The sight of mythical beings battling jets should have been awe-inspiring, yet their absence now felt like a void, a silence more unsettling than the cacophony of battle.

Only a few hours ago, dragons and jets danced intensely overhead. Now, the skies were eerily silent and empty, save for the occasional thrum of helicopter blades hunting survivors and the roar of patrolling American airpower.

Hofmann rubbed his eyes and glanced at DuPont. "You think they're regrouping? Planning something bigger?" His voice carried an underlying note of concern.

"Doubt that," DuPont replied, sliding down from the Humvee to the ground. "They wouldn't have given up airspace if they were." The lieutenant checked his kit to ensure he was good on ammo before striding forward to where the rest of his platoon was waiting. "From what we've seen, they play for keeps. They'd have shown it by now if they had something bigger up their sleeve."

Following his platoon leader, Hoffman squinted at the horizon. "So they just up and left?"

"Seems that way," DuPont responded, his gaze scanning the windows and rubble for any sign of movement.

Hoffman frowned, clearly unsatisfied. "But why? Why attack Ohio? There's nothing here!"

"Why the hell would I know, Hofmann?" DuPont retorted, fatigue lacing his voice. "I'm not paid enough to know. And from the looks of command right now, no one else knows either."

Hofmann grunted and shook his head. As they neared their destination, they overheard an animated discussion among their soldiers.

"You're a furry, Jackson. Between that little lizard thing and the werewolf, which do you think you'd prefer?" one soldier asked, keeping his weapon trained on the front line.

Jackson, the platoon's designated "furry," rolled his eyes as he adjusted the M-249 SAW in his grip. "Seriously? You think now's the time for that shit?" He hesitated, then smirked. "But, since you asked, probably the werewolf."

Laughter erupted among the soldiers, and Hofmann and DuPont stood behind them, exchanging looks that implied they didn't want to be associated with the degenerate in front of them.

"I mean, have you seen the legs on those things?" Jackson pointed out enthusiastically, oblivious to his superiors' discomfort. "Ripped, man. Those powerful thighs and calves. Like, no wonder they run so fast. They've got this wild, untamed beauty about them."

Jackson continued to gush, clearly enjoying himself. "The males tower over everyone. Massive with muscles for days. And those jaws. I wouldn't want to be caught in one.

"And the females?" Jackson's eyes lit up. "They're fierce. Smaller, sure, but just as deadly. I bet their fur is softer and smoother. And those eyes. Man, they'd stare right into your soul."

A wiry soldier named Lee edged closer and chimed in. "Talking about werewolves, eh? But have you seen the goblins?" He nodded toward a short, greenish-yellow figure slumped against a wall.

"Now that's what I call a compact bundle of beauty. I mean, look at her. She's petite, but you can't deny she's well-proportioned."

Lee then gave a chef's kiss. "Far better than your roid-raging mutts. Her posture, even when slumped, speaks of grace and agility. And those sharp ears? I bet she can hear every whisper of our conversation right now."

"Sure, she isn't as voluptuous as the furries, but—"

"What the fuck is wrong with you all?" Hofmann's stern and disgusted voice cut through the conversation. The soldiers turned, heads snapping back to see their platoon sergeant and lieutenant glaring at them with a repulsed snarl.

In an instant, the laughter evaporated, leaving a heavy silence in its wake.

Dupont looked at his men with utter disdain. "You people are fucking *disgusting*. We just killed these *things*, and now you're talking about wanting to fuck them?"

His face paled, his initial disgust giving way to profound disturbance. He looked around, his gaze sweeping over each of the men. Shaking his head, he muttered, "Jesus Christ. I'm leading a bunch of freaks."

Hofmann's jaw clenched, and his usual stoic demeanor momentarily shattered. With a deep sigh, he locked eyes with each soldier, his gaze piercing and unyielding. "Look," he began, his voice gruff, "whatever's been said here stays. For my own sanity's sake, I'm going to pretend I didn't hear a word of it." Without waiting for a response, Hofmann turned sharply and walked toward his Bradley parked a short distance away.

"Were we just kink-shamed by the lieutenant?" was the last thing Hofmann heard as he walked up the ramp of his Bradley to join the rest of his crew.

As the dust settled on the ruins of New Philadelphia, the distant roar of engines began to fill the air. The sound grew louder and more insistent, culminating in a ground-shaking rumble that drowned out the soldier's playful banter. Soon, the streets were filled with the unmistakable shapes of the more modern M1A2 SEPv3 tanks, their heavy treads kicking up dust and debris as they rolled forward in an impressive display of military might.

Behind the leading tanks were columns of Bradley Infantry Fighting Vehicles and Joint Light Tactical Vehicles, packed to the brim with fresh soldiers.

"Looks like the reinforcements finally arrived," Sergeant Kim, Hofmann's gunner, spoke up, trying to mask the emotion in his voice. But Hofmann, knowing the man, could sense the relief, disbelief, and shock behind Kim's words.

"Yeah," Hofmann replied quietly, letting out a slow exhale. "Honestly, I legitimately thought there was no way we were making it out of that alive."

Suddenly, the Bradley's driver, Corporal Santiago, laughed so hard that it rang throughout the vehicle. "¡Qué odioso! Ustedes están bien dramáticos! Come on, man," Santiago grinned, wiping a tear from his eye. "There was no way we were going to kick the bucket. We're like the main characters of a movie, bro!"

"Santiago," Sergeant Kim groaned as he slammed his head against the wall. "Shut the fuck up."

Santiago just laughed louder, "Oye! Just trying to lighten the mood, mi amigo."

Shaking his head, Hofmann climbed out of the commander's cupola and saw dismounting soldiers, starting to slowly but surely comb through the streets and buildings in search of any stragglers. Turning his head, he noticed that his lieutenant was lethargically conversing with what appeared to be the commanding officer of this outfit.

"Colonel Hastings, 4th Infantry," the colonel introduced himself, extending a firm hand towards the lieutenant. "Out-fucking-standing work you and your boys have done here. I've been briefed about the hell you went through."

The lieutenant, visibly tired and covered in the remnants of the city's ash and smeared with blood, offered a weak but respectful salute before taking the colonel's hand. "Lieutenant DuPont, sir. We did what we had to do."

Hastings nodded, taking a moment to observe the men around him. Completely exhausted and battle-worn, warriors everywhere he looked did their best to stay awake and alert as they maintained their fighting positions. "Listen, Lieutenant," Colonel Hastings began, lowering his voice as he leaned closer. "Have you and your boys get some chow and rest? We'll handle the mop-up from here."

DuPont wanted to jump for joy at the words, but it still never hurt to play the big army politics game and get some good officer brownie points. Taking one good look around at his weary crew, the lieutenant looked back at the colonel. "We can still fight," he replied, making his voice a little hoarser than normal.

The colonel gently put a hand on DuPont's shoulder. "You're a fucking hero, DuPont," the gruff man said with a smirk. "But we'd like to blast some alien ass as well. We can't let you have all the fun!"

A light laugh left DuPont's mouth as the tension visibly left his face. "I suppose we can share some of the glory, sir."

"That's the spirit," Colonel Hastings replied, chuckling. "Now get out of here, Lieutenant. You all look beat to shit!"

With the conversation concluded, DuPont saluted once more before turning around and walking away. Quickly turning his head, he saw that the colonel was busy issuing commands to his troops, who were bustling around, setting up defenses and preparing for the cleanup operation.

One more jolt of energy surged through DuPont as he pumped his fist in joy. Finally, someone else was going to deal with this garbage.

"Alright, you freaks!" DuPont shouted to his unit as he rejoined them. Despite their fatigue, the men looked up attentively, waiting for their lieutenant's words. "This is the 4th Infantry's problem now, so let's make ourselves scarce! Find some chow, grab whatever water you can, and find the nearest rock to crawl under!"

The unit responded with a mix of cheers and relieved chuckles. They were all eager to get some well-deserved rest after enduring what seemed like endless fighting. It was time for their fresh and well-supplied contemporaries to take the helm and kick the invaders out of their land. But they knew they would have to get back to the grind sooner rather than later.

There was still a lot of work to do.

Though broken, the horde's armies were fragmented and dispersed into the vast terrain. Creatures and people of all kinds fled en masse into the Appalachian countryside, turning the once-peaceful region into a hotspot of fugitives and skirmishes.

As the sun drifted slowly downwards onto the horizon, painting the sky in hues of orange, the hordes' most dreaded hunters treaded softly through the hills and forest of Ohio. Captain Coleman and his elite special forces team slowly crept through the foliage with guns raised and eyes scanning. Occasionally, the sharp staccato of suppressed gunfire would echo out, followed by a death-curdling screech. They were the predators in this new twisted game, stalking their prey and eliminating them with lethal precision.

As Coleman and his team progressed, a small, errant twitch caused the man to snap his weapon towards a bush not more than ten meters away. In quick succession, the man let loose a 5-round burst from his rifle.

Suddenly, a small reptilian creature with dark scales, sharp pointed horns atop its head, and piercing yellow eyes let out a pained screech and stumbled out of concealment. The creature, garbed in tattered blue robes adorned with worn belts and pouches, tried to scramble away. Its long, sinewy tail trailed behind it as it moved, and it clutched its wounds in its hand. However, the thing only moved a few meters before falling flat on its face.

The creature kicked and thrashed wildly for a few moments, letting out desperate, rasping breaths as it tried to find the strength to flee further. But Coleman mercilessly ended the creature's suffering, aiming his rifle at its head. With a squeeze of the trigger, the small lizard violently seized up before its body finally relaxed and accepted its fate.

Without missing a beat, the group of elite soldiers continued on their path, their boots crunching softly against the forest floor. The dense canopy overhead shielded them from the sun's rays, casting distorted shadows on the ground.

As Coleman approached the body, he kicked it over and stared down at the crude yet intricate designs on its long, padded, and baggy robe. Not too far away, he spotted the thing's weapon. It was an unusual design, seemingly a fusion between a mage's staff and a spear. Intriguingly, a strange, smooth stone was embedded just beneath the blade, encased and protected by sturdy iron bands. The staff spear leaned casually against a nearby tree, suggesting its owner hadn't expected any danger.

Just a few steps from the fallen creature lay an oddity on the forest floor. It looked like a small opening, seemingly inconspicuous at first, but upon closer inspection, it was shockingly deep. It appeared as though something or someone had burrowed into the ground, carving out a subterranean path or possibly a hideout.

"Got something over here," Coleman said, causing his team to stop dead in their tracks.

With a simple hand gesture, the closest members of his team quickly converged on the hole, their weapons pointed at the entrance. Others swiftly formed a protective ring around the area, ensuring no surprises from the surrounding foliage.

Bennett was closest to the team's leader, and together, they moved closer, their boots making almost no sound on the forest floor. With synchronized precision, both special forces soldiers leaned over the hole and thumbed their tactical flashlights, sending blinding beams to pierce the darkness below. With the entrance fully illuminated, they revealed another of the lizard creatures trying to clamber up, its eyes reflecting a mix of pain and fear.

Suddenly caught in the blinding light, the creature let out a distressed chirp and instinctively shielded its eyes. Without hesitation, both Coleman and Bennett unloaded their rifles.

Suppressed crack after crack rang out as the bullets met their mark. The creature tumbled backward, deeper into the tunnel, completely riddled with holes.

Taking no chances, the two moved to neutralize any more threats deeper within. They both reached for the grenades in their pouches and pulled their pins simultaneously. With swift, practiced movements, they threw the explosives into the abyss below.

"Frag out!" they yelled in unison, signaling the impending explosion.

The team instinctively took a step back and waited approximately four or five seconds before a muffled explosion echoed from the depths of the tunnel, followed by a plume of smoke and debris erupting from the entrance. The ground shuddered slightly under their feet, and the muted sounds of pained squeals soon replaced the eerie silence that followed.

Clicking his tongue, Coleman took a deep breath and spun around, "Frag 'em again," he ordered as his hand went to the push-to-talk attached to his plate carrier.

As Coleman walked away, Bennett pulled out another fragmentation grenade and pulled the pin. "Frag out!"

"Warmonger, this is Baron, over," Coleman radioed to command.

A brief pause ensued before a response crackled through the radio. "Baron, this is Warmonger. Send traffic. Over."

Coleman took another deep breath as he glanced over to the deceased creature not too far away from the tunnel's entrance.

"Warmonger, be advised. We've engaged multiple lizard-like hostiles in our AO. They appear to be subterranean. Over."

Chapter 18

Elijah fiddled with the strange spear, his fingers running over its intricate design. It was a strange blend of crude medieval craftsmanship and extremely refined and alien precision. He was still musing over the weapon's construction when Coleman's voice suddenly cut through the air.

"Thirty seconds till impact," his team leader quietly informed the ODA as they hunkered down in their concealed position.

Setting the weapon aside, Elijah clamped his hands over his ear protection and flipped down his Enhanced Night Vision Goggles before pointing his rifle toward potential threats. He figured there'd be plenty of time to figure out what that thing was once they finished roasting some miniature land gators.

The sun had finally set, and in its place, the moon rose, casting a pale glow over the forest floor. While the shadows created by the lunar light danced and played tricks on the naked eye, the ODA sat there and watched their prey with their ENVGs.

A mixture of orange thermal outlines and an ethereal white phosphorus-like picture amplified the ODA's vision as they kept their eyes on the unaware, clumsy reptilians that had emerged from the depths of their underground abode. Thinking they were alone, the creatures communicated in soft hisses and high-pitched guttural chirps while they organized themselves.

Suddenly, the forest's nocturnal symphony was interrupted by an unmistakable whooshing sound, drawing Elijah's focus back to the present. In the distance, the silhouette of a dark rod resembling a sinister dart flashed through the sky.

The sound lasted only a second before the earth violently erupted from the massive explosion that followed. The team had decided to say "fuck it" and drop a GBU-72, a bunker buster, on the bastards. He only caught a glimpse, but the dart had pierced the ground cleanly just behind the lizards before the earth swallowed them in fire and debris.

Elijah felt the shockwave before hearing the explosion, the force pressing against his chest and causing his ears to pop. However, after countless Global War on Terror tours, he had become completely desensitized to its effects.

The lizards that had wandered too close to the ODA's position snapped their heads around, staring at the destruction with gaping mouths before several suppressed rifle shots rang out in the night. Almost simultaneously, the lingering reptilians started dropping, either dead or dying.

After ensuring the immediate vicinity was clear, Coleman signaled to the team. "Move up."

The ODA team advanced cautiously from their concealed position, rifles at the ready, eyes darting around for any sign of surviving threats. But that seemed like a wasted effort as they saw the site of the explosion. The bunker buster had definitely done as advertised and gouged into the earth, leaving only a vast crater littered with debris and burned vegetation.

As they neared the blast's epicenter, the pungent scent of burnt flesh permeated the air. Charred and mangled reptilian bodies lay scattered, some buried under rubble, others thrown clear by the force of the explosion.

The scene reminded Elijah heavily of Iraq and the war against the Islamic State, or Daesh. He had been there as part of a specialized

Crisis Response Force, formerly known as a Commander's In Extremis Force. They embedded with capable Iraqi and Kurdish special forces to conduct direct action missions, including taking down high-value targets and even performing hostage rescues.

One operation in particular stood out in Elijah's memory. His task force had been tipped off about a Daesh stronghold outside their supposed "capital" of Mosul. From the outside, it looked like any other battle-scarred compound, but when Elijah's team and their Iraqi counterparts entered, they found much more than they had been prepared for.

The building led to a network of underground tunnels, a tactic that Daesh had become infamous for. It was how they moved undetected, stored weapons, and launched surprise attacks. The entire operation had been a clusterfuck. Close-quarters fighting in the tunnels had been claustrophobic and disastrous. Every bend and dugout room saw an exchange of so many grenades Elijah wondered where everyone got them. Coupled with the limited visibility and echoing gunshots, every inch of the place was a potential death trap.

With Daesh militants putting up fierce resistance and casualties mounting, Elijah's team and their Iraqi counterparts decided enough was enough. The juice wasn't worth the squeeze, and if the commander wanted to be a martyr so badly, they'd make him one.

As the task force made their way above ground, they signaled their Combat Controller, pointed at the stronghold, and told him to get rid of it.

And get rid of it, he did.

Five GBU-72 Ground Penetrators later, the entire complex was nothing more than a smoldering sinkhole. Each impact shook the earth, felt even from a safe distance, as the explosions collapsed the intricate underground network like a house of cards. Fireballs and plumes of smoke shot skyward, blotting out the horizon as the massive munitions did their job. The ground reverberated painfully for over a mile as massive plumes of smoke and dirt ejected from hidden entrances, casting a dark veil over the landscape.

Elijah's eyes refocused, snapping him back to the present. The vividness of his memory had momentarily blurred the lines between past and present, but as he took in the scene before him, the eerie similarities began to fade. Instead of the human remains of Daesh militants, he now saw the twisted, charred bodies of these strange lizard creatures, their scales seared and eyes lifeless.

"Told ya all we needed is a bunker buster," Elijah said, huffing in amusement as he shot a look at Coleman.

The team leader scoffed and rolled his eyes. "Yeah, yeah, whatever," Coleman replied, brushing some dirt off his shoulder. "I forgot you CIF freaks handle everything through unmitigated violence."

Elijah chuckled as he stepped over part of a corpse. "Some things require a more subtle touch, but sometimes, all you need is a big *boom.*"

"Eh," Coleman shrugged, gazing around the wasteland before them. "I can't really argue with that."

An unsettling realization crept into Elijah's mind as the team swept the area. If these creatures could burrow underground complexes for refuge so quickly, just how many of these burrows dotted the landscape? With the main body of the horde dispersing across the countryside, there could be dozens, maybe even hundreds of them.

And what if they just kept going?

"This is going to be a problem," Elijah muttered, his amusement replaced with a hint of concern.

Bennett, who had been poking at some strange item, turned and raised an eyebrow. "What do you mean?"

Elijah sucked in a deep breath, adjusting his rifle, and noticed the team's eyes on him. "Well, think about it," he said, scratching his short beard. "We found the hole these things crawled out by sheer chance, so what are the odds of some beat cop finding more, especially a year from now?"

Everyone gave him a hard look as he continued. "I mean, an army of what? Tens of thousands literally ran for the hills? We don't even know how many lizards there were in that 'army,' and we barely even killed a quarter of them," Elijah said definitively, waving his hand. "So now I'm just assuming we have several new invasive species."

Coleman rubbed his temples and sighed heavily. "Ah, shit. I didn't think of that." He groaned in mental pain. "And that's just what we saw today. "There's no telling how many of these burrows are out there or how fast they can reproduce."

"Great, I bet these things are going to be fucking everywhere," Lister, the dark-skinned weapons sergeant, mumbled, adjusting his heavy weapon load. He glanced around at the heavily forested hills and frowned. "We're spitting distance from the Appalachian mountains," Lister observed and pointed east. "It's dense, hard to navigate, and full of places to hide. They'll thrive there."

Schwarz shook his head. "And with winter coming, it'll be even tougher to search. If they make it there, rooting them out will be a nightmare."

"Enough," Coleman said, his voice firm. "We're gonna have to leave the what-ifs to someone else. Our current mission is to clear this area and recon south."

The group stood silent for a moment, absorbing how fucked up the situation was. After the surreal combat, each face showed a mix of emotions, but they weren't strangers to scenarios like this.

Just the details.

Slowly, they began to move out. The crunch of foliage under their boots was the only sound as they continued their patrol.

* * *

Lysandra's senses stirred as the unfamiliar hum and beep of strange devices awakened her from a dreamless sleep. A throbbing pain consumed the left side of her face, and her vision was hazy. As she tried to move, her body felt heavy and restrained, as if bound to the bed. Panic began to set in as she realized she had no idea where she was or how she had come to be there.

"H-Hello?" the battered woman called out weakly, her vision struggling to focus. "H-Hello, is anyone there?"

Her frail, raspy voice echoed faintly in the sterile-smelling room. Out of the corner of her good eye, she noticed the soft glow of luminescent apparatuses around her. These odd devices punctuated the stark whiteness of the room, their purpose a mystery to her.

Lysandra tried her best to focus her vision, but everything— colors and shapes—seemed distorted and unstable. To make matters worse, not only did every muscle in her body feel as though it were made of lead, but she also felt the taut pull of cuffs tethering her to the bed. She struggled weakly to free herself, but the metallic links of the restraints only amplified her anxiety and sense of vulnerability.

Suddenly, an authoritative voice sounded in the room, causing Lysandra to stop her feeble struggle. Mustering whatever willpower she had left, she focused her gaze on a pair of those otherworldly soldiers holding their black weapons.

Horror etched itself on her face as she stared at the men speaking to each other in their strange language, though it was clear they were discussing her. Their gestures conveyed urgency and importance, and

Lysandra couldn't help but imagine the worst. Was she to be tortured for information? Experimented on because she used profane magic? Humiliated and executed for her transgressions in this world? The possibilities spun in her head, each darker than the last.

The soldiers, identified by the black "MP" on their arms, continued talking before one stepped forward and pressed a button on the sleek wall panel beside him. The panel lit up, revealing an intercom system. He spoke into it, "Alpha to Med Bay. The subject is conscious. Alert Dr. Kassa."

Moments later, the doors slid open with a quiet hiss, revealing an older woman with a sun-kissed complexion who carried herself with an air of authority. Her hair, intricately woven into long braids that bounced with every step, cascaded down her back. She wore a white robe over bright green scrubs and stopped just in front of Lysandra, looking down at her curiously. Not too far behind, a team of individuals in matching bright green scrubs followed, holding various medical instruments and devices.

Dr. Kassa carefully examined the wounded side of Lysandra's face, her fingers gently probing the tender, swollen skin. With her other hand, she shone a small penlight into Lysandra's remaining eye, checking for any signs of a concussion or other internal injuries. As she did this, another medical team member spoke to the doctor in a hushed but urgent tone, pointing at the monitor that displayed Lysandra's vital signs. "Her blood pressure's spiking," the nurse announced, her brow furrowed in concern.

A hum left Dr. Kassa, who had turned her attention to the monitor. "She's terrified," she replied in a soft voice. Then, leaning closer to Lysandra, she noted how human she looked despite the obvious differences.

Every line of worry, every crease of fear, and the depth of

confusion in her bright yellow eyes were all too familiar. They were the same expressions any human would have in such a horrible situation. Except for the long, pointed ears peeking through her dark blonde hair and the vivid hue of her irises, Lysandra could be mistaken for any woman from Earth. The realization added another layer of complexity to the situation, reminding Dr. Kassa that emotions and experiences might be a universal constant despite being from a completely different reality.

Hoping to comfort Lysandra, Dr. Kassa gently touched the uninjured side of her face. She wished they shared a language and words to convey safety and care, but now, gestures would have to suffice.

Another nurse approached, holding a syringe filled with a translucent liquid. Dr. Kassa nodded in approval as the nurse carefully administered the sedative. They needed Lysandra calm, not just for the medical procedures, but for her own well-being in this alien environment.

As the minutes passed, the sedative's effects became evident. Lysandra's tense posture relaxed, and her rapid breathing steadied. Though still uncertain, her eyes no longer held that wild edge of panic.

"Quite curious, isn't it?" a voice remarked from the back of the room. The anesthesiologist, a middle-aged man with salt-and-pepper hair and thoughtful eyes, stepped forward. "In all the encounters we've had with these interdimensional beings, it never ceases to amaze me how our sedatives and anesthesia actually work and don't outright kill them."

Dr. Kassa nodded thoughtfully. "Yes, it is remarkable. But what surprises me more is how other common medical practices seem to work on them. It's like they share a foundational biology with us."

A third nurse chimed in, her face slightly pale, "Speaking of similarities, the pathologists and other medical examiners have been having quite the time performing autopsies on some of the deceased creatures. Everyone's been in an uproar after they found out that the internal structure of some of these beings only exhibits a handful of differences from our own."

"Really?" Dr. Kassa turned to the woman and raised an eyebrow.

The nurse nodded. "Yes. In fact, what's even more fascinating is the phenomenon observed with those large werewolf-like creatures. After an extended period post-death, they seem to morph. They gradually transform into something more human-shaped, though still significantly larger."

The anesthesiologist looked surprised. "That's unsettling. But why or how would they do that?"

"We're not sure yet," the nurse replied. "But biologists, doctors, and scientists worldwide are scratching and clawing to get here as if Ohio's the new Mecca. Everyone wants a piece of this puzzle. The discoveries made here could reshape our entire understanding of biology, evolution, and perhaps even the nature of existence."

Silence enveloped the room as they tried to understand the implications of another world full of sentient life existing and the reality of magic being a tangible, quantifiable force.

A technician, who had been quietly calibrating a machine nearby, suddenly spoke up, "Can you imagine? If we actually learned and harnessed magic? The entire globe would be turned on its head overnight."

Another round of silence came over the medical team as they exchanged uneasy glances. Each found this reality difficult to accept, but Dr. Kassa, ever the pragmatist, clapped her hands loudly to get everyone's attention. "All right, all right!" she shouted, turning to her team. "You're all professionals, so quit your brooding. We have patients to attend to."

Meanwhile, Lysandra felt as if the world had inverted, gravity had reversed, and she crawled on the ceiling like a damnable monster. Whatever these strange, heaven-forsaken people had given her was beyond potent—not only was every color intensified, but every sound was both muffled and overwhelmingly clear. She stared at the strangers in her room in horror as they seemed to twist and turn in impossible ways while the sterile white of the hospital walls pulsed and breathed as if alive.

Lysandra opened her mouth as if trying to say something, but no words came out. Instead, there was only a whispery gasp, a desperate attempt to communicate her panic and disorientation.

The poor woman couldn't help but curse the demon who had tricked her into coming to this accursed land.

CHAPTER 19

"They still haven't killed me," Lysandra remarked, glancing up at a curious artifact alien to her world. This strange, flat box displayed moving images, constantly shifting scenes before her eyes.

Sometimes, the artifact displayed more otherworldly humans engaged in mundane tasks; other times, it showcased breathtaking cityscapes that Lysandra could only dream of visiting, like the capital of the Holy Dominion or the Magi's Sanctum's various seaborne cities. But what truly captivated her wasn't the mere fact that they were hand-moving pictures, no, no, no. Though rare in her world, those types of magicks weren't unheard of.

No, it was the fact that there was sound. It was *impeccable*.

The voices, the music, the ambient noises—everything was so clear, it was as if she were in the very scenes unfolding before her. The chirping of birds felt so real she almost looked around the room for them. The delicate notes of an instrument made her feel as though the musician was right next to her, playing a serenade just for her. It was a sensory experience unlike any other she had experienced.

She scooped another spoonful of the bland porridge they served her and shoved it into her mouth, the tepid mush barely registering on her taste buds. Compared to the vibrant sounds from the artifact, the food seemed fit only for the undead. As she chewed, she couldn't help but remark, "For beings who can create such wondrous sounds, they sure don't know how to make food exciting."

Occasionally, though, they surprised her. Rarely, but sometimes, these otherworlders brought a dish or drink with such intense, unique flavors that it left her speechless. Lysandra remembered the first time they gave her something called "chocolate." The rich, velvety texture and intoxicating sweetness had left her salivating. But the delight was short-lived—after consumption, their version of "healers" swarmed her, conducting all manner of strange and indecipherable tests.

Over time, Lysandra realized their intentions weren't malicious but curious. Still, she wished they would improve their culinary skills.

Suddenly, the thick metal door beeped and creaked open. In walked a group of three individuals who frequented her room daily. The soldiers stationed in Lysandra's room immediately snapped to attention and saluted the middle figure, a tall, pale woman with dark hair pulled back into a bun.

"At ease," the woman said before turning to an even taller man with salt-and-pepper hair and glasses perched on his nose. He was flanked by a young woman with curly hair and a notebook clutched in her hands, practically bouncing with excitement just to be there.

"Dr. Stenhouse, if you will." The woman gestured toward Lysandra, then stood beside the soldiers.

Dr. Stenhouse cleared his throat, arranging some materials on a nearby table before turning to Lysandra and speaking slowly. "You... feel... today... good?" Each word seemed to be weighed and measured.

Though the sentence was fragmented, Lysandra understood the essence of his question. She blinked, genuinely impressed. "You... learn quick," she responded, matching his halting tone, her brows raised in surprise.

As the older man documented the exchange on his device, the young woman began scribbling furiously in her notepad.

The lead linguist nodded, smiling slightly. "Yes. We try. Understand you."

Lysandra watched them momentarily, marveling at the strides they'd made since their first awkward attempts at communication. It was obvious they had an excellent methodical approach that any academy or school in her world would trip over themselves to acquire. It was truly astounding to break down language to its most rudimentary form and then gradually rebuild it just to communicate with a freelancer.

Emboldened by the exchange, the curly-haired woman inched closer. She pointed at Lysandra and asked again. "You feel... good? No hurt?"

A chuckle escaped Lysandra as she glanced at the woman. "No, Emma, no hurt." She remembered Emma had introduced herself during a previous session. "But I would like some better food, though," Lysandra added with a self-deprecating smirk.

Emma and Dr. Stenhouse exchanged puzzled looks. "Food," Emma murmured, jotting down the word. "That one we got."

Dr. Stenhouse leaned in, adjusting his glasses. "We also got 'better' and 'like,' but I'm unsure about the rest. The syntax is unusual, but let's dissect it."

Emma tapped the end of her pen on the notepad, deep in thought. "Okay, whenever she says 'like,' she usually indicates a preference or desire for something."

Tapping his hand on his head, Dr. Stenhouse nodded. "That aligns with our language. And 'better' typically signifies an improvement or something of superior quality."

Flipping through her notes, Emma stopped on one page and circled a few passages. "If we pair 'like' with 'better food,' she's probably indicating dissatisfaction with her current meals."

After a brief silence, Dr. Stenhouse straightened up and turned toward the group standing apart. "Ms. Toivonen," he called to the stern-looking woman dressed in a crisp, tailored dress suit, "What exactly are we feeding her?"

Toivonen's expression remained unreadable. "Primarily porridge," she replied simply, her tone final. "Until we know more about her biology and what is safe, it's the most neutral thing we can give her. We don't know what might harm the subject."

Emma's eyes flashed with a hint of defiance. "She's not a 'subject,' Toivonen. She's a person. Her name is Lysandra."

The professionally dressed woman regarded Emma for a few moments, meeting her fiery gaze with an icy one. "We don't know what might harm 'Lysandra,'" she said, choosing not to argue further. "Our top priority is ensuring nothing compromises her health."

"Then let's work collaboratively," Emma responded, squaring her shoulders in refusal to back down. "Lysandra has given us so much in terms of communication and understanding. The least we can do is make sure she's comfortable. If she's expressing dissatisfaction with her food, shouldn't we address it?"

Toivonen barely restrained an eyeroll but kept her composure. She glanced at Dr. Stenhouse, silently urging him to rein in his assistant. "It's not our decision to make. If the medical team deems it unsafe, then it's not safe. The decision about Lysandra's food is based on a combination of factors, including her biology and potential allergic reactions. It's a matter of security, not comfort."

Sensing the tension, Dr. Stenhouse intervened and spoke up. "Ms. Toivonen, I understand your concerns, and they are valid. But perhaps we can find a middle ground? Maybe consult the medical team to see if there's any possibility of slowly introducing a variety of foods to Lysandra. Monitor her reactions and adjust accordingly?"

Toivonen exhaled slowly. "It's not about denying her comfort, Dr. Stenhouse. But our hands are tied until we have more information. I'll speak with the medical team, but I can't guarantee anything."

Emma sighed, clearly frustrated. "Ugh, you CIA types always say your hands are tied. All we're asking—"

"What we're asking for!" Dr. Stenhouse interrupted firmly, giving his assistant a stern look. "Is a chance for collaboration and understanding. Now I understand that we're only here because *you* allow us to be here, and no one doubts the importance of security." He continued, silently conveying to Emma to control herself, "But we're also dealing with a sentient being who's been nothing but cooperative. Addressing her basic needs could increase cooperation."

Emma bit her lip, stepping back, acknowledging his unspoken message.

Toivonen's face remained inscrutable as she mentally weighed the pros and cons of the argument. A full minute of silence stretched out, the room's atmosphere growing palpably tense, the hum of the facility's ventilation the only sound.

With impatience starting to win over her better judgment, Emma started to fidget, unable to understand how someone could deny another person their basic human rights. Occasionally, she would glance at Dr. Stenhouse as if seeking permission to interject.

As Emma was about to speak again, Toivonen turned abruptly, striding over to the wall-mounted intercom. With a quick press of a button, she said, "Medical team, this is Toivonen. Please report to conference room three. We have a matter to discuss concerning the patient's dietary requirements."

Emma blinked in surprise, exchanging a glance with Dr. Stenhouse as their handler promptly left the room.

"All you need to do to convince those types of people is to speak their language," Dr. Stenhouse said with a smile, motioning for Emma to follow him to a quieter corner of the room.

The assistant raised an eyebrow and gave Dr. Stenhouse an intrigued look. "And what language is that?"

"Pragmatism," he responded. "Spy types, especially at Toivonen's level, deal in risks, benefits, and bottom lines. They're not heartless, but they've learned to set emotions aside in order to complete their objective. So, when dealing with them, it's essential to present your arguments regarding practical benefits and minimized risks."

A frustrated huff left Emma's mouth as she rubbed her temples. "I really don't like how they can just set aside their humanity just to get a strategic advantage," she said, furrowing her brow. "But I get what you're saying. It's about framing the narrative to align with their priorities."

Dr. Stenhouse simply gave her a wry smile. "I don't like it either, but we have to play their game if we're going to ensure Lysandra's well-being and understand her people. If speaking their language can get us there faster, then that's what we have to do."

Emma frowned, staring down at her shoes. "It just feels manipulative."

"Emma, their job is *to be* manipulative." Dr. Stenhouse placed a comforting hand on her shoulder. "Their entire purpose is to think ten steps ahead, and most of the time, humanity isn't even a factor," he said, glancing back at Lysandra, who was watching them with concern.

A frustrated growl left the assistant's mouth as she ruffled her curly hair. "No, their job is to be *evil!* How could someone treat another living, breathing person as if they're some kind of object?!"

With a deep sigh, Dr. Stenhouse pinched the bridge of his nose. "I don't disagree with you, Emma. But you have to understand, we're in a delicate situation," He explained, turning back to his assistant. "We've been given an infinitely unique opportunity that any academic or scientist would kill for, and they're the ones in control—"

"But it's not right!" Emma interrupted, her voice quivering with anger and disbelief. "They can't just strip someone's rights and dignity away because it's convenient!" she nearly shouted, gesturing animatedly. "When does it stop? When they dehumanize all of them and—"

Before she could continue, Dr. Stenhouse raised a hand, signaling her to halt. His voice took on a chilling edge as he met Emma's gaze with a piercing gaze. "Emma, you need to understand something," he began, his eyes locked onto hers. "These people, this establishment, they operate on their own terms. They can and will do as they please, and the moment we cease being valuable, the moment we're no longer an asset to them? We're gone."

Emma remained silent, gritting her teeth as the weight of his words settled in her heart. Tears welled up in her eyes, not just from anger but from the fear and realization of their precarious situation. "So, what? We just play their twisted games and dance to their tune?"

Dr. Stenhouse sighed again, rubbing his temples. "For now, yes. But we do it smartly, subtly. We use our position to push things in the right direction gently," he said, placing a hand on Emma's shoulder. "If we're too direct, we risk everything. But with a careful approach, we can influence outcomes and even get them to see things the way we do."

Though Lysandra didn't understand a word, the tension in the conversation spiked her anxiety as she lay in her hospital bed. Her singular good eye darted between the two scholars as she tried to figure out what might have gone wrong.

Only the hum of the fluorescent lights and the beeps of strange machines resounded in the room for what felt like an eternity, but it was Lysandra who finally broke the silence. "Problem?" she asked, her tone filled with worry.

The two academics exchanged glances, unsure how to respond, but Dr. Stenhouse gave her a reassuring smile and pointed to himself and his assistant. "No, no. We fix problem." He paused, trying to find the words in his limited vocabulary. "Just... talking. All is okay."

Lysandra stared at them for a moment, her gaze searching and unsure, but then she nodded slowly. "Okay," she responded softly, taking solace in their assurance.

Although the conversation drained both linguists of energy, they continued deciphering Lysandra's language. Emma reopened her notebook, and Dr. Stenhouse resumed his questioning. However, as the hospital room regained its warm atmosphere, the coldness of the facility's hallways intensified with the sound of Toivonen's heels clicking against the sterile floor.

Toivonen didn't care much about the melodramatics of the more emotionally driven university types. To her, there was just too much on the line for anything other than functionality, pragmatism, and clear objectives. Her fingers brushed against the cold metal of the handrail as she marched through the maze of corridors. The walls, painted in the stark whites and grays typical of military and research complexes, seemed to close in around her, echoing her every step.

Though most of the facility was brightly lit, pools of shadows marked Toivonen's path, and her thoughts grew darker. These academics, with their lofty ideals and bleeding hearts, were always a hassle to deal with. They were simply too naïve, failing to see the bigger picture. National security, global diplomacy, and the very fabric of human society were the stakes that had landed squarely on her shoulders, and an entity as alien as Lysandra represented risks and opportunities on a scale even Toivonen could barely fathom.

As she approached conference room three, she took a moment to straighten her jacket and compose herself. With a quick tug at her lanyard, Toivonen ensured her access badge was in place before pulling out a black, featureless phone.

After a few taps, she lifted the phone to her ear and spoke. "It's me. The academics have a new demand. They want to change the subject's dietary needs."

A few moments passed with a few hums and acknowledgments before she continued, "I've already called in the medical team for a review, but between you and me, this is starting to get messy. Stenhouse and his assistant are becoming emotionally invested, and it's compromising their objectivity."

Toivonen paused as a muffled voice leaked through the phone's small speaker. Whatever was said caused a thin line of annoyance to appear on her face as she pursed her lips. "Yes, yes, I understand the value they bring, but there are limits. If they become a liability, I won't hesitate to pull them off this project."

Sighing deeply, Toivonen pinched the bridge of her nose and tilted her head upward to push back against her growing headache. "Yes. Yes, sir. I understand, sir." She closed her eyes briefly, grounding herself before speaking again. "I'll try, sir, but we must set clear boundaries with them going forward. Perhaps a meeting to reiterate our objectives and priorities is in order."

The voice on the other end murmured in agreement, suggesting a time for the meeting. "Tomorrow at 0900," Toivonen confirmed. "And make sure Dr. Stenhouse and his assistant understand that I *will* replace them if they can't grasp the gravity of the situation. We must consider all angles and can't compromise the subject's health."

With a final affirmation, Toivonen ended the call and slipped the phone back into her pocket. The woman kept pinching the bridge of her nose for a few moments before glancing at the closed doors of conference room three, steeling herself for the meeting ahead.

As she entered, she saw the room filled with military and medical personnel sitting around a large, round table covered with documents, screens, and various classified devices.

She acknowledged the staff in the room with a nod. "Alright, ladies and gentlemen. You all know why I've called you here, so let's get down to it. I want a list of what we can safely introduce into the subject's diet without compromising her health."

Everyone in the room exchanged glances before Dr. Kassa threw up her hand and cleared her throat. "Well, we've been closely monitoring the patients' reactions to various food samples we've introduced," she began, adjusting her glasses. "And so far, she hasn't shown any allergic reactions to anything we've tested for. Yet."

The final word made Toivonen's eye twitch as she tapped her finger steadily against her arm. "Go on, Dr. Kassa."

Dr. Kassa took a deep breath and looked down at the documents in front of her. "Well..."

CHAPTER 20

Varian cradled his head with one hand as he stared at the raging fire in his fireplace. In the other, he clutched documents, their edges crumpled, his claws piercing through the thick stack. The words of that damnable devil echoed in his mind as his gaze remained locked on the violently popping embers.

His supposedly easy and bloodless path to becoming a true god had been a disaster.

"No, not a disaster," Varian laughed, correcting his thoughts. "This is a calamity."

His advisors had warned him—hells, even one of the devils had cautioned him against meddling with the unknown. But the allure of true godhood, the temptation to claim an even grander realm, had been too great. The celestial dragon, the heart of their expeditionary force and a symbol of his might, now lay in a recuperative state after the failed incursion. The beast's once-lustrous feathers no longer shone with the brilliance of the heavens, and its mighty roar was reduced to pained groans.

But the open rift was an even greater concern. The swirling vortex that stabilized the abomination marred the skyline of the savage lands, speaking of an inevitable threat.

Yet Varian was not one to be easily deterred. Over the centuries, he had built a vast and intricate web of alliances, dependencies, and rivalries. Each vassal, tributary, nomadic horde, hostile state, and even the untamed lands had a role in his grand design.

For centuries, he had played the game of power and politics with finesse, maneuvering like a grandmaster on the cosmic chessboard. No single entity, be it friend or foe, had truly understood the depths of his strategy or the extent of his reach. But forces able to rival his own without the use of magic had been an unforeseen anomaly—one he needed to keep distant while he searched for a way to handle it.

The fire pit roared and bellowed throughout the chamber as if on cue, jolting Varian from his thoughts. The sudden heat felt more like a gust of icy wind, and Varian shivered. However, it wasn't the temperature that unsettled him. No, it was the figure standing before the firepit, flaring at him with glowing, hellish eyes.

"You cannot close it, can you?" the figure's voice, dripping with malice and discontent, echoed throughout the chamber. And just before Varian could blink, the devil Alastor stood before him.

The devil's form shifted between that of a man and a nightmarish creature with horns and leathery wings. Flames licked the edges of his silhouette, casting eerie shadows along the walls.

Varian's vision swam as the world around him darkened, focusing solely on Alastor. A sharp tug within his mind hinted at a connection between them, as if an invisible thread had always existed, now drawn taut.

"In your thirst for godhood, you have knocked on doors that should have remained closed, Varian." Alastor's voice was hypnotic, forcing Varian to recall every whispered warning and ignore premonition. "I warned you. But in your hubris, you believed you were exempt from such folly."

The emperor's heart raced, but his demeanor remained composed, his gaze unwavering. "The pact," he declared firmly, "still stands between us. By its terms, no harm shall come to me from the hells or their schemes while the deal holds true." The room thickened with tension as the emperor continued, "I have the Banished One within my grasp. You cannot, and will not, harm me, Alastor."

A low chuckle resonated from Alastor, echoing throughout the chamber and filling every crevice with its unsettling cadence. "Bold words from someone who has potentially damned not only this mortal plane but *all* mortal planes!" the devil snarled, his voice dripping with venom. The flames around him flared, casting a sinister crimson hue that bathed the room. "The hells and their devils do not wish to rule over *rubble*, Varian."

With a glint in his eyes, Varian defiantly lifted his chin. "I've always been a gambler, Alastor. I may not understand the entirety of what I've done, but I am more than capable of navigating the storm I've created."

Alastor's laughter clashed like steel, cold and foreboding. "Even now, your arrogance blinds you," he sneered, holding a clawed hand to his head.

"Enough!" Varian's fist slammed down onto his desk. "I have fulfilled my end of the bargain, Alastor." With a flourish, he presented the ethereal contract, its iridescent ink shimmering in the chamber's dim light. The parchment pulsed with a power of its own, an embodiment of the oaths made in the infinite hells.

For the first time, Alastor seemed taken aback. His posture straightened, his attention riveted on the document. "You wouldn't dare."

"I not only dare, I assert!" Varian interrupted with a bellow. "I hereby transfer the ownership of the Banished One to you. And as per the contract's stipulations, my safety and sovereignty are guaranteed! You and your infernal minions can't touch me, nor can any of your damned schemes."

The devil's eyes narrowed, his fist trembling in demonic fury. The firepit and every candle in the room burned brighter, even as the air felt as cold as ice. "You think these mere words will save you? That this contract will be your shield?"

Varian leaned in, his voice dripping with confidence. "They're not just words, Alastor. It's a bond forged in the hells themselves, a promise that even Satan wouldn't dare break. In your eyes, I may be a mortal, but I've played this game long enough to know its rules."

Alastor clenched his teeth so hard it could've torn through steel, his gaze flickering between the contract and Varian. Silence filled the chamber as the devil calculated his next move. The atmosphere grew dense, the weight of decisions and the cosmic game of power pressing down on them.

"Where is she?" Alastor finally asked, barely containing his anger.

A wicked smirk widened across Varian's face as the contract slowly burned from top to bottom after its fulfillment. "Why, she's at the heart of the rift itself, dear Alastor."

Silence reigned as they stared at each other. Varian's expression was smug, while Alastor's seemed to disbelieve what he had heard. Suddenly, the devil erupted into a burst of uncontrolled laughter, pointing a clawed finger at Varian. "You!" he bellowed, clutching his head with his other hand. "You would make a *superb* devil, Varian!"

With that last proclamation, once filled with confrontation and doom, the chamber drowned in the devil's maniacal laughter. Shadows danced with the flames, and the room's boundaries seemed to blur, its edges disintegrating into nothingness.

Alastor's figure grew larger, the air around him shimmering with dark energy. "You think you've won? Because you've traded the Banished One—the very catalyst of the rift—and offloaded the responsibility onto me?"

Varian's smirk didn't waver. "Isn't that how it works? A trade, a deal, an exchange of services? I've upheld my end, and now you have what you wanted."

Alastor looked genuinely thoughtful briefly, his eyes burning with an infernal light. Varian knew Alastor was trying to make him a scapegoat for this fiasco. The devil pondered the near-infinite possibilities before settling on a course of action.

Ever the strategist, Alastor reared his full height and adjusted his stance, appearing more regal. "Very well, Varian," he purred, his voice smooth as honey, yet filled with a venomous undertone. "You have indeed kept to the terms of our agreement, and I am bound by the very nature of this infernal contract. But you seem to forget. While a contract prevents direct harm, it does not limit indirect consequences."

Varian narrowed his eyes. "What are you insinuating?"

Alastor's smile broadened, revealing sharp, gleaming teeth that seemed to absorb all light. "I'm saying that while I cannot lay a hand on you and may not plot your demise, your choices have opened doors. Doors that might allow others, not bound by our agreement nor even aware of me, to take an interest in you."

Varian's claws dug deep into the table, a knot tightening in his stomach. "What are you insinuating?" he hissed.

But Alastor didn't answer. Instead, he let out a hearty, sinister laugh and flicked his hands. A flash of intense heat radiated through the chambers as Alastor vanished in a collapsing ball of fire, leaving only his echoing laughter and the stench of sulfur.

Left alone in the chamber, Varian collapsed into his chair, an ominous chill running up his spine. A sinking feeling of foreboding now replaced the bravado and confidence he exuded. He realized he had a devil plotting against him.

"I need allies," he murmured, gazing at the ethereal contract as it finally evaporated into nothingness. The game was far from over, and Varian understood that the next few moves would be critical. He had to be prepared for whatever awaited him in the shadows of the unknown.

* * *

Coleman and his Special Forces ODA had just touched down at the forward operating base, disembarking from a Black Hawk that had whisked them back from their observation point.

The 160th Special Operations Aviation Regiment, known as the Night Stalkers, had provided their usual exemplary transport when a ranger came in to hit the target they were observing. Just like the Rangers, the Black Hawks were far from standard issue, equipped with cutting-edge avionics, FLIR systems for night operations, and refueling probes for extended range.

But of all the raids he had taken part in or observed, the rangers still managed to surprise him. Coleman still vividly remembered the operation as the 160th SOAR made their approach with an aggressiveness he'd rarely seen, even among seasoned pilots. They came in low and fast, hugging the earth like a long-lost lover and unleashing a veritable swarm of rangers fueled by steroids, Rip Its, and hatred.

As Coleman's boots hit the tarmac, he noticed the activity around the base had intensified. Armored units rolled past, and mechanics and crew swarmed over APCs and IFVs, conducting last-minute checks and repairs. The air buzzed with the whine of turbines as more helicopters landed, unloading their cargo of marines and soldiers before lifting off again in a wash of dust and debris. However, the sight of more rangers loading into the nearby modified Black Hawks made his hair stand on end.

Suddenly, a bout of laughter drew Coleman's attention away from the spectacle. Elijah and Bennett, two of his team members, were ribbing a platoon of SEALs gearing up near their helicopters, readying themselves to replace them as recon elements watching a section of the rift. The SEALs, identifiable by their distinctive patches and the casual swagger that accompanied their precise movements, were prepping for their own observation mission near the rift.

Ever the instigator, Elijah had a wide grin plastered on his face. "Hey, don't forget your fins!" he shouted as they passed the SEALs. "Wouldn't want you guys to drown in that small creek!"

One of the SEALs, a brown-skinned, bald man with a neck gaiter covering half his face, scoffed and shot back, "Shut the fuck up, Eli. I bet you and your bitch boy got lost again."

Knowing they were talking about him, Bennett joined in on the fray. "Try not to write a book about this one, alright?" His jab at the stereotype caused the SEALs to groan and roll their eyes in unison.

However, it was all in good fun as another round of laughter erupted. "No promises! It's gonna be a bestseller called *The Time I Saved an Army Guy*," an extremely pale, short, and stocky SEAL replied. "But don't worry, we'll mention you guys in a footnote."

Shaking his head with a chuckle, Coleman motioned for his team to follow. The humor was fun, but they had their own after-action reports to file and new orders to receive.

Soon, the laughter faded, replaced by the beats of helicopter blades and the whines of engines as the SEALs returned to their preparations. It wasn't long before the frogmen piled onto their designated aircraft and ascended. They were tasked with precisely what Army Special Forces, Rangers, and other special operations units were designed to do: setting the conditions.

Bradley Fighting Vehicles maneuvered through designated areas of the base, their engines growling like caged beasts ready for the hunt.

With their M1125 Strykers, the mechanized infantry units conducted pre-combat checks, ensuring every piece of equipment was functional, and every round of ammunition accounted for. The rumble of heavy steel treads from the M1A2 Abrams added a bass line to the cacophony of the FOB as they lined up, their powerful turbines spinning up.

Artillery units were also busy, with Paladin self-propelled howitzers loaded to the brim with munitions. They would provide the necessary fire support, capable of delivering devastating barrages to soften enemy positions before any advance.

Amid it all, Coleman and his team strode confidently toward the tactical operations center to be debriefed. Inside, the buzz of officers fussing over screens, maps, and radios painted the picture of a nerve center pulsing with information. Coleman's boots thudded against the firm surface of the prefab floor as they made their way to the debriefing area. The team didn't even take off their gear before taking their seats.

In every corner of the room, high-ranking officers stood or sat, waiting for the debriefing while engaged in their own discussions. With the ODA fully present, the operations officer acknowledged the operators' presence with a nod, opened his laptop, and signaled everyone to settle in. A projector hummed to life, casting a high-fidelity video of a drone observing the area of operations as the Special Forces team prepared to recount their observations. The sterile light cast long shadows across the faces of the attending officers and analysts, all poised to absorb the details that could shape subsequent operations.

Coleman, still clad in his dusty gear, stood first. "During our observation phase," he began, his voice steady despite the lingering adrenaline coursing through his system, "we identified a large, spire-like structure at the center of the rift. It appears to function as an energy source—or perhaps it's harnessing energy. We couldn't determine its origin or purpose, but the emissions were unmistakable."

The video then focused on the spire in the heart of the rift, filling the screen. "This structure"—Coleman pointed—"was guarded by individuals who, based on their distinct attire, we identified as potential high-value targets. Their behavior suggested they were either a command element or elite cadre."

A sea of murmurs spread through the room momentarily as everyone watched the feed. The team waited for the chatter to die down before Schwarz picked up where Coleman left off.

"Here, you see the arrangement of their encampment," he explained, standing up and pointing to a cluster of armored individuals with a laser pointer. "Notice the perimeter security and the internal checkpoints. This layout wasn't temporary; they've been here a while."

"We monitored them for a while, but then they suddenly began showing signs of imminent departure," he continued as the video showed the encampment come to life with activity. "Watch their body language here. There is a sense of urgency that wasn't present before. They're gesturing aggressively, which could indicate a dispute or a change in plans."

Coleman pressed a button on the laptop, fast-forwarding the video to show the individuals packing hastily. "We believe some form of communication triggered this sudden change."

The room's atmosphere grew tense as field officers and flag officers began theorizing aloud. "Based on this development," Coleman continued, "we initiated communication with the QRF, but they needed to move swiftly to intercept before disappearing. Unfortunately, we were too late."

The projection flickered as the timeline sped up, showing the sequence of the rangers deploying from the helicopters, fast ropes unfurling, and engaging the guard detail. The aircraft lifted off, but the operation yielded no actionable intelligence, leaving them no closer to understanding what they had stumbled upon.

"With no HVT and no actionable intel, it was best to bug out before the enemy's own QRF responded," Coleman concluded, his expression taut with a hint of frustration.

The assembled officers leaned in, processing the setback. The loss of a high-value target was a setback, but it was not the end of the operation—it was merely a shift.

"This isn't the outcome we anticipated, but it's not entirely fruitless. Every encounter, successful or not, provides us with valuable information," Captain Alleck Dohmer, a Navy SEAL commanding officer, said. "Whatever information they received spooked them enough to get the hell out of there. The question is, what?"

Captain Dohmer tapped his finger on the table and looked around at the assembled Special Operations Command officers. "Perhaps they've got eyes on us and realized we're going to make our own moves soon."

A United States Marine Corps general nodded. "We need to assume they have some level of counterintelligence at play. It's imperative to review our operational security measures and potential leaks."

"My question is, what in the fuck is that thing?" Brigadier General Lawrence Hargrove gestured to the still image of the strange marble spire emitting energy. "Is this a weapon? A communication device? Or—"

"How they opened the rift?" Elijah blurted out, causing heads to snap toward him.

Coleman pinched the bridge of his nose, a hint of frustration breaking through. "Now's not the time—"

Another officer, this time General Michael Jones from the Air Force, raised a hand, stopping Coleman from his reprimand. "No, No. Let him finish. I'm curious."

Suppressing a disgruntled sigh, Coleman shot Elijah a glare. The medic wasn't typically one to theorize, but now he was bolstered by the general's interest.

The room was still, and every officer and analyst was waiting to hear more.

"Sir, with all due respect," Elijah began, his eyes darting nervously between the officers and Coleman. He raised his hands in submission, "I'm just the doc; I don't really know what I'm talking about."

Unsatisfied with that answer, General Jones knocked on the table to get his and everyone's attention. "Your perspective as a medic isn't any less valuable than anyone else's in this room. As a matter of fact, as an operator on this mission, you might have spotted something others missed."

Feeling the weight of the room's eyes—including Coleman's daggers—Elijah had no choice but to elaborate.

"All right," he said cautiously. "I was just thinking that the spire is in the middle of the rift, right?"

The room remained silent, waiting for him to continue.

A cold jolt of nerves shot up Elijah's spine as the pressure mounted. "And this strange material or energy surrounds the entire rift as if it's holding it together. Our HVTs were positioned around it while they were chanting, praying, or whatever. I don't think that was just coincidence—they were either protecting it or maybe channeling something through it."

Murmurs spread across the room like wildfire, with Elijah's words acting as the kindling. Each person pondered the implications of such an absurd theory. It wasn't just the spire's position that was notable, but the behavior of the high-value targets and the enemy's reaction added weight to the idea.

Captain Dohmer leaned forward, catching onto Elijah's hesitant yet insightful observation. "It makes sense, especially since everyone except the HVTs was stopped and turned away..." He leaned back heavily in his chair, arms folded, deep in thought. "We need to secure it, and we need to secure it now."

Suddenly, the captain stood and began marching toward the door. "We need to throw everything at this. I'll divert my boys. Pike, can you get your rangers on it?"

Army Colonel Matthew Pike stood up as well and nodded. "Coleman, get you and your team back on those choppers in ten."

CHAPTER 21

Elijah furrowed his brow as he stared up at the strange, dark, marble-like spire that pierced the earth before him.

It stood like a sinister monolith, its smooth yet impossibly dark surface absorbing light rather than reflecting it. It seemed as though it were a shard of darkness itself, implanted in the ground as an insult to the sun.

However, what really sparked Elijah's interest wasn't the material of its strange construction but the destroyed landscape around it. It was almost as if it had suddenly and violently erupted from the ground.

Scratching his head, Elijah looked around and saw enormous trees uprooted and tossed aside as if they were nothing but twigs. Turning his attention back to the spire's base, he noticed what was left of a shattered rock formation, seemingly turning to glass and clinging to the structure's impossibly smooth, void-like surface. It was obvious that the rock formation had once been atop the spire's origin point. Still, now it seemed as if it had absorbed the very essence of the geological features around it, leaving behind a crystalline residue that shimmered with a strange, unnatural light.

The juxtaposition of light or energy being absorbed while simultaneously trying to escape left Elijah unnerved, as his mind raced to reconcile the scene with any known natural phenomenon. The medic knew enough to recognize that what he was seeing just wasn't right. There was no word in his vocabulary that could adequately describe the aberration before him; it was as if this spire was an abomination, an affront to the natural order of the world, a physical impossibility that defied the rules of the environment he had come to understand.

"Please help." The faint whisper seemed to slither through the air, bypassing his ears and resonating directly within his mind. Elijah winced, pressing the heel of his palm against his temple as if he could physically squeeze out the intrusion. "Release me."

Elijah's head snapped around, looking for anyone in earshot, but he found himself alone. Only the rhythmic hum of rotor blades cutting through the air and the distant sounds of the mixed units participating in the air assault reached his ears.

He blinked for a few moments, attempting to clear his mind.

It must be the lack of sleep.

They had been on edge for days observing this place, and Elijah knew that if someone went too long without proper rest, the mind could conjure all sorts of tricks under stress. Yet, as he took a step back, a pang of guilt tugged at his chest. Elijah felt as if the plea for freedom had been so desperate and sorrowful that it pierced through his exhaustion and skepticism.

Glancing back at the spire, Elijah felt a strange kinship with it. Perhaps his own desire for a break from the chaos of this reality made him imagine the voice and empathize with it. Or perhaps there really was something trapped within that alien column of darkness, reaching out to him specifically.

Yet, as he looked around at the veritable army surrounding him, Elijah couldn't quite figure out why. They had landed without resistance, and there was no enemy presence except for the corpses from the earlier raid. Instead of a quick-reaction force rapidly securing the area as planned, they encountered bizarre creatures with forms and movements alien to their world, scavenging amongst the fallen.

Elijah tilted the headphones, which were hinged to his helmet, and rubbed his temples, but suddenly, a voice resounded next to him, nearly causing him to jump out of his skin.

"Hey, Eli, go touch it," Bennett called out, standing right beside him.

For a moment, Elijah entertained the idea before turning to Bennet with an expression that spoke of disbelief bordering on incredulity. "What the fuck? No. How about you fuckin' touch it?"

Bennett chuckled dryly, though the smirk on his face faltered as he glanced back at the spire."C'mon, you could be the chosen one or some shit and get some funky powers!"

"Shut up, dipshit," Elijah replied, almost deadpan, as he turned away. "The *only* thing I was chosen to do is your mom."

The retort drew a chuckle from Bennett as the medic walked away, shaking his head. Even though he knew it was a joke, Elijah couldn't quite believe how anyone would willingly touch that goddamn thing. He made his way over to where his team leader, Coleman, was deep in discussion with a commander from the ranger company who spearheaded the raid. The two men were huddled over what looked like an alien map, their expressions a mix of confusion and caution.

"Just doesn't make any sense," Coleman muttered as he picked up several more documents and scrolls. "Why the hell would they just leave all this shit here instead of burning it or taking it with them."

The ranger commander, Major William Sutton, scratched his chiseled chin. "Doesn't make any sense to me either. They had plenty of time, so there's no real explanation," he replied, glancing at the strange magical items scattered around. "I'd say it's a trap, but where's the trap part?"

His gaze wandered back to the spire. "I mean, if it's a trap, it's poorly executed. No follow-up, no ambush, nothing."

Coleman poked at a small, strangely ornate device at the end of the table before turning to see Elijah standing there. "You find anything useful?"

"Uh, not really." Elijah shrugged as his gaze drifted over to the device Coleman had been fiddling with. "Just more questions more than anything else."

Elijah then spotted several flasks of various sizes filled with strange glowing liquids. "Everything here is kind of outside my frame of reference, other than video games and media." He gestured towards the flasks with his chin. "I mean, these could be potions that heal you or give you power, but I wouldn't rely on media logic, if you know what I mean."

"Without the right equipment or knowledge, they might as well be radiation in a bottle," the medic said, his voice tinged with a mix of curiosity and concern. "And that," he added, pointing at the spire, "is giving me serious 'do not touch' vibes."

He was lying.

In truth, Elijah still felt drawn to the spire. That pitiful voice echoed in his mind like a silent plea. He felt its pull almost like a tide beckoning him to wade into unknown waters. Despite his dismissal of Bennett, the medic couldn't shake the feeling of a presence within the spire, something sentient and aware. It felt imprisoned, yes, but more than that, it felt like it was betrayed, leading to its confinement.

Shaking his head, Elijah turned his attention back to his team leader and Major Sutton. He had to focus and push the intrusive thoughts aside until he could properly figure things out. "I get it, though. The area looked like a stage set after the actors had long departed." Elijah walked over to the flasks and picked up one with a bright orange glow. "Props left in disarray with no discernible logic, maps and battle plans scattered across the table."

He tilted the flask in his hand, causing the viscous liquid to gently slosh about. Another curiosity his subconscious begged him to explore, but caution stayed his hand. This wasn't a video game where Elijah could just respawn and or revive. It was a stupid thought, but at least this one was his own.

Bennett sauntered over, his eyes flickering across the strange equipment in the tent. "You guys find anything?" he asked, clapping a hand on Elijah's shoulder.

"Yeah, maps, trinkets, and potions or some shit," Coleman answered, poking at another oddity.

Major Sutton picked up a smaller flask containing a blue, glowing liquid that brightened whenever it moved. "Lab rats are gonna have a field day with this garbage

"Man, they'd be on this like a fat kid on ice cream," Elijah agreed with a chuckle as he carefully placed the orange-glowing flask back onto the makeshift table. "I can't blame them, to be honest. I really want to know what this stuff is too—" His gaze inadvertently wandered back to the spire, where he spotted a figure slowly approaching it. "Who the fuck is that?"

Elijah's voice trailed off mid-sentence as his eyes narrowed. Standing in front of the spire was a soldier dressed in familiar camo, yet the details weren't quite right. The pattern on the uniform was a jigsaw that didn't quite fit together; it mimicked their own but was just a shade too dark, a line too straight, or overlapped in ways that weren't standard. The individual's gear was almost a caricature of standard-issue equipment—pouches where no pouch should be, holsters where none should exist, and the weapon's shape exaggerated as if drawn by someone who had only heard descriptions but never seen them.

No one else from Elijah's ODA or the mixed units of rangers, marines, or SEALs were anywhere near the spire. They were spread out, establishing a perimeter or sifting through the chaos of left-behind alien artifacts. This figure was an anomaly, an outlier that sent a silent shockwave of alert through Elijah's already frayed senses.

The medic felt his teammates' curious glances as they followed his line of sight to the misplaced soldier. The individual's foreignness in his gear wasn't lost on them either, especially since the odd man seemed to be alone.

"Does he belong to one of the other units?" Sutton asked, his voice lined with the authority of command but edged with the uncertainty the sight warranted.

Before anyone could answer, Elijah snapped his weapon toward the individual and flipped off his safety. "Stop!" he bellowed, pushing his way out of the tent. "Take one more step, and I'll fucking waste you!"

The figure halted but was already directly in front of the spire. The strange soldier's hands remained at its sides, showing no indication that it understood the threat. Instead, it stood eerily as if waiting for something to happen.

A horrid chill ran down Elijah's spine as he adjusted the rifle in his grip. The tension in the air could have been cut with a knife. Despite the confusion in the encampment, the discipline drilled into each soldier kept the situation from devolving into chaos. The activity seemed to slow as more eyes focused on the unfolding scene by the spire. Some soldiers, unsure of the threat, began to align their weapons with Elijah's stance, while others continued to scan the horizon, their bodies tense with the stress of potential conflict from any direction.

Whispers and muttered questions were drowned out by the crunch of sand under boots and the occasional metallic click of a safety being disengaged. Everyone waited for a cue from their commanders or the mysterious figure itself.

"Hands! Show me your fucking hands!" Elijah ordered, his voice harsh against the low hum of the spire, which continued spewing energy into the rift. However, that hum seemed to rise in pitch, a detail that didn't escape the more observant soldiers. It was as if the spire was excited, screaming at a frequency just beyond human hearing.

Major Sutton stepped beside Elijah, his own weapon pointed at the figure. "Hold your fire. Keep him covered, but nobody shoots unless I give the word."

He turned slightly to address one of his men without taking his eyes off the figure. "Get me comms with the other units. I want to confirm if anyone's missing a man."

Elijah kept his weapon trained on the figure. The order to hold fire battled with an instinct that screamed something was fundamentally wrong. The figure hadn't moved, but its presence was an intrusion that set his nerves on edge.

"If he doesn't move, I don't shoot," Elijah muttered, trying to steady his nerves. His finger slid off the receiver and hovered over the trigger, an action that spoke of both restraint and readiness.

Every fiber of his being screamed to pull the trigger; not killing what stood in front of him felt against every instinct in his body.

Coleman, who had been quietly observing from a few steps back, had never seen Elijah this spooked before. Even in the worst firefights, Elijah had always maintained a borderline sociopathic calm, cool, and collectedness. In fact, most of his rowdy behavior had been more for entertainment than anything else. But now, Coleman could see the strain etched across his medic's face, the way his eyes darted, searching for the slightest movement to justify action.

"Eli, don't let whatever freaked you out get to your head. We need to handle this one step at a time. We don't want a blue on blue." He tried to soothe the obviously frazzled Elijah.

But Elijah's grip on his rifle didn't wane. Whatever the hell he was aiming at wasn't part of their reality—not entirely. The alien nature of it clawed at his mind, urging him to act.

Major Sutton and his adjutant were engrossed in their attempts to try to make sense of the headcount report when the figure made a subtle, almost undetectable move. Its arm remained by his side, but the faintest shimmer, like a heatwave on a hot road, suggested movement.

It was all the provocation Elijah needed. The pent-up tension, the raw edge of fear and uncertainty, exploded into action. Even though his ear protection wasn't on, he didn't hear the deafening blast of the first shot—only the recoil slamming into his shoulder as he unloaded round after round into the figure's back. The harsh staccato of suppressed gunfire erupted, shredding the tense and eerie calm.

Officers and soldiers alike reacted instantly, their yells of "Stand down"' or "Elijah, cease fire!" mixing with the echoes of gunfire. But their pleas fell on deaf ears as Elijah advanced, still squeezing his trigger, emptying the entire magazine into the figure.

Coleman sprinted forward and tackled Elijah as he readied a fresh mag. His shout was cut short as all attention snapped back to the spire. The dark energy pulsing from it stopped abruptly, as if Elijah's rounds had severed a lifeline to the ominous structure.

But what stunned everyone wasn't the spire—it was the figure.

The thing had slowly risen, its body twisting and turning in impossible ways as sickening cracks echoed across the field. A stunned silence fell over the encampment, everyone frozen in place, staring at the surreal scene. Elijah's ears rang, his chest heaved, and in his peripheral vision, he saw rifles slowly rise again, confusion etched on every face.

Sutton was the first to act. He rushed out of the tent, rifle raised. "Waste it!"

A cacophony of gunfire erupted—a thunderous chorus of every caliber imaginable hammered into the unknown. The figure moved with a jerky, otherworldly grace, seemingly unaffected by the barrage. Each step it took toward them felt like a descent into madness. Its form shimmered with the same heatwave distortion, a tear in the very fabric of reality that refused to mend.

Suddenly, a hellish laugh echoed across the battlefield, freezing the soldiers to their cores. The demonic figure, now fully revealed in its nightmarish glory, towered over them. It spoke again in a strange, twisted language, but its malice needed no translation.

"Well played!" The visage of violence itself laughed. "Well done, humans of another world! This servant of Alastor is impressed!"

Elijah, his earlier fervor replaced with cold dread, clung to his rifle like a lifeline—the only tangible thing in a world that had slipped into a twisted fairy tale. Around him, soldiers were backing away, their faces pale, weapons lowered but still ready.

"It is not often I am bested so readily by mortals!" the demon roared, its voice a rumbling mockery of speech. "Your fear gives you strength—interesting," it added, its meter-long claws scraping against the ground.

Despite the creature dismissing their efforts as amusement, there was a subtle shift in the air, a grudging respect that was more terrifying than scorn. The soldiers' continued gunfire seemed to do little but stir the dust at the demon's feet. Slowly, as if by a silent command, the firing ceased.

It was then Elijah broke free of Coleman's grip and pulled out an M320 grenade launcher with its sights chopped off. He slipped in a 40mm HEDP grenade and fired. The weapon gave off a thumping sound before the grenade slammed into the demon's face.

A deafening roar resounded as the round exploded on contact, sending a shockwave through the air. The soldiers flinched, instinctively taking cover. As the smoke cleared, they watched a blend of hope and terror in their eyes.

The demon, stumbling back, emerged from the dissipating smoke and dust. Its hand slid up and traced the gouge left by the hypersonic jet of copper from the small-shaped charge, intrigued. Although its hide had been impervious to conventional weapons, this had piqued its interest; however, the damage was negligible.

"You, so quick to fire—do you not understand the futility?" the demon hissed, its gaze piercing Elijah. The creature seemed more intrigued than threatened, its voice a rumble of distant thunder.

Elijah met the demon's gaze as he loaded another grenade. "Your mom's futile," he retorted.

The demon paused, tilting its head to the side as if processing the human's brazen defiance and peculiar insult. A surreal silence hung over the battlefield for a moment, broken only by the distant crackling of energy from the now-dormant spire. The soldiers held their breath, their grips tightening on their weapons.

Then, a sound no one expected—a low, guttural chuckle— emanated from the demon. The laugh, devoid of warmth, mockingly acknowledged Elijah's audacity.

"No wonder she is insistent on choosing you!" the demon rumbled, its chuckles subsiding into dark amusement. "Very well, I shall grant you your lives as a token for your spirited defense." With a grandiose flourish, the demon extended a clawed hand towards the ominous spire, where a strange dagger was embedded deep within its surface. The blade glowed with an ethereal light, its energy palpable even from a distance.

The air around the shrouded dagger shimmered playfully, as though the blade acknowledged its new custodians with a flicker of luminescence. The demon's gaze lingered on the soldiers before settling on Elijah, who stood defiantly, grenade launcher aimed directly at its face.

Without another word, the demon's form shifted to flames that licked the air without consuming it. In mere seconds, the laughter ceased, the thick malevolence dissipated, and the being that had challenged reality itself vanished into a whisper of smoke curling toward the sky.

Chapter 22

"Fuck me, man," Coleman groaned, his gaze sweeping across the faces around him. Each and every one of them was etched with a blend of awe, confusion, and lingering fear. The encounter had spooked them but hadn't taken the fight out of them.

Each highly trained fighter stood at the ready, scanning every inch of the encampment with their weapons gripped competently in their hands.

If Coleman was honest, he couldn't blame them for their fear—he felt it too. After all, there was a literal *demon* standing before them, straight out of some ancient legend. Horns and all.

"Can someone tell me what the *fuck* just happened?" the team leader yelled as he walked towards Elijah, who re-holstered his heavily modified grenade launcher.

No one seemed to have had an answer as a deep quiet settled over the area. However, one soul's voice broke the silence as they dropped an empty magazine and slotted a fresh one into their rifle. "Eli shot a demon in the face with a grenade launcher." Bennett's matter-of-fact response cut through the heavy air like a hot knife through butter.

The lighthearted reply was met with a mix of amused chuckles and celebratory cheers, but the undercurrent of anxiety was palpable among the servicemen. It was blatantly obvious their weapons were nowhere near effective against the infernal thing. Even the armored-piercing capabilities of their High Explosive Dual Purpose grenades had done little more than scratch it; those munitions could pierce up to seventy-six millimeters or three inches of steel.

Coleman stood for a moment, replaying the scene from just minutes ago in his head. "T-That he did," he affirmed, rubbing the stubble on his chin thoughtfully.

"So, demons are real, huh?" Sutton asked, his voice a mix of skepticism and wonder. He stepped forward, ruffling his hair in disbelief before regaining his composure. "Makes you wonder what the hell else is real."

There was a bout of silence as everyone exchanged uneasy glances. The implications that mythology, folklore, and legends weren't just stories seemed far more likely—and unnerving.

"Yeah, and apparently, they're bulletproof," Elijah added, walking over to where he had shot the demon.

Major Coleman nodded, narrowing his eyes as if sheer willpower would let him spot the demon lurking in their midst. "Well, if the damn thing can be scratched, then that means it might be able to bleed."

"And if it can bleed, then it can be killed," Sutton finished the thought, turning to the surrounding soldiers, SEALs, and marines. "Was anyone recording on their end-user device? We need to get any footage we can to command."

Several servicemen voiced affirmation and stepped forward. Sutton noted their responses with a curt nod. "Good. Those with visual intel, grab maps, scrolls, or whatever you can carry, and prepare for exfil. We need to get this shit up the chain."

While the Ranger company commander issued orders, Coleman switched channels to HQ. "Warmonger, this is Baron. We've secured the perimeter, but we've encountered an unknown hostile exhibiting, uh, supernatural capabilities. Over."

The radio was silent for a moment before Warmonger's RTO responded, "Supernatural, Baron? Say again."

It was Coleman's turn to go quiet. He glanced at Sutton for a moment before responding back on the horn. "We've engaged with an entity resembling a demonic figure. It demonstrated teleportation abilities and resisted conventional weaponry. We've got visual intelligence. Requesting exfil."

"Wait one, Baron," Warmonger replied, and the line went silent.

"I bet you they think we're high as shit," quipped the bald, brown-skinned SEAL Elijah had teased earlier.

The joke felt far too real for anyone to laugh. Everyone seemed to agree with the sentiment as Sutton chuckled, shaking his head. "Hell, I don't blame them. I still think we're hallucinating or something."

A moment later, the radio crackled back to life, Warmonger's RTO with a tone that was all business. "Baron, Warmonger, maintain your defensive posture. Exfil is being arranged. Prepare your intel for transfer and await further instructions. Warmonger out."

The ODA team leader switched to his original channel and looked at the men who had captured footage of the supposed demon. "Alright, grab as much shit as you can and be prepared to hand off everything. We'll hold the fort, but keep your eyes peeled and your heads down. We don't know if that thing was alone or if there are more of them."

Sutton jerked his head towards his rangers, who were waiting for confirmation. "You heard 'em—get the fuck outta here. And fuckin' break anything!"

Amid the controlled chaos of preparations, no one initially noticed Elijah's absence. The seasoned soldiers, hardened by years of training and experience in the sandbox, were thorough in packing sensitive items and setting up a defensive perimeter. The whirl of activity created a cacophony that drowned out subtler sounds of Elijah's steady approach towards the spire.

One could say this was insanely stupid, and they'd be right. Elijah wouldn't deny that curiosity killed the cat, but he'd be lying if he said it was curiosity driving him. There was also something—or someone—else. A palpable yet soft pull asked him—no—begged him to accept her offer of patronage. Earlier, the entity had lingered in the back of Elijah's mind, trying to coerce him into doing its bidding. But now, the entity has made itself *very* visible.

He could feel the damn thing as it tried to ensnare his mind, but he also felt the frustrated screams and tantrums of failure. The entity couldn't understand why it couldn't get a solid hold of him like it had with so many others in the past. But as Elijah stood on the threshold, the presence opted for a different approach. It seemed to recognize that brute insistence was futile and instead unfurled its emotions like a banner in the wind, letting them flow over him.

What hit him was an abstract sensation of need or command and a torrent of raw, unguarded emotion.

He felt the sharp sting of betrayal's blade—so acute it could have been his own—along with an ancient and bone-deep fear, a well of anguish with no bottom. And threading through it all was an aching longing for freedom. It was as if the entity was exposing its soul to him, laying bare a history of entrapment that spanned an unimaginable gulf of time.

"Ah. So that's how it is," Elijah remarked, understanding what lay before him as the connection tightened his chest.

It was a story that resonated with him.

There were no details, but he, too, knew the sharp stab of betrayal and the cold void of abandonment. These were not just memories—they were scars that had yet to fully heal. He understood all too well the value of freedom and the pain of its absence. Yet, even with this tide of shared suffering and the pull on his sympathies, Elijah knew the perils of acting on empathy or any raw emotion.

Even *he* wasn't dumb enough to abandon all sense in his thirst for answers.

Scoffing at the voice in the back of his mind, Elijah threw up a hand and waved it off. "Yeah, sure, you can be my patron or whatever when you get out."

That half-hearted acceptance was all that the entity needed to seal a pact. The dagger sucked itself deep within the black spire with a sound like the world's breath being taken away. Elijah recoiled, his eyes wide with shock as the stone surface rippled violently, as if it were imploding. A torrent of light and energy that had previously spewed into the rift now reversed, spiraling back into the center of the spire and centering on the dagger.

The violent action snapped everyone's attention to the spire, their eyes finally resting on Elijah as he scrambled backward. But as they moved to help, they suddenly found themselves frozen as reality twisted in ways their minds couldn't fully process.

Their horror was only amplified when a single light and dark tendril snaked toward Elijah, who simply stared at it in a mixture of awe and terror.

"Holy shit! What the fuck?!" Elijah shouted, trying to get away from the abomination that was snaking toward him.

The tendril, an aberration of light and darkness mingling in defiance of physical laws, moved through the air with an eerie grace.

Both Coleman and Bennett were in a dead sprint to reach the medic and pull him away, but they were too late. The tendril brushed against Elijah's hand before violently stabbing its way in. Every nerve in Elijah's arm screamed as he doubled over in pain, but the sensation was soon drowned out by a cascade of whispers—echoes of emotions and untold thoughts.

Coleman was the first to reach him, grabbing the back of Elijah's plate carrier and pulling with every ounce of strength. Elijah felt like he was being torn in two, the whispers rising to a cacophony that threatened to overwhelm his senses. Bennett arrived a second later, aiding Coleman. They were locked in a desperate tug-of-war with the unseen force that had anchored itself to their comrade.

"Move, move, move!" Coleman's voice was a distant roar to Elijah, now lost in a haze of alien sensations. The tendrils retreated as suddenly as they had attacked, slithering back into the spire with the same unsettling grace, leaving a trail of shimmering air.

Bennett and Coleman didn't stop to watch the spectacle. They dragged Elijah away, his legs regaining enough strength to stumble alongside them as they sought the relative safety of distance. The entire encampment mobilized around them, forming a protective barrier as everyone pointed their weapons and shouted into their radios.

Elijah's vision was blurred, his mind awash with more than just his own thoughts. He could feel the entity, its essence mingling with his, angrily yelling at him for being so difficult to brand.

But soon, the yelling ceased, replaced by a horrifying silence.

The air around the spire seemed to vibrate with the aftershocks of the reclamation of energy. Once pulsing with malevolent darkness, the black structure was now something different altogether. The final strands of energy withdrew into the spire, centering on the green-leafed dagger at its heart.

With the strange aura now completely consumed, everything around the spire stood still, silent as the eye of a storm. Then, as if exhaling after holding its breath for an eternity, the stone's surface began to change. What had once been an obsidian monolith morphed into something more ordinary yet extraordinary in detail.

The ancient-looking spire no longer had its once smooth, dark features. Instead, intricate, complex patterns were now engraved into it. The patterns resembled an endless labyrinth of mazes winding around the spire in continuous, unbroken lines that intersect and overlapped, creating a tapestry of stone that baffled the mind.

"What the fuck happened to me?!" Elijah shouted, frantically pulling off as much gear as he could. The medic kept looking at his hand, where the tendril had stabbed him, but there was no wound, no mark. The skin was unbroken, as if the entity's touch had been a phantom pain.

"Hey, hey, Elijah, look at me, man." Coleman gripped his shoulder, trying to ground his comrade's panic with a firm but worried gaze. "You're all right, brother. No blood, no entry wound."

Bennett, helping remove Elijah's body armor, spoke up. "This is magic shit! The wound could be internal!"

Elijah's breath was ragged. "I don't know! I don't know! I fuckin' like! I can fucking *feel* something inside me! Something's there, man!" He clenched his fists, trying to shake off the invasive presence. "I can't believe I'm going to die to a fuckin' *rock!*"

That's when Navy SEAL corpsman arrived, sliding next to him and pulling off his med pack. "Let's get him stable," he muttered, moving with practiced urgency. "We need to check vitals and—"

A loud crack echoed across the area, cutting through the soldiers' anxiety and murmurs. They all turned toward the sound, eyes fixed on the spire.

The cracks that had formed along its intricate patterns were now deepening into a network of fractures, spreading like wildfire. Pieces of the spire began to fall away, but each fragment was sucked into the vortex surrounding the dagger.

"The hell is happening to it?" Bennett asked, still in the process of stripping off Elijah's gear.

"It's almost like it's imploding," Sutton added, his voice low with awe and fear.

The spire seemed to collapse inward, its grooves glowing faintly with residual energy, as if the structure could no longer contain the force within. The glow intensified, a low hum filling the air, a vibration everyone could feel deeply in their bones.

Still dazed but aware of the danger, Elijah watched with horror and fascination. The entity within him was silent, but something told him that wouldn't last. The spire finally collapsed into a small, fiery orb.

The orb grew brighter and began to move toward the group, slagging the ground beneath it. But the light was so intense that every soldier shielded their eyes or turned away. As they braced themselves against the unknown, a force swept over them like a gust from an explosion. There was no heat, wind, or sound—just an impossibly bright light that enveloped everything for what seemed less than a heartbeat.

Then, as suddenly as it came, the light vanished with a soft, delicate pop, leaving an eerie quiet lingering in the air.

When they turned back, the spire was gone. In its place was the strangest sight they had ever seen. Just in front of them were liquefied remains of the ground and above it, floating, was a diminutive creature—a stark contrast to the destruction created.

No larger than the palm of one's hand, the creature fluttered about with delicate wings that flickered with iridescent purple hues. Her pointed ears framed a face bearing a smug expression, and her burning flame of hair stood in contrast to the molten ground below, which began to cool and reform as if her mere presence commanded the chaos in order.

"Mmmm. Freedom," the creature moaned in delight, stretching as she showed herself to be something akin to a fairy.

But her smug grin turned into a toothy one, revealing jagged, razor-like teeth as she spotted Elijah. "Well done, mortal!" The fairy creature chirped happily, bolting past the soldiers to hover before the medic.

Elijah's heart hammered against his ribcage, both from the creature's sudden proximity and the intensity of the situation. Despite her small size, he could feel the power emanating from her through their bond.

The soldiers instinctively readied their weapons, but none could get a clear shot with the small creature so close to Elijah.

"You have unbound me," the creature chirped, her singsong voice belied the danger behind her shark-toothed smile. "A deed neither small nor simple. I owe you a debt, *Elijah*."

The soldiers and marines stiffened at the fact that they could understand the being and at the mention of Elijah's name. The creature's knowledge hinted at an unseen connection between her and their medic.

Elijah swallowed hard, his mind racing with questions about what had just transpired and what this entity wanted. Deep in his thoughts, he sensed an unspoken covenant forming—an unsettling feeling that, if he were to ask who she was or how she knew his name, a strange contract would etch itself into his memory.

Zipping around his face, the fairy inspected him, closely, her face filled with befuddlement. "It's quite surprising that mortals were able to break my bindings," she mused before giggling. "I suppose I should thank you properly!"

"W-What? No, no, no! I'm fine!" Elijah waved his hands in denial, trying to edge away.

"Oh heavens, no. That won't do!" Her grin widened. An even more vicious smile spread across her face. "I can't let my slav—I mean, savior go unrewarded!" Another evil giggle escaped her lips.

Everyone stared in shock as the scene played out. "Hehehe! Don't worry, little one!" The fairy zipped right in front of Elijah's face. "I wOn'T HuRt YoU." Her voice distorted, and her eyes flashed brightly.

Elijah threw up his hands, bracing himself.

But nothing happened.

"Huh?" The fairy stared in confusion. She cast the spell again, placing her hand on his head. "Why won't it work?!"

Elijah immediately tried to swat her away, but she teleported to the other side of his head, casting another brilliant flash. He swung at her repeatedly, but the fairy simply dodged each time.

"Is this empty?! Hellooo?" she yelled, bonking Elijah on the forehead with her fist. "Is anyone in there?!"

BONK! BONK!

Every comrade around him seemed to be in complete disbelief as they stared at the spectacle, but Elijah grew increasingly frustrated as he flailed at her. But the fairy dodged each swing with the same bewildered look.

"Can you fuck off already?!" Elijah yelled, drawing his pistol.

"Rude! I'm trying to do you a favor, you idiot!" the fairy retorted, hands on her hips. "I don't know what this 'fuck' means, but it sounds rude!" she reprimanded with a pout and turned away. "You're rude!"

Sutton turned to Coleman with a bewildered look. "What the hell is happening?"

"I don't know," Coleman replied, still staring at the surreal scene before him. "Don't ask me."

Elijah gripped his pistol tightly, his mind racing for a way to get rid of the menace. She was small and impossibly quick, so drawing on her was out of the question, but he was still determined.

"Okay, okay." Elijah took a deep breath to calm his frayed nerves. He holstered his pistol in a gesture of peace. "I apologize for that. It's just a lot to take in. Can we start over?"

The fairy's countenance shifted as her wings slowed their flutter, the iridescence dimming to a soft glow. "Hmm. I suppose I could forgive you," she mused. "Very well, but first, as your patron and master, you must tell me how you're resisting my mind spell."

That's when a thought struck him.

"Sure. Yeah, I can do that," Elijah replied, the gears turning in his head.

Bennett raised an eyebrow, fully aware that Elijah was lying and about to pull some bullshit like he usually did. "This son of a bitch," he muttered under his breath, reading his body language. The engineer knew *exactly* what this devious bastard was going to do.

A cruel smile formed on Elijah's face as he put a little distance between himself and his so-called patron. "Here, I just need you to float in place."

"Like this?" the fairy asked, glancing at her body to ensure she was doing as instructed.

"Yeah, like that."

Suddenly, the sharp crack of a gunshot rang out as the small being exploded into chunks of gore.

Chapter 23

While everyone in the encampment had fallen deafeningly quiet, Bennett decided to roll with the absurdity and voiced his thoughts. "The mere fact that something so stupid worked pisses me off," the engineer muttered, flicking a tiny hand off his sleeve.

Elijah let out a smug huff as he jammed his pistol back into his holster.

Coleman stood completely stunned, staring at what was left of the fairy, unable to fully accept what had just happened. The thing had exploded in a dramatic fashion, showering everyone in its proximity with strange, bloodless gore.

"Is this what happens when you do DMT?" Sutton remarked, entirely at a loss for words. He had trained nearly all his life to think on his feet and handle any situation—except this. There was a limit to what they were prepared for, and this was *far* beyond that threshold. "Because I get the feeling these are the kind of things Joe Rogan sees when he keeps talking about DMT."

"Actually, I feel like this is some Men in Black shit." The brown-skinned, bald SEAL from earlier pulled his neck gaiter down, revealing a scruffy face. "We should probably get this idiot back to quarantine or something." He pointed a thumb at Elijah, who was still being treated by the SEAL's corpsman.

Elijah shot the bald man a glare that could curdle milk. "Fuck you, Mack! How the hell was I supposed to know I was making a deal with some psycho fairy?!" he snapped, the smugness from before wiped away by sheer exasperation. "Goddammit, now those fuckin' nerds are gonna start poking and prodding at me like I'm some kind of mutant rat!"

Mack simply shrugged, a smirk on his face that said this really wasn't his problem. "Hey, I'm not the one with space AIDS. Shoulda thought about that before you started fucking around with the spire."

"Shut your marginalized Mr. Clean lookin' ass up," Elijah retorted, snapping his head at the shiny-headed man, followed by a colorful slew of profanities, each one more inventive than the last. Everyone started to chuckle, but a low, dangerous snarl abruptly cut off the medic from the SEAL platoon's corpsman.

"Stop. Moving." The corpsman's quiet voice carried the authority that made even a hard-headed operative like Elijah pause mid-rant.

Elijah flinched away from the corpsman, who glared at him with zero tolerance for his antics. "We don't know what that spire or that goddamn fairy did to you, so stop hopping around like a dipshit when I'm trying to make sure you don't drop dead from magic fuckery," the corpsman snapped back, forcing Elijah to hold still. "You're a goddamn medic. You should fucking know these things," the SEAL grumbled as he went back to his work.

Having witnessed the entire exchange, Bennett walked over and gave Elijah an insufferable smirk. "Well, well, well. How the turntables."

The stupid reference caused Elijah's eye to flick up at the engineer in irritation, but he couldn't retaliate without drawing the ire of the corpsman, who was checking his vitals.

"Yeah, laugh it up," Elijah shot back with a scowl. "You're just jealous you didn't get to shoot Tinkerbell."

An incredulous look formed on Bennett's face as he shook his head. "Yeah, no thanks. I'd rather eat a turd than deal with whatever cosmic voodoo bullshit you've just signed up for."

A disgruntled huff of air escaped Elijah as he finally sat upright. The corpsman gave him a difficult look as he finished checking his vitals. "I don't know what the fuck is wrong with you." The corpsman stood up and walked away. "Keep your cosmic AIDS away from me. This is the eggheads' problem now."

Coleman watched the exchange with a mix of amusement and concern. He rubbed the bridge of his nose, feeling the weight of command heavy on his shoulders. With a deep breath, he turned to Sutton, who was already looking his way. Both men wore complex expressions.

"We should update Warmonger," Coleman stated with much less confidence than an army special forces officer should. They need the full picture, especially after this fairy fiasco.

Sutton nodded in agreement. "Yeah. This is completely out of both of our pay grades," he muttered before turning around and walking off to organize and oversee the entrenchment of their new beachhead.

Coleman sighed, reaching for his radio's push-to-talk. With a click of the transmit button, the special forces major spoke clearly and concisely.

"Warmonger, this is Baron. Sitrep as follows." He paused, glancing at Elijah, who was busy putting his gear back on. "Post-encounter with the anomaly resulted in the structural collapse of the spire and the manifestation of an unidentified entity."

As the fuss around the medic started to get louder, Coleman turned toward the imploded pillar. "Entity has been neutralized, but we potentially have someone compromised by unknown variables," he continued, observing the slagged rockets that had finally cooled.

"Request immediate medevac for assessment and containment. How copy, over?"

"Warmonger copies all. We were watching. Wait one."

While Coleman waited for HQ's reply, he scanned the perimeter, his push-to-talk in hand. The aftereffects of the day's chaos had left the area looking like something out of a nightmare, with a gaping dark hole where the spire had once stood.

But the landscape around the absent structure was fascinating. Whatever that spire was, it looked like it had suddenly and violently erupted from the ground, scarring the area.

The radio crackled to life again, and Warmonger's voice returned with instructions. "Baron, Warmonger. CBRN medevac en route, ETA five mikes. Maintain security of the area and report the compromised individual's current status. Over."

Coleman glanced at Elijah, now under the watchful eyes of his teammates, ensuring he didn't exacerbate any unknown condition he might have contracted. "Compromised individual is stable, with no visible signs of physical trauma," he replied, looking down into the void left by the spire. "Casualty is exhibiting no immediate symptoms but may have exposure to unknown anomalous effects. Over."

"Roger that, Baron. Keep us updated on any changes. Secure any intel gathered for debriefing upon return. Warmonger out."

With the medevac on its way, Coleman stepped down from his vantage point and made his way back to the team, already going over every detail they would need to report. The paperwork and debriefings involved with this fiasco weighed on him like a ten-ton boulder.

"At least there's no way this day can be even more of a clusterfuck," Coleman mumbled as he rejoined his team. "Alright, shitheads, let's make sure everything's ready for when the bird lands. And someone, keep an eye on Eli—" The words got caught in Coleman's mouth as he stared at Elijah wide-eyed.

Marked by confusion, Elijah looked around as everyone shared Coleman's shocked expression, slowly backing away. "What? What's wrong? Am I growing a third arm?" He looked around and finally noticed the figure perched on his shoulder.

"Hmm," a familiar voice hummed as she bounced her leg over the other. "You mortals can see me? How fascinating," she murmured, intrigued. "Clever too..."

A deafening silence swept over the encampment as everyone stared at a being who, just a few minutes ago, blew into chunks of flesh. The silence shattered when the little creature blinked in front of Elijah's face the moment he stood up, wrapping his face in a wide hug with both hands.

"Holy shit—*AHH!*" Elijah yelped, flailing as he tripped over his med pack.

"I like my servants clever!" the fairy shouted joyously before a vicious cackle escaped her mouth. "Hahaha! Such potential!"

The fairy's laughter echoed through the encampment, reverberating off the debris and remaining structures, sending a shiver down the spine of every soldier present. With her hands still clasped to Elijah's face, a distorted chant resounded, reverberating like an amplified song.

Suddenly, within a blink of an eye, strange marks etched themselves into the ground across the entire encampment. The soldiers, trained and disciplined as they were, instinctively backed away, shielding their eyes from the blinding light emanating from a massive, pulsating glyph beneath their feet.

"AHAHAHAHAHA!" A manic expression painted the fairy's face as she cackled. "You'll make such a promising apostle!" it screeched, concluding that whatever this mortal was must have been extremely powerful to resist the effects of soul magic.

But as one second turned to two, the glyph burned brighter and brighter. "AHAHAHahahaha. Ha. Wait..." A note of concern slipped into the fairy's voice.

Looking around, she noticed that not only was her energy being funneled into the binding spell, but it was also being sucked into the landscape on the other side of the poorly constructed gateway. As a matter of fact, her power was being consumed at an alarming rate.

And it was only accelerating significantly.

"Waitwaitwaitwaitwait!" the thing yelled, trying to stop whatever was happening, but unfortunately, it was far too late.

"NONONONONONONO. Wait! Wait! Wait!" the fairy screamed as she saw her own stolen power flowing out from the world around her. "I didn't mean to bind an entire world!"

Panic filled the tiny being as nearly every ounce of her power drained into the insatiable maw of the glyph. The light became so blinding that none of the soldiers could look directly at it.

"Shut it off! Shut it off!" the fairy screeched, her voice losing its melodic quality, now sharp with fear as she realized the mortal she was trying to bind wasn't from this reality.

By this time, the fairy had already released Elijah and floated up to witness eons of power being consumed by another reality. But as soon as it started, the spell stopped and winked out of existence, causing the fairy to drop out of the air and land directly on Elijah's face.

"Oof!" she yelped in pain before scrambling to her feet.

Elijah, in the process of sitting upright, looked in shock and fear. Checking his body, he saw that he was intact and wasn't growing any extra limbs. However, he also caught sight of an angry-looking fairy with fiery hair standing on his abdomen.

"Y-You!" she shouted, jabbing a finger at his face. "Give it back! Gimme back my power!"

"What the fuck just happened?" Elijah groaned, rubbing the back of his head. He chose to ignore the fairy hovering nearby, wings beating and looked at his comrades, who were also recovering from their stupor.

"You didn't tell me you were from another world! You didn't tell me you weren't from this reality!" she whined, zipping over to Elijah's head and beating on it with her tiny fists. "Gimme it back, gimme it back, gimme it back, gimme it back, you thief!"

Again, Elijah waved his hand in an attempt to swat the annoying thing away from him, fully expecting her to teleport to the other side of his head. But he was surprised when his hand actually connected with her tiny body, sending her rocketing toward the ground.

"Oof!" the fairy cried out as she bounced off the ground, cartwheeling a full meter before coming to a stop facedown. The fairy thing lay still for nearly a minute before finally stirring and struggling to get up.

Bennett, squinting and rubbing his eyes, clutched his weapon tightly with his dominant hand as he scowled. "What the fuck just happened?!" The engineer then looked his body over to ensure he was in one piece.

The other soldiers and marines, all checking themselves for injuries, were equally stunned. Meanwhile, Elijah was still fending off the determined little nuisance. "You." The fairy, wobbling on her tiny legs with tears in her eyes, pointed accusingly at him. "You thief! Why'd you take it all? You took all of it!"

"I only wanted to give you a little bit, but you and your stupid world took it all!" she wailed, yanking at his hair. "Gimme it, baaack!"

Elijah winced as the belligerent fairy grabbed a handful of hair under his helmet. Fed up, he reached up and grabbed her, causing her to squirm. "Can you *stop?*" he demanded, glaring at the tiny, snarling gremlin.

"You can't do this to me! I'm a goddess! A real one!" the fairy protested, trying to resist his grip "I curse you! I'll damn you! I'll eat your soul! I'm a goddess, ya know?!"

Never in all his years had Elijah wanted to squeeze the life out of something so small until he ran into this insufferable little terror. It amazed him how something so cute could be so annoying, troublesome, and, most of all, persistent.

"How about I just break every bone in your body—Ow, fuck!" Elijah tried to threaten the tiny thing, but she retaliated by biting his hand with her razor-sharp teeth.

By reflex, Elijah flinched and released her, only for her to bite again, this time at his face. He cocked his arm back and let loose a full-powered punch, connecting and sending her hurtling toward the ground.

"GWAK!" the fairy yelped as she crashed into a small pile of rocks.

With an audible crack, the poor fairy slumped over, her neck twisted at an unnatural angle as she stared lifelessly at her attacker. Elijah, however, wasn't fooled as he waited for the damn thing to come back.

"Status!" Sutton yelled into his headset, his voice cutting through the chaos and snapping everyone to attention. Momentarily stunned by the surreal events, the rangers, marines, and SEALs fell into formation, their training overcoming the shock.

Meanwhile, a strange pop resounded as the supposed goddess regained her form and charged at Eljah's face at full speed, her choppers at the ready. The Fairy growled, biting his hand again.

"Are you all okay?!" Coleman shouted to the team, ignoring Elijah's struggle as he flailed in the air, swatting at his attacker.

Both Bennett and Schwarz just stared at the bizarre scene of Elijah comically dancing around in disbelief. This whole thing felt like a twisted joke some weirdo was playing, yet here they were.

Glancing down, the engineer started pinching himself in different spots to see if he might be dreaming or in some kind of coma, but each pinch brought only disappointment.

"Nah, this is some PCP shit," Lister, the team's weapon sergeant, muttered, straightening up. "What the fuck is next? We see some kind of—"

"No, shut the fuck up!" Coleman snapped, raising a hand to cut him off. "Not another fucking word. You know damn well *anything* is on the table now, and your dumb ass is going to manifest it!"

Suddenly, the evil cackles of their medic resounded, causing everyone to look at him again. "Ha! Got you!" Elijah yelled out, grabbing hold of the tiny, winged Fairy with a rag he randomly found and wrapping it tightly around his hand.

The fairy ignored the man's every word as she continued to try to bite down, but unfortunately, her teeth weren't long enough to fully penetrate the cloth.

"Let me go, you—! You thief!" she yelled, struggling. "I'm your patron! I'm your goddess! You should obey my every order!"

Realizing he couldn't kill her, Elijah's brain went into overdrive, desperate to find a solution. "Look, can we talk? Let's talk," he pleaded at his wit's end. "Let's give peace a chance and talk like rational beings, okay?"

Seeing no other option without her soul magic or any other way to threaten this mortal, the Fairy tilted her head, pouting at Elijah. "Okay, fine," she said reluctantly.

Elijah looked around to see his team and the remaining soldiers keeping their distance. Their silent message was that he was on his own, and they were staying exactly where they were—far away from *that* thing.

Worry etched the medic's face as he took a deep breath. With a heavy sigh, Elijah deliberated on what to do, but he knew sooner or later he would have to let this thing go. After a few minutes, he finally loosened his grip, allowing the fairy to hover in place as he waited for her inevitable attack.

Elijah exhaled a deep sigh of relief as the immediate chaos seemed to subside, the adrenaline ebbing from his veins. "All right. Can you explain what just—Ow, fuck!" His question was abruptly interrupted by a set of sharp teeth sinking into his hand.

Elijah's attempt at peace and resolution had failed; the tiny being had bit his hand once again.

"Peace was never an option!" she declared, her tiny teeth chomping down relentlessly.

Chapter 24

Yzael was walking down the strange, bright hallway of a heavily guarded healer's building when her hand unconsciously slid onto her abdomen, where she had been wounded.

By all accounts, she should have died from such an injury, but the marvels of this magicless world had pulled her back from the brink. The fabric of her tunic, foreign yet adapted from materials given to her by the local healers, was smooth under her dainty fingers—a stark contrast to the roughness of her battle-worn gear. She paused, her eyes reflecting a turmoil of gratitude and disorientation. This world, so starkly different from hers, had seemed a crucible of survival, yet it felt more akin to her homeland's academies or healing houses.

She glanced back at her escort, a stern yet not unkind soldier trailing behind her, holding his strange, tiny black staff in a relaxed manner. He was one of many wardens she'd had, but this man occasionally struck up conversations, only to fall silent in frustration after remembering they couldn't understand each other.

However, that slowly started to change after her many encounters with this world's scholars. Yzael could now manage simple conversations, eroding the language barrier a bit more each day. This was partly due to the natural inclination of high elves toward scholarly or magical endeavors, though Yzael herself had always had an ear for languages. It was a necessary skill in her line of work, where contracts and alliances were as varied as the realms themselves.

Yet the tongues of this world were intricate in a challenging and frustrating way. English, as it was called, seemed to have many unnecessary or even contradictory rules, often feeling like arcane spells written in the shifting sands of the Wailing Dunes. Yzael had discovered that context was as crucial as the words themselves here and that tone nuance could alter a phrase's meaning entirely.

A voice suddenly called from behind her and her escort. "Hey Mike, babysitting again?"

They both stopped and the escort—apparently named Mike—shot the newcomer with a weary look. "Yeah, pretty much," he admitted, rubbing his eyes. "You know, when Brass said we'd be overseeing a bunch of magicians or something, I figured they'd be all fire and brimstone, trying to escape or hex us. But look at them." He gestured loosely to Yzael and then to the others nearby. "More than content just to cooperate and do whatever they're told. It's boring."

Yzael, who had been listening intently, tilted her head in curiosity. Doing something like setting a fire or trying to escape would guarantee her death, and although she was centuries old, she very much liked living. The long-eared woman cleared her throat, drawing Mike's attention. "It would not make sense to make trouble," she said, her English rough but intelligible. "You treat well. I have no path to return." She searched for the right words. "No... no place to go."

Mike's eyebrows shot up in surprise, his posture straightening as he turned fully to face her. "What the fuck? You speak English?" he asked, his voice tinged with newfound respect and a hint of embarrassment for his earlier words.

"I am learning," Yzael affirmed with a small smile. "Your world is... different. But fighting, escaping... not always the path of wisdom."

Silence lingered in the hallway as Mike turned and exchanged a look with the other guard, who seemed equally surprised. "Huh. Well, I'll be damned."

The other guard chuckled, shook his head, and ducked back into the room he was in, leaving Yzael and her escort to their own devices.

A newfound curiosity started to seep into Mike as he scratched his head. "Well, that's impressive," he admitted, rubbing the back of his head. "I didn't expect you folks to pick up on things so quickly." He glanced down the hallway as if ensuring they were alone before leaning in slightly. So, if you don't mind me asking, why cooperate? I mean, if I were in your shoes, I'm not sure I'd be so accommodating."

Yzael considered the question, sensing the depth of what he was truly asking. "In my land, we have a saying," she began, choosing her words carefully. "'To know the river is to avoid the flood.' I am not of my own realm, and your people hold the... um... what is the word?" Yzael furrowed her brow, wracking her brain. "Power! Your people hold the power."

Mike nodded, the lines on his forehead easing as her words sank in. "Makes sense," he conceded. "So, what's your plan, then? You just gonna wait it out, learn what you can, and hope for the best?"

The blending of the words "going to" into "gonna" caught her off guard for a moment, but Yzael's smile turned wistful. "Another saying, 'Even the smallest seed can one day be the largest tree.' I will learn and grow. When the time is right, perhaps I will find my way home. Until then, I will flourish in the soil where I have been planted."

Mike chuckled as he adjusted his weapon to a more comfortable position. "You've got more patience than me, I reckon," he mused, his gaze drifting off. "If I was thrown into some foreign world, I probably wouldn't listen so well."

There was a moment of shared silence before Mike's curiosity piqued again. "You seem pretty smart, so what made you, uh..." He paused, searching for a more tactful way of asking. "Why did you come here, to our world, I mean?"

Yzael stiffened as a grimace started to spread across her face. Anger and disgust welled in her stomach as her eyes dropped to the floor, and for a brief moment, she seemed smaller, burdened by the weight of those she'd lost and those she had yet to find. "I—no, we were tricked," she admitted, her voice a mere whisper. "They said I would be stopping criminals and bandits, not invading."

She had a similar, much more hostile version of this conversation the other day with men and women who saw her as a threat. It had been a trying ordeal that tested her patience and resolve as they pushed her to her limits to see how she would react.

But the conversation was now more approachable. The genuine curiosity and willingness to listen gave her a sliver of hope that understanding might be reached. Although she couldn't blame the others for their suspicion and prodding, it seemed to be their way of making sense of her and her people's sudden appearance.

"I have not been treated with cruelty," Yzael clarified to Mike, a note of earnestness in her voice. "There has been no torture, no violation, no stripping away of my dignity or necessities, so I have no reason to, um, not listen so well?" She turned away to walk back to her room.

Her memory drifted back to the interrogations—their grating, incessant questions that poked at every piece of logic she offered for hours on end. It was exhausting, especially with her command of the language still developing.

As Yzael moved away, her mind inevitably drifted back to Gideon. He had been a steadfast presence in her life for years, a comrade in arms, and his absence now left a hollow space within her.

Many of her kin would call her a fool for feeling so strongly about a presence only there for a fraction of her life, but Yzael had learned that wasn't how relationships worked. Someone could be in your life for mere moments yet impact you deeply. A lesson her people, with longer lifespans and insular ways, hadn't learned.

Many she had known and worked with had fallen or disappeared in the ensuing chaos of their unexpected transition to this world. Gideon had been among those who had vanished in the tumultuous battle that had taken place. The memory of the explosion that had nearly claimed her life was as clear as the bright hallway she now walked. Gideon had pulled her from the brink, finding shelter in a decrepit building as the world outside succumbed to madness.

The hubris of the Sepharic Empire led them there. In a desperate bid for victory, they unleashed a horde of wereman, usually held in check by shamans but now intoxicated through profane rituals and driven into a frenzy. The beasts raged and howled, attacking friend and foe alike as they descended upon the town where Yzael and Gideon took shelter.

She remembered the terror, the acceptance, and then Gideon's eyes. He had that same look of determination when he was about to do something foolish. With a promise of salvation, he disappeared up the stairs of the crumbling building, and that was the last time she had seen him before darkness claimed her.

The next thing Yzael knew was the painful and disorienting white lights searing into her eyes, the cold touch of metal against her skin, the beeping of strange arcane machines, and the sensation of a tube shoved down her throat. They had saved her, yes, but at what cost?

"Where are you?" Yzael whispered as she gazed out of the window, something she found herself doing often these days. She wondered if he was looking up at the same sun from a different corner of this vast, strange world each time. Logic whispered he was likely gone and that she should prepare for that reality. But the heart, especially one beaten for centuries, wasn't so easily swayed by logic, regardless of what her people liked to say.

Yzael held onto the hope that Gideon had somehow survived and that he had escaped the horror of their last stand and found safety. Yet, as days turned into weeks and no word of him reached her ears, that hope began to dim.

Heaving a sigh, Yzael quickened her pace, eager to return to the solitude of her room and the comfort of her own thoughts. As she turned a corner, however, she caught the sight of Emma and Dr. Stenhouse entering a room she had passed dozens of times over. The scholars had been her bridge to understanding this world, and their patience and warmth were a welcome respite from the cold, brutal interrogation rooms.

"Emma! Dr. Stenhouse!" Yzael called out, speeding up to a jog.

The two scholars snapped their heads around and welcomed her with the same warmth she had grown accustomed to. "Yzael!" they shouted, opening their arms into a hug.

As she approached and accepted their odd but intimate greeting, Yzael glanced into the room. Her heart leaped into her throat. Amidst the clinical ambiance was a familiar face marked by a strange black patch over one eye and ears shorter yet equally pointed as hers.

Lysandra.

Yzael froze, eyes locked on her kin. Lysandra had survived. Relief washed over her, and for a moment, she could only stare, taking in the sight of her former commander.

Lysandra turned, and their eyes met. A myriad of emotions passed between them: relief, sorrow, joy, and unspoken questions of how they had both come to be here, in this world so far from home.

"Y-Yzael?" Lysandra's voice was choked, but its strength was undeniable. She stood cautiously, unsure of her body's limits in this place.

Yzael pushed past the scholars and stepped into the room, her previous destination forgotten. "Lysandra, by the heavens, it is you," she whispered, moving closer.

But the sudden barks from the guards stationed in the room broke the reunion's trance. "Stop! Stay where you are!" they ordered sharply, raising their weapons and assessing their situation.

Dr. Stenhouse and Emma quickly intervened, recognizing the tension building in the room. They raised their hands in a calming gesture and moved forward, positioning themselves between the guards and the two elves.

"Please, stand down!" Dr. Stenhouse's voice was authoritative and urgent. "This is a critical moment, a delicate reunion! There's no threat here!"

However, the guards remained resolute, their training taking over. Unmoved by Dr. Stenhouse's plea, they focused solely on maintaining what they perceived to be a secure environment.

"Stay back!" one guard reiterated, his tone leaving no room for negotiation. The other guard, meanwhile, raised her radio, and clicked the button to communicate with the command center.

"Command, we have a situation in the east wing, room seventeen. Possible security breach, over," she reported in a standard, concise manner.

The response immediately crackled through the radio. "Roger that. Maintain your position, reinforcements are en route. Contain the situation. Over."

Emma moved swiftly, placing herself between the guards and Yzael. Her voice was raised in a mix of anger and desperation. "Don't you dare!" she yelled at the soldiers. Her past confrontations with authority had left a sour taste, but none so bitter as this. "She's not your enemy! She's not a lab rat for your sick fucking experiments!"

Mike, however, just stood there, his weapon at the ready. He knew Yzael wasn't the threat they thought she was after his conversation with her, and he remained conflicted. Should he perform his duty, arrest her, and resolve this misunderstanding? Or should he intervene and try to defuse the situation, risking a court martial?

But that all went out the window when Yzael threw up her hands. She felt it, just as Lysandra did—a violent surge of magic rushing through them both, filling their veins with power she hadn't felt since arriving in this foreign world. It was overwhelming, like a dam bursting within her soul. The mana-starved agony she had suffered was now replaced with an excess she couldn't even possibly absorb all at once.

Then, realization struck. Yzael's eyes widened as crackles of fluorescent blue lightning shot from her fingertips, the energy striking the ceiling with a sound like thunder. The room filled with an eerie light, causing everyone to shield their eyes. Shadows danced wildly on the walls. Unprepared for such a display, the soldiers instinctively raised their weapons and fired. Their bullets ricocheted uselessly off the magical shield Yzael had conjured just in time.

"No!" Lysandra screamed, springing into action.

Still a seasoned freelancer and hardened warrior, the elven woman used the influx of mana to empower her movements. She became a whirlwind as she tackled the female soldier, slamming her against the wall with a force that left a crack in the plaster. The soldier's weapon clattered to the ground, sliding far out of reach.

The second soldier tried to pivot his weapon toward the new threat, his finger tensing on the trigger. But Lysandra, with reflexes honed over decades, was quicker. She grabbed the gun's barrel, yanking it downward as the soldier fired, rounds embedding in the floor in a burst of dust and debris. With a swift, fluid motion, she wrenched the weapon from his grasp and swung it like a club, the stock shattering against his head with a crack. The soldier crumpled, dazed, and vulnerable on the ground.

The room fell silent for a heartbeat. The only sounds were the painful ringing from gunfire in an enclosed space and the labored breaths of soldiers and elves alike. Lysandra, her face a mask of fear and regret, let the broken rifle drop from her hands and backed up, pressing her back against the wall. She looked at her comrade, both women wide-eyed, realizing what they had just done.

The door burst open, and heavily armed soldiers flooded the room, their weapons drawn, pointed directly at the two elves.

"Get the fuck on the floor! Show me your goddamn hands!"

Chapter 25

Toivonen sat alone in the conference room, leaning as far back in her office chair as she could manage. Her hands cupped her nose and mouth as if trying to relieve the mounting pressure on her head. Around the wooden table, her staff members sat in varying degrees of unease, occasionally glancing at the ominously ringing cell phone in the center.

The phone, a harsh reminder of the chaos unfolding just beyond the conference room walls, had been ringing incessantly. It lay there, vibrating with yet another unanswered call, its screen displaying a scrollable list of missed calls.

A young facility staff member, new enough not to recognize the peril of approaching Toivonen in this state, cleared his throat. "Ma'am, shouldn't you—"

However, his words were abruptly cut off.

Toivonen's eyes snapped open, fixing the man with a glare that was as sharp as any knife, though deceptively calm. Her look carried a not-so-subtle threat that if he dared finish that sentence, his next of kin would soon receive notice of his sudden and inexplicable demise.

The man clammed up immediately and looked away while the black, featureless phone continued to buzz, echoing the tension in the room. Each staff member exchanged uneasy, knowing glances with a mixture of fear and relief that they weren't the ones in the hot seat.

The silence deepened, punctuated only by the phone's persistent ringing. It was a tense, almost oppressive quiet, filled with unspoken thoughts of the staff members and the palpable stress emanating from Toivonen.

Finally, as if responding to the collective anticipation, the phone stopped clamoring. Almost in relief, the staff let out a collective sigh, only for the device to spark back to life, its shrill tone demanding attention again.

This time, without a word, Toivonen slowly reached out and grasped the phone. She brought it to her ear with a resigned slowness that betrayed her inner reluctance. "Toivonen," she answered crisply, the single word signaling her readiness to take control of the conversation, regardless of the tirade that might follow.

"The fuck is going on over there?!" The voice was loud enough that snippets of the outburst traveled across the room, the caller's anger unmistakable.

A stream of obscenities followed, painting the air blue. Toivonen listened in silence, resting her elbows on the table and pinching the bridge of her nose. Her leg, however, bounced up and down, causing her heel to click against the floor in a rhythmic, agitated pattern.

"No, sir." Her voice cut through the tirade with surgical precision. "Yes, sir. Understood, sir."

The room was utterly silent now, save for the one-sided conversation. Each "sir" punctuated Toivonen's grasp on professionalism despite the storm of profanities coming from the other end.

The staff dared not move, their eyes carefully avoiding Toivonen in fear of being drawn into whatever hell was unfolding. They could only imagine the verbal barrage their stoic superior was enduring, each terse reply a testament to her restraint.

"Yes, sir, we'll—" Toivonen's words were cut short by the abrupt click of the line going dead. She sighed deeply, one hand sliding to cover her eyes, the other propping up her head, her elbow resting heavily on the table. The room held its breath, the staff members frozen in a tableau of anticipation and dread.

After a moment that stretched too long, she finally spoke, her subdued voice echoing through the room like a bomb. "Prepare for the director's arrival," she said, causing everyone to stiffen.

A senior staff member, a man who'd been part of the most adverse operations in the Middle East and Eastern Europe, let out a low, nearly inaudible "Fuck." It was a word that seemed to resonate with the collective sentiment of the room, a succinct summary of their situation.

But as they stood to get to work, their personal devices blared, indicating an incident in the interrogation room that required all hands.

* * *

Yzael found herself in quite a predicament.

Darkness engulfed her world as the pitch-black burlap sack over her head blocked any glimpse of her surroundings. But the rough fabric scratching against her skin wasn't the only reminder of her ordeal in Lysandra's room. No, the ominous sac was joined by a gag in her mouth that prevented her from casting spells and tight iron shackles that forced her hands behind her back, preventing any gestures.

This wasn't a completely foreign experience, though. As a high elven academic student, she and another rather rambunctious peer had delved into arcane knowledge that was frowned upon, if not outright forbidden. It was a time of reckless curiosity, driven by a hunger to push their magical limits.

As her mind wandered, a mix of nostalgia and distraction, she recalled secret meetings under the veil of night, the thrill of exploring uncharted magical territories, and the frantic escapes as staff chased them throughout the school. The two troublemakers explored perilous methods of magic.

While Yzael herself pursued the forbidden arts of manipulating mana, pushing the boundaries of what was deemed safe or permissible by their elders, her academic colleague chose other specialties.

Wracking her brain to remember her name, Yzael could only remember the ambitious, redheaded woman who was always more daring than prudent and had a particular fascination with witchcraft. She viewed it not as the profane art most believed it to be but as an untapped well of potential. Together, they experimented with incantations whispered in hushed tones—spells that could tap into the banished fae Goddess's essence.

What fun they had, pushing the limits of their abilities, reveling in the raw power they could summon. Their experiments, often teetering on the edge of control, drew them into a world of arcane secrets and mystical discoveries. The red-haired high elf, whose name still eluded Yzael, was a whirlwind of energy and ambition, always eager to push further to unravel the next mystery.

It didn't take long for them to leave their studies behind and venture out into the world, but eventually, their paths diverged as their interests deepened. Yzael focused more on the refined control of mana, seeking to understand and master its practical application as a freelancer. Her colleague, on the other hand, delved deeper into witchcraft and the powers that drove the hells, drawn to the wild and untamed aspects of magic, which often left Yzael both in awe and concerned.

Now, in the darkness of her captivity, Yzael drew upon those memories, those experiences from a past long gone. The knowledge she had gained during those heady days of forbidden study might be her only key to escape. Without the ability to chant or gesture, she would have to rely on her magic's more subtle, intrinsic aspects.

After the unfortunate events that may or may not have led to the death of two human warriors, her demise seemed increasingly likely. Yzael focused on her breathing, calming her racing heart and channeling her thoughts inward. She sought to tap into the raw, untamed mana she had once toyed with, now coursing through a world flooded with strange energy. It was a dangerous game that required immense concentration and control—especially without the usual outlets of spoken words and hand movements.

Channeling her focus, Yzael began the slow, meticulous process of drawing mana around her.

Energy started to course through her, reigniting a faint glimmer of hope so long as she maintained control.

Gradually, she directed the mana towards the burlap sack over her head, feeling the energy accumulate at a small point. With a metal push, she released it in a controlled burst, causing the fabric to smolder and singe, creating a tiny hole. The faint light that filtered through was a welcome sight—a small victory in her dire situation.

Peering through the hole, Yzael surveyed and recognized her surroundings. She was in the same gray and featureless room they'd interrogated her in. Her eyes turned to the large mirror stretching across one wall; it was clearly a two-way. Her people had used similar setups to observe students, which meant she was probably being watched.

Realizing she had to take a risk, Yzael decided to act. She needed more visibility to work on her shackles, which meant removing the sack entirely. Bracing herself, she focused her mana again, directing it toward the burlap fabric.

With a subtle manipulation of her energy, she increased the

intensity of the burn until the fabric smoldered away. Yzael shook her head free, ignoring a few singed strands of her silver hair as she blinked against the sudden influx of light.

Standing up cautiously, Yzael scanned the room. The mirror was silent; no sounds or movements indicated the presence of observers. After a tense moment of waiting, she seemed alone for the time being.

A small, triumphant smile crossed her lips. "Wonderful," she whispered, a mix of relief and satisfaction in her voice. It was a small victory, but in her current situation, any victory counted. "Perhaps they've gone to lunch."

She then examined the intricate shackles binding her wrists. Unlike the simple iron bands of her world that she could just break with a spell, these were complex, with a locking mechanism requiring a key. Physically breaking them seemed nearly impossible without injury, so she had to sit down and attempt a more delicate magical manipulation.

She carefully sat, positioning herself to access the handcuffs. Closing her eyes, Yzael focused her mana on the lock mechanism. She had to be precise, as the slightest mistake could set her back or, worse, trigger a mechanism to tighten the cuffs.

Yzael visualized the inner workings of the cuffs as her senses extended through her mana, feeling the pins and tumblers inside. She gently nudged and tapped, seeking the slightest movement, but her eyes shot open at a faint click. All she did was apply pressure to the mechanism holding onto the teeth and felt it click a little looser.

"Huh," she murmured, staring at her now-free hand in a mix of disbelief and relief. "That was simple." She stood and cautiously tested the door. As she instinctively suspected, it was locked.

With one hand now free, Yzael studied the unfamiliar lock, a mechanism more akin to goblin engineering than anything she knew.

In her world, doors were often reinforced with enchantments or relied on basic latches requiring rudimentary keys. This modern deadbolt and sophisticated locking system were new to her, almost like a new puzzle—one she didn't have time for, though.

Extending her free hand, Yzael focused her mana on the lock and, with a subtle gesture, applied a shearing force. A loud snap resounded as the deadbolt gave way, and the door drifted open. She cautiously poked her head out, preparing to cast a barrier spell in case one of the guards was waiting to end her little foray.

But to her surprise, the hallway was empty. The usual hustle and bustle of the facility's guards and staff had given way to an eerie emptiness and silence, which only added to her unease. As Yzael stepped out, she heightened her senses, alert to any surprises.

With twitching ears listening for the faintest noise, she moved cautiously, mulling over the thought that she might be walking into a trap. But at the same time, people as logical and meticulous as her captors wouldn't rely on contrivances if they intended to capture or kill her.

If they truly wanted to end her, they would have truly done so from the start, or at least gagged and bound her in the interrogation room. "No, there must be something else at play," she murmured, hand outstretched as she peered around another corner. "Maybe something had happened that caused an evacuation?"

The thought lingered in Yzael's mind as she navigated the corridors. Her elven instincts told her that something significant must have occurred to cause such a drastic change in the facility's usual rhythm—an evacuation, a lockdown, a security breach, or maybe a renewed attack.

There were numerous possibilities, and none of them offered any real comfort.

As she ventured deeper, her thoughts snapped back to the present with the faint sounds of shouting and a scuffle down the hall. Despite the danger, Yzael threw caution to the wind, taking off at a run. Her heart pounded with dread, hoping Lysandra wasn't the epicenter of this conflict. After Gideon's disappearance, she couldn't bear the loss of another ally—not here, not now.

Ignoring the cold tile floor on her bare feet, Yzael ran through the corridors and approached the noise, bracing herself against the familiar yet particular sensation of a powerful, ancient, arcane energy in the air. It reminded her of the forbidden arts she had once studied, sending her instincts into overdrive.

Yzael's senses screamed at her to turn away and run back to that tiny room she had crawled out of, but her curiosity got the better of her as she peered around the corner. There, she saw a column of soldiers clad in armor with large shields raised to form a formidable wall. Their uniforms, blotched in irregular patterns designed for camouflage, featured peculiar face coverings. With prominent, transparent lenses for a wide field of vision and filters resembling snouts, masks lent them a mythical, beast-like appearance.

"Ma'am, we don't want to hurt you! Please walk out—" the lead soldier shouted, glancing back at an unarmored figure who stood with a look of disdain. "Float out with your hands up!"

"Bro, she's going to fuck all y'all up," the unarmed soldier warned with a chuckle. "I've killed this fucking menace probably ten times over. What the hell do you even think you're going to do?"

Yzael's curiosity deepened after the cryptic statement. The casual mention of killing someone multiple times puzzled her. Death, in her world, was final. Only gods could claim multiple lives.

Was this a figure of speech or an exaggeration? Or some darker magic or technology?

Her thoughts were interrupted by a loud thump as one of the soldiers shot a canister into the room, releasing a thick, billowing smoke. At the lead's command, the soldiers advanced with their strange staffs, shields, and club-like weapons.

Yzael instinctively recoiled, pulling her head back as the canister discharged its contents. She recognized that similar tactics were used to flush out more entrenched foes, such as kobolds and scroungers.

Tucked away in the corner, Yzael debated her next move. Whoever was inside the room was unlikely to be Lysandra, considering one of the otherworlders had evidently "killed" them. Still, the arcane energy lingered, tempting her with the mystery.

Shaking her head, Yzael turned to continue searching for her commander. Her primary concern was Lysandra's safety, and the faster she found the good commander, the faster they'd get out of there.

But just as she was about to turn away, the sounds of pain and yelling reverberated through the halls, drawing her attention back to the scene. Yzael cautiously peeked around the corner to see a chaotic retreat of soldiers stumbling over one another in disarray.

The soldiers who had confidently entered the room moments ago were now scrambling to get out. Their gear was shredded and bore light, magical wounds from burns, frost marks, and electrical scorching. It was clear they'd been on the receiving end of a powerful, varied, magical onslaught.

"Tried to tell you," the unarmed soldier said, fanning his face as the smoke leaked out.

CHAPTER 26

"Apostle!" the little fairy snapped angrily, buzzing out of the interrogation room. "How could you just stand there and allow these stupid... *stupids* to treat me in such a manner?!" She pointed an accusatory finger at her claimed human, her voice indignant.

However, Elijah stood there, unimpressed, as the military police in riot gear flailed helplessly to extinguish the strange fire or swat away the ice spreading over them. "Can you put them out, please?" he asked, pinching the bridge of his nose. "Things are gonna get really complicated for me if any of them actually get hurt or die."

However, the great Yanaiyániuoa's face contorted more angrily. "Those idiots insulted me with their stupid questions! I'm a goddess! A real goddess! Not one of those pathetic pretenders who need mortals to keep praying to them!" She barked with shrill indignation. "They should be bowing, worshiping, and offering tributes—not daring to question my divine presence!"

Elijah's expression was hollow, his gaze blank as he looked at the tiny goddess. The entire day had felt like a horrible, drug-fueled hallucination—one he couldn't escape.

"Okay, look, Yana," Elijah said. "You need—"

"*Yana?!*" the goddess bellowed, her eyes flaring with violet fire as she hovered before Elijah. Her tiny form radiated a fierce energy that belied her size. "How dare you! Do you not understand the disrespect you show to my divine being with such casual familiarity?!"

Elijah remained unfazed, staring at her with a leveled gaze. "Look," he huffed, placing a hand on his head to dispel his headache, "by your own admission, you've lost most of your power." Agitation flared in his voice. "And somehow, you've managed to drag me into whatever bullshit... this is!" He gestured around as the soldiers struggled in the hallway, frantically slapping at small patches of fire that ignited on their gear or brushing off chunks of ice that had kept springing up on their armor.

But worst of all, the hallway beyond was a scene of destruction—scorch marks marred the walls, bullet holes poked the surface, and concussive forces shattered sections of the structure.

"So we!" Elijah gestured aggressively to himself and Yana before continuing, "And I mean, *we* are not exactly in a position to demand anything right now! So, could you please stop doing whatever it is you're doing to them?"

Yanaiyániuoa hovered before him, arms folded, a snarl on her face. "Hmph," she huffed, turning her head haughtily. With a flick of her hand, she dispelled the creeping flames and ice that plagued the soldiers. "Annoying! I have the most annoying mortal ever!"

As her magic unraveled, Yanaiyániuoa grumbled, "And this stupid world! Why don't my curses and soul magic work on any of you?! It's stupid! Stupid, stupid, stupid!"

"Fuck off before she changes her mind," Elijah said to the soldiers as the chaos from the fairy's magic subsided. "And tell the spooks to stop sending fucking MPs down here! Nothing you're gonna do is gonna work!" He pointed to the section leader with his entire hand. "Just let me talk to her, okay?"

The MPs, still regaining their composure, regarded Elijah with a blend of relief and apprehension. The captain, a veteran of high-stress situations, appeared out of his depth but gave a firm nod.

"Understood," the captain replied, his tone betraying both his reluctance to leave the matter unresolved and his eagerness to avoid further conflict with this fairy. "This shit is way above our pay grade anyway."

Elijah exhaled deeply as the soldiers regrouped and retreated, casting uneasy glances at the fairy. Once they'd disappeared around the corner, Elijah turned to face Yanaiyániuoa, still hovering with her arms folded with an indignant expression. "Yana," he called out calmly, "we really need to work together on this. I know it's frustrating not to be worshiped or whatever anymore but causing a scene like this isn't helping."

The little goddess' eye twitched at the casual shortening of her name as she continued to glare daggers at her human. "You are the *worst* apostle ever," she hissed. "I give you my divine blessings and authority, and this is how you treat me?!"

"Gift?" Elijah raised an eyebrow, meeting her heated gaze. "Yana, this is a gift I neither asked for nor wanted," he replied with a hint of exasperation and a roll of his eyes.

"You!" Yanaiyániuoa's arms shot out in anger. "You ungrateful little human!" she exclaimed in outrage. "You should be honored to even be in my presence!"

As the two bickered, Yzael watched from a distance, her face a mix of disbelief and fascination. The fairy just down the hall was supposedly an all-powerful being, straight out of ancient tomes and lore—entities scholars warned against dabbling in.

But here she was, staring at Yanaiyániuoa—a goddess from before the earliest records of high elven society. Seeing this being, albeit diminutive and in a petty squabble, was nothing short of astonishing.

While Yzael was absorbing the fact she was staring at a living, breathing deity squabble with some mortal, the elf decided to enhance her perception and see if she could glean anything interesting. She whispered an incantation, "Súlë Níra," under her breath. Known as the Eye of the Star, it amplified her vision to perceive magical energies otherwise invisible. Her eyes shimmered momentarily as the spell took effect, granting her a deeper view of the world.

And with that, any lingering doubt vanished. The mana in the air, the residual energies from the fairy's outburst, matched the ancient magics Yzael had studied in secret.

Meanwhile, Yanaiyániuoa continued her tirade. "You're such a stupid, stupid head! So stupid that you don't even realize the grandeur of being blessed by me!" She thrust her finger at Elijah one more time. "You're so stupid you don't even realize you're standing in front of a goddess, and you treat my gift like it's—!"

Abruptly, her rant was cut short. Sensing a faint flow of magic, the little goddess immediately snapped her head toward Yzael, her eyes narrowing. The subtle spell was meant to be undetectable, but the great Yanaiyániuoa's divine senses picked up on it despite her diminished power.

Fear shot through Yzael as she ducked back.

She had been noticed.

She spun around to flee but found herself face-to-face with Yanaiyániuoa. The goddess's tiny form radiated a powerful presence as she floated inches away, violet eyes taking in every detail of Yzael with a discerning gaze.

Yanaiyániuoa's expression shifted from smugness to contemplative as she observed Yzael. "My, my," she began, her voice mingling with a hint of respect. "The descendants of my former worshippers have come a long way." Her gaze focused on the elf, detecting the potent, finely tuned mana coursing through her.

"It seems that after locking me away, your kin and those other traitors haven't been idle," Yanaiyániuoa remarked, as if seeing straight through Yzael's magic and bloodline.

Caught off guard by this sudden encounter, Yzael struggled to find her voice, aware of the historical weight between her people and the ancient goddess. But that seemed to matter little at the moment. All that she could think of was just how absolutely fucked she was at this current moment.

She gathered as much courage as she could, her voice wavering. "Oh G-Great Y-Yanaiyániuoa," she stammered with wide eyes. "I... I am Yzael of the High Elves, j-just a simple arcane user, detached from those who plotted against you!" Her words were careful, respectful, and tinged with a healthy dose of fear.

Yzael's heart raced as she spoke, knowing full well the volatility of the deity before her. "Your recognition of our progress, while it is an honor, is also... quite overwhelming," she added, her voice barely more than a whisper.

Yanaiyániuoa observed Yzael's reactions, her smug smile growing wider. "Overwhelmed? Oh, you should be!" The goddess said with glee as she twirled around playfully. Her violet eyes seemed to glow brighter as she floated closer, inspecting Yzael with a curiosity that felt almost invasive. "A simple arcane user, you say? Detached from the old conflicts? How quaint."

Before Yzael could open her mouth and respond, Elijah's voice suddenly echoed from behind. "Yana! What the hell are you doing, and where the hell did you go?" His tone was a mix of confusion and frustration. "Wait, how did I even know where to find you?"

Before Yzael could turn, the little goddess reached out and touched her face. A flash of violet light enveloped the area, and Yzael felt an overwhelming energy surge through her mind and soul. Her vision blurred, and she collapsed to the floor, barely managing to prop herself up with her hands, her pupils glowing violet.

Floating above, Yanaiyániuoa wore a contemplative expression, seemingly ignoring Elijah's questions. "Hmm. Why couldn't I gain complete control over her?" she mused, more preoccupied with this new puzzle than Elijah's presence.

Baffled, Elijah rubbed his eyes from the bright flash before frowning. "Yana, what the hell just happened?"

Yanaiyániuoa, now lost in thought, suddenly screamed in realization. "Ahh! This human! This world! They took all of it!" Her face shifted to horror, and she bolted to Elijah, hitting his forehead with her tiny fists. "Stupid, stupid, stupid human! Your stupid world! It's all your stupid fault!"

"Can you—" Elijah grimaced and swatted at the fairy. "Can you fuckin' stop?!"

Meanwhile, Yzael clung to her consciousness, the ancient energies within threatening to consume her. Grounded by the need to save her friend, she held onto her last thread of awareness amidst the chaos.

The poor elf could do nothing but focus on grounding herself as the voices of the goddess and the unknown human echoed around her. She couldn't comprehend what they were bickering about, but the tone and intensity of their argument suggested a deep frustration—perhaps even a history between them.

"Ugh! You're impossible!" the fairy lamented dramatically. "Of all the mortals that could exist, I had to end up with the most stubborn, annoying buffoon!"

Elijah, seemingly used to such outbursts, responded with exasperation."Excuse you. You have no one to blame but yourself for this."

Yanaiyániuoa growled as she floated around Elijah in a huff, her tiny form casting flickering shadows in the bright corridor. "If I had half the mind, I'd incinerate you where you stand and with it!" she barked, jabbing a finger at him. "But I've foolishly invested too much in you already!"

"Does this empty vessel have any idea how much energy it takes to bind an apostle?!" she yelled, bonking him on the head with her tiny fists. "Let alone one from another plane of reality?! I can't just kill you outright and find another! That would be such a waste!"

Suddenly, Yanaiyániuoa's demeanor changed dramatically. Her eyes widened, and she clutched her head, letting out a shrill scream of mental anguish. "Ahh! That's right! This is another world!" she yelled, remembering her own folly. "Of all the stupid things I could bind, it had to be a stupid human from a reality that doesn't even acknowledge my existence!"

As her outburst echoed down the corridor, Elijah simply stood there, arms crossed, the very image of exasperation. "You literally did this to yourself," he began, his voice tinged with sarcasm.

But before he could elaborate, Yanaiyániuoa cut him off with a sharp and loud "Shut up!" and smacked him on the head once more before turning her attention back to the high elf, who still trembled on the floor like a shaking leaf. The poor girl's face was a mixture of horror and pain as Yanaiyániuoa scrutinized her with a calculating gaze.

"Hmmm..." the fairy hummed in contemplation, then clapped her hands together. "I have decided. You shall be my servant!"

Elijah, perplexed by this sudden decision, interjected with a confused expression. "But why?" he asked, his voice trailing off as he tried to make sense of the goddess's whimsical decision.

Yanaiyániuoa turned sharply to Elijah, her eyes flaring with annoyance. "I said shut up! Apostles are meant to be seen, not heard!" she snapped.

"What the fuck am I, a battered housewife?" Elijah muttered under his breath. Glancing at Yzael, he added matter-of-factly, "Yeah, well, you can't have her." He swatted the fairy out of the air. "She's a prisoner of war or some spook science experiment or some shit."

The fairy recoiled from Elijah's swat but quickly fluttered back. Her face twisted into a scowl, and her violet eyes blazed with anger and disbelief. She was momentarily at a loss for words before finally bursting out.

"You!" she began, her voice rising in pitch and volume. "You are the rudest, most insufferable human I have ever encountered!" Her tiny hands balled into fists, shaking with indignation. "Rude! Rude, rude, rude, rude, rude!" she punctuated each word with a point at Elijah.

Elijah simply rolled his eyes and turned to the elf, who was still visibly shaken and disoriented from the fairy's spell. He carefully grabbed her arm and lifted her, nearly balking at her compliance despite her incapacitated state. The elf's response was almost robotic, lacking the typical resistance of someone suddenly hoisted to their feet.

"Huh," Elijah remarked, eyeing the elf with curiosity while his patron continued to yell at him.

As he observed the elf's terrified yet vacant expression, he guided her experimentally down the hall, noting her eerie, automated compliance. "It's like she's a robot or something," Elijah mused, scratching his beard.

His expression shifting to concern, Elijah's gaze returned to Yana. "What did you do to her?" he asked, his tone serious now. "It's not permanent, is it? They're going to be pissed if it's permanent." He continued moving the elf around. "She's just following along."

Still hovering, Yanaiyániuoa observed the interaction with a mix of irritation and curiosity. She sighed dramatically, placing her tiny hands on her hips. "I dominated her soul," she declared with a dismissive wave. "But apparently, I didn't have enough power to do it properly, so she's stuck in this limbo state—not quite here, not quite wherever." The fairy tossed a hand over her shoulder in an aloof gesture.

Her glowing violet eyes then fixed on Elijah, her expression shifting from annoyance to disdain. "But that's not the problem right now!" she pointed at him accusingly. "You are the problem! You're a terrible apostle! How am I supposed to regain my powers with someone like you?!"

Still experimentally moving Yzael, Elijah stopped and looked at his supposed "goddess" with a raised eyebrow. "Me? I didn't ask for any of this, remember? You're the one who decided to 'bless' me or whatever," he retorted, voice flat. "I'm the property of the US of A. You're gonna have to negotiate with them first."

Yanaiyániuoa blinked at Elijah in utter confusion. "Negotiate? With the what of what?" she sputtered, her voice rising. "What do you mean I have to negotiate with someone? I claimed you!" She floated energetically around Elijah, flailing as if shuffling invisible objects to emphasize her point. "The entire point of claiming someone who hasn't been claimed is to have them, completely and entirely!"

A smirk of sadistic amusement spread across Elijah's face as he watched her animated display. He knew for a fact the upcoming shit show between him and Command was going to be biblical, and he'd have front-row seats. "Yeah, well, that's not how it works here. You can't just go around claiming people willy-nilly, especially not when they're already under the jurisdiction of a government like mine."

Yzael, still dazed, stood limply, eyes unfocused and distant, a passive bystander to the bizarre exchange.

"This is!" Yanaiyániuoa huffed, placing her tiny hands on her hips as she faced Elijah again. "This is preposterous! I am a *goddess!* I do not negotiate! Especially not with mortals!" Her eyes blazed with the same violet light that had overwhelmed Yzael. "I demand to speak to whoever's in charge! Take me to your leader!"

Chapter 27

Every single shred of professional decorum had indeed left Toivonen's body. She sat with her head in her hands, struggling to process the surreal scene unfolding before her. In the middle of the high-security CIA facility was her boss—the Director of the CIA, Mich O'Reilly—in a heated argument with a diminutive supernatural fairy.

"What do you mean I can't own *my* human?! He's mine!" Yanaiyániuoa's voice, shrill and filled with indignation, cut through the room.

The director glanced at Lisette Ford, his colleague from the State Department—an African American woman swiftly summoned to address the unexpected situation. She stepped forward, exuding both experience and gravitas, ready to tackle the diplomatic challenge.

"Madam... Yanai... Yanaiyá..." The diplomat fumbled slightly over the fairy's complex name.

"Just call her Yana," Elijah interjected casually.

"Yanaiyániuoa!" the fairy barked, irritated by the casual address. Her newly claimed apostle simply rolled his eyes in response.

Trying to regain her composure, the diplomat continued, "Madam, I must explain that in our world, the concept of owning another person—especially a *citizen*—is not only legally unacceptable but also morally reprehensible. It's a fundamental violation of human rights."

She paused to let her words sink in before adding, "This is

particularly true in the case of specialized military personnel like Mr. Drake here." She glanced toward Elijah, who just sat there with an expression suggesting he was done for the day already. "They are protected by laws specific to their service and status. Owning or claiming ownership over them is not only illegal but also a matter of national security."

Lisette maintained a respectful tone, aiming to bridge the gap between vastly different worlds and cultures. "We must find a solution that respects our laws and your unique circumstances. This requires understanding and cooperation from all parties involved."

O'Reilly nodded in agreement while Yanaiyániuoa seemed to ponder, weighing the diplomat's words against her own understanding and expectations. The room held a tense silence as everyone awaited her response, hoping for a resolution to this unprecedented dilemma.

"That's stupid," the fairy rebuked, her wings fluttering in agitation. "He's my apostle, so he belongs to me!"

Elijah sighed, rubbing his temples as the argument circled back to where it had started. "Yana, shouldn't you at least stop doing whatever it is you're doing to that elf?" he groaned, looking up at her with tired eyes. "It's been hours."

In the tense conference room, the little goddess turned sharply toward her human and prepared to berate him but paused before her eyes flicked towards Yzael. With an annoyed click of her tongue, Yanaiyániuoa gestured at her victim and unraveled the spell that had ensnared Yzael's mind.

Yzael's reaction was immediate and visceral. She jolted as though waking from a deep, disorienting dream, her eyes widening in horror. Her gaze darted frantically around the room, taking in the unfamiliar surroundings, the air of cautious vigilance, and the soldiers lining the walls with weapons held ready but not aggressively. Her eyes settled on the people at the table, including Toivonen, whom she assumed was in charge—

An assumption proved wrong, given Toivonen's posture and the two authoritative figures standing before her.

Yanaiyániuoa, floating above the table, glowered at Elijah. "There, happy now?!" she barked before turning to Yzael. "I'll deal with *you* later!"

Still reeling from the spell's control, Yzael nodded weakly, recognizing she was in an extremely precarious situation. She resolved to stay quiet, hoping to blend into her seat and be forgotten.

"She wants the elf, too," Elijah casually blurted out, pointing his thumb toward Yzael.

Yzael stiffened.

The Director, accustomed to high-stakes situations, addressed Yanaiyániuoa diplomatically despite his frustration. "Madam... Goddess," he began, deliberately avoiding her name due to its complexity, "you can't simply declare people to belong to you. It's not how things work here."

Yanaiyániuoa's response was swift and sharp. She scanned the room, her expression mockingly surprised. "Oh? Why not? Is there another goddess here? I don't see another goddess," she retorted with heavy sarcasm. "Would you like to point me toward this supposed deity?"

The small goddess's incomprehension of the human perspective was evident as she floated, her aura radiating ancient authority that clashed with the conference room's modern atmosphere. "What is so difficult to understand?" she asked, exasperated. "I am a true deity, not like those idiots who play at it, leeching off systems that were never built for them. Claiming a mortal's soul is as natural for us as mortals claiming food for nourishment."

"Think for a moment!" The fairy pointed at her head with both hands. "How many times have you idiots tried to kill me?! Did you dummies think I'm subject to your laws, or what is it called again?" She glanced at her apostle.

"Human rights," Elijah sighed.

"Yeah, that! Did you think I was bound by your 'human rights' or whatever nonsense you came up with?!" she shouted, frustrated.

A tense silence reigned as the atmosphere shifted, the diplomatic effort faltering. The fairy had a point; they'd tried nearly everything to kill her short of a nuke. Yet she always returned. For all intents and purposes, she was immortal.

While everyone racked their brains to try to find a solution to this colossal problem, Toivonen spoke, her voice tinged with fatigue and sharp insight. "That's stupid. You can't even get your own 'apostle' to listen to you, and you've been throwing a temper tantrum ever since you got here."

The room fell into a deeper silence as Toivonen's blunt observation hit a nerve. Her directness contrasted sharply with the diplomatic efforts that had spiraled in circles.

"You think we haven't seen your lukewarm results with poor Yzael over here?" Toivonen gestured at the elf, who jumped in her seat. "Your attempts to exert any kind of control here have been half-baked at best."

Taken aback by Toivonen's directness, Yanaiyániuoa floated, her wings fluttering in agitation. She opened her mouth to retort but found herself at a loss. Instead, she looked at Elijah, seemingly seeking support.

Elijah leaned back in his chair, fixing her with a casual gaze. "She's got a point. She kinda got you there," he remarked in an offhand, matter-of-fact tone.

"Traitor!" she hissed, levitating a pen cap and throwing it at him. "Who's side are you on?!"

Caught off guard, Elijah winced as the cap struck his eye. "God-fucking-dammit!" he cursed, rubbing his eye with one hand. He glared at the tiny goddess, patience wearing thin. "The one who actually pays me, you tiny winged menace!"

The room fell silent except for barely contained chortles from the soldiers.

Lisette cleared her throat, attempting to regain control. "Alright, let's try to keep this civil. We're here to find a solution, not to escalate tensions further."

The director nodded. "Yes, we need to find a practical way forward," he added, addressing the goddess. "Our goal is to work out an arrangement that respects your... uniqueness while adhering to our laws and norms."

"We should probably define what she means by 'own' or 'claim' and not immediately jump to slavery," Toivonen interjected, gesturing tiredly toward the goddess. "It's evident we're operating on two completely different levels of understanding, so some clarification is in order," she continued, pragmatic as ever.

The director and Lisette exchanged glances.

"That's quite fair," O'Reilly tentatively agreed, nodding toward Lisette. "Thoughts?"

Lisette paused, choosing her words carefully, then addressed Yanaiyániuoa. "Madam, when you speak of 'claiming' or 'owning' a soul, could you clarify? It's crucial we fully understand your perspective," she asked diplomatically.

Yanaiyániuoa regarded Lisette with mild incredulity. "What? When I claim a soul, it's not some mere possession like your stupid writing tool over there," she said, gesturing dismissively toward a nearby pen. "It's about becoming the arbiter of their fate. They become representatives of my authority, extensions of my will and power. It's an honor bestowed upon them, granting a portion of my divine strength."

"And since this one has yet to be claimed, I claimed him!" She flew over to Elijah, sitting on his head. The man had no energy and barely reacted, staring blankly at the far wall, wishing he were anywhere but here.

Then, the goddess gestured vaguely toward Yzael, crossing one leg over the other. "And that one, too," she declared as one leg bounced on top of the other. "No other god is going to want her anyway because she's using my little brand of magic."

The room's atmosphere shifted palpably as Yanaiyániuoa's declaration settled over them. Her nonchalant claim over Yzael, based solely on the high elf's use of her magic, added a new layer of tension to the negotiations.

Under the scrutiny of everyone's gaze, Yzael's mind raced. Her use of Yanaiyániuoa's magic, deemed a form of heresy, was punishable by imprisonment, death, or worse—crippling—if any faith's authorities discovered it. Shifting in her seat, her hands moved to her sides as if to flee, feeling like every eye drilled holes into her.

But her worry seemed futile; the conversation continued as though no one cared about her heretical magic.

The director, humming with interest, remarked, "So, this is akin to knighthood and vassalage." He rubbed his clean-shaven chin thoughtfully, steering the conversation toward the goddess's terminology and away from Yzael's magic.

"What? What does being a knight or what?" Yanaiyániuoa looked down at Elijah, puzzled.

"Vassal."

"Yeah, that!" She waved dismissively. "What does that have anything to do with me claiming my mortals?"

Seizing the opportunity, Lisette stepped in. "It's just a bit of our history," she explained. "In medieval times, knights were warriors who swore loyalty to a lord in exchange for protection and land. Vassals were similar, offering service or loyalty for certain privileges. The key point is mutual agreement, where both parties benefit."

This explanation struck a chord with Yanaiyániuoa, who curiously tilted her head. "So, these knights and vassals chose to serve for protection and rewards?" she asked, intrigued by the concept.

"Yes, exactly," Lisette replied. "It was based on mutual consent and benefit. Perhaps we could view your 'claiming' as a mutual agreement, where both you and the mortal benefit."

Yanaiyániuoa dangled her leg thoughtfully. "Hmm, loyalty and mutual agreement," she murmured, then suddenly exclaimed, "Wait! You're not loyal at all!" Without warning, she kicked Elijah in the head.

"Hey, you little shit! I didn't consent to a goddamn thing!" he snapped, trying to grab at the menace.

Floating just out of reach, Yanaiyániuoa pointed an accusatory finger at the man. "Yes, you did! Yes, you did! You accepted me when I left my prison—you accepted my power. That's consent!"

Everyone turned to Elijah, who looked away, recalling a vague memory. "No, I didn't! So what, you're gonna start making shit up now—" He paused, realization dawning. "Ah, shit."

His indignation faded, giving way to begrudging acceptance. "Ahhh, shit... I did say something, didn't I?"

Yanaiyániuoa floated closer, triumphant. "See! You did agree! You acknowledged my power, so you belong to me!"

A defeated groan escaped Elijah as he ran a hand through his hair. "Fuck me, dude." He looked around, frustration and resignation on his face. "Fine. I may have said something, but it was sarcastic—not a real well-thought-out argument."

Lisette stepped in, her voice calm though concerned. "It sounds like there was some level of acknowledgment, even if it wasn't formal." She glanced at the director. "But it seemed to be enough to form a binding pact."

O'Reilly, noting the seriousness, leaned forward. "So this goddess can form a contract even if it's a verbal joke?" he asked, looking around.

In the tense and complex moment, Yzael hesitantly spoke, her thick accent adding weight to her cautious words. "Um... if I may," she began, "Yanaiyániuoa is... uhh... more than just a goddess. I-In our history, she is also known as a high judge in a... a Fae Court." Her hands fidgeted slightly, betraying her discomfort.

The members of the room turned to her and nodded encouragingly.

"The Fae are known for their... uh..." she began, struggling to find the right words in this foreign tongue, "contracts. These contracts are not simple; they are complex, with... what's the word? Yes, binding terms. People fall into them without fully understanding."

Her gaze drifted as if recalling tales and warnings from her world. "These contracts can have... specific clauses, often harmful or leading to death. The Fae play with words and intentions. What is casual to us can be binding to them."

Her explanation illuminated the perilous nature of dealing with beings like Yanaiyániuoa. O'Reilly and the others absorbed her words, understanding the need for caution in every word.

"This means that a casual remark to us could be a binding agreement to them," Lisette said grimly, looking at Elijah, who pinched the bridge of his nose to squeeze the headache away.

"Jesus Christ," he muttered. "So what does this mean? I'm stuck with this annoying shithead—"

"Rude!"

"Until I'm dead?" Elijah finished, clearly exasperated.

The room fell silent, and the director contemplated his predicament. He glanced around, searching for any loophole that might allow Elijah to escape this situation.

Then everyone turned to the goddess, who sat on a stapler with a haughty expression. "What makes you think death would free you of our contract?" she chimed, her tone playful. "I'm a *true* goddess, and you're my apostle!" she giggled, floating over to the man. "So that means your *soul* belongs to me, dummy!"

Elijah shut his eyes and slammed the back of his chair. "Of-fucking-course!" he groaned as the little fairy cackled.

"Your soul is mine, mine, mine!" she sang, circling his head. "You belong to me!"

Lisette cringed at the idea of being bound to this entity eternally, shocked to learn the fate of their souls after life and death. "Is there any way to... nullify this pact? Are there any conditions under which it could be dissolved?" she asked, her eyes focused on the small deity.

"Nope! It's eternal, just like me!" Yanaiyániuoa declared, playful yet firm. "Eternal and unbreakable, just like the bonds of true divinity!"

As everyone grappled with this revelation, Yanaiyániuoa turned her attention to Yzael. Floating closer, her expression grew expectant. "Now, about you," she said, pointing a diminutive finger at Yzael. "You've been using my magic, so it's only right you accept your position as my servant and worshipper."

Already overwhelmed, Yzael looked visibly uncomfortable. "I... um, I already follow a god," she stammered hesitantly. In truth, her devotion was loose, practiced mainly to avoid the scrutiny of zealous followers.

Yanaiyániuoa laughed heartily, slapping her knee. "Oh, that's good!" she chuckled. "Using my magic—the kind that would get you burned at the stake—and yet you hesitate?" Her tone was teasing, edged with a sharp truth.

Shifting uneasily, Yzael glanced at Elijah, now slumped over with his face buried in both hands. The thought of sharing a fate like his was daunting. "I-I don't think that's wise," she said slowly, carefully choosing her words. "I believe I should stay faithful to my current deity." After witnessing Elijah's predicament, she had no desire for a similar binding.

Yanaiyániuoa's smile widened maliciously at Yzael's hesitation. "Oh? Oh, oh, oh? Is that so?" The fairy zipped around her, making Yzael flinch.

"Is that so? Is that so?" Yanaiyániuoa taunted, hovering close enough that Yzael couldn't look away. "What about your little friend? Don't you want to keep her safe?"

Yzael froze instantly, her eyes widening.

"I can keep her safe, ya know! I can tell these humans not to touch her, ya know?! I'm a goddess, ya know?!" The little fairy grinned toothily.

The mention of Lysandra made Yzael's heart race. Yanaiyániuoa's words cut deep; Lysandra was why Yzael took such risks. The idea of her commander's safety struck a powerful chord. The high elf looked at the fairy, her eyes reflecting a mix of fear and uncertainty. Slowly, she opened her mouth. "H-How do you know?"

"What?" Yanaiyániuoa looked at her as if she was stupid. "What do you mean how do I know? Do you not remember me dominating your soul—"

"Failed to dominate." Elijah, being petty as usual, heckled his patron.

"Shut up!" the goddess roared, snapping at him before turning her piercing gaze back to Yzael. "Anyway, do you not remember me casting a domination spell on you?"

A wave of dread swept over Yzael as the memory surfaced: being trapped within her own mind, a prisoner to forces far beyond her comprehension. The helplessness—the dreadful feeling of wandering through an arcane labyrinth with no way out—remained vivid. She shuddered at the recollection, her eyes darting nervously around the room.

Swallowing hard, Yzael lowered her gaze, her thoughts racing. The prospect of forfeiting her soul to such a notorious goddess was beyond terrifying. Yet, the thought of losing another companion was equally unbearable. Though Yzael wasn't as close to Lysandra as she was to Gideon, her commander shared the same indomitable spirit— cut from the same cloth, forged in the same trials.

And that was enough.

"I..." Yzael squeaked, her voice hoarse.

"I accept."

A brilliant violet flash engulfed the room as Yanaiyániuoa placed a hand on Yzael's head, the binding spell sealing their pact.

Chapter 28

Varian, Emperor of the Seraphic Empire, was the offspring of a union between a goddess and an ancient dragon. He sat at the head of the vast marble table with regal composure, his councilors, advisors, and generals—members of various races—fixing their gazes upon him.

Yet his majestic appearance could not conceal the thinly veiled frustration and the gnawing tinge of fear in his heart. The aftermath of his ambitious but disastrous attempt to invade another world through a gateway constructed by an imprisoned divine entity weighed heavily upon him. His dream of ascending to true godhood—worshiped by an entire world's populace—had been shattered by modern weaponry and tactics. It was a bitter pill for an emperor and would-be deity to swallow.

And to make matters worse, the imprisoned entity had been freed, its bindings crumbling to dust.

A deep, uncomfortable silence filled the council chamber as Korthax, the dragonkin general adorned with white feathers, concluded his grim report. This was not merely a military defeat but a catastrophic blow to the empire's image of unassailable might, threatening its carefully maintained deterrence.

But what made the atmosphere oppressive wasn't just the revelation of the otherworlders' unconventional methods of warfare. No, it was what Korthax proposed next.

The room's occupants stared at Korthax as if he were mad when he requested the emperor's permission to withdraw their forces from territories they had painstakingly assimilated over the past century. His plan was to abandon these vassals and allies, turning regions into buffer states against the inevitable advance of the otherworlders. The general cited the slow yet relentless buildup of metal beasts and war machines on the other side of the gateway as evidence of the looming threat.

The proposal was met with immediate outrage. A cacophony of voices erupted as the council—comprising seasoned generals, shrewd advisors, and influential nobles—voiced their disapproval while visibly agitated.

"General Korthax, have you lost your mind?!" bellowed Councilor Silvianor, a dark elf and a veteran commander of many campaigns, his voice reverberating off the high ceilings. "To abandon our territories and our vassals? This is not merely cowardice—it is a *disgrace!*" He slammed his hand onto the marble table, cracking its surface.

Another member, Noblewoman Elenariel, a sun elf duchess, rose from her seat and leaned forward aggressively, her hands pressing into the table. "How dare you propose such an abomination after suffering a humiliating retreat!" she sneered, her fury evident. "We are the Seraphic Empire, not some frightened fledgling kobold cowering before a dragon!"

Similar sentiments rippled through the chamber as council members shouted in indignation. Advisor Aurelianthrax, a vibrantly red-feathered dragon known for her usual calm, hissed with disbelief. "General Korthax, your plan reeks of defeatism," she hissed, her eyes narrowing dangerously. "What of the years of effort? The resources spent? The irreplaceable forces and personnel lost? Are we handing over these lands to serve as a buffer for an enemy we scarcely understand?"

Korthax stood firm, trying to maintain his composure while he smoothed his ruffled feathers. "Councilors, generals, advisors, I understand your concerns. But we must face the reality of our situation." He gestured broadly around the room. "Our incursion into that world has revealed an enemy whose capabilities surpass our expectations. We cannot afford further losses to our draconic forces—especially now that the otherworlders have freed The Banished One!"

The mention of the newly liberated divine entity momentarily quelled the room's silence, reminding everyone of their precarious situation. After a long pause, Varian, who had remained silent, rose to his feet. His voice cut through the tension like a blade. "Enough! We must not let emotion cloud our judgment." He sat back down in his opulent chair, his tone authoritative. "General Korthax, explain the rationale behind your proposal in detail."

Grateful for the emperor's intervention, Korthax gave a respectful nod. "Thank you, Your Majesty." He adjusted his ceremonial uniform, steadying his nerves. "Our primary objective is the preservation of our empire. By withdrawing from these territories, we conserve our draconic forces and establish a strategic barrier. The lands we vacate will pose significant challenges to the otherworlders. Hostile entities surround them, and they are fraught with treacherous terrain, savage wildlife, and dense foliage." He paused, letting his words sink in while brushing down a few feathers on his hand. "This delay will grant us time to fortify our defenses, better understand our enemy, and uncover what has become of The Banished One. Rest assured, when the gods demand answers, they will seek more than simple explanations."

The room grew quiet once more as the council members considered the weight of Korthax's argument. The bitter reality of their circumstances was undeniable. They were at a crossroads, and the decision made now would shape the empire's survival amid divine scrutiny.

Korthax pressed on. "Furthermore, we must consider the political implications. While our portal led to the otherworld, the otherworlders released The Banished One," he explained, glancing around the chamber. "With some astute political maneuvering, we can redirect blame toward the true culprits."

This struck a chord. The councilors shifted uncomfortably, their minds racing with the implications.

"This is not merely a military strategy but a diplomatic one," Korthax elaborated. "We can use this opportunity to unite various factions and entities against the otherworlders, redirecting hostility away from our empire."

It was a pragmatic strategy that reeked of betrayal and desperation—but desperate times demanded desperate measures.

"By refocusing scrutiny on the otherworlders, we can emphasize that, while we instigated the situation, they were the savages who unleashed the harbinger of apocalypses upon the world. With some reframing, we can garner sympathy and support, potentially even from those who have historically opposed us," Korthax continued, his voice gaining confidence as he outlined the potential benefits. "This could lead to new alliances or, at the very least, a redirection of hostility."

Advisor Aurelianthrax interjected, her tone measured but sharp. "So, you propose we use your failure to our advantage?" she asked, her words carrying the weight of both an accusation and a strategic consideration. "We reshape the narrative to strengthen our position, both militarily and diplomatically?"

"Exactly," Korthax affirmed without hesitation.

The atmosphere shifted from overt hostility to grudging consideration. General Solien, a sun elf renowned for his tactical acumen, nodded slowly. "It's a distasteful proposition but one that could buy us the time to regroup and assess the situation more effectively."

Varian, who had been silent for most of the discussion, finally spoke. His voice, resonating with the authority of his divine lineage, cut through the tension. "We are at a critical juncture," he began. "The survival and future of our Empire hang in the balance. General Korthax's plan, while unpalatable, offers a viable path forward in these trying times. We must be willing to adapt and make difficult choices for the greater good."

He paused, allowing his words to sink in before continuing. "However, we cannot ignore the potential consequences of such actions. Betraying our vassals and allies could have long-lasting repercussions, damaging our reputation and honor. We must weigh these risks against the potential gains."

Councilor Silvianor leaned forward, his expression grave. "Your Majesty, the risks are indeed significant. But we still need to show token support for those barbarians on the periphery."

Varian nodded slowly, his gaze sweeping across the faces of his council. "Very well." He turned to Korthax. "General Korthax, proceed with your plan but assign a few legions of our less effective forces to support those on the periphery. This will include our less competent commanders, nobles who have proven themselves more of a liability than an asset, and corrupt lords who have been a cancer to our society. Let them serve a dual purpose in these trying times."

Korthax inclined his head, grasping the layers of the emperor's strategy. "A wise decision, Your Majesty. It will cleanse our ranks of long-standing hindrances while presenting a façade of support to our border territories."

Advisor Luminarion, one of the emperor's Seraphic political strategists with ethereal purple feathers, knocked his fist on the table and spoke. "I know quite a few dissenting—and potential dissenting—voices within our sacred empire. Those who have been a thorn in our side can now be put to use in a manner that benefits all."

"Exactly. We cannot afford to carry dead weight," Varian agreed. "Every decision, every action, must serve the greater good of the empire."

The council members exchanged understanding looks, recognizing the harsh but necessary nature of their Emperor's orders. In unison, they stood and bowed toward the emperor. "By your will," they said, their voices echoing wondrously throughout the council hall.

Wearing a magnanimous expression, Varian waved his hand, dismissing them. Each member turned and marched out of the room.

Varian's face remained stoic and commanding as they left, but as the large, ornate doors of the council hall closed with a resonant thud, his carefully composed mask began to shift. His calm sovereignty for his councilors morphed into an expression of unbridled fury.

Alone in the vast council hall, Varian's gaze remained fixed on the closed doors. The room's silence seemed to amplify the storm brewing within him, his anger festering like an unchecked wound.

Finally, unable to contain the tempest raging inside, Varian slammed his fist onto the thick marble table. The force of his divine strength shattered the stone, sending shards scattering across the floor. "Alastor!" he roared, his voice filled with a rage that shook the very foundations of the hall.

His outburst was more than just a scream of anger; it manifested his frustration, disappointment, and fear. Rising from his seat, Varian's entire body trembled with fury. "You coward!" he bellowed, his voice echoing off the high ceilings. "You treacherous, spineless wretch!"

Varian paced back and forth, his footsteps heavy and resounding. "If you were ever a mortal, I would find your kin and slaughter them *all!*" His voice grew louder, dripping with venom. "You dare bring me this debacle?!"

His eyes burned with fiery intensity, his face contorted in anger. "I should have known! Trusting a devil from the hells—what folly!" He cursed Alastor's name, each insult dripping with bitterness over his shattered dreams and the disastrous campaign.

As his tirade continued, the air in the hall grew heavy, charged with his fury's raw, unchecked power. The Emperor of the Seraphic Empire stood amidst the ruins of the council table, his rage unabated—a ruler betrayed and burdened by the weight of his ambition.

After several long, furious outbursts, Varian's breathing began to steady. The red haze of anger faded, giving way to an emperor's cold, calculating mind. Straightening his posture, he adjusted his imperial uniform, smoothing the fabric as he reasserted control over his emotions—and the situation.

Varian's thoughts shifted. Swift, decisive action paired with cunning would be necessary to expand upon General Korthax's proposal and ensure the empire's survival.

His thoughts turned to the border territories and the surrounding powers as he pondered his next steps. Deploying a token force of the empire's less competent elements was merely the beginning. Subtler, more insidious strategies would be required: carefully placed promises, the strategic deployment of powerful magical artifacts— just enough to sow chaos and entangle his enemies in perpetual conflict.

Taking a deep breath, Varian strode out of the council chamber, pushing open the doors to confront a startled guard standing nearby.

"Fetch me the Minister of Artifacts."

* * *

Screams and guttural laughter resounded as Gryki Fizzspark dragged her small green body across the scorched ground, leaving her shattered flame spitter behind. Pain and fear consumed her thoughts as she used her only good arm to claw forward.

Once a haven of goblin innovation, the burning city had become a hellscape of fire and death. Gryki's movement was a testament to her resilience, but her resolve faltered as a menacing voice thundered behind her.

"Where d'ya think you're goin', gobo?"

The deep and guttural voice was laced with sadistic amusement. Gryki froze in terror, terror gripping her as she turned her battered body. Her wide eyes met the towering figure of an orc, seven feet of pure muscle. His dark green skin glistened with sweat and soot, and his jagged teeth bared in a cruel grin.

The orc gestured grandly to the burning city around them, where the victorious, guttural laughter of ogres and orcs drowned out the screams of innocents.

"Pretty hard ta run when yours legs don't work," the monstrous being laughed as it slowly approached.

Covering his arm was the source of his might: a large, strange gauntlet that looked more like a product of arcane sorcery than any weaponry the horde could have mustered. The massive gauntlet hummed with energy; its intricate mechanisms and glowing runes gave the orc otherworldly strength.

The orc let out a deep, guttural laugh, his eyes fixed on Gryki as he spoke mockingly. "Look at you, tiny gobo. Yous thought yous coulda says no to me? Fight against me and the boys?" he sneered. The orc's grin widened, revealing long, jagged teeth—signature to orcs.

"Yous runnin' for help? Is dat it?"

Gryki's heart pounded in her chest, each beat echoing the dread that filled her. The orc's towering presence loomed over her, his shadow engulfing her small form. As he reached out with his giant, gauntleted hand, she tried to scramble away, but her injured body betrayed her.

The orc's laughter filled the air, cruel and mocking, as the menacing hand, clad in the techno-magic gauntlet, closed around Gryki with an ease that belied its massive size. Gryki screamed in pain, the pressure of his grip threatening to crush her already battered body.

"Yous ain't goin' nowhere, gobo," Grotmash Bludfist growled, his voice filled with malicious glee. "Ain't nowhere for yous gobos to go."

A horrid scream resounded as Gryki felt the awful gauntlet squeeze and crush her already mangled side. Bones snapped, and torn flesh ripped under the immense pressure. Tears streamed down Gryki's face, not just from the physical pain but also from the sight of her beloved city in ruins, her people suffering.

Grotmash Bludfist leaned closer, his foul breath hot on her face. "Awww," the monster cooed in false sympathy. "Yous want the pain to stop, little gobo? All yous had ta do was bow to da Bossman, Fraka. Bow ta me," he sneered sadistically.

"P-Please," Gryki pleaded through gritted teeth, the agony overwhelming her resolve. Her voice was ragged, barely audible over the crackling flames and distant screams. "Stop."

Fraka, reveling in her pain, tilted his head, examining her like a predator assessing its prey. His eyes, cold and merciless, reflected the fires that raged around them. "Stop, eh?" he mused aloud. "Maybe I will, maybe I won't. Depends on how much fun I be havin'."

The sheer malice in his voice was like a physical blow, and for a moment, Gryki lost all hope as the pain made her consciousness flicker. Another jolt of pain coursed through her as she toppled to the ground. Fraka stood above her, his wicked smile unrelenting. His words jolted Gryki back to harsh reality as his tone shifted, adopting an air of twisted ownership.

"Yous know what, little gobo?" he said, his voice low and menacing. "I've decided. Yous ain't gonna die here. No, yous are part of da Horde now. Yous are one of Fraka's boys."

Gryki lay cradling her ruined arm and leg, her tears soaking the singed grass. She didn't speak, but her answer was clear—her head remained lowered, submissive.

Another cruel laugh echoed as Fraka mocked the very essence of Gryki's spirit. "That's right, little gobo." He towered over her; his overwhelming power and brutality cast an oppressive shadow. "Yous understand now. Yous got no choice but to serve. Fraka Gar Orak has claimed you."

Broken and defeated, Gyrki felt deep despair engulf her as her thoughts turned to her people. The reality of their situation was crushing—not only had she witnessed the destruction of her home, but now she and her people faced a future of servitude under the very monster responsible for it all.

Chapter 29

Lysandra's face was etched with a mix of frustration and dread as she sighed heavily. Glancing down, she examined the metal cuffs clasped tightly around her wrists. Each one was connected to thick metal chains, anchoring her firmly to the all-metal table in front of her.

Looking around, she found herself again in the stark, featureless room that had become an all-too-familiar setting. It was a place of endless, meaningless conversations passed off as interrogations. Every once in a while, they'd ask her something meaningful, and she'd half-heartedly ramble off an answer. But in the end, it always circled back to trivialities.

Lysandra's patience was wearing thin, and the repetitive nature of these sessions was becoming increasingly grating with each visit. Glancing around the room, she focused on the one-way mirror that housed her observers. It was like a silent, unblinking eye, constantly watching and judging. She wondered if they were searching for weaknesses or cracks in her resolve or simply trying to understand the enigma she presented.

"It's not like I have anything to hide anyway," she muttered, letting out another defeated sigh as she hung her head.

In the cold, hard silence of the room, Lysandra's thoughts turned inward. She contemplated the series of events that had led her here to this moment of isolation and scrutiny. Her actions, driven by a mix of protective instinct and a rush of emotions, now seemed reckless in the harsh light of their consequences.

And to top it all off, she felt foolish. Yzael wasn't just some damsel in distress or a mediocre mage unable to function when something got too close. No, Yzael was a seasoned and powerful high-elf mage, likely several times older than Lysandra.

As Lysandra sat there, her thoughts wandered to Yzael's vast repertoire of spells and centuries of experience wielding magic. She could only imagine the depth of Yzael's magical knowledge—the countless spells and incantations she must know by heart, the arcane secrets she had unraveled over her long life. Yzael, in many ways, was a living archive of magical lore, a testament to the power and longevity of her kind.

However, she didn't regret a single thing.

Just as the thought crossed her mind, the room's door creaked open, pulling her from her reverie. To her surprise, Dr. Stenhouse, a scholar from this world whom she hadn't seen in what felt like ages, walked in. Her good eye widened in shock, and she moved to greet him, but the heavy bindings and heavily armed soldiers walking in behind them stopped her.

"Ah, hello, Lysandra," Dr. Stenhouse greeted her, his tone tentative, almost cautious. Lysandra could sense a distinct change in his demeanor since their last interaction. He seemed more reserved, his usual academic enthusiasm dimmed by whatever had occurred outside this room.

"H-Hello, Stenhouse," Lysandra replied, her voice tinged with relief and concern. "It's been some time."

As they conversed, it became evident that Dr. Stenhouse's grasp of her language had improved significantly. Though still marked by hesitation and occasional fumbling, his sentences were more coherent than before. This improvement, however, was overshadowed by the palpable tension in the air.

Lysandra's mind returned to the matter that troubled her the most. "Where is Emma?" she asked, looking past the scholar expectantly. "Is she doing alright?"

Dr. Stenhouse hesitated, his expression clouded with something Lysandra couldn't quite decipher. The way he avoided her gaze was telling. "Emma is no longer working with us, Lysandra," he said, his voice tinged with a mix of regret and discomfort.

Furrowing her brows, Lysandra struggled to understand his words. "No longer working with you? What do you mean? Where is she?" Concern was evident in her voice, her single eye searching his face for answers.

Dr. Stenhouse took a deep breath, his shoulders noticeably slumping as he looked down. "Emma has left the project. There were, uh, disagreements, and she has gone elsewhere." His words were carefully measured, but the underlying tension was evident.

The revelation left Lysandra with mixed emotions. Emma and Dr. Stenhouse had been a bridge between her and this strange new world, a friendly face among those who saw her as a threat. Emma's departure left Lysandra feeling even more isolated and vulnerable.

"Is she safe, at least?" Lysandra pressed, her voice laced with worry.

"Yes, of course," Dr. Stenhouse replied, his voice softening slightly. "She's fine. She has returned to her studies elsewhere."

Lysandra absorbed this information with a mix of relief and sadness. Emma was safe, but the circumstances of her departure remained a mystery. Before he could speak further, Dr. Stenhouse interjected, his tone more somber than before.

"And, Lysandra, I am also leaving the project," he announced, his gaze meeting hers directly.

Lysandra stared at him, her mind racing. "Why?" she asked, her voice barely more than a whisper.

Dr. Stenhouse sighed, his eyes filled with deep regret. "We made... a mistake," he admitted, his voice weighed down with meaning. "It cost us dearly and nearly got others killed. The decision was made that it would be best for me to step aside."

Lysandra read the lines of stress etched on Dr. Stenhouse's face. It was clear he didn't agree with this judgment, but she remained silent, understanding the situation's complexity all too well. She, too, had contributed to the chain of events that had led to this moment.

"I came to say goodbye," Dr. Stenhouse continued, his tone tinged with sorrow and resignation. "My leaders granted me this courtesy for all the hard work and cooperation, for willingly turning over scholarly things. I will pass them on to my successor."

Lysandra's heart sank as her gaze fell to her shackles. "Goodbye?" she repeated softly, the word lingering in the air, heavy with sorrow.

To her, Dr. Stenhouse had been more than just a researcher—he had been a bridge to understanding this strange, baffling world. His departure felt like another door closing, leaving her even more isolated.

Dr. Stenhouse gave a slight nod, his expression a mix of sadness and resignation. "Yes. Goodbye."

"I wish it didn't have to end like this," Lysandra said quietly. She could tell it wasn't easy for him to walk away, just as it wasn't easy for her to lose another ally. But she understood. The man must have already faced immense constraints and pressures; that little scuffle in her room must have pushed everything over the edge.

A small smile spread across Stenhouse's face as he stood. "Me too. But we have to accept what is given." He glanced at the guard, who simply nodded.

Standing to leave, he added, "Take care, Lysandra. I hope you find your way."

Lysandra was left alone with her thoughts as the door closed behind him. She realized she was now just another stranger in a strange land.

She wanted to be angry at these mundane and inert humans around her but couldn't bring herself to do so. They had treated her with more respect and dignity than anyone in her world would, especially given her circumstances.

Lysandra glanced around the bare room, the weight of her situation pressing heavily on her. She was truly alone. She should have never come to this heaven-forsaken world. The decision to take up a freelance contract had been driven by greed—the lure of riches and adventure. In hindsight, it seemed foolish and shortsighted. What she had envisioned as a straightforward task, a simple in-and-out job, had spiraled into a conflict spanning worlds, leaving her a pawn in a game far beyond her understanding.

Her thoughts turned bitterly to the Seraphic Empire—the pompous, arrogant, feathered bastards who had sparked this entire fiasco. They had thought they could waltz into another reality and claim it as their own, giving no thought to what lay on the other side. A surge of anger coursed through her at their hubris. Their unbridled ambition had landed her here, trapped and alone in this cell.

Yet, here she was, chained and restrained, while those responsible for the invasion likely continued their machinations unscathed. The injustice gnawed at her. Once a free agent, a master of her own destiny, she was now a captive, her fate in others' hands.

But Lysandra was not one to wallow in self-pity or resign herself to her circumstances. She had always been a survivor, someone who adapted and overcame. As dire as it was, this situation would not be her end.

The former commander looked up at the false mirror and opened her mouth, but once again, the door creaked open. In stepped the dark-haired woman—Toi… something. She regularly accompanied the scholars during their previous visits, standing stoically beside the guards and overseeing the learning sessions.

Lysandra's gaze lingered on her momentarily, recognizing the familiar face. It had been a while since she last saw this woman, but her presence didn't elicit any particular reaction. She was just another player in this ever-evolving drama. But just as Lysandra was about to lower her gaze and resign herself to another round of questions, she caught a glimpse of Yzael following close behind the guards who entered.

"Y-Yzael?!" Lysandra practically yelled, her shackles straining as she tried to move forward.

Relief, confusion, and desperation swirled in her eyes as she watched the dark-haired woman and Yzael take seats in front of her. "Yzael, what's going on?"

Yzael's expression remained composed, starkly contrasting Lysandra's evident turmoil. The high elf turned to Toivonen, who simply nodded, granting her permission to speak. Turning back to Lysandra, Yzael's eyes conveyed a seriousness that demanded attention.

"Lysandra, I need you to listen carefully and answer as truthfully as you can," Yzael instructed firmly yet reassuringly.

Lysandra's heart pounded as she tried to process the scene before her. Yzael was unshackled, sitting across from her, and seemed to have assumed a role far different from that of a fellow captive. "Have you joined them?" Lysandra asked, her voice reflecting a mix of disbelief and concern.

A difficult look spread across Yzael's usually stoic face as she slowly looked away. "It's not about joining them, Lysandra. It's... it's complicated."

"But why are you free while I remain bound?" Lysandra couldn't mask the confusion and hurt in her voice.

Before Yzael could respond, Toivonen interjected, her voice calm yet authoritative. "Yzael, please begin the questioning. We need to understand the full extent of Lysandra's involvement with her employers."

Yzael hesitated for a moment, her gaze lingering on Lysandra's pained face before letting out a sigh. "Lysandra, we need to understand why you came to this world. Can you tell us about the contract you accepted from the Seraphic Empire?" Yzael's voice was gentle, but her words had an undercurrent of urgency.

Lysandra's face was etched with a mix of confusion and frustration as she gave Yzael a stern look. "Why are you asking me this, Yzael? You took the same contract. You should know," she replied, her voice tinged with a sense of betrayal.

"Yes, I was aware," Yzael admitted. "But, as I'm more than sure you've noticed, these humans are meticulous and redundant." She acknowledged Lysandra's frustration, her words attempting to soothe her former commander.

The response seemed to resonate with Lysandra. She let out a tired sigh, resigning herself to the situation. "Fine," she whispered wearily.

"The contract I took was straightforward. Taskers sponsored by the empire offered it," Lysandra explained, her voice tinged with regret as she recalled ignoring Ulina's warnings—the owner of a tavern and a small freelancer guild. "I was to provide my services as a mercenary—nothing more. It was just specific tasks like recon, escort duties, and occasionally dealing with bandits and criminals. The pay was good. Very good. I didn't ask questions; I never do. It's cleaner that way."

Toivonen listened to Yzael's translation attentively, taking mental notes. "At any point, were you made aware of their broader intentions? The invasion?"

Lysandra looked to Yzael, who reiterated Toivonen's question and shook her head. "No. They never shared their plans with hired help. I knew they were ambitious—the empire always is—but an invasion of another world? No, I didn't see that coming."

Yzael translated, her expression neutral. Toivonen's analytical gaze remained fixed on Lysandra as though trying to discern the truth behind her words.

"Did you have any interactions with higher-ups? Anyone who might have hinted at something more?" Yzael asked, continuing Toivonen's line of inquiry.

Lysandra thought for a moment. "Not really. My only interaction with anyone of note was with a draconic officer who warned us about..." She trailed off, glancing toward Toivonen. "Their capabilities. By that time, we were already in the field."

Toivonen nodded slightly, jotting down notes on her pad as she listened to Yzael. She leaned in, her eyes sharp. "And what is your opinion on the empire?"

Lysandra let out an annoyed sigh, her head dropping in frustration. "I've answered these questions a hundred times over."

"Lysandra, I know, but please answer the question." Yzael's tone softened as she looked between Lysandra and Toivonen. "It's just their way. Please."

With a twitch of her eye, Lysandra shook her head and relented. "Ugh, fine," she groaned. "My feelings about the empire haven't changed. They're overambitious, overreaching, and now, clearly unfathomably reckless.

Yzael continued to translate, her tone steady and neutral. Lysandra noticed a flicker of understanding in Toivonen's gaze, though the officer's demeanor remained strictly professional.

"And what is her opinion of the forces of the world the empire invaded?" Toivonen asked, glancing at Yzael, who relayed the question with an emphasis on honesty.

Lysandra's annoyance faded, replaced by a contemplative silence. She looked down at her shackled hands, her expression distant as memories flooded her mind—memories of friends and colleagues she had led to this world, promising adventure and riches. Instead, they found death and tragedy.

The taverns where they had planned their exploits, the laughter, and camaraderie—all now distant echoes. They had trusted her, and she had led them into a disaster.

So, who was to blame? The people of this world who had swung the death blow in defense of their home? Or the empire, whose reckless ambition had thrust them into a nightmare?

Guilt, anger, and sorrow churned in Lysandra's gut as she focused on her twiddling hands. "I don't know who to blame," she admitted, her tone heavy with pain. "My friends are all dead. They died at the hands of this world's defenders. But we were the invaders, misled by the empire's folly."

She raised her hand toward her missing eye, only to be stopped by the chains binding her to the table.

Yzael translated her words slowly, her voice tinged with empathy. Toivonen listened intently, her expression unchanged as she glanced toward the two-way mirror.

"Thank you, Lysandra," Toivonen said after a brief pause. "Your perspective is invaluable in understanding the complexities of this conflict."

The room's tension was palpable as Yzael awaited Toivonen's next move. Toivonen leaned forward, her piercing gaze fixed on Lysandra.

"I've been informed that the empire you fought for withdrew from the battlefield," Toivonen said, her voice steady. "They left mercenaries like your team to cover their retreat." Yzael translated, her tone grave. "It seems they promised reinforcements, gold, land, and status to those who stayed behind. But that support—it never arrived."

Lysandra's reaction was immediate and visceral. A dark, hollow laugh escaped her lips as she dropped her head into her hands, her shoulders shaking with anger and despair. Yzael translated the laughter, her scowl betraying her own frustration.

Toivonen waited patiently for the laughter to subside, her expression unreadable. The room fell into an oppressive silence, the weight of Lysandra's realization hanging heavy in the air.

Finally, Toivonen spoke again, her voice rough with effort as she addressed Lysandra and Yzael in their common language. "Do you want revenge?" Her accent was thick, her pronunciation hesitant, but the intent was clear.

Lysandra slowly lifted her head, meeting Toivonen's gaze. Raw emotion burned in her eyes as she silently wrestled with the question's weight.

After what felt like an eternity, she finally spoke. "I want to hurt them."

Toivonen nodded toward one of the guards. "Inform the Goddess she's ready."

Chapter 30

Weeks had passed since the Ohio Incident, a surreal event that had thrust the small country town into the global spotlight. Just south of the epicenter, where two worlds had violently collided, there now lay a seamless tear in reality, blending the fantastical with the mundane.

The armies of the otherworld—strange and fantastical beings—had been pushed back to just outside New Philadelphia, their advance halted by the might of modern weaponry and tactics. While many from the shattered army had retreated through the rift, countless others had scattered, disappearing into the countryside.

Efforts to round up survivors and insurgents continued, but the task was daunting. The creatures that had crossed over were elusive, their strange magics and alien biology complicating the search. Military and local authorities reached a grim consensus: finding everyone and everything that had crossed over was impossible.

The focus had now shifted to the area surrounding the rift itself.

Where once a shimmering portal and a strange, blackened spire stood, there was now an expanse of unsettling nothingness. It was as if the two worlds had stitched themselves together at this specific location, creating a surreal landscape that played tricks on the minds of those who gazed upon it. The rift's glow had faded when the spire collapsed, leaving behind an area that defied explanation.

Overseeing the anomaly were the stalwart defenders of this once-ordinary world. What had started as a modest forward operating base had grown exponentially, transforming into a sprawling military complex. The ground trembled with the constant movement of armored vehicles—some conducting field exercises, others vigilantly guarding the rift against any signs of renewed assault. They were determined not to be caught off guard again.

Protected by these sentinels, scientists and researchers from around the globe flocked to the site, eager to study this mind-bending phenomenon and the magics that now seemingly permeated the Earth. They set up their equipment and ran countless tests and experiments, yet the rift remained an enigma. No meaningless hypotheses had emerged to explain what they were experiencing.

Amidst this backdrop of military might and scientific inquiry, the area around the rift had taken on an almost surreal quality. Once fearful and uncertain, the local citizens slowly adapted to their new reality. Stories and rumors circulated: some spoke of strange sightings in the woods, others of mysterious happenings near the rift.

As day turned into night, the area around the rift took on an eerie calm, punctuated by the thudding of helicopter rotors and the rumble of armored vehicles. The lights from the military base cast long shadows across the landscape. Occasionally, the distant echo of an explosion or the staccato burst of gunfire reminded everyone of the volatile and dangerous nature of the other side.

"This fuckin' place," Lieutenant DuPont grumbled after one of his Bradleys tore into a bear-like creature the size of a pickup truck.

He hated to admit it, but these encounters near the rift were becoming less unsettling. Every hour of every day brought multiple incursions from strange monsters, each more peculiar than the last. This particular creature stood out for its sheer size and fearsome appearance. However, the bear-like beast Lieutenant Du Pont's unit encountered was a terrifying amalgamation of Earth's wildlife and something far more alien. It resembled a massive grizzly bear crossed with a wolverine, and its physique was both awe-inspiring and horrifying. On all fours, it stood as tall as a large SUV. Its body was covered in thick, matted fur—dark, almost black, with streaks of red running along its spine. The fur bristled with primal energy, enhancing its menacing appearance.

Its head, reminiscent of a marsupial's, featured a broader, more powerful jawline filled with razor-sharp teeth that gleamed in the faint light. Its eyes glowed with a deep, unsettling intelligence, starkly contrasting its otherwise brutish appearance.

Most terrifying of all were its muscular and robust limbs. DuPont was convinced the creature could overturn an armored vehicle if it got too close. Its massive paws, ending in claws like curved swords, seemed capable of easily tearing through metal and flesh.

"At least you're loud as shit," DuPont muttered, clicking his push-to-talk. "Hit the fucker again. Make sure it's dead."

The Bradley's heavy weapons roared to life once more. DuPont squinted as the muzzle flashes lit up the darkened landscape. His grip tightened on his weapon as the beast suddenly twitched, then sprang to life. The damned monster had been playing dead. Under the relentless hail of armor-piercing rounds, its hulking body thrashed violently, letting out a guttural roar that echoed through the night.

"Jesus Christ!" DuPont yelled, opening fire alongside his men.

In a primal surge of rage, the monstrous bear charged toward the armored vehicle that was threatening its life. Its massive form, illuminated by bursts of gunfire, moved with a speed and agility that belied its size.

The soldiers reacted instantly, their training kicking in as they unleashed a torrent of fire. The Bradley's 25mm gun found its mark: an armor-piercing round struck the creature square in the head. The impact was instantaneous and devastating, its body stiffening as death claimed it.

Momentum carried the creature forward. Its massive bulk tumbled and skidded across the terrain, narrowly missing DuPont and his men, who dove out of its path. The ground shook as the carcass came to a halt, dust and debris setting in its wake.

Quickly scrambling to their feet, the soldiers warily approached the still body with their weapons raised. As time went on, these incursions started to become more frequent. Just how many more of these creatures had slipped through?

"Check it," DuPont ordered, despite the lingering adrenaline.

The soldiers hesitated, but two soldiers cautiously advanced. A jab to the beast's lifeless eye confirmed its death.

"Yeah, it's dead," one soldier confirmed, exhaling deeply.

Turning to his men, DuPont nodded. "Secure the area. Make sure there aren't any more of these things lurking around."

As the soldiers spread to carry out his orders, DuPont muttered, "Goddamn things playing dead. Fuckin' great, just what we need." DuPont had seen his fair share of combat and bizarre situations, but this new reality, where creatures straight out of myth could feign death and almost overrun a platoon, added a new level of unpredictability.

"What's next? Skinwalkers or some shit? I mean fuck, we've already been blasting goddamn dragons, so why the hell not?" he mused to himself, half-joking but half-dreading the possibility.

While the platoon swept the area for potential threats, DuPont monitored the rest of his Bradleys as they maneuvered, using their optics to scan the horizon. His gaze shifted to the light orange glow on the horizon, signaling the approach of morning. For a moment, his thoughts drifted to the base and the sheer scale of the military buildup there—an unprecedented show of force unlike anything he had ever seen.

It was a surreal experience, especially with the increased patrols, constant drills, and influx of troops and equipment. Everything pointed to the military setting the stage for something significant, and DuPont had his suspicions. It all seemed to lead to one conclusion, yet he couldn't help but wonder what they were preparing for.

Or, more aptly, what they were preparing to do.

His thoughts turned to the special operations units flooding into the base. Every branch and unit had been increasingly active in the area, but these "spooky types," as the soldiers called them, operated with a heightened level of secrecy that piqued DuPont's curiosity.

Lieutenant DuPont's interactions with one particular Army Special Forces team provided valuable intel—about the theater's operations and the various races from the other side. He had fought alongside the ODA during the invasion's initial stages, enduring the crucible of blood and Dragonfire. However, in recent weeks, that Special Forces team had become extraordinarily tight-lipped—a stark contrast to their earlier camaraderie.

This shift was another red flag for DuPont. Special Forces teams are naturally secretive, but this sudden reticence suggested something more. They were no longer just fellow soldiers shooting the shit; they were preparing for something. Whatever it was, it was part of a more extensive, more mysterious operation—one DuPont could only speculate about.

The usual banter about their latest "safari"—what they'd seen or killed—had dwindled to brief, terse remarks. Any attempts DuPont made to delve into what they might have been up to were met with non-answers or deflections.

It felt as though an invisible wall had been erected between them.

DuPont respected the need for operational security, but he couldn't shake the feeling that these men were at the center of whatever was coming. And as time went on, his gut feeling was slowly being vindicated.

From DuPont's perspective, the activities of the special operations forces were becoming increasingly conspicuous, especially near the rift. Occasionally, he'd catch glimpses of them lurking around the anomaly or returning from its direction, their Polaris Dagor vehicles and ATVs bristling with heavy weaponry. Their excursions often coincided with disturbances near the rift. DuPont's unit had been called upon as Quick Reaction Force more than once, racing to the breach to provide support. Each time, they'd find the special ops teams retreating at full speed, hostile entities from the other side hot on their heels as they fired back.

It wasn't hard for DuPont to put two and two together. These special operations guys were poking and probing the rift, testing its defenses. Each foray seemed like a calculated effort to push boundaries and gauge reactions. They weren't just gathering intelligence but actively shaping the battlespace for what DuPont suspected was an inevitable conflict.

"Tie it up and hook it up to one of the Bradleys!" DuPont barked, shaking himself from his thoughts. "The eggheads back at the base will probably want to see it."

* * *

"Oh, look who's back!" Coleman shouted, leaning back on the couch as Elijah entered the team room. "Hey, magic boy! We missed you," the ODA team leader cooed sarcastically with an annoying smile.

Elijah glanced at Coleman, his expression oscillating between annoyance and indifference. "Go fuck yourself," he shot back, walking past the group, who all wore identical shit-eating grins.

As he moved further into the room, Bennett, another team member, chimed in with genuine curiosity. "How'd you manage to convince the nerds to let you go? Thought they'd have you chained to a lab table by now, with all that freaky cosmic bullshit you got going on."

"You can go fuck yourself, too," Elijah retorted in the same flat, agitated monotone as he flopped onto an empty couch, letting out an exhausted groan.

Bennett chuckled, "Touchy today, aren't we? Did they do butt stuff and probe you?"

"I fucking wish," Elijah muttered, rubbing his temples. "That'd be more enjoyable than sitting around and playing fuck-fuck games with spooks and scientists because my goddamn spiritual hitchhiker refuses to talk to anyone normally."

The team erupted into laughter, though Elijah's humor didn't reach his eyes. He leaned back, his gaze distant. "I mean, seriously. You'd think a millennia-old entity would be more cooperative. But no—it's like pulling teeth to get a straight answer. And I'm the middleman in this cosmic comedy."

Coleman peered over his shoulder and raised an eyebrow. "How'd you escape?"

Elijah exhaled, his frustration evident over the disbelief. "Escape is a strong word. It was more like a temporary reprieve. The eggheads kept asking Yana—the fairy—questions. She kept demanding their souls in exchange for answers."

The room collectively winced, bracing for the inevitable stupidity, especially concerning a capricious deity.

"And get this," Elijah continued, his tone bitter. "One scientist, cocky little fuck, actually laughed at her. Said, 'Oh sure, take my soul, like that's a real thing.'"

The team members exchanged uneasy glances.

This time, Lister spoke up. "What? What the fuck? And then what?"

Elijah looked slowly at the man and shrugged nonchalantly. "Yeah, that didn't end well. In all her glory, Yana took him up on it and, uh, consumed his soul. One minute, he's laughing, and the next, he lights out. The body functions, the brain has activity, but no one's home."

A heavy silence fell over the room.

Bennett ran his hands over his head and slowly pushed them outward as if his brain exploded. "Man, that's dumb as fuck. Imagine consigning yourself to oblivion because you can't stop being an asshole."

"Yeah. Yeah, it is." Elijah nodded, the situation's absurdity not lost on him. "And that's not even half of it. The whole thing turned into a complete shitshow. CIA handlers started freaking out, scientists were screaming, and everyone in general was scrambling, trying to figure out how to handle a goddess who just does that."

Coleman leaned forward, intrigued despite the grim subject matter. "So, how'd you get out of that mess and back here?"

A wry smile tugged Elijah's lips as he ran a hand through his hair. "Honestly? Yana threw a fit." His smile widened into a grin, albeit a tired one. "She got pissed at the CIA Director for not giving her 'apostle' what he wanted and started ranting about respect, power, or some other cosmic bullshit. It was like watching a child throw a tantrum—but with the ability to delete you."

The men around the room exchanged glances, a mix of disbelief and amusement on their faces.

"So, they just let you go?" Schwarz asked, skepticism lacing his voice.

Elijah gestured toward the sniper with both hands. "What are they gonna do? Kill her?" he asked incredulously. "Do you know how many times we"—he pointed to himself and everyone in the room—"tried that? Like, c'mon."

Schwarz shrugged and conceded the point. "Okay, fair."

"I think they were just glad to get rid of us, to be honest," Elijah mumbled. "Yana kept making threats, and they couldn't really contain her. So, they told me to 'keep my mouth shut' and to please fuck off. They were probably hoping she'd follow and leave them alone." He stretched his neck to one side.

Coleman chuckled. "Well, I guess that's one way to deal with bureaucracy. Have a temperamental goddess on your side."

"So where is she now?" Bennett asked, looking around. "You said they wanted to get rid of both of you, right?"

Looking over his shoulder and around the room as if searching for someone, Elijah shrugged. "Fuck if I know. Last time I saw her, she was bitching at the spook handler they sent with us or some shit."

The room filled with chuckles and relieved sighs. The thought of Yana—a deity with the temperament of a petulant child—haranguing some unfortunate CIA case officer was oddly comforting in its absurdity.

Coleman clapped his hands together, bringing the focus back to the present. "Alright, we've got a lot on our plate. Elijah, you're back with us, so let's brief you on the latest updates. We're being more proactive and have increased our activity on the border to—"

"We're invading, aren't we?" Elijah interrupted with a smirk on his face.

"We're setting conditions," Coleman replied with a coy smile.

Chapter 31.

Mikael looked up toward the sky as the Finnish winter cast its serene, icy blanket over the countryside. The snowstorm from a few days prior had transformed the landscape into a picturesque scene of snow-laden trees and frosted fields.

Dressed in a thick, insulated jacket and a woolen beanie, he exhaled a visible breath into the crisp air. His youthful face, framed by his tight and high haircut, was flushed from the cold. As Mikael's boots crunched softly in the fresh snow on his way to his family's home, he glanced up to see the front door burst open.

"Mikael!" his sister's voice rang out, and before he could fully process it, she was charging toward him at full tilt.

Mikael's heart swelled with joy. It had been six long months since he'd last seen his family, and he eagerly anticipated this enthusiastic greeting. He opened his arms wide, expecting the warm, loving embrace that usually followed his prolonged absences.

But as Enni closed the distance, something felt off. She didn't slow down as expected. Instead, her pace remained steady and determined.

Before Mikael's instincts could kick in, Enni launched herself at his waist, tackling him with a surprising force. The momentum sent both of them tumbling into the snow. Mikael landed on his back, Enni sprawled on top of him, both covered in a dusting of fresh powder.

For a moment, Mikael lay there, stunned, staring at the sky now framed by his sister's grinning face. "Enni! What the hell?!" he exclaimed, half-laughing and half-gasping for air.

Enni laughed, her eyes sparkling with mischief. "You've been gone for too long! I had to make sure you haven't gone soft in the military," she teased, offering a hand to help him up.

"Soft?!" Mikael shot back in mock outrage. Quickly recovering from his initial surprise, he shifted into a defensive position, wrapping his legs around Enni's waist and pulling her down into a full guard—a move straight from his Finnish Defense Forces training. "Soft, she says!" he teased, keeping a firm grip on his sister. "If only you knew the 'kenttäkeittiö' life!"

Enni struggled playfully, trying to break free from his hold. "Oh, so you're a tough 'intti' guy now, huh?!"

As they playfully wrestled in the snow, Mikael launched into exaggerated tales of military life, his tone light but filled with pride. "And don't even get me started on those awful battle drills where you crawl through the mud and pretend you're some action movie hero!"

The laughter echoed across the yard until the front door flew open again. Their father appeared in the doorway, amused and exasperated.

"Perkele, Mikael ja Enni! Lopettakaa se hulluttelu heti!" Jukka called out in Finnish, his voice booming across the snowy yard. He then seamlessly transitioned to English, a tactic he often used to drive his point home. "Stop fooling around, you two! You're dragging half the mud on the ground into the house!"

Mikael and Enni froze, looking sheepishly at their father, who had his hands on his hips and wore a sheepish smile despite his stern words.

"Stop being idiots and come inside. Your mother's busy cooking, and she wants to see you!" Jukka continued, his tone light but firm.

"And you'd better clean up before stepping in here, or I'll hose you down in the yard!"

The siblings exchanged a quick glance before bursting into laughter. As soon as Jukka disappeared inside, they scrambled to their feet and brushed the snow off their clothes.

"All right, all right!" Mikael raised his hands in mock surrender. "We're coming in. No hosing, please!"

Once inside, Mikael was immediately greeted by a chorus of cheers. The cozy living room was packed with family and friends, all gathered to celebrate his return after completing conscription. The atmosphere was joyful and proud, with warm embraces and heartfelt laughter filling the space. The scent of home-cooked food wafted through the air, and the fireplace cast a soft glow.

Mikael's mother emerged from the kitchen, beaming as she wiped her hands on a paper towel. "Mikael!" she exclaimed, rushing over to hug him tightly. "We're so proud of you!"

Jukka clapped Mikael on the back, his usual stoic expression softened by a smile. "You've done well, son. We've all missed you."

Mikael's friends came forward one by one, clapping him on the shoulder and exchanging jokes and stories. Among them were Joonas and Armas, childhood friends who had already completed their own stints in the military.

"One of us!" they shouted in unison, pulling Mikael into a playful group hug.

"You're finally in the veterans' club now," Joonas teased. "No more greenhorn status for you."

Armas chimed in, his eyes twinkling with mischief. "Yeah, now you can join us in complaining about early mornings and endless drills."

The men in the room erupted into laughter, nodding in agreement. They had all endured the miserable yet oddly rewarding experience of conscription in Finland. At one point or another, each of them had woken up before dawn to crawl through the mud or lie in some godforsaken, snow-covered foxhole, simulating ambushes. They had trudged through long marches in harsh forests, laden head to toe with anti-tank mines, and dragged their buddies along after they'd been "wounded."

Feeling a surge of pride and belonging, Mikael joined the conversation, sharing his own tales from recent months. "You guys remember that thirty-kilometer trek with full gear? Yeah, that was a nightmare," he said, rolling his eyes in mock frustration.

"Enough, enough." Mikael's mother waved her hand, silencing the group. "The food is ready. Come, let's eat already!"

The jovial atmosphere shifted as Mikael's mother announced her arrival. Like ravenous dogs, everyone's attention turned to the dining room. On the massive dining table, an array of piping-hot dishes lay, their delicious aromas wafting through the air, signaling a hearty, home-cooked meal awaited.

Silence reigned as each person licked their lips like a starving scavenger, eyeing both the food and each other with equal intensity. The unspoken rule of "first come, first served" hung in the air, and everyone was poised on the edge of their seats, ready to make a dash for the first serving.

Before chaos could ensue, Mikael's mother, fully aware of the impending mess her "buffoons" were about to create, raised her voice. "Ei, ei, ei! Stop right there!" she commanded in a tone that brooked no argument. The room froze, and everyone looked at her sheepishly.

She then turned and gestured towards Mikael's father. "Jukka, you first," she said, a smile on her lips.

With a massive smug grin, Mikael's father rose from the group. Enjoying his moment of privilege, he sauntered toward the table, grabbed the serving spoon, and tantalizingly dipped it into the salmon soup while the rest of the group glared at him with a mix of resentment and envy.

"Why does he get to go first?! Isn't this my party?!" Mikael protested, shooting his mother a pouty look.

His mother shot back a sharp glance, the kind only mothers can give, and retorted, "Shut up, Mikael. You'll get your turn." Her voice was stern but tinged with affection.

Knowing better than to argue further, Mikael looked away and muttered under his breath, "Just saying."

A chorus of laughter erupted from the exchange as Mikael's friends nudged him playfully, teasing him about still being under his mother's thumb.

The rest of the family and guests proceeded to serve themselves in an orderly fashion, filling their plates with the sumptuous spread. The meal was a feast for the senses, featuring traditional Finnish dishes like salmon soup, Karelian pasties, and mouth-watering roast meats.

The room buzzed with conversation and laughter as they sat down to eat. Stories about school and conscription flowed freely, crude and innocent jokes were exchanged, and heartfelt memories were recounted. It was a celebration of Mikael's return and a testament to their small, tight-knit community's strong bonds of family and friendship.

"Gah, don't get me started on the KVKK!" Mikael groaned, rolling his eyes and waving his hand dismissively. "That old, ugly piece of garbage should've been replaced long ago! At least give us MG3s!"

A chorus of agreements echoed around the table. "Right? I mean, Germany is just right there!" Joonas gestured aggressively in the direction he assumed was south. "I mean, we're in NATO now! Why can't we get the good stuff?!"

The lively dinner atmosphere continued as plates were passed around, and everyone dug into the hearty meal. Amidst the clinking of cutlery and laughter, the conversation naturally veered back to their shared military experiences.

After taking a hearty bite of his Karelian pasty, Armas leaned back and sighed. "You know what I don't miss? Those damn bicycles," he said, his words muffled by a mouthful of food. "Carrying those goddamn things was so damn annoying. Just let me walk."

"At least you're not in America right now," Mikael's father chimed in, holding a piece of Finnish rye bread slathered with salmon spread.

The table paused as everyone absorbed Jukka's comment. There was a collective understanding: the topic had shifted to something more serious. The recent events in America, particularly the combat footage circulating on the news, had captured their attention.

Joonas turned to Mikael. "Did you see that footage? With those... what were they, werewolves?"

Mikael nodded, his expression contemplative as he poked at the last bit of his salmon soup. "Yeah, I saw them," he said, scratching his head. "It was brutal. Nothing like what we've trained for."

Armas, who had been quietly sipping his glass of milk, chimed in, his voice tinged with concern. "As cool as that air war was—with those flying lizards and all—it must've been hell for the pilots. Imagine staying awake for over thirty-six hours, locked in that cockpit, only to land, rearm, and go right back up. No rest, no mercy."

The table fell silent as each person lost themselves in thought. The idea of an entire world invading another seemed like something out of a movie or a video game, yet here they were. Nevertheless, as they continued discussing the strange monsters from another world, the conversation was abruptly interrupted by the sound of a phone ringing.

Enni's eyes lit up as she glanced at the caller ID. "It's Juho!" she exclaimed, her tone shifting from concern to excitement. Juho, her and Mikael's older brother, was in the professional Finnish army and was often busy with his own exercises and duties.

Mikael looked up, a small smile forming. "Juho? Maybe he's calling to congratulate me," he mused, feeling a surge of pride at the thought of his brother acknowledging his completion of conscription.

But as Enni answered, her expression quickly shifted from excitement to worry. "Juho? What do you mean, 'turn on the TV'?" she asked, her voice laced with confusion and concern.

After a brief exchange, she hung up and walked over to the television. "Juho said to switch to the news. Something's happening," she said, unease evident in her tone.

The room grew quiet as everyone turned toward the TV. Enni changed the channel to a news station that was broadcasting an emergency NATO announcement. The NATO Secretary General, a former Swedish general named Gustav Lindberg, stood at a podium, addressing his colleagues in Brussels, NATO's headquarters.

Cameras snapped incessantly, and whispers filled the grand hall as the camera focused on Lindberg. His expression was grave, and the urgency in his voice was unmistakable.

The room fell into a tense silence as the Secretary General stepped forward.

He looked at the audience with a steady, resolute gaze before turning slightly to acknowledge the cameras live-streaming his address to millions worldwide. He cleared his throat, and the sound echoed somewhat in the hushed room.

"Ladies and gentlemen, esteemed members of the North Atlantic Council and allies across the globe," he began, his voice calm but heavy with significance.

Breaths were collectively held in every home and every room. It felt as if the world itself had paused to listen. Mikael and his family and friends leaned closer, their eyes glued to the screen.

"I address you today in Brussels, the heart of our sacred alliance, under unprecedented circumstances." The audience, a mix of hardened journalists and seasoned diplomats, stiffened in their seats. "Our meeting is being live-streamed to millions across the world." His eyes flicked briefly to a screen displaying images of dragons soaring through the skies and mythical creatures roaming the streets. "Screens in homes and public spaces alike are filled with scenes that defy belief—creatures of myth and legend soaring through the skies and walking through the streets."

"We find ourselves in a moment of history that, in a thousand years, we could never have even fathomed." He paused, allowing the gravity of his words to settle over the room. "The United States of America, a pillar of our alliance, has endured an unprovoked and barbaric attack that claimed the lives of thousands and displaced countless more."

Mikael's heart pounded in his chest as he listened, each word painting a stark and harrowing picture. He glanced around the room, noting the disbelief and worry etched on the faces of his family and friends.

"Even now, the death toll rises as emergency services continue to identify the fallen," the Secretary General continued. His voice was cold but controlled, laced with a calm fury. "This is not merely an act of war as we know it. This is an invasion of our reality by forces unknown and beyond our current understanding."

"The North Atlantic Treaty Organization," Lindberg said, "has always stood for the collective defense of its member states against any threat to their territorial integrity and security. And today, our great and esteemed ally has invoked Article 5 of the Washington Treaty."

The room fell into a stunned silence. A low murmur swept through the grand hall as Lindberg allowed the weight of his declaration to sink in. Then, gripping the edges of the podium, he spoke again, his voice firm and resolute.

"And we *will* answer that call."

Lindberg's presence on the screen exuded calm determination. His words were carefully chosen to convey both the gravity of the moment and the strength of NATO's resolve. "At this very moment, we are mobilizing NATO forces to provide full support and aid to the United States in response to this unprecedented threat. Our unity is our strength, and we will work tirelessly to safeguard our people and uphold the principles we hold dear," he declared.

His voice took on a righteous timbre as he continued. "This is an extraordinary situation that demands an extraordinary response. Our alliance, forged in the fires of war and tempered by a commitment to peace and security, now faces a challenge unlike any we have known. But I assure you, we are prepared to meet it with unwavering resolve and an unshakable commitment."

Looking directly into the camera, his gaze fierce, he declared, "To the people of the United States of America, you are not alone. We stand united and unbreakable."

Addressing the global audience, he added, "To our citizens watching, our allies, and the world, NATO stands together, or not at all." His voice grew firmer.

Turning a page on the podium, Lindberg wore a solemn yet determined expression. "We are convening an emergency session to coordinate our response and mobilize our forces. We will then provide support, share intelligence, and deploy the necessary resources to aid our American allies."

The room remained silent, each word resonating with profound significance. "Per the principles of the North Atlantic Treaty, and in response to this crisis, I officially invoke Article 5. An attack on one is an attack on all."

He paused, letting the magnitude of his statement settle in. "This evening, I informed the United Nations Secretary General of our decision and our steps. We will work closely with our international partners to address this crisis unified and coordinated."

Straightening up, Lindberg shifted his gaze, glancing at the room one final time. "Thank you," he said simply before stepping away from the podium.

The screen cut to black as the broadcast ended. Mikael's phone buzzed in his pocket. Pulling it out, he scanned the screen, which lit up with a flood of notifications. His commander's name flashed repeatedly, accompanied by a daunting tally: twenty missed calls and a single text message.

The room's attention shifted to him, and the faces of the people present were etched with a mix of concern and curiosity. Before anyone could speak, Mikael broke the silence in a quiet, somber tone.

"They're calling me back," he mumbled, his eyes fixed on the screen. "I have orders to report to the barracks by tomorrow morning."

Thank you for reading a MoonQuill original novel. More exciting stories can be found on at www.moonquill.com.

We would greatly appreciate it if you could take a moment to leave a review. Each one helps the author and supports their ability to continue writing fantastic books for everyone to enjoy!

Scan the QR code below to subscribe to our mailing list and be notified of new releases. You'll receive 4 e-books for free!